THE KINGDOM OF RUIN

KC KEAN

The Kingdom of Ruin
Heirborn Academy #1
Copyright © 2024 KC Kean

The moral right of the author has been asserted.

Without in any way limiting the author's, KC Kean, and the publisher's exclusive rights under copyright, any use of this publication to "train" generative artificial intelligence (AI) technologies to generate any works/images/text/videos is expressly prohibited.
The authors reserve all rights to license uses of this work for generative AI training and development of machine learning language models.

Cover Design by Dark Imaginarium Art
Interior Formatting & Design by Wild Elegance Formatting
Editor - Encompass Editing Service
Proofreader - Sassi Edits
All rights reserved.

No part of this publication may be reproduced or transmitted by any means, electronic, mechanical, photocopying or otherwise, without the prior permission of the copyright owner.

ISBN: 978-1-915203-46-5

The Kingdom of Ruin/KC Kean – 1st ed.

To waking up every day and choosing to live.
To surviving the storm that takes aim on us.
To being the baddest bitch you deserve to be.
To making sure everyone gets some good dick. Even if it's only on the pages.
We can take care of the rest ourselves!

KC KEAN

I'm not just doing this for myself. I'm doing it for my sister, my father, my people; For the Floodborn Kingdom.

– Addi

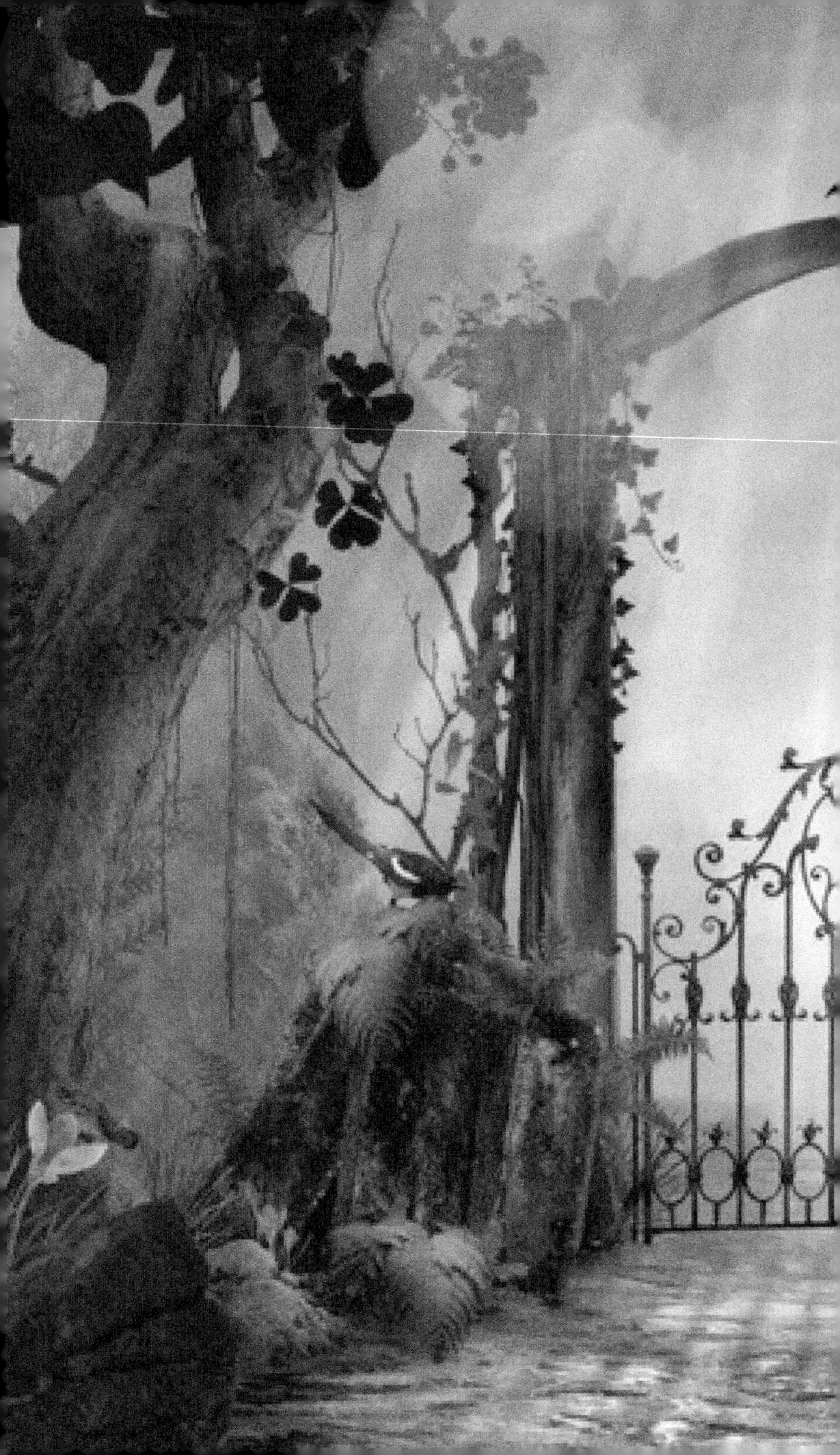

Prologue

"Once upon a time, there was a princess."

"A princess?"

"A princess," he repeats, smiling softly as he nods.

"Oh my, I want to be a princess!" I squeal, excited as butterflies flutter in my tummy.

"You are, my love. Now, forever, and always," he promises, tucking the sheets around my body before swiping a loose blonde curl behind my ear. "But tonight, you must sleep. For the nights will grow dark and the earth sodden beneath our boots."

"I don't like the sound of that." I grumble through a yawn.

"I don't either, but one day, a new dawn will pass, blessing all those who follow the light."

My nose scrunches in confusion. "Do we follow the light, Daddy?" I ask, gripping the robe fastened around his waist. He places his hand over mine, and the warmth from his touch is soothing.

"We do, my love," he confirms, kissing my forehead, and my eyelids slowly start to flicker closed. "Now sleep, for tomorrow awaits."

THE KINGDOM OF RUIN

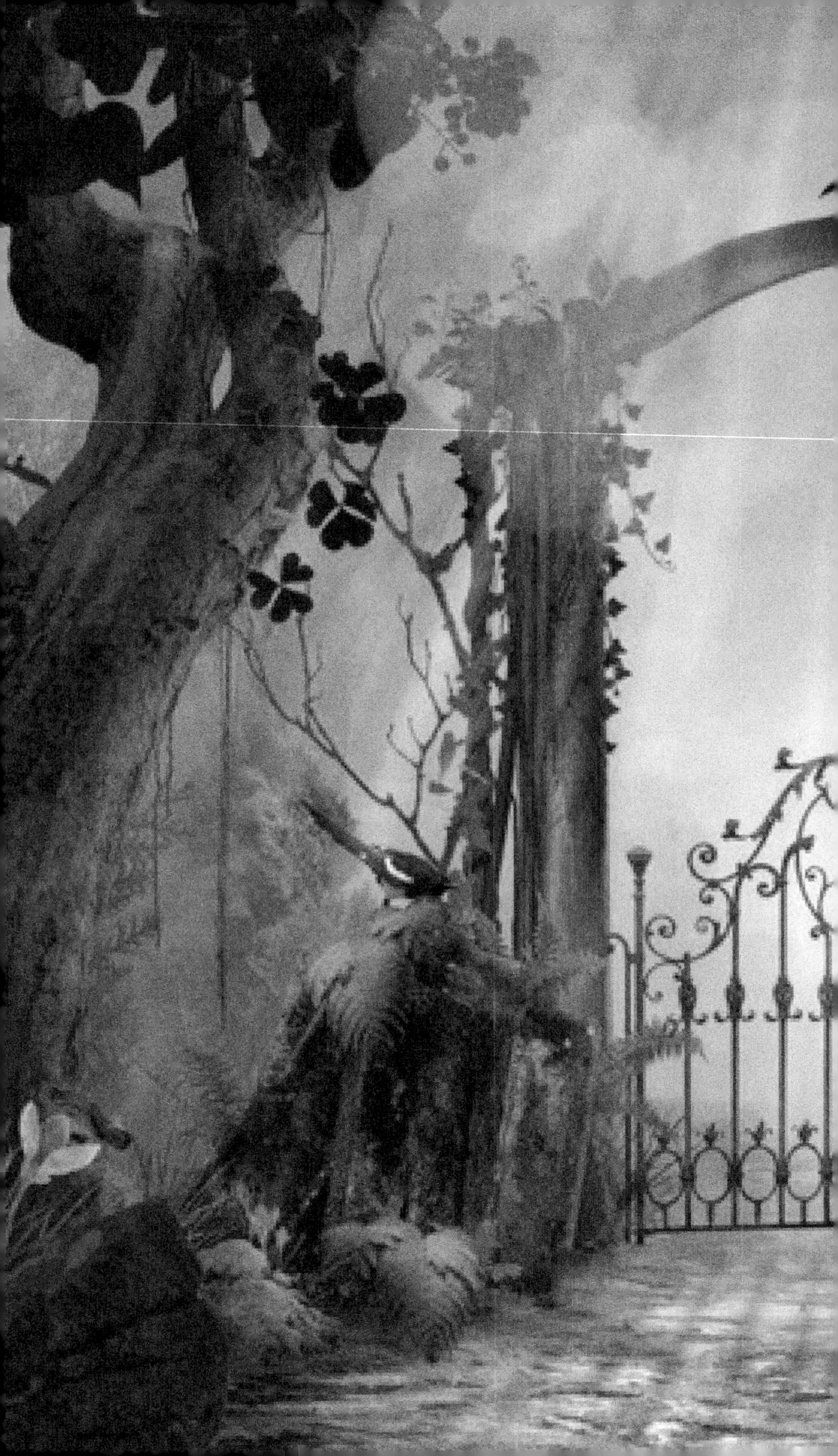

ADDI

1

I tug at the edges of my oversized hood, making sure to shield myself from view as best as I can. It's noisier today. More hectic. Which is understandable, but it doesn't make weaving through the cobbled streets any easier.

I'm used to sweeping through the shadows, hiding from the sun's glow; not because it can hurt me like it can others, but because my objective is to remain hidden. Always. Well, it was. Things are most definitely about to change.

My feet ache already and I mentally berate myself for not breaking in my new boots before today, but there's been so much to prepare for and little time to consider something so minuscule.

Dragging my hand over the stone wall to my left, I

keep myself pressed as close to it as possible as another hoard of people charge by me. The buzz in the air is electric, infecting everyone, and I can't deny the thrill of excitement that burns up my spine with anticipation.

It's been a long time coming, and although I may be twenty years old—twenty-one in two weeks' time—it officially feels as though my life is finally beginning.

The City of Harrows.

It's drawn me in, and with every step I take, I feel another dose of determination and righteousness consume me. I take a deep breath, trying to quell the nerves that threaten to rise along with it, just as someone barges into me, slamming my shoulder against the wall.

I bite back a grunt, fighting the urge to find out who knocked me into the wall as I straighten my hood and continue down the narrow pathway. When it widens into the open square, I slow, pausing by the fruit stall that always makes me smile. I don't know what it is about the smell of oranges, but it offers me a sense of comfort that I can't seem to get anywhere else.

Plastering my back against the wall behind the stall, I pause for a moment to take in the bustling square. The clock tower stands tall and proud at the other end of the space, the large golden bell shimmering in the mid-morning sun. The water in the fountain spouts up in the air, making the small children gasp and giggle as they watch with a sense of wonder you don't get to retain as an adult.

I don't let myself embrace their joy for too long, looking at the rest of the people scuttling through the square with purpose. Everyone has a purpose today; to take part or observe. Either way, there's a level of exhilaration I've never felt in the air before.

"Do you think all of this will be worth it?"

I peer at the fruit stall owner as he speaks with the person beside him. They shrug in response, folding a variety of fabrics along their stand. "Is anything really worth it? We're lost to whatever The Council decides at this point."

"We'll see many losses, I'm sure. But we're already facing too many of them as it is, don't you think?"

My fingers flex at my sides as I listen, enraptured.

Losses.

That's all the Floodborn Kingdom has experienced for as long as I can remember. Longer, if history stands correct. I shake my head, pressing my eyelids closed as tightly as possible and working to get my breathing under control.

Anger and rage don't solve any situation, my love. Be controlled, considerate, and level-headed.

My father's words play in my mind as I count down from ten. He's always the voice of reason, especially mine, but that doesn't stop my emotions wanting to get the better of me.

A horn blares in the distance, pulling me from my thoughts, and I glare at the source of the sound. Amidst the traditional stalls, pretty fountain, and clock tower, revs a sports car. Not just any sports car, a flashy red one, worth more money than I can consider, with music blaring.

It didn't used to be like this.

Once upon a time, history says that the Floodborn Kingdom was home to the fae. Filled with wonder and a simple life. It has since been tainted by everyone else who chooses to walk the kingdom. The City of Harrows is the focal point, drawing everyone in, with the castle still perched heart-achingly high upon the hilltop in the distance. Uninhabited and darkening with every passing day.

Now, people of all kinds walk these streets; a fact I believe makes it a better place. Except for the damn vampires and their excessive lifestyle. They drive me insane whether they try to or not, and no matter what I do, no matter how hard I try to remain level-headed, considerate, and controlled, it means nothing when they're around.

People part ways for the sports car to get through. Nobody is really grumbling, despite the clear inconvenience it causes. My eyes narrow as I watch it slip under the arch and speed off, heading in the same direction as everyone else.

The sea of people regathers once it's gone, and it blows my mind how seamless everything becomes once again. I try to focus on a few people, attempting to guess what they are and where they come from, but it's not easy in this kind of setting.

A fact I'm certain will change once I reach my destination.

Status is going to mean everything, and I know I'll be in the minority. I'm prepared for that. I'm more than expecting it. I just need to remember my breathing exercises to keep a handle on my emotions.

"I think it will either be a vampire or a wolf that ascends the throne," the fruit stall owner states, making me purse my lips in distaste.

He can think whatever the hell he pleases, but that doesn't mean it's going to be the truth. Pushing off the wall, my hands ball into fists as I trudge behind the remaining stalls, the spike of determination back in my steps as the bell chimes from across the square.

Dammit. I'm definitely late.

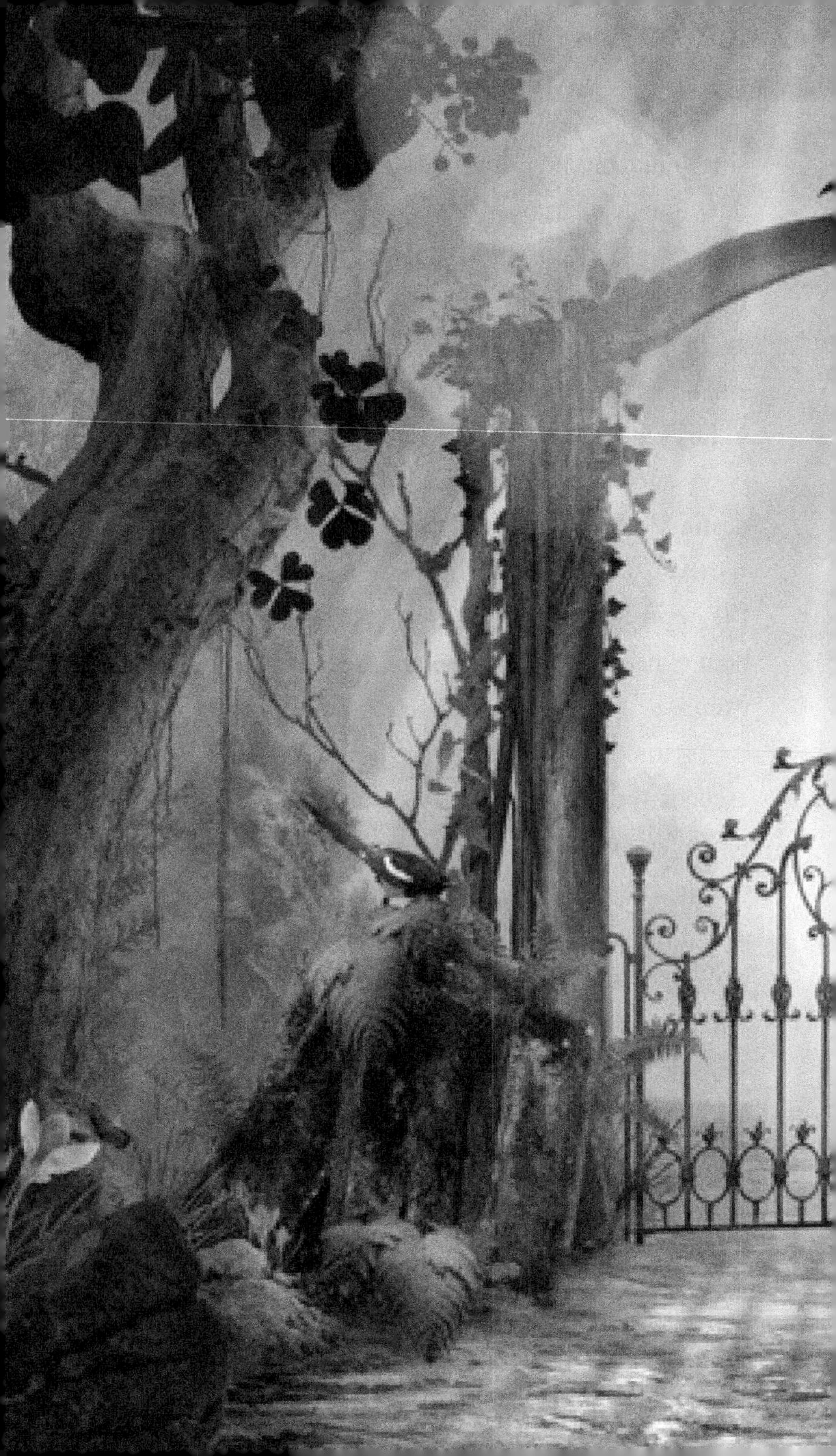

ADDI

2

I barrel ahead with less finesse and care than moments earlier, shouldering past someone as I move under the archway, my steps faltering as my destination comes into view. Even among the hoards of people approaching, it still captures my attention, stealing my breath without any preemptive thought.

I wet my dry lips, failing to add any moisture as the new addition to the Floodborn Kingdom stands tall and proud. The narrow bridge connects the main city walls to a floating island. The thought of it sounds wondrous and magical, but the jagged roofs and endless turrets tell a different story.

Keeping to the left, I take a deep breath and trudge forward with my head bowed and gaze aimed at my feet as I try to remain as invisible as possible.

Adrenaline courses through my veins the closer I get. It's daunting as hell. This is everything I've been building up to. This is the moment everything begins to change. I've waited so long it doesn't even seem real.

The wind whips wildly around me as I dart over the bridge, the grip on my hood tightening. All it does is fuel the excitement coursing through me, hurrying my steps before I barge into the courtyard.

I find a small nook along the wall and tuck myself away as I take a moment to stare up at my future.

Heir Academy.

Gulping, I let those two words repeat in my mind as I absorb my new reality, manifesting everything that will follow. With every breath, I solidify the fact that I'm exactly where I'm supposed to be.

"Entrants, please make your way onto the grounds; proceedings are about to begin."

A buzz zings down my spine, encouraging me to put one foot in front of the other as I follow the other attendants. Guards stand between the pillars, keeping a watchful eye on the bodies, and I think I've managed to slip past unnoticed until a hand clasps around my upper arm, halting me in place.

"No hoods," he grunts, yanking mine down before I can even consider a response, and I glare up at him. His eyes narrow, his grip tightening around my arm, bringing me so close to the brink of responding rashly before someone else gains his attention.

"Gray, come and look at this."

He dismisses me without a second glance, shoving me through the passage before offering me his back.

My lips purse as I clench my fists at my sides, counting down from ten as I take deep breaths. Once my mood seems a little more under control, I run my fingers through my hair, tucking the loose curls behind my ear before turning to rejoin everyone.

I feel exposed without my hood up. I've never walked a step in the City of Harrows without it, and although I knew it was coming, I wasn't ready for the rawness of it. It's a safety blanket I've grown accustomed to; a fact that instantly irritates me and only confirms that I won't be wearing it any longer.

The space grows wide, filled with bodies, and I instantly acknowledge the groups. It's not purposeful, but we're drawn to our own kind. Always. I keep to the side of the large square enclosure, opting to stand in the spot where the sun beats down as I take everyone in.

The gathered attendants to the far right stand tall and proud. A level of righteousness seeps from them, exposing the natural superiority that oozes from them effortlessly, making my lip curl in distaste. They're draped in luxury, dressed in designer clothes, with flashy gadgets and an air of regalness.

Vampires.

I peer to their right and find myself a little stunned to see the group standing so close to them. A different vibe emanates from them altogether. Everyone's shoulders rub as they all stand closer than necessary, an air of familiarity and family pouring from them. They're the second largest group here, but instead of designer clothes and the latest tech clinging to their every limb, they're mostly in ripped jeans and open checkered shirts with tanks underneath. Males and females included. They laugh loudly, a bubble of excitement enveloping them.

Wolves.

Pressing my lips together, I move to the group standing in the center of the space, a quaint, almost solemn vibe coming from them. They're all-knowing, studious, and proper. Draped in cloaks similar to my own, they talk in quiet, hushed tones, always carrying some kind of book with them. It's almost cute and nerdy until they open their mouths to express how wrong you are and how right they are.

Mages.

My gaze travels to those in the far left area, their group smaller than the others, and although you get the sense they aren't as close as some of the other groups, there's still an air of serenity and adventure that bubbles around them.

No one looks the same; no one acts the same. They're all individual and unique, and they own it.

Shifters.

Similar to the wolves, but completely different all at once. They're not packs, they're not a family, and they don't shift into wolves. They shift into whatever the fates decide they are.

Nerves bubble from the group near them, with a sense of wonder and panic twisting in the air. Ordinary. Mundane. Giftless.

Humans.

With gadgets tucked in their hands and a need to prove themselves drifting from them, they're desperate to belong, to fit in—as they rightfully should. It's just a shame that the actions they take don't mirror it. They should be the most frowned upon group, but they're not.

Which leaves the smallest group standing closest to the podium. The group that makes my heart sink. Everyone affords them a wide berth as the members shuffle nervously from foot to foot. It's the uncertainty that comes from them that confirms what they are without you having to look for the most obvious point. Pun intended.

Fae.

Once the leaders of the kingdom, now the remnants of a nightmare. Simply an afterthought of atrocities that brought the kingdom down and left ruin in its place.

"Which group are you?"

I startle at the interruption, glancing up at a man dressed in a perfectly pressed navy suit. The black framed glasses on his nose somehow make him seem approachable, but the tightness of his jaw and squint to his eyes tell a different story.

"Why?"

He narrows his eyes, irritated with having to waste more time on me than necessary and completely unimpressed with my inability to be immediately pliant and at his will. "Because you're standing alone, and the groups have been formed," he states, and I cock a brow.

"I was under the impression we are here as individuals, that what or who we are doesn't matter," I counter, making his eyes narrow further.

"Be as you will, but you may seek strength from those around you. Alone…you won't last long, I'm sure." He smiles, the display not reaching his eyes as they darken. I can read between the lines and understand what he's not saying.

He thinks I won't last two minutes alone. Maybe he's right, or maybe I am.

Time will tell.

Channeling my father's words, I put a wide smile on my face and nod. "Thank you for the advice."

I know I don't really have a choice in the matter. I've

already heard the rumors that everyone will be housed according to their origins when we step inside the academy. There's no point delaying the inevitable, but what can I say? I'm stubborn and I'm not going to fall under someone else's thumb so easily.

Especially not a vampire's.

Turning away from the irritation spoiling my observations, I roll my shoulders back and cut through the crowd, slowing to a stop at the front of the podium. Along with my kind.

Fae.

The nerves and panic that drift around them threaten to seep into my bones, too, but I push it back, slowing my racing heart as I channel every ounce of strength, determination, and power I have. It doesn't help when I can feel people looking at me. Or is that the anxiety attempting to get the better of me?

Dammit.

"Are you with the right group?" a girl asks, and I turn to look at her with a frown. It's on the tip of my tongue to question whether she thinks anyone would actually choose to stand here if they didn't have to, but I manage to keep my mouth shut and simply nod instead. That doesn't seem to appease her, though. Her gaze shifts to my ears and back to my eyes. "It's just you don't…"

"Have pointy ears," I interject, giving her a pointed

look. "I'm aware. Would you like to look closer to see the scars from where they were snipped?" I grunt, annoyed that I briefly reveal my feelings. The only effect that ever has is that someone obtains the upper hand over you, but to my surprise, it's pain that flickers in her gray eyes instead.

"Oh my gosh, I'm so sorry." Her hand lifts to her mouth and I'm not sure if she's going to cry or not, but I can't deal with that.

No. Way.

"You didn't do it. So don't apologize." I try to offer her a smile, but I know it's weak, and there's no rectifying it. So I turn my attention to the people gathered on the podium, murmuring among themselves as we all wait. The alternative would be to reach for my ears and feel the smooth edges to the tops, along with the slightly raised scar that serves as a memory sharper than any other.

Everything happens for a reason. Everything is meant to fall into place. Everything is okay.

"I'm sorry. I'm an apologizer. I'll even apologize for apologizing," she continues to ramble, standing at my side. I nod, hoping that will be enough of a response for her to back off, but apparently, my usual resting bitch face vibes aren't in full effect today. "I'm Flora, by the way."

Clearing my throat, I peer at her out of the corner of my eye, taking a moment to actually take her in. Her vivid orange hair falls around her shoulders in loose waves. Her big gray eyes are filled with a sense of hope, but they're also tainted by the panic and worry that wars within them. She's about my height, an inch or two taller if I'm being completely honest with myself, and her frame is small. She's going to need to work on that while she's here; otherwise, it will be pointless.

My hands flex at my sides. *That's not for me to worry about.* Or is it? Is that not the entire end game of all of this? Taking a deep breath, I turn to face her properly.

"I'm Addi."

"Nice. Addi, as in…"

"Just Addi will do."

My throat clogs as it does every time someone takes the time to press me for details about myself, but thankfully, she doesn't push, turning to face the podium again.

My gut clenches as I listen to the fae around me, the worry thick in their voices as they try to decipher everyone's intentions. They probably need to be more focused on their own—another fact I may have to add to my to-do list. To prove myself as a fae among these people, I need to first prove it to my own kind. If it's the last thing I do, I will make a positive name for us among this madness.

We are our people, Addi girl. We will always stand strongest when we are together and united as one.

My father's words echo in my mind, guiding me as always, despite the fact that I have so many arguments

I could throw back. As if our strength may have been stronger if we were united in this moment too. This is my first interaction, properly, with another fae, and it feels... weird. Maybe not weird, but it's not my norm, yet I'm supposed to act like it is.

"There you are. I was wondering what was going on." I glance at the guy approaching, but his gaze is on Flora, who blushes.

"It's not like there's really a sea of fae for you to lose me in," she retorts, the pink of her cheeks deepening, and he grins at her before turning to me.

"Arlo, nice to meet you." He offers his hand, a natural and calm smile on his face, effortlessly putting me at ease, which immediately sets me on edge. I don't trust anyone, and I'm not about to start with him.

"Addi."

He quirks a brow at me when I don't immediately take his hand, but after a beat, I relent, just as Flora plants her hand on his arm. "She's focused, give her some space."

It's my turn to raise my eyebrows at her, but she simply shrugs in response. I am focused. She's not wrong. But, am I also that obvious? It doesn't matter. As long as she didn't come up with any other assessments that may weaken me.

"Focused. Nice. I—"

Whatever he's about to say is cut off by a siren ringing out around the huge space, drawing the murmurings to a halt. All eyes turn to the podium where a lady stands. Her white hair is pulled back into a messy braid, silver glasses are perched on the tip of her nose, and she's wearing a florescent pink blazer and skirt set with a white silk blouse underneath.

She looks over the crowd, her smile growing when she turns toward the vampires, confirming what she is before she moves toward the slim, silver microphone perched atop the podium.

"Welcome, everyone, to Heir Academy."

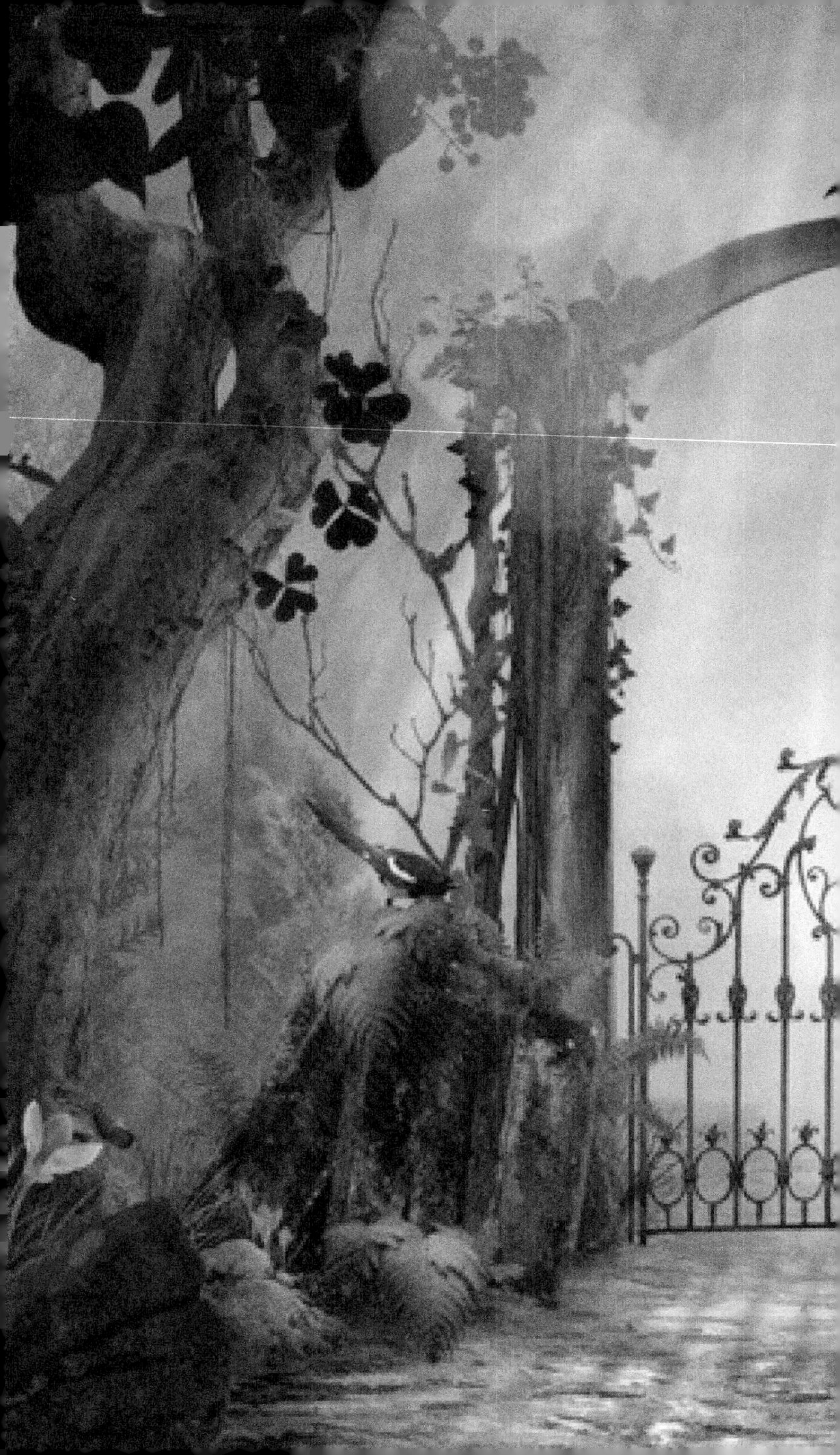

ADDIE

3

Her voice instantly sets me on edge, offering no kind of warmth or excitement to be here. Not that it's the approach she was going for, but still. We're hopefully here for the long haul, building for the new future they're insisting on, but what do I know?

A lot more than they think you do.

"Thank you for gathering here this morning. It brings me great pleasure to welcome you through the academy's gates with open arms." She pauses, lifting her arms in a fake half hug that looks awkward as hell before she drops them back down to her sides. "There is much for us to learn about one another, much for us to learn about our past that we don't want to repeat, and much to embrace about where we hope the future will take us."

"As long as you're a vampire, she means," Arlo

whispers under his breath, making my teeth sink into my bottom lip to stop the smile from spreading. Flora, on the other hand, swats him in the stomach, her cheeks reddening once again. At least I'm not the only one coming to the same assessment of the woman before us.

"My name is Mildred Bozzelli. You may call me Dean Bozzelli. After much consideration among The Council, I have been appointed as the dean of Heir Academy, and it's my utmost certainty that I will ensure everyone remains focused and dedicated to the cause we are undertaking." She smiles proudly, reveling in the title she's earned herself, and I feel the nervous energy around me increase. "But, less about me and more about all of our fine attendees today. Don't you agree?"

Cheers echo around us, and when I peer over my shoulder, I find the wolves, mages, and shifters joining in with the vampires, while the fae and humans remain a little more stoic.

"Firstly, I believe we should start at the beginning. As many know, Floodborn Kingdom rose from the seas many years ago, led by many, but most recently, King August Reagan." My chest aches as disgruntled mumbles spread among the crowd. "He was the last of the fae to lead us and the remnants of his rule still echo around us." Her face is full of sympathy, but her words remain just as quick and sharp. "After all of the mistakes, The Council was formed, uniting the origins of our kingdom. Now, however, the time has come for us to find our new leader, one forged in stone by hard work and determination, fortified with the will to lead all of our people. No matter the cost, here at the academy, we *will* find the one who will lead us and unite us all, for the sake of our kingdom."

Her gaze glances dismissively over the fae and humans again. She offers the wolves, shifters, and mages an extra moment, but she lingers on the vampires. It's clear who she believes should rule.

Part of me wonders why the rest of us are even here, but then my heart skips a beat, reminding me exactly why I am here. There's a lot to prove.

There hasn't been a queen in over five hundred years, and the thought of a fae retaking the throne won't come easy to many in the kingdom. I'm here to prove them all wrong.

"Our aim is to find the new heir among you. There will be trials, tests, and moments where we will push you beyond your limits; all to determine who that is. It won't be easy, but if the past has taught us anything, it's that we must not succumb to kindness that can linger in our hearts. This kingdom deserves a dedicated leader whose strength and cut-throat loyalty can do what's best for the people above all else, someone ruthless enough to do what needs to be done for the best interest of Floodborn."

Another round of cheers fills the air, and this time, it includes a few humans and some of the fae around me. I jab my hands into the pockets of my cloak, clenching them into fists in anger.

Paper brushes against my knuckles, making me frown, and I pull out a small folded sheet. With my gaze locked on Bozzelli's, I meticulously unfold it until there's nothing left to do before I peer down. My eyes skim the scratchy words scrawled across it. My heart instantly aches, but the warmth that blossoms in my chest almost floors me.

Quickly glancing at Bozzelli again, I'm relieved to see I've gone unnoticed as I refold the paper and return it to my pocket.

"In a few moments, registration will begin for everyone and we'll filter you all onto the official grounds of the academy. Once in there, you will have the remainder of today to get comfortable, but everything begins tomorrow. Not everyone will make it. Not everyone will want to. But coming here today confirms your trust in The Council and your loyalty to the Floodborn Kingdom. I can't wait to embark on this journey with you."

"Why does she look so bloodthirsty when she says that?" Arlo whispers, nudging Flora with a twinkle of mischief in his eyes.

I school my features, pretending as though I don't hear him as I watch six additions join Bozzelli on the podium.

They stand shoulder to shoulder, three on either side of the dean, before she begins to point them out.

"On the end to my left, you have Professor Alyx Sorrow. She will be leading the mages. Followed by Professor Landon Fairbourne, who will guide the fae." Her nose turns up slightly as she says it, but if anyone notices it, they don't bother to say a word. "With Professor Garrick Knight beside me, who will assist the shifters." They each wave at their introduction before Bozzelli lifts her other arm, indicating the three remaining professors beside her. "Professor Harrison Amos, to my right, will be here for the humans. Beside him is Professor Connor Whitlock. He will be commanding the wolves. While Professor Maxima Holloway will escort the vampires the best she can."

I repeat their names a few times in my head as I stare at their faces, committing them to memory. Once over, I wouldn't have remembered a single name she just said, but with my father's guidance, I now understand the importance of remembering names and faces. Both to leave a good and lasting impression on them, while also remembering who may or may not betray you in the future.

The latter is more likely than I care to admit.

"As you are already in your groups, I will have each professor call out the origins before they guide you inside. They will go through the timetables, attire, accommodation, and dining details that will pertain to you for the next two years. Unless we find our heir before that time, of course," she adds, twitching with excitement. I'm certain she's going to bounce out of her shoes at any given moment, but before I can see if that's likely to happen, Professor Alyx Sorrow calls out the mages.

She waves them forward as she steps down from the podium, leading them through the stone archway to the left. They follow her wordlessly and I take a moment to really absorb what's happening right now.

There's no going back, no alternatives. We're going to walk under that archway and either die at the hands of Heir Academy, lick our wounds when the heir is declared, or bask in triumph as the crown to the kingdom is placed upon our heads.

I turn in the direction of Floodborn Castle, but it's obscured by the academy so I picture it from memory instead.

"Are you nervous? I can't really sense it from you like I can everyone else." It takes me a second to realize Flora is asking me.

Shrugging, I shake my head. "Nervousness isn't something I really struggle with." Not in the way everybody else here does. "You can sense that?" I query, and she nods shyly, her hair covering her face for a split second before Arlo elbows her.

"Flora is the best fae with mind magic I've ever met,"

he insists, revealing that familiar pink tint to her cheeks again.

"He's overhyping me," she mutters, fidgeting with her fingers, but I store the tidbit of information away. Knowing the strengths of those around you only makes you stronger yourself. Just as the weaknesses that grasp you, if not balanced perfectly, could find you dead.

"You know I'm not," Arlo retorts, and I offer her a smile, which seems to help her relax again.

"Fae. Follow me." Professor Landon Fairbourne's voice booms around us, carrying more strength than you would expect, given the fae around me, and I immediately like it.

This man could be an asshole for all I care, but carrying himself the way he is only impresses me. Hopefully, he will find a backbone in some of those around us. I can sense Arlo is already open to saying what he thinks, and Flora can handle him just fine, but I get the feeling she doesn't use that same level of strength with others.

I keep to the back of the group, Flora by my side, with Arlo flanking her. I try to assess him out of the corner of my eye now that I have a moment, but it's not so easy with Flora between us.

He's clearly over six feet, that's for certain. I'm standing strong at five-foot-seven inches, and he towers over both of us. His messy brown hair makes his blue eyes seem brighter, twinkling with mischief, and although he seems slim, the set of his shoulders and power in his stride tells me there's more to him than meets the eye. He catches me looking, throwing a wink my way, and I quickly turn to follow the professor once again.

He probably thinks I'm interested now. I'm definitely not. Besides, I can sense the air of affection between him and Flora. Nonetheless, I'm focused on my mission. There's no time for distraction.

I'm pulled from my thoughts as we take in the cobbled walkway. The academy building itself comes into view, but we walk around it. The pathway forks off from a central fountain in six different directions. One for each origin.

Fae.

Humans.

Mages.

Shifters.

Vampires.

Wolves.

"Form a line, registration is about to begin."

THE KINGDOM OF RUIN

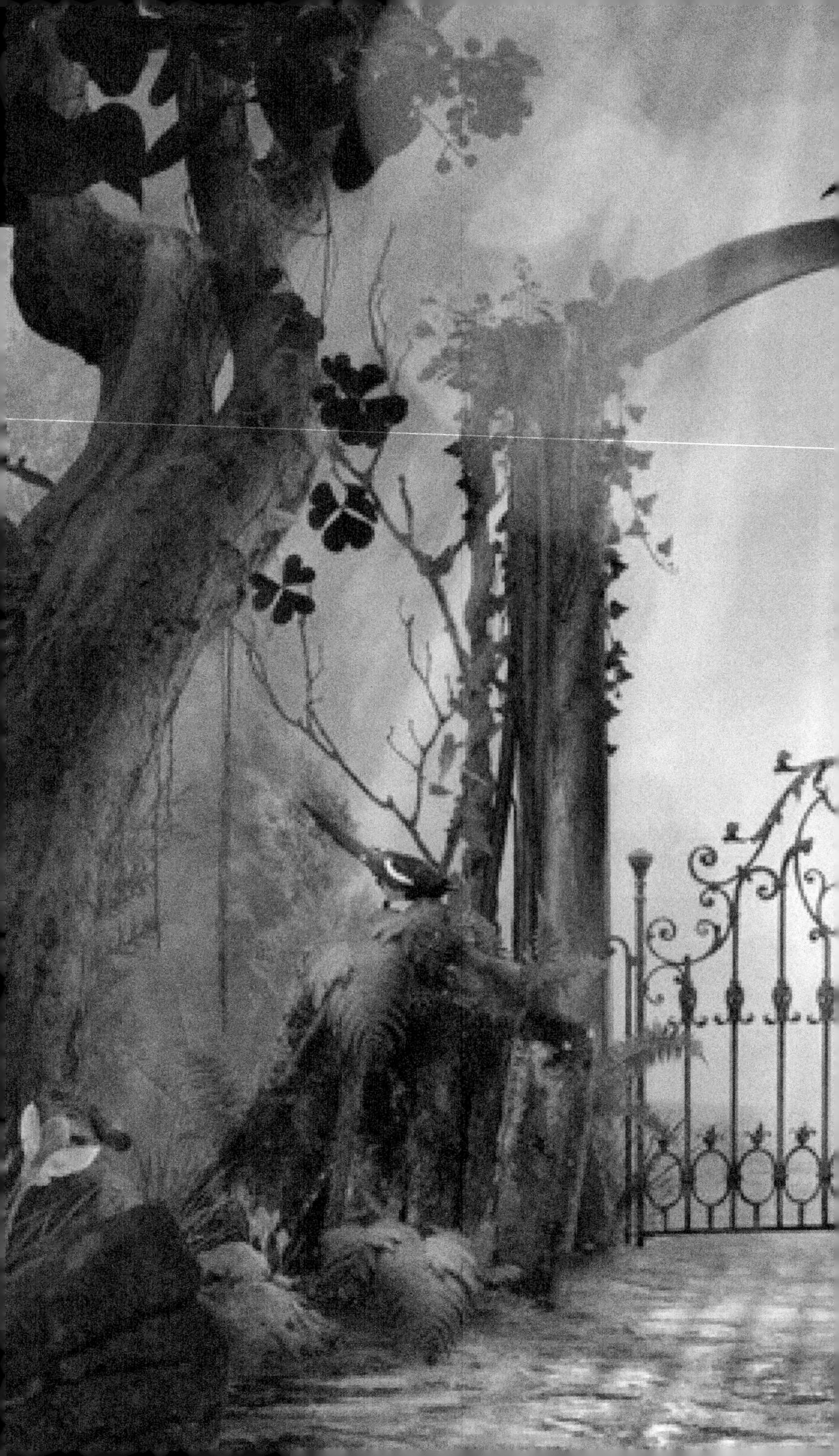

ADDI

4

The order rings out, and the student body falls into formation without a word. Peering around at everyone, the size differences between each group becomes more magnified when you consider the size of the lines forming.

Murmurs pick up as we wait as patiently as possible. I can sense Flora attempting to start a conversation with me multiple times, but each time, she rocks back on her heels, slamming her lips shut. By the fifth time, I can't take it anymore, and I turn to face her. I hope the smile I'm attempting isn't off. I am actually trying to be nice. I think.

"Small talk isn't really my thing, I'm more likely to ask you what weapon you prefer rather than reference the weather. So, you're going to need to spit out whatever is on the tip of your tongue because I really can't guess it."

Arlo chuckles, nudging Flora with his shoulder as her cheeks turn pink again. I've barely met the girl, but I already get the feeling I'll be noting when her cheeks aren't bright rather than when they are since it seems to happen so often.

"I, uhh, I was just curious what you did before you came here."

Reasonable question. I can answer that. "I worked for my father. Our ranch is…isolated, but it gets us by. A huge contrast to this." I nod at the looming academy building behind her and she nods in agreement. "What about you?"

She beams, lacing her fingers together as she bounces on the spot, and I feel a sense of pride seeping from her. I'm not joking when I say small talk isn't my thing, much to my father's disappointment, but seeing her response makes me reconsider my distaste for it. "I was interning. I only just finished school last year, and Summer Oak doesn't have many jobs that can facilitate my powers."

It's on the tip of my tongue to ask what specifically she was interning as, but I'm interrupted by a sneer.

"Move out of the fucking way." I turn to my right, staring up at some ass who seems certain his glare is going to off me. When it doesn't, and I don't instantly move, his eyes narrow further and he folds his arms over his chest. "Are you dumb? I said move."

Flora, Arlo, and I are standing as close as three people

can, talking in a small group. Looking over my shoulder, I notice there's a huge gap since I haven't been moving along with the line to register. This idiot is just interested in causing a scene.

"There's already plenty of space for you," I state with a smile as I turn to him, pointing over my shoulder, but that only seems to make his nostrils flare.

"Come on, Addi, let's—"

"You don't look like a member of the fae origin. Why don't you go and join the line that you are connected with." I recognize Professor Fairbourne's voice from a few moments ago and he appears in my peripheral a moment later, but I keep my eyes locked on the guy beside me.

His lips are pursed, as though he's considering whether or not to persist. His eyes widen with a sense of humor to them, but not the kind that has you preparing to laugh.

"That's what I was doing, but this bitch doesn't want to get out of my way."

I grind my teeth, ready to give this guy a piece of my mind while my brain tries to settle on what he is. He seems to think he's superior, but it doesn't appear to be as natural as it is for vampires. There's no warmth to him, no sense of endless knowledge.

He has to be shifter.

"I'm sure you could walk around *this bitch* easy enough." Professor Fairbourne cocks a brow at the unwanted guest, who takes the hint but doesn't miss the opportunity to shoulder past me as he goes. I sink my teeth into my tongue, forcing myself to let the moment pass as Fairbourne turns his attention to us. "You're up next. Move along."

He walks off without a backward glance as I spy Flora gulping nervously.

Rolling my shoulders back, I do as he says. Facing forward again, I have to admit that despite the grandeur of everything so far, the registration seems a little lackluster. A lone woman sits behind a table with nothing but an electronic device in her grasp. "Name," she calls out, not bothering to look up at me.

Clearing my throat, I keep my voice low. "Addi, Addi Reed." My heart races, my pulse ringing in my ears the moment the words slip from my mouth as I anticipate the world folding in around me. But a moment later, she nods and waves her hand dismissively. "Off you go."

I blink, and blink again before I finally move, a sense of bewilderment in my step now as I rejoin the back of the fae line.

We're done far quicker than the rest, and Professor Fairbourne wastes no time directing us down the path that leads to the fae building.

The smaller buildings are all visible from what seems like a communal area, and it's no surprise to see that the fae building is the smallest. They either anticipated low numbers from us or didn't care either way.

Professor Fairbourne doesn't say a word until we come to a stop in front of the graystone building. There are four floors in total, and as I peer out toward the other origin buildings, I notice that even the human accommodations appear to be six or seven stories high. The accommodations for the vampires and wolves are double that.

"The first floor is your main communal area. The second floor has been assigned to the females, and the third and fourth floors are for the males. Each floor also has its own designated communal bathing room, however, because of the numbers, you are all welcome to enjoy your own rooms. Any questions?" Fairbourne rocks back on his heels, assessing each of us as he awaits an answer. When no one immediately speaks out, he sighs. "Okay, well, the food hall is in the main academy building, and I believe it is well signposted. Otherwise, you will find your names engraved on plaques on each door. Inside, you will find everything else you will require to begin classes tomorrow."

I rattle my mind, eager to think of something to ask, but I'm coming up blank since there's so much we're not actually being told. Before I can come up with anything, he shakes his head. "Everyone here is between the ages of eighteen and twenty-two, and you're here because you chose to be, not because you were called upon. We're searching for the new leader of the Floodborn Kingdom. If you can't come up with a simple question when asked, fates help us with anything else."

My eyes narrow at him as he waves us off, trudging back down the path we just came down without a backward glance.

"Asshole," Flora mutters under her breath, and I have to stifle a smile at the surprising outburst from her.

Everybody else ushers inside, and I count eighteen other fae attendees, plus me, confirming just how outnumbered we are.

The note from earlier flashes in my mind, bringing a smile to my face as I repeat it to myself word for word.

To Addi,
I'm so proud of you, and I'm saying this before you even leave the house. No matter what, you will always be the best big sister that ever existed. Dad's telling me to put something specific, regal or some crap, but you don't need any of that from me. You just need to know that I think you rock. Today, tomorrow, and every day that follows.
Be safe, because if I have to wait until death to see you again, I'll find a way to bring you back and kill you myself.

I love you.
Nora x

I let the words reignite the embers of determination licking through my veins as I repeat the biggest mantra in all of this.

I'm not just doing this for myself. I'm doing it for my sister, my father, my people.

For the Floodborn Kingdom.

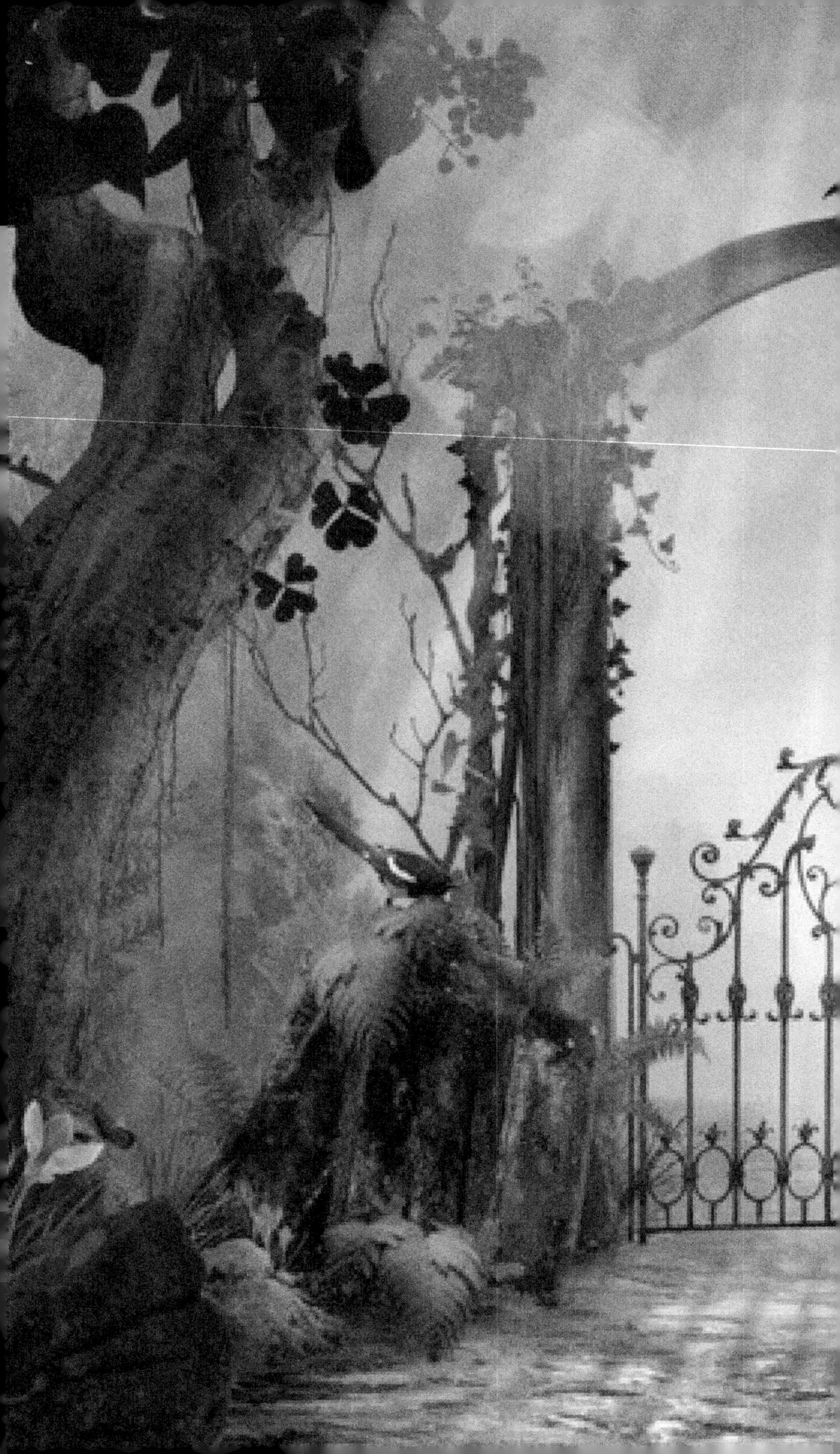

ADDI

5

The communal area doesn't really register in my mind, apart from noting the exit points. Otherwise, I hurry up the stairs among the small crowd in search of the space I will call my home for the foreseeable future.

The wooden floor creaks under my boots as I reach the second level. Guys carry on ahead up the remaining staircase, while the girls around me all squeal when they see their names displayed on the doors we come across. It's the oddest reaction, considering the circumstances, but it seems we're not all approaching this with the same regard.

I note that the door at this end of the hall has a sign for the communal bathroom, so it's no surprise that I find my room at the other end, and I'm even less surprised to find Flora's door to my right.

As Professor Fairbourne mentioned, there's a small golden plaque on the dark wooden door engraved with *'Addi Reed'* and my date of birth underneath. Why does my date of birth need to be on there?

"Hey, it's your birthday next week," Flora states, pointing at my door. "We should make plans," she adds, and I hum in response, neither confirming nor denying my commitment to make plans. "If you need me for anything, you know where I am," she offers, pointing at her door as her cheeks tinge pink, and I nod, grabbing my doorknob and stepping into my new room.

I make a mental note that the doors don't seem to lock. There's not even a latch from the inside, and I won't be able to sleep a single second if I can't rectify that. First, though, I need to take in my room instead of dwelling on that or the fact that this is the first birthday I will spend alone without my sister or father.

The door falls closed behind me as I brace myself against it, head falling back with a sigh as my mind whirls with memories from every birthday I remember up until this point.

The joy, the laughter, the happiness despite difficult times. All of it.

Just the three of us.

Me, Nora, and our dad.

My mother is a different story altogether. There's little

I remember about her at all. What I do recall is a blur. A flash of blonde curls, the pinch of her brows, the feeling of disappointment constantly weighing on me, even at such a young age. But her absence doesn't haunt me like it once did, which feels like an accomplishment in itself.

I know my past, I know the pain she left in her wake, and I'm glad I have no recollection of any of that. Sometimes, I wonder if I really don't remember or if it's my subconscious guarding me. Either way, I need to shake it off and focus on the here and now.

Blinking my eyes open, irritated that I don't recall closing them, I peer around the space now branded as mine. A surprisingly large window fills the wall opposite me, with thin beige curtains draped over them. They're going to do nothing to block the sun, but I'm sure I can figure something out.

The carpet matches the shade of the curtains, along with the sheets covering the single bed pushed against the left wall. It's clean, at least, but it looks ridiculously dated with the oak bed frame, desk, and chest of drawers that complete the room.

A small closet is to my right, enclosed with the same oak wood as the door, and I sigh.

It's not much, but it will do. It's home, for now.

Moving toward the window, I brace my hands against the frame and peer down at the quad below. It's easy to see the different origin buildings that frame the communal walkways, except for the humans' building, which is directly beside us. Not that it matters. As long as I can protect these four walls while I'm inside them, that's all that matters.

From here, Heir Academy seems huge. Whoever the architect was made sure to go for dramatic effect, and a lot of effort was put into its construction, that's for sure. It looms perfectly in the distance, daunting and wondrous all at once.

I stare to the left of it, squinting in hopes of catching a glimpse of the building that holds my one true goal, but it's just out of sight from here yet again. I make a mental note to find a spot where I can see it from campus. Because nothing will help me visualize and manifest the future I deserve more than seeing it with my own two eyes.

Turning my attention back to the room, I let my shoulders fall, relaxing the tension inside me before I shrug off my cloak and remove my concealed backpack. There was an option to have your belongings collected from home and delivered to your room, but that was completely off the table. Just like the use of my full name was.

Which means I've had the pleasure of fitting my entire life into the backpack now resting on my bed. I may have used a little of my magic to make it more compact, but there was certainly a lot I left behind. The reality is, none of it mattered all that much anyway.

Except the one thing I wanted to bring more than anything but couldn't.

Photos.

As I empty the contents of my backpack, it becomes more real. No matter how many of my things I have here, it's not truly mine without a photo of my family, but it wasn't safe. It never is. But that's all coming to an end, I swear it.

For now, I'll have to piece together the vision of my family through memory alone.

Discarding my backpack, I look down at everything I brought. My cell phone, as useless as it really is, the usual essentials like underwear, a few outfits and shoes, along with the measly cosmetics I have.

Everything else of importance is attached to me. More specifically, the ribbed waistcoat fastened over my long-sleeved black tee which sheathes a few daggers in various shapes and sizes, as well as a few other weapons I've found useful along the way.

Any concerns about a security search before we entered are now no longer a concern. They were more bothered about my hood being up than the weapons concealed beneath my cloak. I won't be able to carry them around campus at all times, but at least I have them with me.

Grabbing my clothes, I shuffle over to the closet to find

the attire previously mentioned by the professors. There's a gray cloak hanging beside a single long-sleeved gray t-shirt, a pair of leggings in the same color, with matching sneakers nestled on the floor beneath them. A folder sits beside it, and I lift it into my arms before sauntering back over to the bed, flicking through the pages as I take a seat.

A letter is perfectly centered in the first pocket.

Welcome to Heir Academy.
Your attendance is greatly honored, and you should be proud of yourself for taking the necessary steps to aid our kingdom.
Many have traveled from near and far; no matter the distance, your presence is noted.
Two years seems like a long time, but after the struggles we have faced, The Council believes it's an appropriate amount of time to help us find the best-suited heir for our people. Our kingdom.
It is no secret that we intend to push you to new limits while also increasing your knowledge and wisdom along the way. The kingdom still faces many threats, which we believe have only increased with the origins closing ranks among themselves. We're aware we have chosen to house you in such a way, but those arrangements may evolve with time as the mission of this academy is, above all, learning to reintegrate the origins.

For now, get comfortable and familiarize yourselves with your new surroundings, but most of all, prepare for greatness.
The Council.

My finger trails the words as I go over them again, trying to read between the lines and decipher any hidden agendas, but they're far too vague for me to piece anything together. Pursing my lips, I relent and continue through the folder.

There's a note on attire being of our choice, as long as we wear our designated cloak when moving around campus, and gym wear for any sporting classes. I can't help but scoff at the fact that they made a damn point in the letter, stating they wanted to help merge the origins together, yet they've added another factor into the mix that only helps distinguish who is who.

Fae are to wear gray.

Vampires - red.

Wolves - green.

Mages - purple.

Shifters - blue.

Humans - cream.

Shaking my head, I continue on, coming across my class schedule next, and my eyes widen in surprise when I note every class is mixed with other origins. At least they're attempting it somehow, but they're still creating unnecessary status symbols based on our cloaks.

The timetable is a bit of a blur, the information not really important to me right now, and I find myself losing interest quickly. Looking around the room, I know I need to change something up so I can get my head back on straight. I'm useless if I'm zoning in and out.

I can't just sit around here waiting for everything to fall into my lap. If I want to survive this place and come away with the crown, then I can't stop moving. Maybe right now, that means focusing on something else outside of these four walls first. Then I can return and tear my schedule apart in preparation for tomorrow.

Nodding to myself, I leave the folder open on my bed and stand, rolling my neck as I consider my clothes. Technically, the attire set by The Council begins tomorrow, along with classes, so for today, I can wear what I please.

I consider my boned waistcoat, heavy against my body from the weapons. To wear it or to leave it?

My gut twists as I reach for the top button, pausing me in my tracks.

I follow my gut. Always. Now is not the time to make exceptions.

So I grab my black cloak, drape it over my shoulders, and head out to see what awaits me inside the walls of Heir Academy.

THE KINGDOM OF RUIN

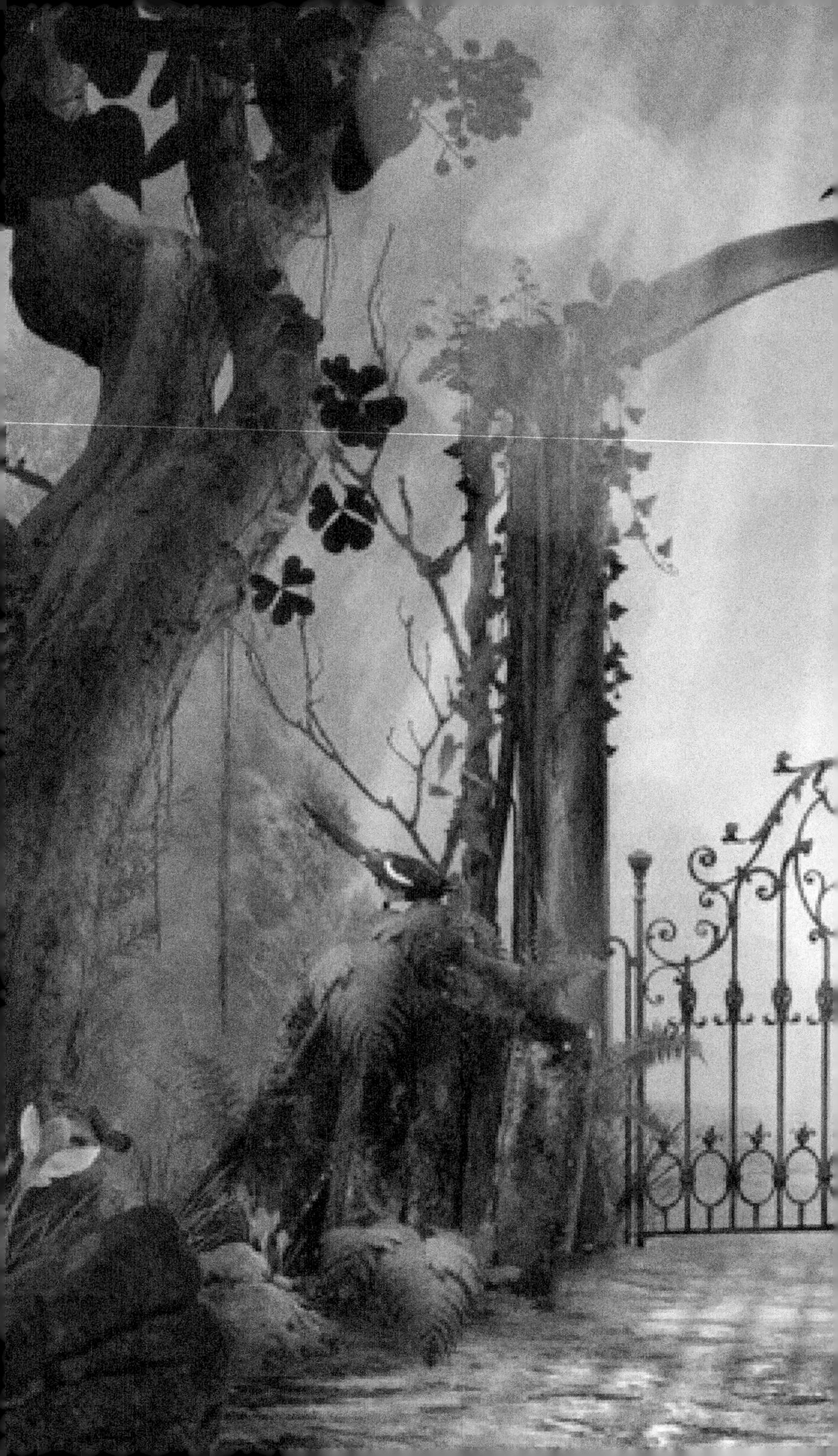

ADDI

6

Exploring the grounds in my full gear seemed like a good idea at the time, but now that I see the expanse of it, I almost wish I hadn't. I can already tell I'm going to be out here running laps in my spare time, working on my stamina while taking in the impressive space.

Being draped in my black cloak, however, makes that impossible for right now. It does serve its purpose of concealing my weapons, though. And I should probably train with it on instead of creating a mental blocker in my mind. Although, I just want to get familiar with my surroundings before I start putting myself through tougher paces.

Quaint little patches of grass are scattered everywhere, picnic benches dotted throughout, with winding pathways and treelines that make the place feel far more whimsical in comparison to the academy building.

I wish Nora could see it. She would love it. I can picture her curled up on a picnic blanket under the large oak tree to my left, a book in hand, a bag of grapes at her side, and a wistful smile on her face. She would preen over the sounds of the birds tweeting in the distance, like it's cute or something, while I stood guard, watching anyone and everything that may near.

My heart aches at the thought of being away from her, my father too, but Nora and me? We're inseparable. Or we were, until now. I've never spent a day without her, and as much as it pains me, it won't be forever, and it will be for the greater good.

With that in mind, I add it to the ever-growing list of positives to fuel me.

As I round a bend in the path, reaching the crest of the hill that leads back down to the lush grounds of the academy, a turret in the far distance catches my attention, rooting me to the spot.

The walls are worn, but the work has begun to bring it back to its full glory. The once cream exterior is now a mottle of copper and brown, but the stained-glass windows still shimmer in the sunlight, even from here.

Floodborn Castle.

The last to walk those halls no longer remains in control

of the kingdom.

King Reagan. The fae king. Tarnished and broken, the fae desperately need a new sense of hope in the kingdom, and I'm going to provide it.

Seeing it standing in the distance, a beacon of fae strength, sends a warmth down my spine that lifts the corner of my mouth. The breeze around my face feels gentler, the air warmer than a moment ago, and the zing that glosses over my skin cements this moment forever in my mind.

That's where the heir will reign.

That's where *I* will reign.

My nostrils flare as I take a deep breath before slowly exhaling and continuing along the path.

Reaching the bottom of the incline, I notice the tree line grows thicker, the lush green leaves forming the perfect archway over the path as I slink into what seems like a forest. White snowdrop flowers grow sporadically throughout the grassy area, with a few sprinklings of berry shrubs and daisies.

It's undeniably breathtaking, but it has a strange way of setting me on edge. Like it's out of place here. Maybe that's the point of it: to catch us off guard.

Well, consider my guard well and truly in place. Thank you very much.

The sound of music playing drowns out the tweeting

birds, and every step I take makes it louder. I purse my lips, considering whether to continue on ahead and risk bumping into whoever is playing the awful tune that fills the air or turn back around, slink back into the shadows, and walk the long way back.

My stomach grumbles in protest, reminding me that I haven't eaten anything since yesterday evening, but the indecision still wars inside of me. Curiosity gets the better of me when I spy two guys by a fallen tree trunk.

I slow my pace, sticking to the opposite side of the path to where they are as I take them in. One has a soccer ball in his possession, tossing it up in the air and catching it while he lays on the grass beside the trunk, whereas the other guy sits with his elbows braced on his knees.

They're chatting and laughing, none of which is actually audible with the music playing, but the familiarity and calmness between them is clear. Which is crazy as hell because I can tell they're not from the same origin.

The guy on the grass has messy brown hair, emerald green eyes, and a noticeably broad frame, even from this distance. The guy with him has jet-black hair swept to the side with precision and deep brown eyes that seem to be calculating everything, even while he's seemingly relaxing.

A glance from anyone else may seem irrelevant, especially from this angle where you can't see any more significant details about them, but my father trained me how to confirm someone's origin. It's an ability I like to keep close to my chest. Especially here.

Secret or not, the two origins I find laughing together now are at opposite ends of the spectrum.

A wolf and a vampire.

The origins with the largest populations, making them the top two origins likely to produce the new heir. The thought alone makes my jaw clench and my eyes narrow as I stare at them, even though they've technically done nothing wrong.

A twig snaps under my boot, a sound not noticeable above the music, not to the naked ear at least, but it drags both of their gazes in my direction. It takes everything in me to school my features and keep my feet moving, despite their attention, but it's impossible to tear my eyes from them.

The air shifts around me and the wolf forgets his ball, bracing on his elbows as he glances over at me. The vampire frowns, the tick to his jaw noticeable from here. My presence is clearly not wanted. Maybe turning around earlier to go unnoticed was the better option, but it's too late for me to change my mind now.

Rolling my shoulders back, I wet my dry lips as I strain every muscle in my neck to look away from them, but just because I'm not looking at them doesn't mean they're not looking at me. My body tingles from their attention, and as much as I will it away, it only grows stronger the closer I get.

Just follow the path, Addi. Pretend they're not there and get the hell out of here before you open your mouth and cause any unnecessary drama.

"I don't know who suggested you go for a walk through here, but let me make it clear: no humans are wanted along this path."

"Not human, but thanks," I bite back before I can stop myself.

A flash of movement flickers in the corner of my eye, and a moment later, the pathway in front of me is blocked. The green-eyed wolf stands with his arms folded over his chest, a step behind the vampire who leers a little closer than I'm sure is necessary. He taps at his chin as his gaze drifts over me from head to toe, the cloak concealing most of me from them.

Thankful for the floaty layer, I slip my hands inside to hold onto the first weapon I can get my hands on. Just in case.

"Well, you're not a vampire, as there's nothing flashy about you," he states, turning his nose at me, but I keep completely still, refusing to react.

"Definitely not a wolf. She's not warm and welcoming," the guy behind him adds, making the vampire nod.

"Not a human, so she says, and she's missing pointy ears. Sure, she's wearing a cloak like a mage, but she doesn't have the air of regal wisdom like Abel does. Wouldn't you agree?" He doesn't bother to glance over his shoulder at his companion, who nods in agreement.

"If you're done with your assessment…" I start, but the vampire's gaze darkens as he shakes his head at me. Which only serves to annoy me more.

"Which only leaves a shifter, but there's just… something missing from the equation." He edges in closer, making my spine stiffen. "So, we're back at the beginning with you being a human. Lying about it is never going to change that fact."

I refrain from rolling my eyes, barely, as my mouth parts, ready to put him back in his place, but the shrill sound of girls giggling bursts the little bubble we seem to be in. My lips mash together and I sink my teeth into my tongue, willing myself to keep tight-lipped.

Glancing over their shoulders, I track the new arrivals: three girls and five guys. I feel both pairs of eyes remain on my face for a moment longer before they follow my line of sight.

Use this to your advantage, Addi. Get. Out. Of. Here.

They're standing in front of me before I can make my hasty exit.

"Who is this?" one of the girls asks, peering down her

nose at me with an air of superiority that instantly reveals her as a vampire.

"Wait, isn't that the weirdo with no fae ears that was standing with them?" One of her friends stares down at me with the same expression as she makes her jibe, and I take two rushed deep breaths, trying to calm my instinctive reaction, but it does little to quell the annoyance simmering in my veins.

The feeling only intensifies as the girls laugh at her appraisal, while the black haired, sharp jawed vampire who called out in the first place tries to meet my eyes.

Don't react. Don't react. Don't react.

"She's fae? But how?" The wolf asks, flicking his own ear, earning another chuckle from the growing group.

"Ew, fae, why are we even having this conversation right now?"

The taste of copper fills my mouth as I use all of my might to just keep my mouth shut, even though I want to jab a blade into this girl's neck and make an example out of her.

I really should; it would be a lot of fun, but I don't want to reveal my hand so soon. If the alternative is them underestimating me, then so be it.

Taking a deep breath again, it works a little better than my last attempt and gives me enough fuel to put one foot in front of the other, side-stepping the group as a whole, but

I'm halted just as quickly.

"Fae are as low as they get. You're going to find yourself very, *very*, lonely here," Mr. Vampire grinds out as he stares down at me with a sneer lifting his upper lip.

I feel the snap inside of me as my tongue falls from my teeth, which I bare in what I'm sure looks like a twisted, feral smile that does nothing to make me look good.

"Oh, I can get lower," I murmur, stepping closer to him this time. A move that makes his eyes widen just a fraction. *Good, you know I'm not afraid of you.* "When I drop to my knees for a dick worth submitting for, I can get way, *way* lower." My nostrils flare as my breaths come in short, sharp bursts. I stare him down, hearing the gasps echo around me at the crude words that fall from my mouth, but this is who I am. Some days containing it is a little harder than others. "Have a nice day," I add, attempting a sweet smile now, but I know it's still nowhere close to friendly.

I don't wait around to find out, though. He gives me an inch and I take it, hightailing it out of there before I utter another word.

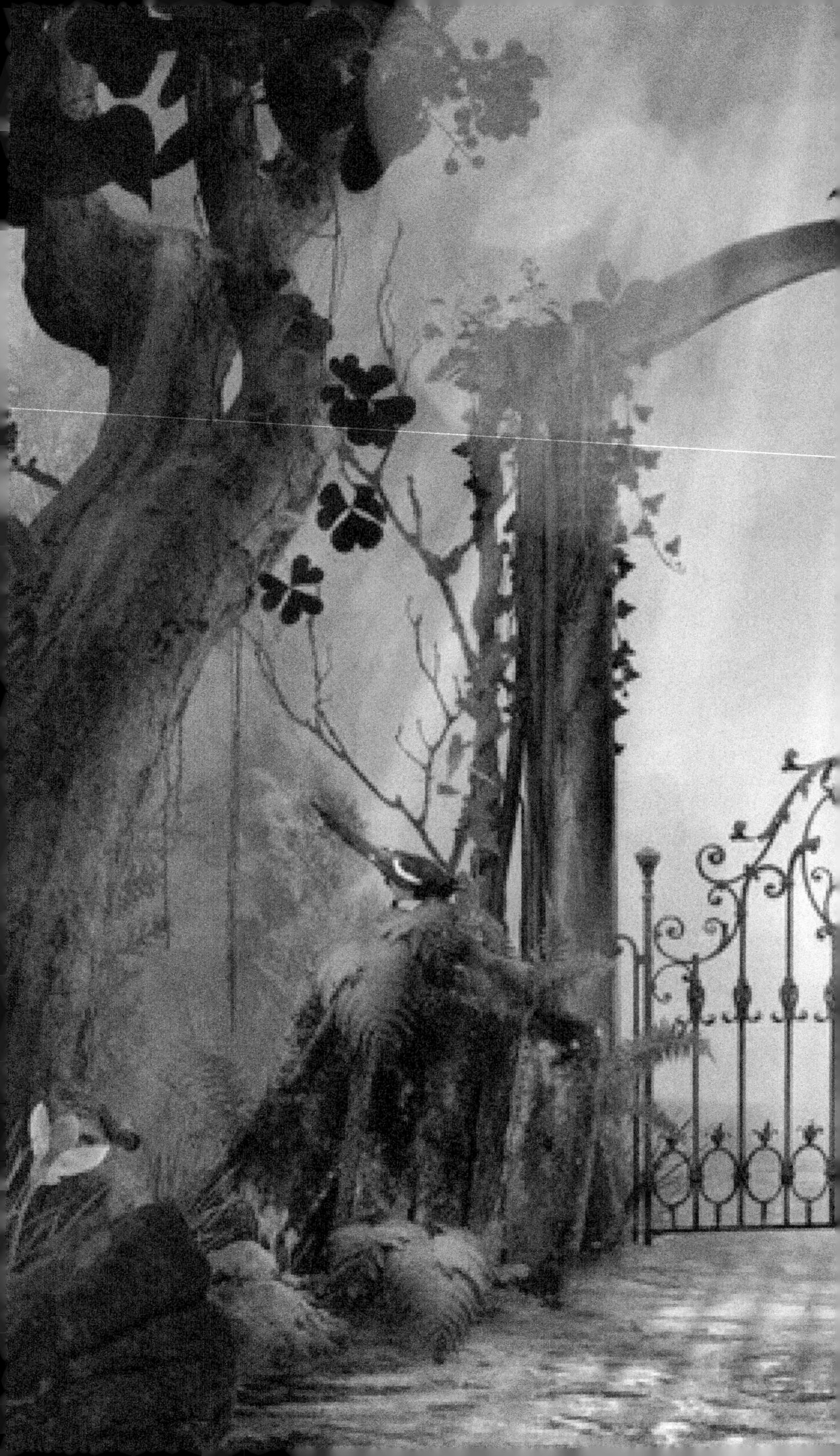

ADDI

7

Gray...is kind of my color, it seems. It makes my eyes look lighter and my hair almost whiter. I kind of don't hate the academy-issued cloak that now drapes my shoulders, but the purpose and meaning behind it still irritates me.

It doesn't wrap around me like my black one does, so I can't wear my dagger-filled waistcoat underneath. I still have a few blades concealed where I can, and my chest is lighter, at least.

Running my fingers over the intricate braid I've twisted back off my face, I make sure it's completely secure. There are a few loose tendrils poking out, but that's unavoidable with my unruly curls.

I need to leave for breakfast, which means a grand trip to the dining hall. I stopped by yesterday, managing to grab some food and slip back to my room without any further issues, but my gut tells me I'm not going to be as lucky this morning.

Visions of jet-black hair and deep brown eyes flash in my mind, merging with messy brown hair and eyes greener than my own.

I should have kept my mouth shut, but sometimes it's just impossible. Giving in and offering any kind of response only encourages them further, and I really don't need the distraction. Hopefully, I can avoid the other origins enough to fly under the radar while stoking fire into the fae I'm with so we can all envision a strong end goal together.

Shaking my head, I set those thoughts aside for now. It sounds complicated, how I need to be and act to have the right impact around me, and I don't need to falter under the pressure of it when I haven't even completed the first day of classes.

My gaze drifts to the desk drawer, and I hurry over, wanting to see the letter one more time before I leave. When I returned last night and went through my things properly, I found another heartfelt letter with my name scrawled across it. Only this one was from my father.

Addi,

My love.

You are strong, you are brave, you are everything you

were destined to be.
Stay true to yourself, follow your heart, and you'll make a positive impact on the world around you.
No matter what may follow, I am proud of you, I am in awe of you, I love you.
Don't forget to prioritize yourself among the madness to come, and don't worry about Nora and me.
All my love,
Dad

I should be concerned that they both managed to slip a letter into my possessions without me noticing, but I'm grateful for it no matter what. Folding it with precision, I tuck it away and get ready to leave again.

Once I've done one final sweep around my room, making sure everything is safe and secure, I finally head for the door. The hallway is quiet as I step out, and I bask in the silence as I head for the stairs. A few people are seated in the communal lounge, offering nervous smiles my way as I step into the room. I plaster a smile on my own face before heading outside.

"There you are."

I startle as Flora waves at me enthusiastically with Arlo beside her.

"She was waiting for you. Insisted on it even though my insides are about to fall out with how hungry I am,"

Arlo groans dramatically, clutching his stomach as Flora rolls her eyes at him, and I grin.

It's impossible to deny that they're quite funny and have an easy-going vibe that surrounds them.

I should decline and head to the dining hall alone, but that completely defies the point of us being here. How am I going to win this place and become the heir of Floodborn Kingdom if I'm too antisocial to deal with other people?

With my mind made up, I take a step toward them and they automatically fall into step with me. Comfortable silence drifts around us as we head down the path, passing the large fountain that connects all the different origin buildings along the way.

"So, Addi, where are you from?" Arlo cocks a brow at me, a look I'm getting familiar with already. It means he's challenging me, just like yesterday, but in the calmest and politest way possible, if that's even a thing.

"You don't have to answer that," Flora interjects, eyes widening at her friend, who shrugs in response.

"What? We're fae from Summer Oak, just like everyone else we recognize. There are only a few fae I don't know, and Addi is one of them. I'm curious," Arlo insists, like it's totally fine. So why does my heart quicken and my palms feel sweaty?

Luckily, they are fae and not another origin who would be able to pick up on those tells. I need to get myself together. I may have lived a quiet and isolated life, but that's all changing now.

"I grew up here, on the outskirts of the City of Harrows. We tried Summer Oak for a while, but the warmer climate wasn't to my family's preference," I rattle off, not exactly lying, but definitely omitting some casual truths. It seems to do the trick, though.

"What do you mean? It's absolutely freezing here. I'm already missing the lush heat and summer days of home," Flora admits, her eyes glazing over as she envisions it.

Shrugging, I take the three steps up to the academy entrance, ignoring the glares from the other origins that gather in small groups at the entryway. "I like wearing layers. I can't do that in the sun."

I don't glance back to see her response, focused on my surroundings as I note every door along the hallway before reaching the dining hall. The murmur of voices becomes loud as I step through the double doors, and I instantly hate that there's nowhere quieter to fuel up for the day.

"I didn't see you for dinner last night. Did you eat?" Flora asks, and I nod.

"I just grabbed something small and took it back to my room." I don't know why I'm answering her; it's not really any of her business, but I guess it doesn't matter all that much.

It's a lot busier in here this morning than yesterday

afternoon, and it's a complete sea of colors now as everyone wears their academy issued cloaks. Red and green are prominent, with a few flashes of creams and blues, but the purples and grays are significantly lacking.

"Losers," someone grunts, shouldering past me with a sneer. I manage to remain on my feet, but as I glance over my shoulder, I can't tell who it is I need to retaliate against.

"Are you okay?"

Taking a deep breath, I nod to Flora while keeping myself moving to the food counters.

"I've heard the rumors," Arlo states when I grab a tray, eyes glancing over the offerings.

"What rumors?" Flora asks.

Admittedly, I'm just as eager to know what rumors he means too.

"That there's a target on all of our backs."

"All of our backs? What does that mean?" Flora questions, her eyes pinching in confusion.

"I'm assuming he means the fae. We're going to be targeted by everyone here, but mostly the vampires and wolves who make up the largest numbers of those in attendance," I state, and Arlo snaps his finger at me with a nod.

"But why?"

I look at Flora. Like, really look at her, and it's my turn for my eyebrows to draw together.

"Before you ask, yes, our Flora here is slightly more sheltered than others. She doesn't realize how much the fae as a whole are disliked in the kingdom," Arlo explains, and I shake my head in disbelief.

"Why did you decide to come here then?" I blurt, internally cringing when Flora's cheeks turn pink, but I'm next in line to be served, so I turn away to select my food. Pancakes, too many pancakes, with blueberries and two extra servings of raspberry compote poured over the top.

I murmur my thanks, grabbing an orange juice before turning to the tables.

This is where it gets more awkward than I would prefer. The desire to slip back to my room is strong, but Flora stops me before I can take a single step.

"Let's sit with the other fae, shall we? May as well sit strong in numbers if we're going to be targeted unnecessarily," she grumbles, slipping past me, and without a word, I'm following after her.

Arlo presses his lips together and follows, as if he's simply here because Flora is. A sense I seem to resonate with since I find myself moving along with her too, despite my initial thoughts to decline. I'm questioning myself with every step I take, worrying if I'm too soft for all of this if I can so easily follow her suggestion, but in reality, I'm simply showing strength like she said. That's what I'm sticking with anyway as we approach the table where five fae are already eating breakfast. They all look up, but no one says anything as we sit at the other end of the table. It's long enough to hold twelve people, leaving only a few open chairs between us, but it still feels like the gap could be a million miles.

"So, explain it to me. Why is there this invisible target on my back?" Flora asks, digging into her bowl of cereal. My gaze flicks to Arlo first, who nods for me to take the lead. Reluctantly, and with a heavy sigh, I do.

"Apparently, King Reagan's sins are ours too." The words taste like acid on my tongue, and they don't seem any better to hear as Flora's face twists in distaste.

"But he didn't have any sins. It was his wife...wasn't it? That's what my mother always said."

I shrug. "That doesn't matter to anyone here. All they care about is their own origin taking over the kingdom. We're just another hurdle for them to overcome. Except, given our history, it gives them a sense of validation to hate on us."

"She's right, Flo. The thought of fae taking the throne again isn't one the other origins are happy to suffer," Arlo adds, and I take the opportunity to stuff my face with food.

I can feel eyes on us from all over the room. I know it's a feeling we're going to have to get used to, but I really would just like to eat my breakfast in peace.

Flora clears her throat, gaining my attention, and when

I look across the table at her, she's already staring at me. "I'm here because my mother advised it. I want to be too, for sure, but being the heir to the kingdom isn't really my end goal."

I chew the food in my mouth, considering her words, but they don't make sense to me. "I don't understand."

Flora peers at Arlo for a split second, who lifts a shoulder at her before her eyes are fixed back on mine. "My mother believed in King Reagan and what he stood for. I'm not a leader, that's for sure, but I do have good skills that I can offer if a fae is selected."

"So you're here to gain connections to aid the throne when the time comes?" I clarify, and she nods with a soft smile.

"Yeah. My mother refuses to let me consider that the fae might not retake the throne, so I haven't. I'm set on my path. I'm here to learn, to grow, to get stronger, and be of assistance to my people."

That's…impressive.

"What about you?" I ask, glancing at Arlo as I stuff my mouth with food again, and he shrugs.

"Pretty much the same. I have no interest in the stress that comes with being the heir, but my people deserve my support. Besides, I couldn't let Flora come here all alone now, could I?"

There's something he's not saying. Not in relation to

being here, or his reasoning behind it, but more specifically in relation to Flora. There's something between them; I can sense it in the air, but it doesn't feel like they're more than friends.

Before I can formulate a question to dig deeper into the pair of them, a shadow casts over us from the head of the table and my spine stiffens.

"If it isn't the foolish fae girl from yesterday, Raiden. What did you say you would do the next time you saw her? I forgot."

Pouty red lips, high cheekbones, and layers and layers of mascara framing deep blue eyes stare down at me with a smugness you couldn't even comprehend unless you saw it in the flesh.

It's the vampire girl who interrupted the assessment that was being made of me yesterday, who called me out for standing with the fae when I don't have pointy ears. Her presence instantly irritates the hell out of me.

Another looming shadow approaches a moment later, and I don't have to shift my gaze to know who it is.

Black hair, brown eyes, a chiseled jaw, and a hateful look of distaste at the mention of fae rings true around him. I can't stop my eyes from flicking to him though. It really is shameful for someone so good looking to be such a dick.

Raiden.

That's what she said his name was.

Raiden the vampire.

Setting my fork down, I stare up at him as he continues to look down on me, not reiterating whatever his threat was yesterday that the lovely vampire beside him so eagerly mentioned.

"Can I help you?" I mentally high-five myself for keeping my voice calm and my heartbeat steady. The last thing I want any of these fools to think is that I'm afraid of them.

Far from it.

"Can you help us? Do you hear yourself?" the girl remarks with a scoff, tossing her brown curls over her shoulder with a sense of sass that I really can't handle this early in the morning.

"I didn't say us, I said you. *I* was talking to *him*," I retort, keeping my eyes on the dark and devilish vampire piercing me with his deathly stare. He keeps his lips pressed firmly together, but I'm certain there's the smallest flicker to his top lip. It happens too quickly for me to be certain, and before I can press the matter, the sass queen beside me continues.

"Do you even realize who you're speaking to? I'm Vallie Drummer. Highly regarded within the vampire origin, and you're…a lowly fucking fae who is only here because The Council *had* to include you, even though we all know you will never get your hands on the crown again." She slams her hands down on the table, anger getting the better of her as I repeat two words on a loop in my head.

Calm. Collected. Calm. Collected. Calm. Collected.

My fists are balls in my lap, refusing to relax despite my little mantra, but at least my facial expression remains intact.

"I'm going to take your silence as confirmation that there is, in fact, nothing I can help you with," I state, tilting my head as I ignore her little tangent and hold the stare of the vampire who really, *really* shouldn't look this good.

Ignoring her fuels the fury consuming her, just as I expect, but despite her lightning-fast moves, I still anticipate the action and grab her wrist before she can wrap her fingers around my hair.

This is exactly why I braid the damn stuff to my head, so it isn't so easy for bitches to get their hands on in times like this.

Pulling my stare from Raiden, who has yet to say a word, I use my hold on Vallie's wrist to yank her toward me, making her stumble forward with a yelp of surprise while sending my other hand toward her face, punching her straight between the eyes.

The second I connect, the throb dancing along my knuckles, all hell breaks loose.

We tumble to the floor, arms and legs swinging for contact as we both try to gain the advantage. With a swift jab to her gut, followed by her fists smashing against the side of my head, I manage to dig my elbow into the weak spot between her shoulder and chest to place myself above her.

The second I do, arms band around my waist, and I'm hoisted in the air. I brace my leg, ready to strike out, while lowering my chin to my chest so I can throw back one hell of a head butt when the time comes, but all of that is halted when I recognize the voice of the person behind me.

"That's enough."

I freeze, heart racing wildly in my chest as I pant with every breath when I turn my head to see Professor Fairbourne over my shoulder.

Fuck.

Of course it's the professor for the fae breaking us apart.

Glancing toward the screeching that still sounds out from Vallie's red lips, I find it's Raiden who has gotten a hold of her in a similar grip, but his eyes are firmly fixed on me.

Fairbourne is trudging away in the next breath, with me still in his grasp, and I smile wide as I offer a one-finger salute to the vampire who seems happy to bring disarray to my life for the whole two days he's been in it.

I keep my mouth shut as he marches down the hall and out onto the grounds, but the second the fresh air hits me, so does the ability to use my tongue again.

"You can put me down now," I grumble, and to my surprise, he does just that.

"What the fuck was that?" he barks, pointing behind him like I don't know what he's referring to.

I straighten my cloak and run my fingers over my fitted top and pants. "Me losing my cool. It won't happen again," I admit, scrambling for the words to remind myself that I need to have a more positive outlook.

"It fucking better."

My gaze darts to his as I frown. "What?"

His shoulders relax as he looks me over before folding his arms over his chest. "You're not like the rest." I tilt my head at him, lifting a brow for him to expand upon his observation, but it only earns me a smirk. "Yeah, definitely not like the rest." He takes a step back, swiping a hand down his face, and I take note of his eyes fixating on my ears for a moment before he meets my gaze again. "Something tells me I'm going to have my hands full with you."

I offer him a fake smile, standing tall as I turn away and head down the path. I have no idea where I'm going, but that doesn't matter right now. "I take it you're not good at being out of control," he hollers, humor in his voice, but I don't bother to respond. "You know you're going the wrong way, right? Your first class is this way."

My body tenses and a shrill growl of exasperation burns out my throat as I push past every objection in my body to turn around, stomping past him without a single millisecond of eye contact.

Fucker.

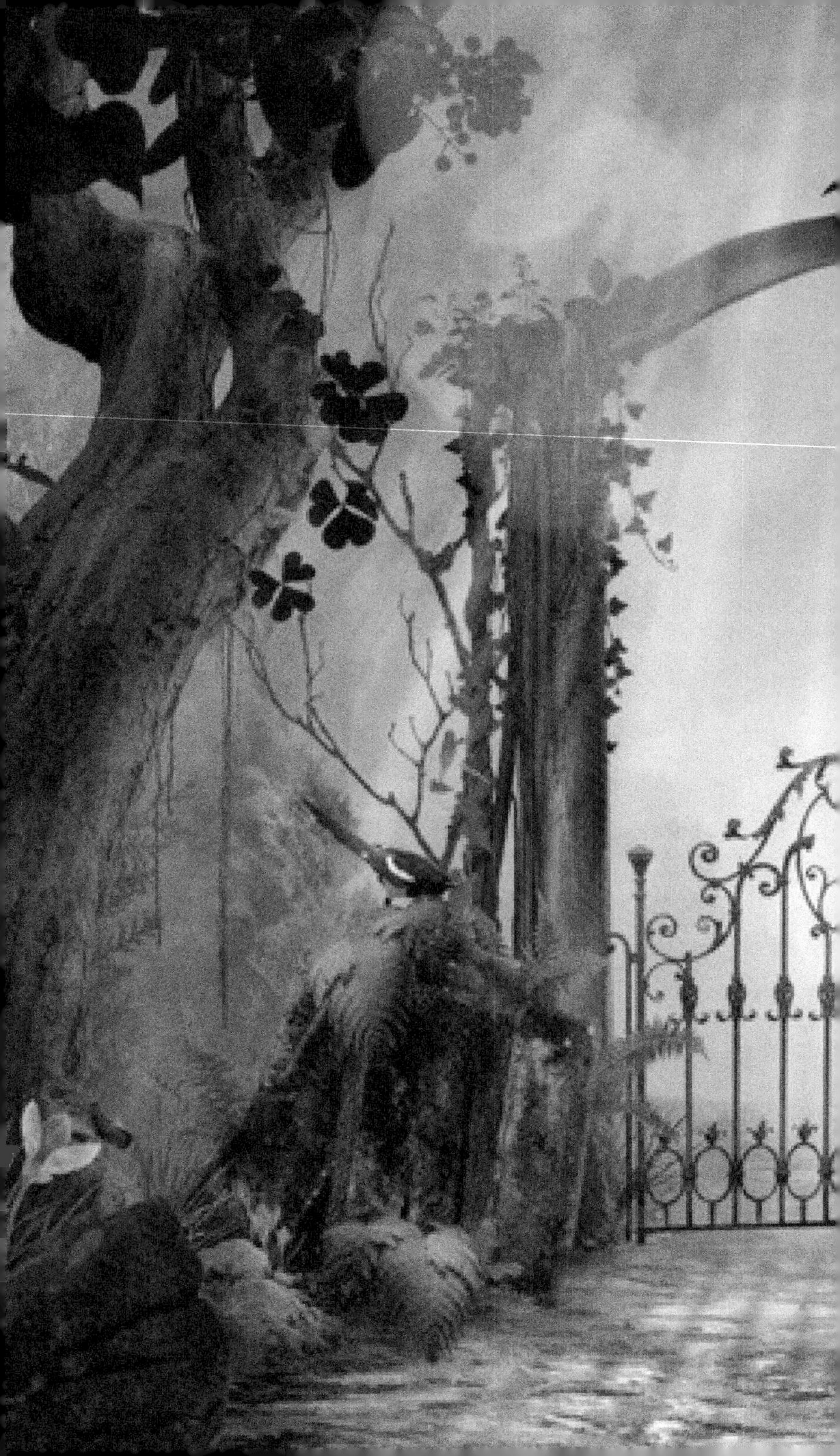

ADDI

8

Irritation still stirs inside me as I fumble into the classroom. A woman stands at the front of the room, circular glasses perched on her nose as she silently assesses everyone. Long wooden tables are lined up in front of her, three rows deep, but no one is seated. Everyone stands at the back of the class, huddled in their origins while waiting for their first direction from the professor.

Glancing around the students present, my gaze instantly latches on to deep brown eyes and perfectly styled black hair as their stare penetrates my skin, threatening to infiltrate my mind.

Raiden.

It seems like this guy is everywhere.

It takes far more effort to tear my eyes from him than I would like to admit, but when I do, I also notice the same wolf from yesterday. His brown hair is just as messy as it was then, like he makes a habit out of running his fingers through it. He's wearing the forest green cloak designated for his origin with a pair of faded jeans and a checkered shirt underneath.

He exudes a different kind of presence than Raiden, but it's still just as enticing and consuming if you let yourself fall under his spell. Not that I would. I one-thousand percent do not have the time for that.

With that reminder firmly swirling in my mind, I search for the gray cloaks in the room and find Flora standing with Arlo and a few others. I can still feel the intense stares from the group at the far end, but I force my eyes to remain locked on the fae as I approach.

Flora's eyes widen with relief when she spots me, and as I come to a stop beside her, she rubs my arm gently. "Is everything okay? I don't even know how to begin unpacking what any of that was," she murmurs, eyes peering toward Raiden, who now has Vallie vying for his attention again.

Not that I care or would even know if I. Just. Stopped. Looking.

"It's all good. I guess this is what's to be expected with that target on our backs," I admit, folding my arms over my chest as I turn to face forward, only to find the professor already staring at me with a raised eyebrow.

"I'm glad you could join us, Miss…"

Everyone follows her line of sight, finding me under her watchful eye. I clear my throat as my shoulders roll back, and my defenses instinctively rise.

"Addi."

She tilts her head, waiting for my last name. She can have it if she wants, but she's going to have to repeat herself if she does. The stare-off lasts a whole ten seconds before she nods, and I could swear there's a smile threatening to tilt her lips, but she looks away before there's a chance to confirm it.

"Miss Addi," she states, clasping her hands together. "Take a look at those in here with you now. This is the same group you will have all your classes, trials, and tests with going forward," she explains, making my spine tingle.

Raiden, Vallie, and their group that appears to bleed into the other origins is going to be a pain in my side for the foreseeable future it seems.

Peering around the crowd again, I notice a few mages huddled together, a flash of auburn hair among the shifters, and a gathering of humans who look like they're ready to throw hands at any moment.

It's crazy how we're all here for the same thing, yet we're all so different. It would be exciting if I weren't concerned for my safety on top of it all, but that's the reality of this life and not something I will ever have the luxury of being free from. So we're rolling with it instead.

A flash of red flutters forward as Vallie steps toward the professor. Her hands are braced on her hips, and even from her side profile, I can see the sly tinge to her smile before she even speaks.

"Can someone explain to me why there has to be any fae in attendance? It's wasting all of our time." She looks over her shoulder for added effect, her eyes finding mine instantly. I don't think I've ever seen someone look so smug.

Ever.

My hands curl into fists, the words *calm and collected* swirling in my mind, but doing little to actually make me either of those things.

"And you are?"

My gaze pulls from Vallie to the professor, who stares at my least favorite vampire with a quirk to her eyebrows. At least it's not just me who earns that look from her.

"Vallie. I'm Vallie Drummer." She preens—literally freaking preens—extending her fingers and batting her eyelashes like she truly believes she's that fabulous.

"A vampire. Typical," the professor says with a sigh, pinching the bridge of her nose for a second before she pushes her glasses back into place and looks back at Vallie. "Miss Drummer, have you been crowned the heir of Floodborn Kingdom?" I frown, as do quite a few others, the question catching us off guard as we wait to see where this is heading. "I'm going to take your silence as a no. That being the case, why do you think anyone needs to explain anything at all to you?" An air of awkward silence drapes over the room, everyone staring between the professor and Vallie, who is getting redder in the face with every passing moment, but she still doesn't utter another word before the professor continues. "And would you look at that? It seems that it's actually *you* who has wasted our time."

Snickers echo around me through the crowd as Vallie steps back, glaring at everyone in her wake, me included, but I opt to keep my gaze set forward. I really don't need to cause more drama so soon after the dining hall. I need to at least try and make it through the first lesson.

The intense stare burning into the side of my head seems to be coming from a slightly different direction, and despite how much I tell myself not to, I take a quick look out of the corner of my eye.

Auburn hair. Deep black eyes. Chiseled cheekbones that look tough enough to cut diamonds. Avoiding his eyes, I note he's wearing a blue cloak, labeling him a shifter. I know he's watching me, but I can't pull my eyes away until the professor clears her throat, regaining control of the room.

"I'm going to seat you in order of your last names. Maybe it will help squash any of these *rights* you feel you have simply because of your origin. Whatever special treatment your family name may get you back home is irrelevant. It means nothing here, and there's no better place to get used to it than in your intro class."

"I can't decide whether I love or hate this woman," Flora whispers, and I hum in agreement. I'm definitely leaning toward the more positive side, but the jury is still out.

She starts to rattle off the list in alphabetical order based on our last names, and I get uncomfortable waiting for her to get closer to the end. It's a strange dynamic and concept, especially since I spent my entire childhood being homeschooled by my father, but I guess it makes sense, and no one else seems to be irritated by it.

"Raiden Holloway." The brief calling of his name garners my attention, and I watch the dark and looming vampire slip into a chair in the front row. Vallie is already seated a few spots to his left, looking at him longingly, and I quickly turn away.

There's no way in Hell you will catch me looking at someone like that.

I focus on the students taking their seats instead, noting that Raiden's wolf friend is named Cassian Kenner. I don't know what it is about the name, but the way he carries it… damn. It suits him.

Irritated with my train of thought again, I startle when

I hear my name called out. "Addi Reed." I follow the moving students and slip into the next seat in a rush as the next name is called out. "Kryll Tora."

My attention is on the blond mage to my left, my thoughts spinning, trying to remember the name called out before mine, but I'm drawing a blank. He turns to me, as if sensing my stare, and smirks.

"Addi, nice name." His blue eyes twinkle with mischief, a trait you don't often see with mages.

"I didn't catch yours," I admit, clenching my hands in my lap to refrain from trying to touch my hair, even though I'm aware it's braided to my head.

"Brody."

"Nice to meet you, Brody," I reply, his name rolling off my tongue as if I've said it a thousand times before, and his smirk only grows.

"I'm sure it is. Don't worry, I have that effect on people." He winks—fully winks—before turning to face forward like he didn't just say…whatever the hell that was.

A shadow casts over me as Kryll Tora falls into the spot beside me, and I startle when I catch a glimpse of auburn hair again. I don't feel the intensity of his stare this time, though. He relaxes back in his chair and faces forward with his hands resting on the table before him. Black ink marks his skin, peeking out from beneath the sleeves of his blue cloak.

He must sense me looking because a moment later, he lifts his sleeve slightly. "They cover my entire body," he states, his voice deep yet smooth as it washes over me. "I can show you if you like." Brody laughs as Kryll rolls his blue sleeve back down, and I sink my teeth into my tongue, fighting the urge to blurt something at him in response. But this ass beats me to it. "Or do you only want a glimpse if you lower yourself to your knees? Because let me tell you, it's worth it. Am I right with that, Brody? I can't remember it word for word since we weren't there to catch her offer in person."

Despite my efforts, I can feel my cheeks heat. They're obviously friends with Raiden. That, or my snarky exchange with him yesterday has spread like wildfire. My money is on the former, especially when I realize I'm sitting right behind the vampire himself. He looks over his shoulder, glaring at me before his eyes soften when he makes eye contact with Brody and Kryll.

Fuckers.

It's official. They're all fuckers here.

"And that leaves us with Arlo and Flora Zeller."

My head whips around so fast I'm certain I'm going to pull a muscle. I find Arlo and Flora taking the final two seats at the end of the row behind me. As if sensing my surprise, Arlo winks while Flora hides her face in her hands.

"Isn't she the cutest little stepsister you've ever seen?"

His words only fan the flames on Flora's cheeks, who looks down at the table with a sense of sadness I feel in my bones. That would explain the weird dynamic between them. The sense of familiarity tinged with longing that floats around them like a second skin.

Turning around to the front, I lace my fingers on the table. Now that I'm seated, I instantly miss the idea of sitting beside Flora. Not that it had been mentioned, or even thought, but subconsciously, it was there. She reminds me of Nora.

Flora and Nora. They even rhyme.

The familiar warmth from her must be what draws me close. I can't decide if that's a good or bad thing, but either way, I need to make sure I'm thinking logically and purposely and not just leading with my feelings.

Despite the occasional stare from either side of me, I keep my face forward and listen to every word the professor says.

"Today, I have been asked to do a small overview of each class you have so you will be better prepared for the rest of the day, along with the coming week, as we adapt to the new changes for us all." She lifts a piece of parchment from her desk, walking around to the front to lean against it before she continues. "Combat class. I think that's self-explanatory, don't you? You'll need your fitness clothes for this class, and combat will range from hand-to-hand training to weaponry." She purses her lips, her eyes flicking over the document. "History class, another easy one. You're going to learn everything about what went wrong in the past so we don't make those same mistakes in the future." My fingers curl tight, turning my knuckles white, and I slip them off the table and into my lap to hide them away from any watchful eyes.

"Those mistakes are exactly the reason I don't think the fae should be here," Vallie reiterates, tilting her head so her nose sticks a little higher in the air.

This time, the professor doesn't even bother to acknowledge her, and I can't deny that makes me like her a little more.

"Origins class is where you will work on your individual abilities as well as learn about each other so that when the heir is selected, there's a wider understanding and appreciation among everyone. The potions and incantations class will be for everyone as well. Not that everyone will excel in those areas, but there are certain skills that can come in handy, and if you don't even know they exist, you'll never learn, am I right?"

I glance around the room, expecting someone to answer her, especially a mage, but to my surprise, everyone remains quiet.

"Then we have the kingdom classes, which are broken

down into three different sections: kingdom visits, kingdom etiquette, and kingdom services."

"What does that mean?" a guy from the front row asks. I haven't seen him before, but the purple cloak confirms he's a human.

"If you let me get to the end of this, you'll find out," the professor retorts, not bothering to lift her head as another round of snickers echo around the room. "Kingdom visits are just that; you will travel to all parts of the kingdom to see everyone and everything. What is an heir to the throne if you haven't walked among the people, seen all the pain and love mingled among them?" Her words hang heavy, but excitement fills me at the prospect of traveling. "Kingdom etiquette will cover what being the heir is all about when you're not dealing with wars, blessing babies, or any of the other boring stuff," she explains, waving her hand dismissively. "And kingdom services just might be my favorite. It will require each and every person in attendance at the academy to offer some form of service to the kingdom. It may be your magical ability or an afternoon of picking up litter in the park. You'll know on the day and provide whatever services the kingdom requires to prove to the people outside these walls that you love this land as much as they do."

I strangely like the idea of that too.

"Finally, this is your form class. We will gather every

Monday morning like this. It gives us a chance to provide you with any important information, allows you time to catch up on anything you're struggling with, and gives you the opportunity to bring any queries forward that you haven't had the opportunity to speak with your head of origins professor about."

Someone clears their throat from the left behind me, and I glance back to see a small girl in a gray cloak. Fae.

"Will our voices be heard?"

"I'm sorry?" I'm unsure if the professor simply didn't hear her, or if she needs further clarification. Either way, my pulse quickens as I watch the girl falter under everyone's stare. When she remains quiet, I open my mouth, ready to repeat the question for her when she manages to pull the strength from within and do it herself.

"Our queries, will they be listened to?" It's an honest question, more valid than anything else I've really heard today, and when I turn back to the professor, I can sense the same level of understanding in her eyes.

"As strongly as I'm listening to you now," she vows, the snarky comments and sternness no longer present as she nods at the fae girl. Rising from her desk, the professor discards the parchment, pacing a few times in front of us before she exhales slowly. "Let me make myself clear. I don't care if you're a vampire, a wolf, a mage, a shifter, a human, or a fae. I honestly couldn't care less if my life depended on it. I won't let vampires walk in here and dictate to me like they have the ability to do elsewhere, and I won't overlook fae simply because the kingdom has a history. This academy is here for everyone, but most of all, it's here for the kingdom. The kingdom deserves us, deserves this level of loyalty from its people. *That* is what I am here for. That is what *you* should be here for."

I feel like I can barely breathe listening to her. Her words ring true. Not just for me, but for all of us. Possibly not the vampires because they'll get pissy that they can't just rule everyone, but hearing her list off all of the origins, humans and fae included, feels validating.

"The last time it was reigned over like this, it didn't end well," Vallie remarks, and the professor instantly shakes her head.

"The last time the kingdom was reigned over, it was lonely at the top. Not only will the heir be the best of the best when the time comes, but those who stand around them will be just as honorable, just as strong, just as determined. We're not here to find a diamond in the rough. We're here to forge something never seen before that can face any storm, weather any war, and remain unwavering throughout."

Yes. Yes. Yes.

Fuck it. Screw my chances, give this woman the role. She knows what it's about.

A bell rings, shattering the moment, and everyone starts to stand. I follow suit, acutely aware that I don't recall the professor even telling us her name. Maybe next week.

"I'm here for you all. That's my role. We'll meet once a week, just like this, but my office is always open at any other time, too," she adds as we all head for the door.

I slip from between the two guys that were flanking my sides moments ago, rushing for the door with as much speed as I can without all-out running. I have no idea where I'm headed after this, I just need a minute to breathe and refocus before I go anywhere.

Barely making it over the threshold, a hand wraps around my arm, nails biting into my skin as a familiar voice rasps against my ear.

"You're not running away from me for the third time."

THE KINGDOM OF RUIN

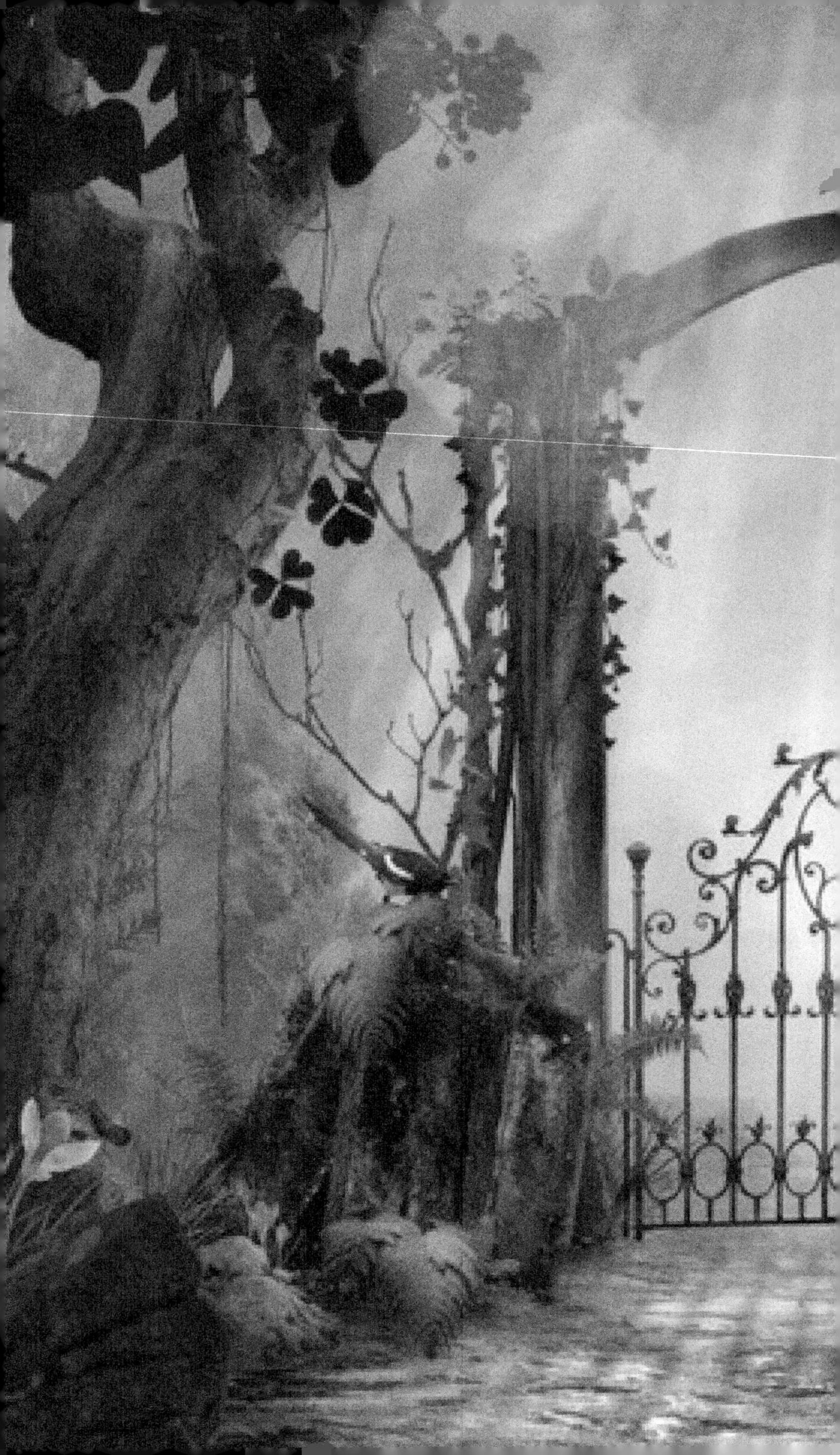

ADDI

9

My back hits the wall with a thud, stiffening every muscle in my body as I glare up at the self-righteous vampire. His facial features give nothing away, not even a sneer, and it makes me want to put one there. I'm not sure what it is I've done specifically that's put the biggest target on my back, but it doesn't look like it's going anywhere anytime soon.

"Addi." The worry in Flora's voice is clear. This isn't something she needs to get herself involved with. The last thing I want is for Flora to be on their radar.

"I'm good, Flora. I'll meet you there." I don't look away from Raiden, trying to keep my voice as calm and unfazed as possible. I don't actually know where *there* is, but whatever this issue is, it's between Raiden and myself, and getting her away from it is my first priority.

"Addi," she repeats, her insistence both surprising and irritating me. Glancing in her direction, I try to offer her a smile, but I know it falls flat. I don't have time to deal with this. Tilting my face to Arlo, I narrow my eyes. Thankfully, he takes the hint, slipping his arm around her shoulders and guiding her down the hall. She still peers back at me a few times as I watch her go, and I exhale with relief once she's out of sight.

I give myself a second to gather myself before turning my attention back to the asshole in front of me, whose grip on my arm only tightens. The rest of the students move around us like we're not even here, confirming that we're not yet willing to defend each other.

This is for me to solve, and me alone.

With the clarification clear in my mind, I consider my next course of action. The instinctive desire to ask how I can help him takes over, the same level of snark as earlier, but I bite it back. I refuse to play the same game with him again. Instead, I opt to remain silent, eyes boring into his as I wait to see what he actually wants.

One of the first things my father taught me was the art of silence. It can be comfortable, it can be unsettling, it can be everything in between. Channeling the vibe you're going for will only work to your advantage.

Awkward it is.

With every second that extends between us, his nails

bite deeper into my flesh, despite my long-sleeved shirt covering my arm. Is that a vampire thing or a Raiden thing? I'm not sure. I've never been this close to either until I got here.

My interactions with other origins has been limited to mainly humans with the odd shifter here and there. Wolves usually prefer to isolate themselves in their own spaces, mages usually have their heads in a book, and vampires are just…vampires. They think far too much of themselves to bother interacting with those of us they consider beneath them.

If anyone else were in his grasp right now, especially another fae, they would likely wince, but I've been trained to take more than the pinch he's inflicting.

"Addi Reed." His voice is raspier than I expect as he says my name. He makes it sound like a sin. Like my entire being is antithesis to the good of the world, yet it still sends a shiver down my spine.

Twisting my lips into something that resembles nothing of the smile I'm going for, I return the gesture. "Raiden Holloway."

His grip tightens further, but I still don't grimace at the pressure as he seems to stand taller, looming over me even more.

"Your mouth is your first problem," he states, eyes penetrating mine, and I make a flourish of rolling them.

"I'm sure that would depend on whose perspective we were considering."

"Exactly my point," he retorts with a nod, as if I've just proven him right.

Ass.

"I don't know, I kinda like her lips." My gaze darts to the blond mage who sits beside me in the class, and my jaw falls a little slack at his statement.

"Of course you would," Raiden grumbles as a hand smacks the back of Brody's head, and I quickly realize there's an audience.

Glancing around the watchful stares, I note Cassian and Kryll are also present. The wolf and the shifter. Behind them, I can also see Vallie with a few girls glaring in our direction. I can't deal with that on top of this too, so I opt for the easiest option, which is to center my focus back on Raiden.

"Are you going to release your hold yet?" I ask in a bored tone, but it only grows tighter. "Noted," I mutter with a sigh. "Are we going to get to the point then?"

Right on cue, The squeak of Vallie's voice echoes around us. "Raiden, what are you doing?"

"Move along, Vallie," Cassian grunts, earning my attention, but the second I catch a glimpse of him, Raiden adjusts his stance so all I can see is him.

"But, Raidy," Vallie pushes, and I have to slam my lips

together to hold back the chuckle at her nickname for him.

Raidy. Freaking Raidy. I've never met a guy who suits his full name and nothing else until I met the one standing before me. I don't know anything about him, not an ounce, but I know with certainty he's no *Raidy*.

A grunt vibrates from someone behind Raiden, likely Cassian or Kryll, it sounds like a shifter, but since Raiden is crowding me, I can't know for sure. I refuse to break eye contact with him to confirm it. A dramatic sigh echoes around us a moment later before perfectly polished red nails wrap around Raiden's upper arm and Vallie's face appears a moment later.

"Fine, deal with the trash. I'll meet you there."

Her words go right over my head as she glares at me for an extra beat or two before sauntering off down the hall. It's on the tip of my tongue to see if she knows where *there* is, but I decide keeping my mouth shut might bring this all to an end more quickly.

Raiden's stare remains fixated on mine, waiting for her to leave with her friends before he takes the smallest step back. It doesn't change the grip on my arm, though. There's going to be a bruise, for sure.

"Why aren't her ears pointed?" Cassian steps forward, green eyes raking over me as he waits for someone to answer him. If he's expecting it to be me, then he's in for a long wait.

"She's got scars." The answer comes from Brody, the mage who seems to be the most observant of the bunch. People don't usually notice them unless I point them out, but it appears he's not regular people.

"Who did that?" Cassian grunts, eyes latching on to mine. I can't tell if it's concern or something else in his eyes, but they're swirling with something.

"Who fucking cares?" Raiden responds before I can even consider if I want to answer or not.

I cock a brow at the irritating vampire that continues to infiltrate my life as he steps closer again, this time bringing us chest to chest.

"This is the only warning you're going to get. Otherwise, I'll do just as Vallie recommended and deal with the trash." The warning is clear in his tone, but I've never been one to listen well.

Exhaling heavily, I rest my head back against the wall. All of this for a warning? I'm sure that could have been achieved without any physical touch, but apparently, he really wants to assert his dominance. Yay me.

"What are you warning me about, exactly?"

The desire for clarification clearly pisses him off since his nails dig even deeper into my skin, deep enough to be drawing blood at this point.

"Leave. Go home. Fae mean nothing around here, and whether you're here to attempt to be the heir or train to be a part of their team when the time comes, you're going to fail."

Ah, I thought that might be what he was hinting at. "Is that all?"

"She's not hearing a word you're saying," Brody states, a level of amusement in his tone as he inches closer.

"Because she's stupid," Raiden remarks, bringing me to the brink of my limit.

"No, she isn't," I grunt, internally cringing at myself for talking in the third person, but it's hard not to when they're discussing me like I'm not here.

Channeling the irritation, I drop my weight, managing to catch myself before my ass hits the floor. Having achieved my goal of breaking Raiden's hold on my arm, I swoop to the left and step out of his space, acutely aware that this guy and half his friends have the benefit of incredible speed on their side. Surprisingly, none of them move.

I straighten, running my hands down my combat pants before straightening my cloak. "Thanks for the heads up. The threat wasn't entirely necessary, but we can hopefully work on your manners in some of our classes. To clarify: your warning is wasted, your threats will go unnoticed, and anything else you can think of, I don't care. I'm not going anywhere, and I certainly don't care what you think of the fae people because all that matters is that I don't fail. Ever."

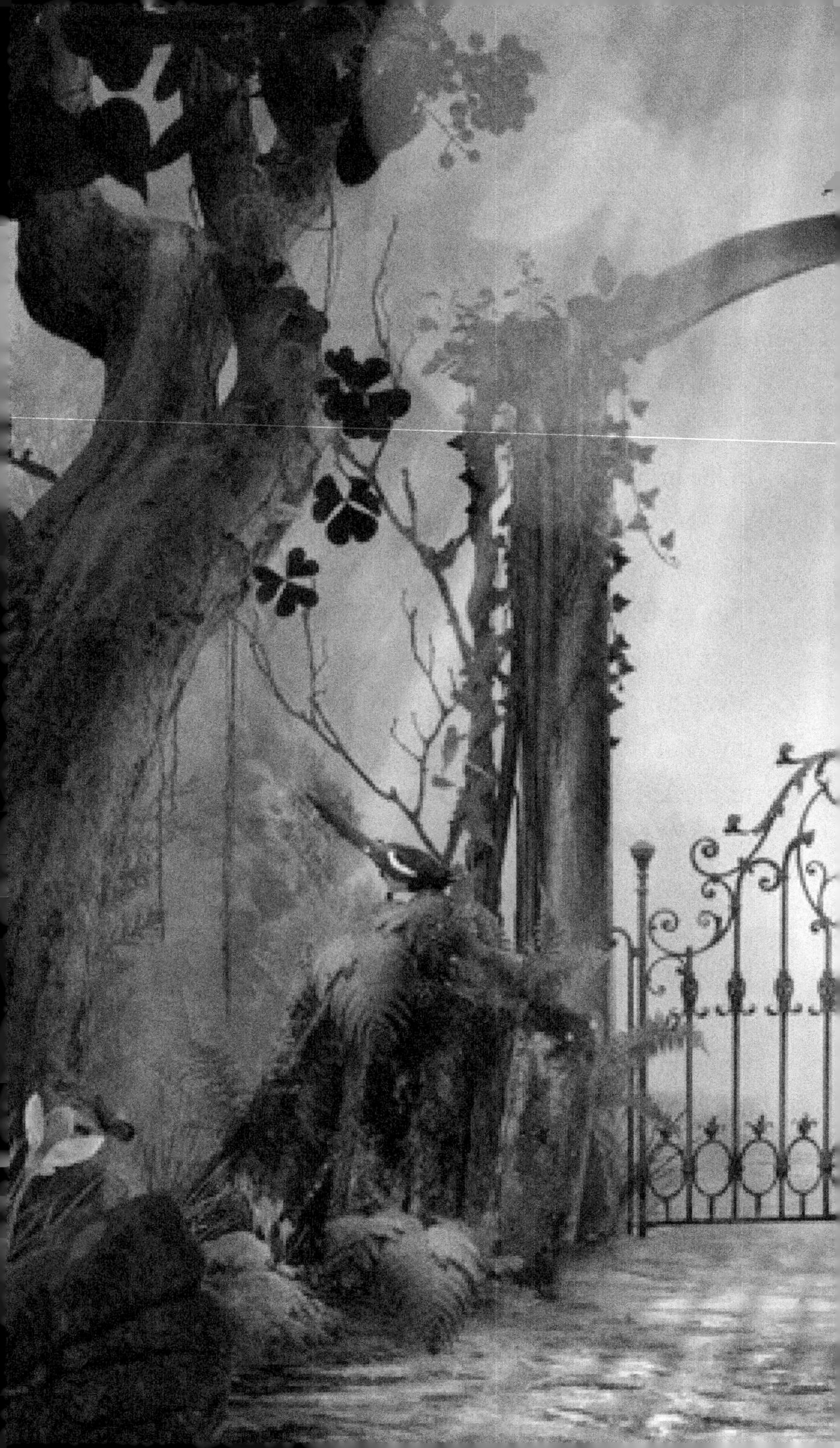

ADDI

10

Thankfully, I caught the tail end of the students from my class making their way to the next stop on our timetable, but my inability to focus meant the kingdom class went straight over my head. I learned nothing but the feeling of eyes burning into my head from all angles.

It seems it's very much the general practice so far for the students to be seated by their last names, earning me the honor of being placed between Brody and Kryll again. Thankfully, neither of them attempted to talk to me, but that didn't mean I couldn't feel their assessing eyes on me.

I could sense it when I first got here, knew it before the academy opened, but the clarity is undeniable: everyone sees the fae as weak. Even the humans glare when they can, an air of defensiveness surrounding them, as if they're ready to fight, and I can't help but wonder if everyone has forgotten that fae do have the ability to channel magic.

The professor talks, addressing no one in particular, as I continue to get lost in my own mind. There's no point trying to waste energy on this class at this stage. It's almost over, and I'm in no position to retain anything.

Instead, my thoughts trail back to how much the fae are underestimated. The elements are our best friends, a part of us more than anything else in the world, but no one seems to care about that.

Water. Air. Fire. Earth. Mind.

We led the kingdom for so long because we could, because we had the strength and capability, until the ground was shattered beneath our feet and we were left pained, heartbroken, and in need of time to heal. Love destroyed it, nothing else. That's something we can all fall victim to. Well, not me. That's never in the cards for me.

I will never offer out my love to anyone. Not when the ramifications of it have destroyed our kingdom, our people, our hope. Never.

Instead, my focus is on my magic. Each fae is born into an element. That's where we pull our strength from while replenishing it, too. King Reagan and every member of the royal bloodline harbored the ability to connect to every element. Otherwise, you dedicate yourself to the one element that runs through your veins and grounds you.

Earth. Water. Fire. Air. Mind.

It's a piece of you. Of who you are and who you shall forever be. It courses through your veins along with your blood, connecting you to your surroundings and the kingdom around you.

Standing barefoot on the ground for an earth element is like resetting your heart. Water fae take to any form of water at every opportunity because it completes them. Fire burns deep inside the red-hot faes, yet I've been told they're usually some of the sweetest people. Air fae bring chaos in the most beautiful ways possible. Storms and destruction. That's who you have to watch out for. Mind fae, however, face some of the hardest challenges. Shutting off from the world takes years of practice and learning boundaries even longer, but seeing the joy come when they sense inner peace and calmness is practically euphoric.

To someone of a royal bloodline, touching base with each of those magics is something chartered off the scales.

The bell rings, pulling me from my thoughts, and I rush to my feet, making sure to step out of the room and walk swiftly down the hall and make my way outside. I'd rather not be accosted again so soon. The sun beams down on me as I step out into the fresh air and slow to a stop, heaving a sigh as I soak it in.

My stomach grumbles, reminding me that it's lunchtime.

"Finally, lunch. I'm starving," Arlo states, coming to a stop beside me with Flora.

Thankfully, neither of them have asked about earlier, and honestly, I wouldn't even know how to describe it. I haven't been tempted to look at my arm yet, but I can do that in my room later.

"Food? I feel like we only just had breakfast," Flora mutters, and the reminder of this morning's events makes my muscles clench. To the point I'm considering whether it's worth going or not.

As if sensing my thoughts, Flora places her hand on my arm. "Do you want to get food and eat outside on the lawn? It's so nice out here," she offers, a soft smile on her lips, and I find myself nodding before I've actually considered what she's saying.

There's a glint in her eyes. I know she's getting a read on me. She really does remind me of Nora in so many ways, but I can't start breaking that down on day one. It will only bring my emotions to the surface, and I don't need to deal with that. I have to remain impassive, focused, and not let my feelings and friendships get in the way of anything.

If that's even what this is; friendship. It's not really something I'm all that familiar with.

Before I can waste too much time deciphering it, I fall into step with Arlo and Flora as we head for the dining hall.

We manage to slip inside, load up our trays with food, and make it back outside unaffected. As we get comfortable at one of the picnic benches out on the lawn, I let my body relax a little, letting a calmness wash over me.

None of us speak, the three of us all content to enjoy our food, the sunshine, and the fresh air. A few other students slowly settle in at the other tables but pay us no mind. Once I'm done eating, I tilt my face to the sky, enjoying the heat against my skin as I try to envision the future I want, but the idea is quickly cut off when I hear commotion from across the lawn.

"Why am I not shocked that she's involved again?" Flora grumbles as I pry my eyes open to seek out the source of the noise.

Vallie.

She really is well-versed in causing drama it seems. Not only with fae, though, which is a fact worth noting. This time, she's causing chaos with a human girl.

"She definitely has a penchant for drama," Arlo states, and I hum in agreement.

"It's annoying as fuck," I admit, watching the scene continue to unravel.

The human girl is sitting at a table with a few other people, none of whom are offering to interject on her behalf, while Vallie hovers over her, finger wagging in her face. She has a mini freaking army of vampire followers behind her too. All girls. All feasting on the frenzy she stirs.

Hopeful that Vallie will leave her alone soon enough, I reach for my drink, but the moment my water bottle touches my lips, Vallie reaches for the girl's throat, lifting her off her seat, the girl's feet dangling in the air as she makes a point of showing her strength.

She continues to snarl in her face, gasps echoing around the lawn as the human girl struggles to get out of her hold. No one at the table with her considers that now might be the time to interject and I can't stand it any longer.

Pushing to my feet, Flora's hand grabs mine on the table. "What are you doing?" Her eyes are wide, panic contorting her face as I shake my head.

"I'm not just going to sit here and watch her treat people like that," I bite out, my anger aimed at the dramatic vampire continuing to cause a stir.

"Why deal with drama that's not yours?" Flora pushes as I slip my hand from hers, but there's no time to respond when an almighty scream reverberates around us.

I take off toward them, watching in horror as Vallie sinks her teeth into the human's throat. Crimson stains her cloak a moment later as I increase my speed, but I'm going to have to connect to my magic if I want to bring this to a stop now.

Without slowing my pace, I focus on the ground beneath Vallie's feet, letting my magic sink into the earth.

Vines rise, thick and fast, twisting around Vallie's legs and climbing to her torso before she even realizes it.

The girl lands with a thud, but I don't stop my magic from consuming Vallie until her arms are pinned to her sides, holding her in place.

She screams, her friends squealing along with her, but the noise becomes like static in my ears as I drop to the ground beside the human girl, whose cries are burning into my brain. The pain is clear, the terror enough to haunt us all.

Sweeping my hand over her face, she's warm to the touch, tears streaming down her cheeks as the two puncture wounds at her throat continue to spill blood onto the grass beneath her.

"I need a mage who can help. Now!" I holler, not caring that Vallie is still causing a scene. She fucking started this. When no one immediately appears at my side, I glance around the space, noting everyone watching me from a distance. "I said I need a fucking mage," I bite, irritation getting the better of me. My eyes lock on Brody's as he stands with Kryll, Cassian, and Raiden. He's a mage. "Can you help?" I blurt, and he simply shrugs, not moving an inch.

"Release her!" one of Vallie's little followers screams, pointing down at the annoying vampire who is struggling against the vines to no avail, but I pay her no mind as I look around at the entire lawn, making eye contact with as many people as possible while the human girl continues to cry out in agony.

"Why the fuck is anyone here if you're not going to help each other? The whole point of this damn place is to do just that. If you're going to attack each other and lord your origins over one another, then we're never going to change. Our kingdom will never grow, and we will stay in this state forever. This is our kingdom! If we aren't going to save each other, then who will?"

Silence greets me, causing even more unnecessary distress as I turn my full attention back to the girl. "It's okay. I'm going to help the best I can," I promise, pressing my palm against the puncture wounds, and causing her to cry out a little more. Dammit. "I can help with the punctures, but the burning through your veins isn't going to leave for a couple of hours."

I hiss as a hand lands over mine, stilling me.

Murmured chants echo in my ears as the screaming from the injured girl quiets. Slowly, slipping my hands from between the hand and her throat, I tilt my head to see which mage actually stepped up. I'm floored when I find it's Brody.

I gape at him, my pulse ringing in my ears as I watch him heal the poor girl beside me. He's not checking the wound, though, his eyes are locked on mine, holding me in place as my heart rate finally slows from the thunderous pace it was at.

It takes me a few seconds to realize his lips are no longer moving, and a second later, the girl slowly rises to sit up. I tear my gaze from his, blinking rapidly to shake myself into the present, and find the girl staring up at me in surprise.

"Thank you," she rasps, her hand wrapping around her throat as she gulps a few times. "Thank you. Both of you," she repeats, and I scramble to figure out what to say in response but come up blank as I turn to gape at Brody again. My throat thickens with emotions I don't want to address when a voice bellows around us.

"Miss Reed. Office. Now. And release Vallie from your magic immediately."

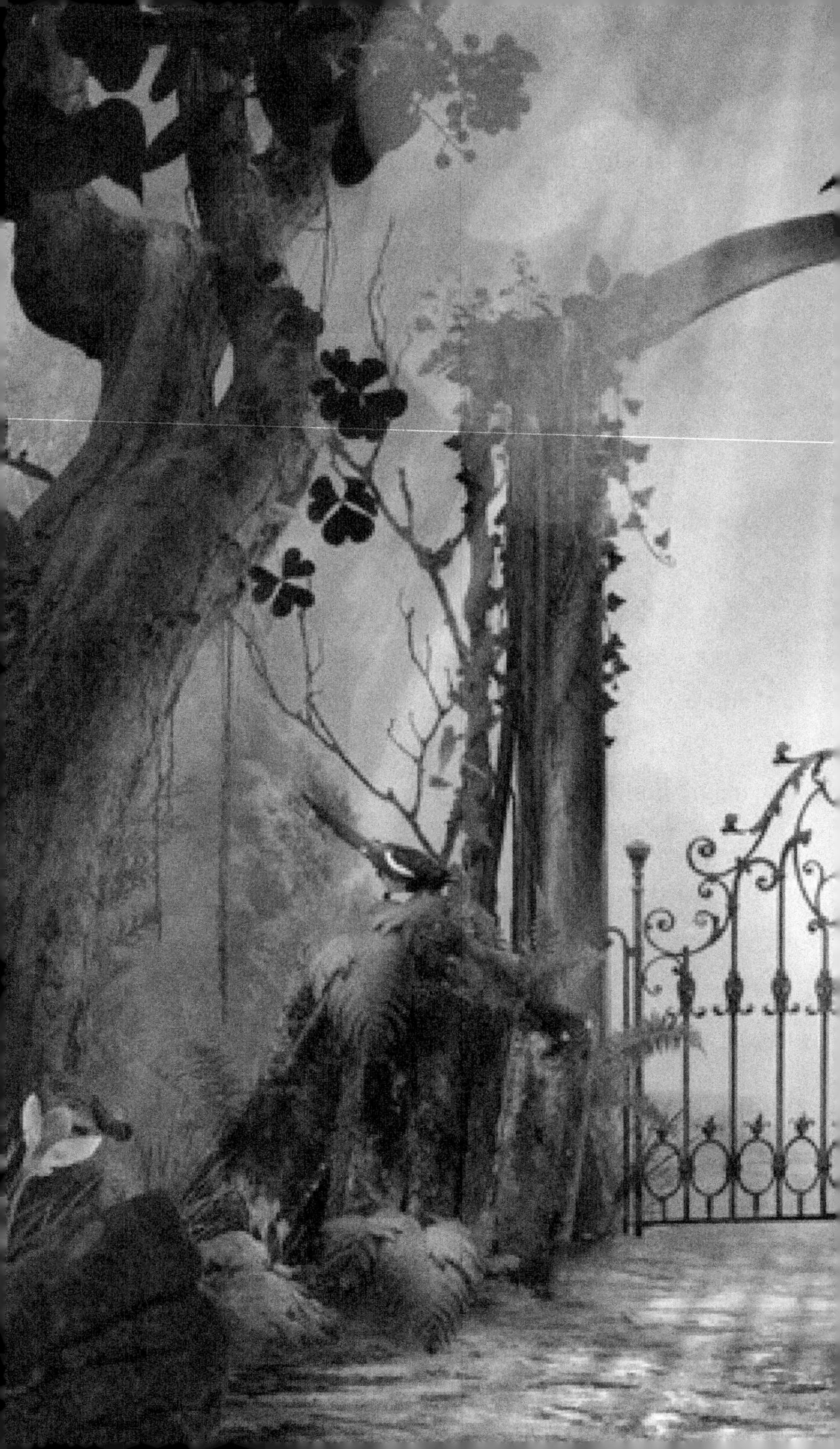

ADDI

11

I thought Professor Fairbourne was here to guide and aid the fae. Yet I've been summoned by this man twice in the same day. Why isn't Vallie being called out for her actions? I came to that poor girl's defense.

Anger vibrates through my body as I step into his office, and it only continues to build when the door closes behind me. I pay no attention to the room as I stare at the man in his high-backed chair, his elbows braced on the desk between us as he cocks a brow at me.

That look alone makes me want to rush back outside and unleash my magic on Vallie again. I think that's what has me more pissed; releasing her from the vines. She deserved to stew in helplessness for a little while longer.

A part of me wishes, deep down, that I could do more damage, but that would only serve to make me a hypocrite.

As much as I may dislike someone, I can't allow the first course of action to be death. That's what my father told me, at least, but with her, she's cutting it real fine.

Brody, on the other hand, he…helped. But that's definitely not something I can dig deeper into just yet. For some reason, that feels raw and I'm not touching it.

"Take a seat," Fairbourne finally says, pointing to the chair in front of me. I eye it, considering whether to let my defiance seep through me in this moment like I want to or get it over with as quickly as possible.

I opt for the latter, dropping into the seat with a sigh.

Sometimes, my father's lessons irritated me. Training to be a leader, an heir, isn't all about showing power and strength like my instincts tell me to. Sometimes, you have to seem pliant, open to negotiation, and agreeable. I hate it.

The distaste for the feelings that coil inside me when I offer any kind of pliancy is strong, but the panic that those feelings stem from my mother instead of my father forces me to swallow it down and accept it.

"I've received some complaints about you," he states once I meet his eyes.

"In less than twenty-four hours?" I question, wondering when anyone would have time to do anything other than focus on adjusting to their new environment.

"That's exactly my concern," he retorts, and my eyes narrow.

"What issues do I seem to be causing?" I bite out, still trying to rack my brain to figure out how I'm the problem here.

"You're a fae."

His words make me pause, waiting for whatever else is to come, but he remains silent as he leans back in his chair, eyes assessing me.

"And?"

"Just a fae," he confirms with a shrug.

I nod, turning away from him for a moment as I try to wrap my mind around the idiocy of this situation. Clearing my throat, I turn back to him. "Well, that's not something I can change."

"As a fae myself, I'm aware." A soft smile touches the corner of his mouth, but it doesn't reach his eyes.

"So why am I here?" He knows there's nothing I can do about being a fae. This conversation is utterly pointless.

Leaning forward again, he gives me a pointed look. "Because it's been less than twenty-four hours and this is the second time I've had to pull you away from drama."

"Drama I didn't start, I might add." I match his stare with one of my own.

"I'm aware." Silence descends around us, but this time, I'm at too much of a loss to be the one to control the energy it creates. It's not awkward, though, just…stilted. "I heard what you said," he finally states when I brace my hands on the arms of the chair, ready to leave. I frown at him, and he takes that as a hint to continue. "About the kingdom needing change."

Shrugging, I relax back in the chair. "It does." I'm not going to deny it. I know I'm not wrong.

"I agree."

I nod softly, impressed that he does, but two people among a sea of thousands aren't enough. Especially when those two people are both fae."Not many here do, though. That seems to be the issue."

"We've got two years to hopefully adjust the perspectives of closed-minded people," he quickly replies, but I can't bite back the scoff in time.

"Maybe."

Silence falls on us once again, this time a little more comfortable, but there's still a level of awkwardness since we don't really know each other that well. Certain that there's nothing left to say, I stand.

"Anything else?" I ask, knowing my next class starts in five minutes, and I'd rather not be late because of some stilted silence.

He shakes his head and I turn for the door, but the second my hand wraps around the handle, he speaks. "I checked the data files."

Glancing back at him, my eyebrows pinch together with confusion. "Okay."

He assesses me for a moment, lips pursed, before he seems to settle his mind on something. "There's no record of an Addi Reed."

My body stiffens from head to toe, panic flickering to life as I school my features and simply blink back at him. It takes everything in me to keep my heart rate calm and facial expression neutral.

"That's strange," I murmur.

"It is," he agrees with a nod before standing. He steps around his desk to lean against it, arms folded over his chest as he speaks, "You know, many years ago, I was on King Reagan's council. I saw what it was like and felt the full effect of a kingdom led by the fae. I also watched it crumble."

"Unfortunately for me, I was too small to recall such tragic matters." My chest is tight, a lump in my throat bigger than I can handle.

"I think you might be the hope the fae people need, and the kingdom needs. Even if you are keeping secrets."

My pulse is racing so fast it feels like my body is vibrating as I nod.

Clearing my throat, I turn to face him. "Do I need to be concerned?"

"No. Not from me, at least. But if I can check so effortlessly, so can others. Which means you need to keep your head down."

That feels much easier said than done because we both know drama is following me around with no effort on my end. Hiding away from it will only make me look weak and unfit to be the heir.

"Thanks, I'll try my best," I mutter, accepting his nod as confirmation that the conversation is over.

Swinging the door open, I pause midstep when I find the other vampire driving me insane on the other side. His eyes are narrowed, jaw tight, but his hair is perfectly styled and the red cloak draped over his shoulders is definitely working in his favor.

I startle at his proximity, worrying over what he may have heard, but before I can panic about it, Professor Fairbourne speaks from behind me.

"My office is concealed. No vampire hearing can penetrate these walls. I'll seek out the professor organizing the enchantments and potions class so you can do it to your room, too."

"I don't think she'll be here long enough for that," Raiden grunts, taking a step back, but I still don't move.

Fairbourne remains quiet at the remark, leaving me to handle the situation myself, which I don't mind at all, but it's slightly amusing that he was just telling me to keep my head down and clear of trouble. Now, I'm openly walking into it.

"What do you want, Raiden?" I grumble, stepping over

the threshold. The instinctive desire to fold my arms over my chest is real, but any reaction to his presence would just make me look vulnerable. I can't afford that. I need to be alert at all times, especially around this guy and his friends.

"We need to talk."

"I'm good, but thanks," I reply with a fake smile taking over my face, and his eyes narrow to slits.

"Great, but I wasn't asking. Now, are you going to play nice, or do I need to escort you a little more physically?"

He wouldn't.

The look in his eyes tells me he definitely freaking would.

My nostrils flare with annoyance. If I put up a fight, I'm still going to end up hearing what he has to say. I know it. But this doesn't feel like one of those times where I should be pliant or agreeable.

Open to negotiating it is.

Straightening my cloak, I stand tall. "We can talk after classes end for the day. That's my offer. Alternatively, I will cause so much of a scene that you'll have a quieter time with Vallie around."

My words hang in the air as he continues to glare down at me, but I spot it...the moment he concedes. He steps back, Adam's apple bobbing slightly as he nods.

"At the fountain that joins all of the origins' houses.

Keep me waiting and I'll make you wish you never stepped foot on campus."

"Too late. I wished that before I got here. Your shameful attempts to threaten me aren't going to change it, but please, keep your efforts up. It's amusing to watch."

THE KINGDOM OF RUIN

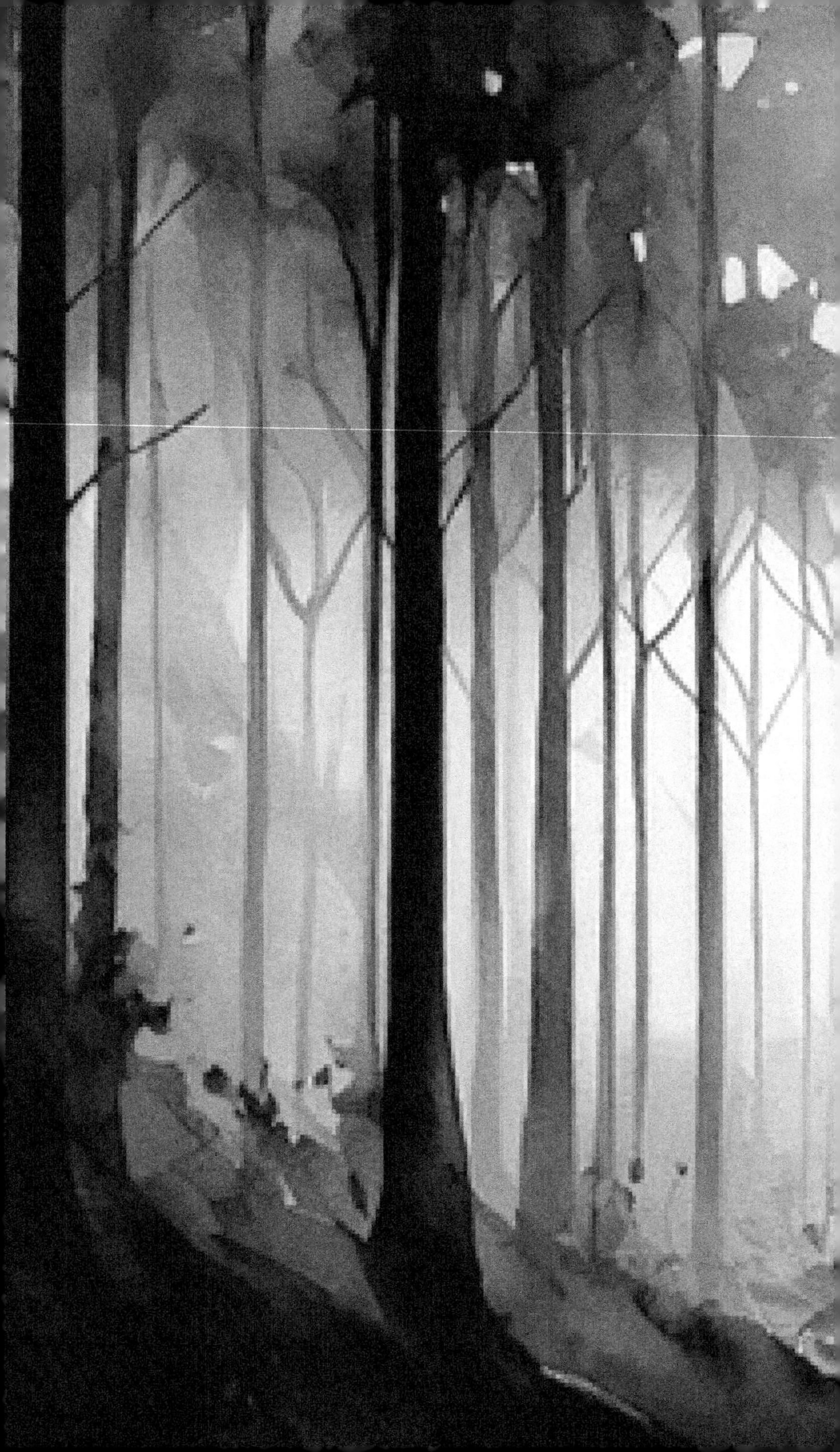

RAIDEN

12

Who in the ever loving fuck is this girl and why is she everywhere? Never in all of my life has someone been so damn present. There's no exaggeration in it, either.

E.V.E.R.Y.W.H.E.R.E.

Yesterday, when Cass and I were talking about our plans for the coming week, I could sense something was different immediately. Her scent filled the air, all vanilla and musky, and ever since, I can smell it everywhere I go.

Big green eyes, curly blonde hair that looks too damn soft, and a toned body that is firm and soft in all the right places. Then she frowns, with her snipped ears and fucking fae abilities, and my mind is conflicted.

If she were a vampire, this entire issue would be completely different, but it's just my luck that she's as far from a vampire as possible. She's the fucking enemy.

Fuck. I can't blink without her infiltrating my vision. There's no getting away from her. That's why we need to talk. She needs to leave. Today. I've got too much riding on this entire academy venture and I don't need the distraction. Especially not one as sinful as her with her sensual looks, snarky comments, and pouty lips.

I spot Cassian ahead and bound toward him with the same ferocity as I had when I stormed away from Fairbourne's office.

His eyes widen, then quickly narrow as I approach. "You don't look like you've had a talk," he states, tucking his hands into the pockets of his jeans as concern dances in his eyes.

"What *do* I look like?" I push, knowing his wolf nature is eager to take over. That's why his hands are stuffed in his pockets, because he knows I don't like to be touched, and his instincts are screaming at him to fucking hug me.

"Pissed as usual, but not in the victorious way you love or the furious way like you did before when she got one over on you," he states, eyes narrowing as he continues to assess me.

My jaw clenches as I frown at him, but it does nothing to shake him off. It never does.

"Nope, still not getting a read."

The voice gets under my skin instantly, just as he

intended. I turn to the source to see my least favorite mage to ever exist. "Fuck off, Brody," I grunt, and his smile grows, much to my annoyance.

"Nah, you love me too much for that," he retorts, clapping me on the arm with a wink, and I want to wring his fucking neck.

Stepping into the classroom, I have no idea what's next on the timetable. I'm too caught up in origins distracting me to give it my full attention. A fact I need to change as soon as possible. Starting now.

I turn to Cass as I walk through the rows to take my seat. We haven't been in here yet, but the layout is the exact same as every other class we've been to so far. Seat assignment has been the same all morning, I'm going to assume this afternoon is the same. Stopping by the seat I'm assuming is mine, I glance at Cass. "Cass, please just—"

He shakes his head from farther down the row, not even letting me finish. "I'm not dealing with his shit. I have enough going on." His grunt is final as he sinks into his seat, head down and body tilted away enough to double his efforts at labeling himself off limits.

Asshole.

Guilt burns inside of me, knowing things are a mess with his father, but fuck, there's nothing he can do about that right now, so why not distract himself and handle this instead?

"Maybe I'll ask her what happened when she gets here," Brody hollers. When I glare back at him, he wiggles his eyebrows.

"Why the fuck are you here again?" I snap, aware that a few people are peering at me because of my outburst, and that fact only irritates me more.

"Because you love me," he sings, ruffling his hair.

"That's definitely not it." My hands clench on the desk as Kryll takes his seat, leaving one between him and Brody for the irritating blonde hell-bent on making my life painful.

"Because we're building a future, and despite how annoying he is, he's useful," Kryll explains, the words very true, but already leaving me questioning myself.

"I'm more than useful," Brody insists, and I scoff.

"Please, I'm sure we could find another mage to do the exact same thing, but without making so much noise."

"Where would the fun be in that?"

"Nowhere. That's the point," I snap as my eyes latch on to my walking nightmare as she enters the room. Quickly diverting my gaze, I find Brody grinning at me.

"Definitely didn't get to have that word you wanted. Noted." He winks, turning his attention to Addi as she slips into the spot next to him.

I turn away, somehow even more pissed than before as I consider why my closest friends are the way they are.

People aren't my thing, mostly because I'm above them, better than them. There's no use denying it or wasting time pretending that I'm not. But if I want to change how this kingdom operates, changing our surviving into thriving, then some concessions have to be made.

This kingdom will be most optimized if we unite the origins. A fact that was hard to swallow, and the only people who know I believe it are Cassian, Kryll, and Brody.

We met years ago, when the vampires were on the rise and I watched the actions of my father, taking in as much as I could from him. We're all completely different, from entirely contrasting backgrounds, but it works. Despite how annoying some of them may be, I trust in them more than anyone else.

Brody is the youngest, most irritating, and the best at peopling. He has a level of charisma that I can't deny, even if I despise it. His potion making abilities are undeniable and his incantations are actually his strongest suit, which means I was totally lying out of my ass before when I said someone could take his place. They really couldn't. I just need to learn how to shut him the fuck up.

Kryll is nothing like Brody. Mostly. He's almost worse with people than me. Not because he doesn't like them, he was just a nomad for so long that he doesn't know how to interact with others, and really doesn't care all that much for trying now. I've never seen anyone shift like him. It's effortless, almost freeing to see, but completely deadly, and he knows it.

Cassian, on the other hand, is my complete opposite. I'm closed off, he's warm and welcoming. I act first, ask questions later, while he wants to understand the ins and outs of everything before making a decision. Our similarities are just as strong, but none of them come down to who we are and what we want, it all relates to our heritage and origins.

Family isn't all it's cracked up to be, as a vampire or a wolf. Everything is laid out for you, especially when you're highly regarded within your origin. They say money gives you freedom, but in my instance, it has resulted in anything but. With the wolves, they say family gives you strength above all else, but in Cassian's case, all it's done is squash who he is for the betterment of the greater good, which someone else gets to decide.

The professor still isn't here, and I'm a glutton for punishment. Before I can talk myself down, I glance over my shoulder. Blonde braids meet my vision, but they're quickly interrupted by another blond who is nowhere near as enticing to look at.

He wiggles his eyebrows again, getting under my skin.

"You know your reaction is what brings him joy," Kryll states, twirling a pen in his hand as he looks at me. Addi had been looking down at her hands twisted together on the table, but she looks up the moment he speaks.

"It's going to bring him to his death sooner, too," I threaten, hoping she will take the warning as well, but Brody's laugh makes it impossible.

"I'm glad you've got jokes when you're still this mad," he boasts, making my eyes narrow.

Jokes? These aren't jokes. My blood is simmering, my brain scrambled, and it's all because of that fucking girl. I glare at her, slightly startled that she's already looking in my direction. Her eyes widen at my scowl, likely wondering what she did now. *Simply existing*, I think, but manage to keep it to myself as Brody continues.

"So, no talk?" Brody pushes, glancing between us.

"After classes at the fountains," she murmurs, getting involved in a conversation that has nothing to do with her.

"Seems specific," Brody adds, turning to face her with his cheek resting on his palm.

"She was negotiating, but I will make all the final decisions," I bite, continuing to scowl at the side of his head when he doesn't bother to turn and look at me.

"Sounds about right."

I'm quickly forgetting all of the reasons I find him useful right now. Killing him feels like the better option.

"Raidy? I was waiting for you to come find me at the medical center. Where were you?"

My body turns to stone at the sound of Vallie's voice,

but I keep it together, refusing to let my annoyance surface as I take the opportunity to retreat from Brody and his bullshit. Vallie is standing on the other side of my desk, hands on her hips as she pouts, and I immediately wish I could deal with Brody's drama instead of hers.

Her pulse quickens as she gains my attention, reminding me how pure her origin is. To be born from vampires is nothing like being turned by one. Blood runs through my veins, as it does hers, and it irritates the fuck out of me. Just like she does.

"Why would I come find you?" The words are like acid on my tongue, but I don't care. I'm way past worrying about how I'm coming across now. Today is a mess, and she's half of the fucking reason thanks to her penchant for the dramatics.

"Because I was injured!" Her exasperation is clear, but I sigh, slouching in my chair slightly as I wave my hand dismissively.

"The point of being at the medical center is to be healed, right?"

Her eyes narrow, not appreciating anything I'm saying as she starts to tap her foot. "Well, yeah, but—"

"So why would I be there?"

"For me."

She means it. She actually fucking means it, and it takes everything I am to refrain from placing my head in my hands. Vallie is a difficult subject, one I would love to throw in the trash, burn into cinders, and never have to look at again, but life has distinct plans for me that are not by my design. So, for now, I have to play along, not push back too hard, and not snap her damn neck for irritating me.

"Good afternoon, students. Please, take your seats." I'm saved by the professor as she saunters into the room, eyeing Vallie, who dramatically rolls her eyes and takes her time moving to her seat.

"Remind me why she has to be here again?" Brody whispers, knowing I can hear him, and I know Vallie likely can, too.

"Vampire politics," Kryll grunts, matching my own thoughts.

"I hate them." For once, I agree with Brody.

Tell me about it. Try living it. He actually has a nice family, barely any rules in his life, and a desire for a good time at all times. Maybe he annoys me because I'm jealous of the luxuries he has. But that would be ridiculous because I'm jealous of no one.

Ever.

All I have to do is get through this afternoon, have the grand chat with the damn fae, then it will all be laid to rest. I can go back to focusing on what's important.

There will be no more stressing. Just focusing on

winning the crown. One step at a time. I can go through the motions, especially if it places me at the top as the heir to the Floodborn Kingdom.

My gut twists, a telling sign that I'm really not going to be that damn lucky.

THE KINGDOM OF RUIN

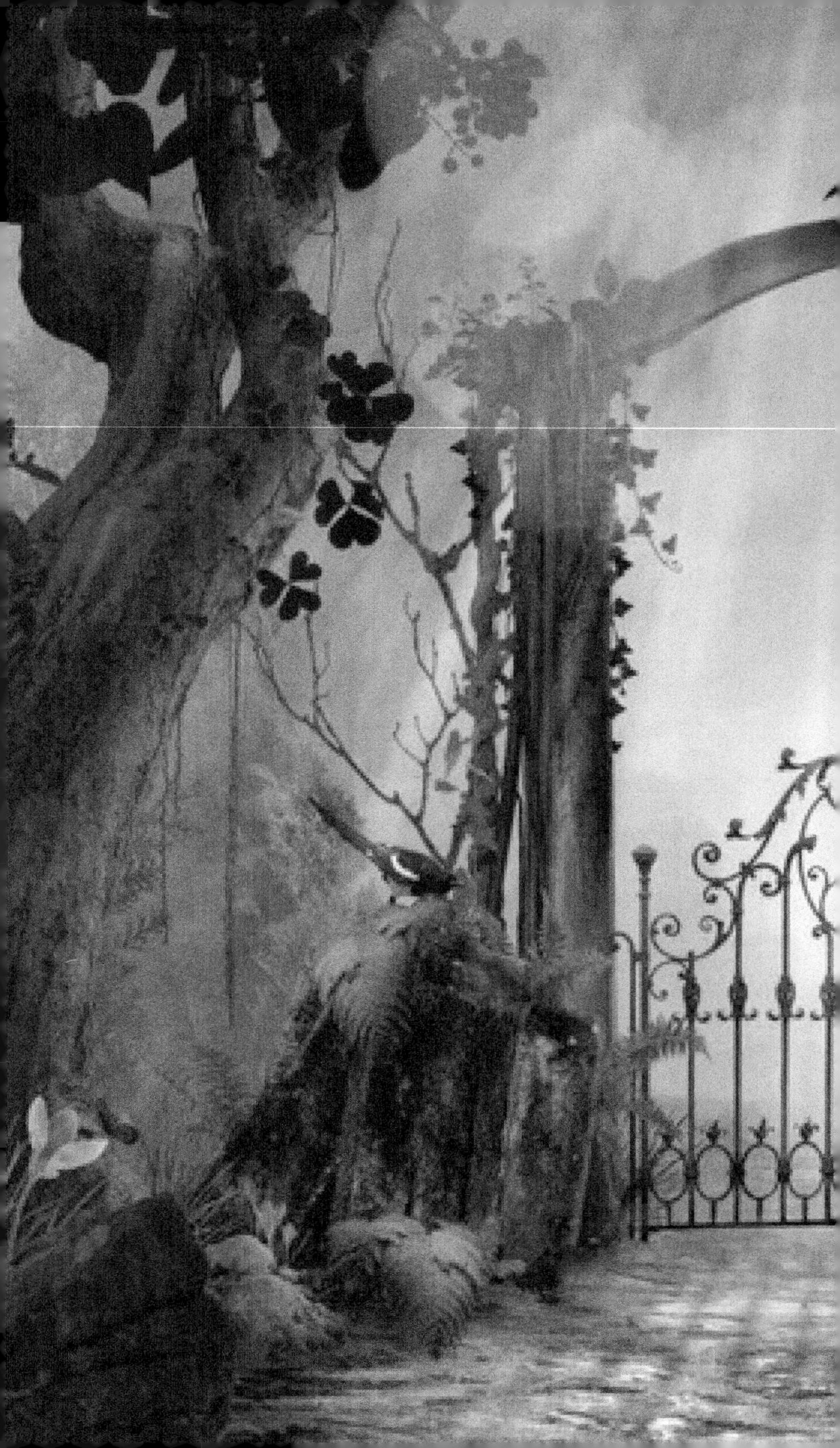

ADDI

13

My entire body is filled with nerves and trepidation, and when the bell sounds out, dismissing the final class of the day, dread sits heavy in my stomach.

Dammit.

I've learned nothing all day because I've been in my head about these guys—guys who have no business being in there. It's irritating. More so that I'm letting them get under my skin, despite my best efforts. I promised myself I wouldn't be distracted. Yet here I am, day one, and everything is already going to Hell.

Everything I am, everything I know, is riding on this, and I'm losing it without even trying. An inkling trickles into my thoughts, but I quickly squash it down. I'm meant to be here. This is my path, and no self-doubt is going to tell me otherwise.

I deserve a reward for handling Brody, or, more specifically, not. He's spent the past two lessons nudging me non-stop. Despite how wicked his smile is, I can't give in to him. It's clear he's the kind of guy that is given an inch and takes a mile.

I'm not encouraging that. Definitely not.

The knowing look Flora gave me between classes confirms it's not a secret, but I gave her my own challenging glance back because I sure as hell am not talking about any of this. There's nothing to discuss. Period. Although, when she insisted on walking back to the house with me, I had to explain that I couldn't. I didn't go into detail, but the glint in her eyes told me she didn't need any.

I should have just had the talk with the damn vampire outside Fairborne's office, then I could have avoided carrying the weight of it on my shoulders all day. That damn hindsight is a bitch. I've never felt dumber than today. It's been a clusterfuck, and I'm aware I've been at the center of every issue. Even when it didn't involve me, I involved myself. Maybe I need to consider that this is actually my fault, my drama, and no one else's.

Pushing up from my seat, I keep my head raised and shoulders back as I turn and head for the door. I keep my steps measured and purposeful, refusing to look like I'm running away, but I'm also praying like hell that Brody quits his attempts.

Thankfully, it's an uninterrupted walk down the pathway, surrounded by students oblivious to the mess I seem to be in while they go about enjoying themselves. As I step around the high bushes, the fountain comes into view, and it's no surprise at all to find Raiden already there.

Fucking vampire speed.

I take a moment to even out my heart rate as I approach, noting both Cassian and Kryll seated on the edge of the fountain behind him. Perfect, he brought an audience.

I'm slightly surprised Brody isn't—

"Phew, I thought I might have missed it. Proceed."

There he is. I really should have known he wouldn't be far behind.

His voice echoes from behind me, slightly breathless from running as he smiles wide, slipping into the gap between Cassian and Kryll at the fountain. When we don't instantly *proceed*, he waves his hand encouragingly.

Give me the strength to handle this guy. Hot damn.

I can feel eyes on me, and when I peer over my shoulder, I find everyone glancing our way as they pass, slowing their pace. They're probably expecting another dramatic scene involving a fae, but I think I've given them enough of that today.

Eager to get this over with, I turn back to Raiden with a sigh. His brown eyes cut to mine, his jaw tightening like my presence causes him issues, but he was the one to insist on this. "Fire away, Fangs," I grumble, nodding for him to proceed.

His eyes narrow, his nose crinkling with distaste. "Fangs?" he spits as Brody snickers.

I shrug, plastering a smile on my face. "I think it suits you." He's plotting my death. I can practically see it in his eyes. His knuckles are white at his sides as he continues to assess me, not actually getting to the point of any of this. "You wanted to talk, but you're not saying much."

"There are too many eyes," he snaps, glancing over my shoulder.

"That's not my problem. You chose the location, remember?" I've never met a man who glares so well in so many different ways.

"Tell me it's fun getting under his skin," Brody hollers, a giddiness dancing in his eyes, and I have to press my lips together to bite back the smile threatening to take over my face.

"Don't rile him up any more than he already is, asshole," Cassian grunts, elbowing the blond menace while his gaze lingers on me.

"But she knows what I'm talking about," Brody insists, pulling me from the stare-off with Cassian.

Squeezing the bridge of my nose, I take a deep breath, attempting to count to ten slowly and calmly, but unless he's actually going to say his piece, the stress inside of me will not subside.

"Are we done here, or…"

"We're not fucking done," he snaps, anger vibrating from him.

He takes a step, and in the next breath, my feet are off the ground. The world moves around me at a speed I can't even explain, and I think I'm going to be sick. Everything comes to a standstill a few moments later, but no sooner do my feet touch the ground than my back is slammed against a hard surface.

I'm disoriented, slowly taking in my surroundings as the world continues to tilt beneath me. Blinking repeatedly, I finally realize where I am. We're in the forest, in the spot where I first saw him and Cassian. My back is pressed against a tree while Raiden looms over me as menacing as ever.

"What the fuck?" I yell, disbelief flooding my body as I glare at him.

"Too many eyes."

Too many eyes? Too many fucking eyes? He thinks that's a good enough excuse?

"Don't fucking do that," I bite out, prodding his chest with my finger as nausea continues to swirl in my stomach.

"I'll do what I please," he retorts, with that air of superiority only a vampire can exhibit.

"A little warning wouldn't go amiss," I push, refusing to give in as I straighten my cloak and smooth my hands over my t-shirt. Taking a deep breath, I meet his glare with a challenging stare of my own. "Please, give me the almighty speech you've been preparing so I can get the hell out of here."

He looks up to the sky, eyelids falling to half-mast as he mutters under his breath. It's irritating, and I'm about to tell him that, but his glare lands on my face again a moment later. "Do you cause such a scene everywhere you go?"

"That's not really any of your concern."

Right now, my head is too scrambled to confirm whether the issues are emanating from me or them, so I'm neither confirming nor denying at this stage.

He scoffs. "You're making it really hard for that to be the case." He steps closer until we're chest to chest, revealing his height advantage. "When I'm crowned the heir, I'm going to have to prove I can handle people like you."

I bark a laugh of my own as I roll my eyes. "Please, people like me? You can't even control some whiny little bitch," I snipe, and he knows exactly who I'm referring to.

His hand is around my throat in the next moment, clenching, testing the weight of my neck in his hand as his nostrils flare even more. "You don't know anything about what you're stepping into. I'm struggling to comprehend why you even bothered applying to attend Heir Academy to begin with."

"The fact that I'm on your radar tells a different tale." Anger coils in my veins. I can match him with everything he's got, but one thing is for certain, when someone is crowned heir of the kingdom, they will have to handle all different kinds of people. But it will be me handling *him*. His hold tightens around me, trying to prove his strength, but I just grin. "Please, tighter. I love the idea of your fingers leaving bruises on my skin," I rasp, my throat constricting beneath his grasp.

It has the desired effect and his jaw falls slack, his hold loosening ever so slightly.

Balling my hand, I slam my fist into his throat at the same time I kick at his knee. He stumbles backward and I rush the few steps it takes to reach the pathway, putting me out of his reach. His deathly glare remains on me the entire time, and it only darkens when he sees the smugness on my face.

I can't hide it.

I've gotten out of his hold twice now.

Take that, asshole.

"You think because you have earth magic, you can defeat me?" he growls, making me frown. I didn't use any magic then. That was all physical combat, nothing else.

Understanding quickly dawns on me when I recall my run-in with Vallie earlier and the earth magic I used to hold her in place.

I don't clarify that with him, though. Instead, I sneer at him.

"I don't think anything concerning you."

"You want to tell that to your little racing heart?" he retorts, slowly strolling toward me with his finger aimed my way before he taps at his ear.

Fucker.

Gulping, I roll my eyes, trying to fight back the panic. "The bruises, remember? I wasn't joking." I mean, I wasn't, but that's beside the point right now. His eyes narrow as he stands on the pathway, his chest rising and falling rapidly. "How about I stay out of your way, and you stay the fuck out of mine?"

"It's not me who needs the reminder," he retorts, so sure that none of this is his fault.

"I'm trying," I snap, but he snaps louder.

"Try. Harder." He comes to a stop in front of me, so we're toe-to-toe, and as much as I want to put some distance between us, I refuse to back away.

"Fuck you," I sneer, making his lips lift in a somewhat smile, but there's no humor there.

"You wish."

"Maybe if you just got your little dick out, you could

penetrate me with it while I pretend to feel it. Then all your pent-up tension would disappear and you would leave me the hell alone," I growl, my face heating as my frustrations all rise to the surface.

So much for remaining calm. Counting to ten won't help me relax at this stage.

"I vote for that."

I startle, turning to find Brody, Cassian, and Kryll all watching with different emotions flashing in their eyes. Cassian seems concerned, Brody entertained, and Kryll impassive. I think.

That's all I need to encourage me to get the fuck out of here. Now.

Smiling wide, I salute them. "Have a good night, boys," I holler, taking a step back from Raiden and heading for the quickest way back to my room.

"We're not boys; we're men," Brody yells, making me snicker, and I'm thankful they can't see me.

"The fact that you need to clarify that is dumb," Kryll grunts, forcing me to press my lips together as I continue to walk away.

"Whatever. She likes me," Brody insists, making my eyes widen.

Get out of here, Addi. Get out now.

This whole back and forth is exactly what I enjoy, but not here. I have more to deal with than boys with little dicks and big mouths. I need to remember that. No matter how hot my skin prickles in their proximity.

As if sensing my need to cool down, Raiden speaks, pouring an ice bucket over me with a finality that hurts more than I care to admit.

"She's a fae. You're not allowed to like lowly scum like that."

THE KINGDOM OF RUIN

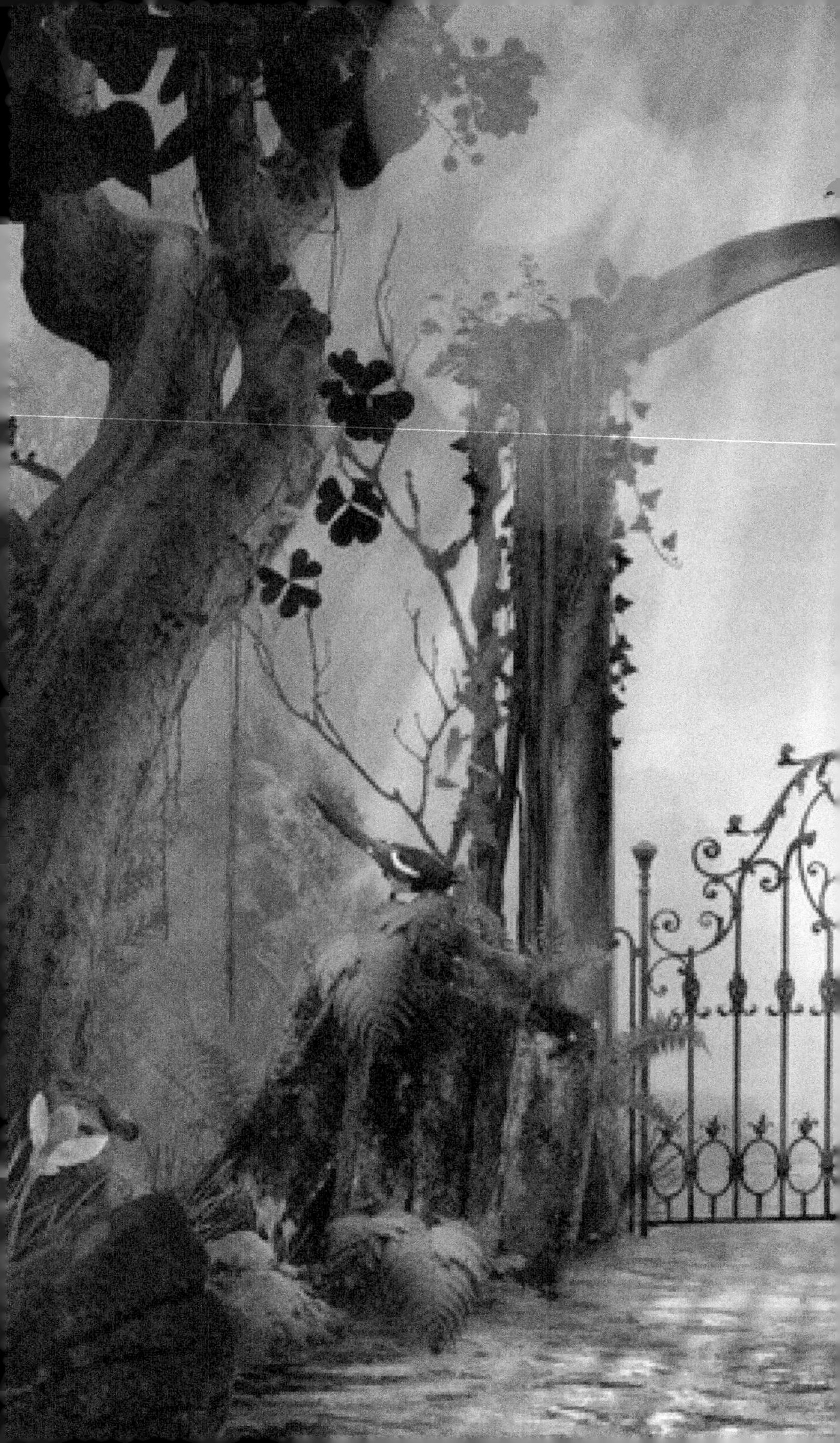

ADDI

14

Thankfully, the food hall was quiet last night and again this morning, but the glint in Brody's eyes as I walk into history class the following day tells me I'm in for a full dose of his charisma this morning. It's too damn early. I barely slept. I couldn't settle because I was beating myself up over being so easily distracted, and when I did eventually fall asleep, I was taunted by the stern scowl on Raiden's face, the smirk on Brody's lips, those piercing green wolf eyes of Cassian's, and the black ink I've only ever seen painted on Kryll's skin.

Fucked.

I'm completely fucked.

Or I was, but I decided upon a new mantra this morning, and I'm sticking to it.

No boys—or *men*, as Brody so helpfully clarified. No

male distractions. My head is firmly in the game and I'm ready to prove that I'm worthy of being the heir. I'll prove it however necessary.

Dropping down into my seat, I feel his eyes on me immediately, while Kryll doesn't even bother to acknowledge my existence. He might just be my favorite person for the day. No conversation, no knowing glances like Flora keeps giving me. Nothing.

It almost gives me the illusion that I'm a little wallflower, blending into the academy without anyone being aware of my presence, but deep down, I know it's not true, and I don't want it to be. Not if I'm to rule this kingdom. I should be memorable, just for better things than causing problems.

"Good morning, Miss Reed," Brody sings. I can't stop the eye roll that takes over my face, but I manage to keep my focus aimed forward. I'm taking that as a win. One point to me. "Cupcake, you can't ignore me forever, you know. Especially since I jumped to your aid yesterday with the little human. You owe me."

I turn and gape at him before I can think better of it. Dammit. One-one.

"I don't owe you anything for doing the right thing," I snap, sensing green eyes peering at me from farther down the table.

"Ah, so she does speak."

My gaze narrows at the annoying mage who isn't just good at getting under Raiden's skin; he's excelling at doing it to me too. It's not so good when you're on the other side of it. Go figure.

Clearing my throat, I turn away from him, staring straight ahead to find the back of Raiden's head now spoiling my view.

Fuck.

"I don't owe you anything," I repeat, desperate not to turn back to him.

"Sure you don't." The underlying humor in his tone grinds my teeth together as my hands ball into fists in my lap. Silence stretches between us when I don't respond, and I'm certain he's found something else to entertain him until I sense him leaning in closer. "I'll take payment in the form of a date. Friday night," he adds to be specific as I scoff.

Fuck. That.

Before I can conjure the words to knock him back, Raiden whirls around in his seat, a deathly glare blazing in his eyes. Is he aware that the look is so common on him that the effect is losing its potency?

"No. You. Won't." The bite in his words hits harder than the harsh look on his face and a reminder of what he said last night twists my stomach.

"He's right," I breathe, turning to Brody with a

sickly sweet smile on my face. "You can't like fae scum, remember?" I wink for added measure before I turn forward again, my smile aching as Raiden glares at me, but I don't miss the confused look on Brody's face.

"Who the fuck said that?"

I don't bother to turn back to him, internally pleading for the professor to make an appearance sometime soon to save me from this conversation.

"I did," Raiden replies, his eyes fixated on me, but I look right through him, staring at a small mark on the wall behind his head. At least he doesn't deny it. But that fact doesn't make the words hurt any less.

My jaw clenches, irritation burning through me that I'm letting him get to me still. I'm more mad at myself than any of these assholes right now.

"Raiden does *not* speak for me, thank you very much. Besides, if you behave, I'll even let you irritate this ass with me. It'll be the highlight of your evening until I show you my dick, then you'll be obsessed with me," Brody promises, his words lightening the rising tension inside of me as I turn to him once again, despite my desire not to.

I clear my throat, ready to give him some sophisticated response, but Kryll speaks first. "He's not like any mage you've ever met before in your life, is he?"

I spin my head his way, noting the smirk touching the corner of his lips.

"That feels like an understatement," I grumble before straightening in my seat and focusing ahead for what I hope is the last time. "Thanks for the offer, but I'm good."

My pulse quickens and I hope like hell he'll take the hint and leave me be. I'm barely ten minutes into the day and he's already banging at the walls I've spent all night putting in place.

"Do I need to channel my inner Raiden and say, 'It's not a question or an offer. I'm taking you out on Friday night. Be ready at seven'? Because I can totally do that if that's what you're into."

"Be—"

"Okay, class, welcome to history." The professor interrupts the retort on my tongue and I can't decide whether I'm relieved or irritated by it. "Since we got introductions out of the way yesterday, we're going to dive head-first into our history today. An overview of the old kingdom will set the foundation, then we can begin to dissect everything in more detail before we move on to other sectors of the history of the origins," she rambles, completely unaware of the situation she's defusing.

Relaxing back in my seat, I focus on her words, startled for a moment that we did indeed have this class yesterday afternoon, but I was too stuck inside my head to recall. Thankfully, it doesn't seem like she covered anything important. So as long as I can focus now, I should be good.

Welcoming the focus of the whole reason we're here, I give the professor my utmost attention, even though I can't remember her damn name. She turns to gather something from the drawer in her desk and I feel Brody's knee press against mine.

Fuck.

Don't react. Don't react. Don't react.

If I pull away, I'm sure he'll just follow, and it feels like a reaction nonetheless to this insane mage. But if I leave it there, is he going to get other ideas? No way. I'd slice his dick off and hand feed it to him if he tried to put it anywhere near me without my permission.

No, Addi. There will be no permission. Ever.

"How's her heart rate, K?" Brody whispers, leaning forward to talk around me while I remain rigid in place.

"It's high, but I can't tell if it's because she wants to hit you or Raiden. It's slightly amusing, I'm not going to lie."

The shifter has humor. Who knew? I almost want to high-five him, pat him on the back with a big thank you, but that's still against the mantra. So, instead, I do nothing. That includes not moving my leg. If I pretend he doesn't exist, he'll get bored and go away eventually.

Then I can bask in the serene peace and quiet that it will come with.

The professor slams the drawer shut with a thud, regaining my attention as she shuffles the papers in her hands. "I'm sure you will use electronics in all of your other classes, but this won't be one of them. There is no better way to record the past than with first-hand accounts in the form of pen and paper." She waves the papers in her hand with a prideful smile on her face as the class groans in protest. "Hush yourselves," she grumbles, disregarding the complaints as she perches herself on the edge of her desk, casting her eyes over everyone in attendance.

She flicks through a few pages, smiling when she finds the one she wants before she nods and reads out the details. "King August Reagan was our last king and leader of the Floodborn Kingdom."

My heart stills as I realize quickly that we're likely going to spend the entire class going over the pain inflicted on the fae people, but from the perspective that they were the villains in the entire story.

Gut clenching, I instantly wish I could find a distraction right about now.

"King Reagan was considered a mighty leader. Fair, kind, and approachable. While cut-throat, deadly, and relentless when necessary."

That sounds like a decent assessment. It's one I would be impressed with if it was said about me.

"Except for when it came to getting his dick wet," someone says with a chuckle, and murmured laughs echo around the room. I don't laugh. Nor do any of the other fae, and to my surprise, I don't see a glimpse of a smirk on Brody or Kryll's faces either.

"Thank you for your insight…" The professor looks to the student who commented. They're sitting in the row behind me to my left, but I refuse to turn around and look. He doesn't deserve any kind of acknowledgment from me.

"I'm Ross." He says it proudly, and I bet with all that I am that he's a fucking vampire, but I still refuse to turn and look. Although, the sound reminds me of the guy who made a point of shoving into me as he came to Vallie's aid the other day.

"Well, Ross. In the future, keep your mouth shut." Her snarl is surprising, and when I actually choose to pay more attention, I notice her pointed ears.

She's fae. Like me.

Clearing her throat, she places the papers on the table beside her before lacing her fingers together and looking at everyone. "Love is a fickle thing. It affects many. Painful, heartwarming, disastrous, breathtaking, toxic, and all-consuming. There are always two sides to any coin. How many of you here think love is beautiful?" Her eyes scan the room as she counts the very few hands lifted in the air. I'm not surprised to see Vallie's hand raised high, along with a few of her friends and only one guy. "And who believes love is pointless?"

I lift my hand, as do many others in the room, especially

the other fae. We've seen the disaster it causes, the heartache and pain. It's etched into our history, ensuring we never forget it.

"Don't worry, Cupcake. I don't have to love you to fuck you. You're good," Brody whispers, and I don't know whether to laugh at his bullshit or punch him in the face. Somehow, I decide on neither, secretly proud of myself when I offer him no response at all.

The professor presses her palm against her chest, right where her heart is. "It's devastating that so many of you feel this way. Not all love is like August and Constantine's," she insists, the latter name like acid through my veins at the mere mention of it. "August was unfortunate. Without a strong network around him, for himself and his two beautiful girls, he was helpless to the fall."

"Where are they now? There's never been any record of the king or his family after their fall," a mage asks from the other side of Raiden, making my heart race wildly out of control in my chest.

"No one knows, and I think that's best. They deserve peace and serenity in this life. They've been through enough pain and suffering."

"We all have, and we're the ones mending everything back together while he cowers away and hides," Raiden barks, slamming his fist on the table with more force than is necessary, which only serves to spike the anger coursing through me.

The professor looks at him with a sadness in her eyes that I feel down in the pits of my soul. "You know nothing, vampire. Nothing but what the world has offered you. You wouldn't survive a day in my shoes, or any other fae's for that matter. Everyone has pain, every origin has a trauma that consumes us, but don't ever pass judgment on those around you that you know nothing about. It won't serve you well, and it's certainly not a trait I would expect to find in our future heir. Would you?"

The room is draped in silence as I gape at her in awe.

Fuck Kryll being my favorite person; it's her.

THE KINGDOM OF RUIN

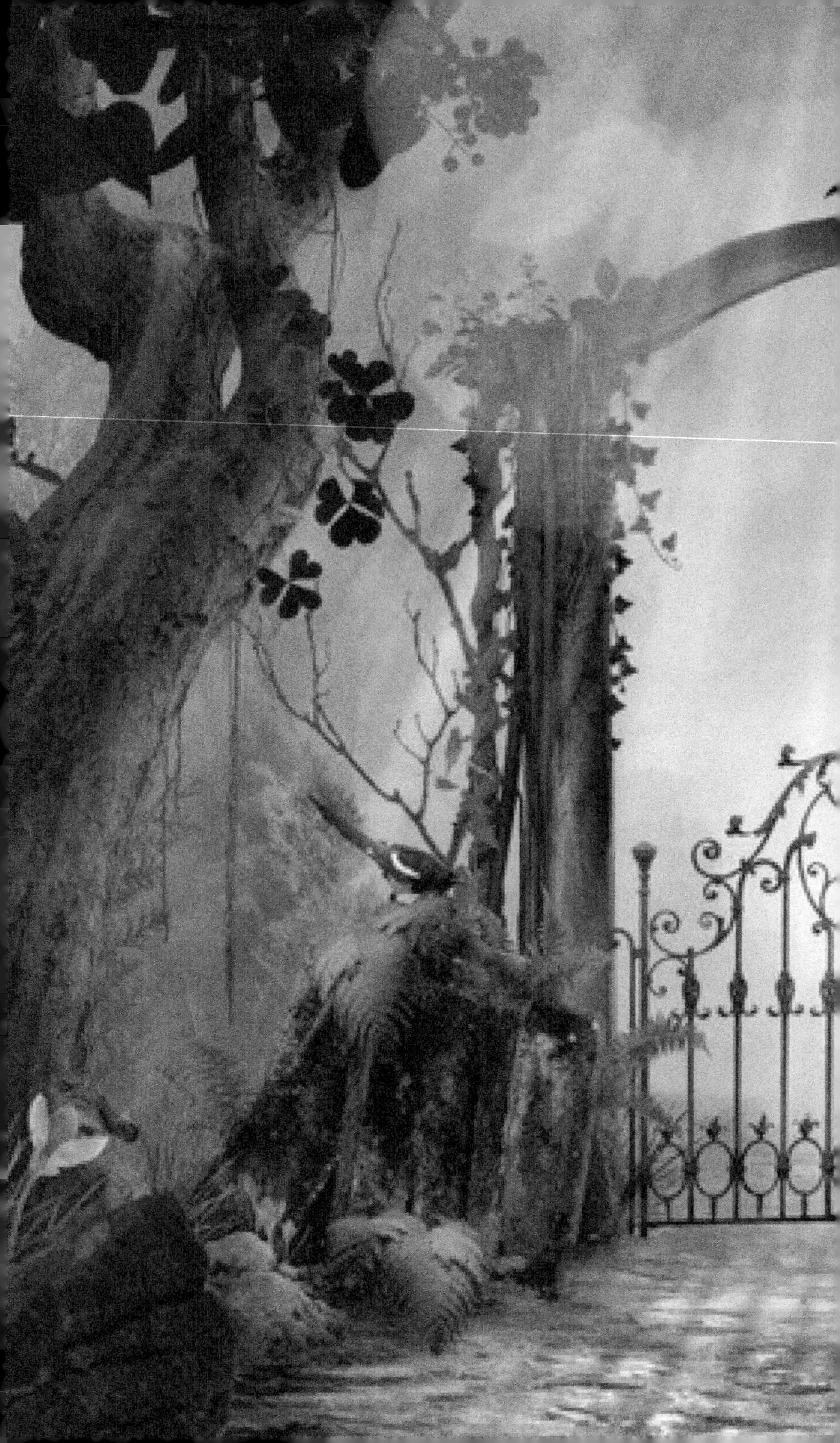

ADDI

15

I don't know how I've made it to lunchtime without being approached again by Brody, but here I am, gathering my trash with what almost feels like a successful smile on my face. Sure, he's continued to press his knee to mine for the rest of the morning, but there's been no other interaction, and I'm counting that as a win.

Two-one. To me, of course. Not that I would ever tell him that. Imagine Brody with the awareness of a challenge in the air. That would only double his efforts. I know it. So, I'm focusing on pretending he doesn't exist until he, eventually, leaves me alone. I already feel like it's working.

"I'm excited to have our first incantations and potions class next," Flora muses with a smile, and I nod in agreement.

"It'll be good for us to be able to implement things

without requiring a mage all the time," Arlo states, stuffing the last bite of his food into his mouth.

"I mean, we'll likely need them from time to time, but I think it's going to be good for us to have a general grasp of it," I add, trying to see it more practically. Just because we're taking the classes doesn't mean we're going to excel at it like the mages do. Their abilities are in their blood.

"Are you always so logical?" he asks as we rise from our seats, dropping our remnants in the trash as we head toward the academy doors.

I'm about to confirm that I definitely am as logical as possible when my brain isn't scrambled, thinking about guys, but I don't get to open my mouth before someone grabs ahold of my arm. I freeze, spinning defensively toward whoever has the balls to touch me right now, only to find a guy I don't recognize.

Instant assessment tells me he's a human and not one from my classes.

"Yes?" I bite, staring down at where his hand remains on my arm. He quickly releases it, clearing his throat as he takes a step back, leaning against the picnic table behind him.

"Thank you for saving my sister," he murmurs, making me frown.

"Sister?"

"Yesterday," he clarifies, and understanding dawns

on me. I don't really know what to say, so I offer him a simple nod instead. I didn't help her for praise or attention. I helped her because it was the right thing to do. Like we all should. A thought strikes me, and before I can weigh out whether to say it or not, I blurt it out.

"Where were you?"

His brows furrow as his head rears back. "I'm sorry?"

"When it happened, where were you?" I repeat, watching his eyes widen as he rubs his lips together nervously.

"I was here." The admission is quiet, a lot softer than his appreciation a moment earlier, and I think we both know why.

I size him up. He's not small by any means. He's stacked, taller than me, with bulked-out muscles and a mean jawline that I'm sure can look menacing when tense. He's here because he's ready to face everything the kingdom is up against—or as ready for it as a human can be.

"And you did nothing?"

"I—"

I wave my hand, cutting him off before he starts stammering like a fool, making sure the disappointment is clear on my face.

"I don't want your thanks again. I want you to stand your ground. That's what we're all here for. Are you here to be the heir or to aid?" He simply gapes at me, eyes darting around as he tries to come up with some kind of answer. "Because you did neither of those things yesterday. Consider that. Consider what a leader or an aid to a leader would do when someone is in need. One that isn't catty among bitchy women." I exhale, letting the tension that quickly consumed me dissolve as I sigh. Turning away, I find Flora and Arlo smirking at me and I shake my head, but before I leave, I glance back at him with a softer touch to my eyes this time. "I am glad she's okay, though," I add before sauntering away.

"You are such a freaking badass. It's not even funny," Flora says with a chuckle, and Arlo nods vigorously in agreement.

"You two are shit stirrers who don't know what they're talking about," I grumble, which only makes them grin wider.

"We know," they respond in sync, and I shake my head in disbelief as we walk toward our next class.

Thankfully, I arrive before Brody or Kryll, so I have the luxury of getting comfortable in my seat before either of them can make an appearance. I'm straightening the neck of my cloak when a shadow looms over me, but the sweet smell of overly flowery perfume burns my nostrils, confirming who it is without me even looking.

When it doesn't drift on by, I know I'm going to have

to look up, and that irritates me even more than the scent. I'm greeted by the forever-friendly face that belongs to my favorite vampire of all time: Vallie.

Her lip is curled in a sneer, her nose flared and her eyes narrowed as she glares down at me with that irritating vampire superiority they all have.

I smile, lips pressed together as I lace my fingers, staring at her expectantly. Silence extends around us and I bask in it, letting it blanket me with the sweetest sense of awkwardness as possible. It takes a few beats, but she discreetly shuffles from foot to foot and I know I have her.

"You're in my way."

I widen my eyes, making a grand gesture to look from side to side before meeting her eyes. "I don't know how that's possible. There are plenty of clear walkways around me, and—"

"That's not what I mean and you know it," she interjects, palms hitting the desk between us as I blink up at her innocently.

"I really don't."

Her lips purse as her face reddens, and it takes everything inside of me to bite back the smile that threatens to consume my face. "Don't play dumb with me. It doesn't suit you. I'm only going to say this once, so you better listen, and listen good." She prods her finger against the table, getting closer with every word while I remain still as stone. "Stay the hell away from Raiden and his friends. You won't like what will happen if you don't." She stands tall, pleased with herself as she flicks her hair over her shoulder and smoothly moves to her seat.

Why does she have to go and say that? That's exactly what I'm trying to do, but now that she warns me to stay away, I suddenly have the urge to get in their space.

Damn bitches and their big mouths. Why do they have to spoil things for me and leave me so conflicted?

I don't get long to fester in my irritation before I'm flanked on either side. Kryll takes his seat without a word or glance in my direction, reminding me why I silently like him so much, while Brody oversteps my personal space just enough for it to be noted as he follows suit.

His knee is pressed against mine, immediately sending goosebumps up my thigh, and for the first time, I instinctively retreat. Internally berating myself, I sense his reaction as he shifts his leg, touching me once again.

"Tell me you don't want my warmth pressing against you, Cupcake, and I'll move." The challenge is clear in his tone, but I refuse to give in. Speaking with him will only give him what he wants, and after an almost successful morning, I'm standing my ground.

I let his body touch mine and focus on the professor as he steps into the room. The frown line between his brows is permanently present and it makes me wonder whether

Raiden will end up with one like that, too, considering how mad he is all the time.

Thankfully, he wastes no time getting straight into the lesson. "Good afternoon, students. I'm Professor Morgan, and I'll be guiding you through incantations and potions for the foreseeable future. The first task of the day is going to be to learn how to ward your rooms, as it's been brought to my attention by another professor that this may be of use and importance to you." His brown eyes find mine and I recall the conversation I had with Professor Fairbourne yesterday.

Would he call me out like that? That's not exactly keeping me off the radar at all.

I keep my face impassive, forcing my breaths to remain even as I wait for him to proceed. There's no point in worrying over anything he may have said right now when I can't control it, especially when I really do need to focus on this because it will come in handier than he knows.

"To ward rooms, it's an incantation, along with a sprig of sage and a good helping of lavender. Get used to the smell of both. They're going to be everywhere."

"I'm practically made from both of them. You can smell me if you like it…" Brody offers, and I don't know whether to laugh or frown at his craziness, but I manage to keep it together and remain focused on Professor Morgan.

I murmur my thanks when I'm handed both items,

clasping them together as if someone's going to take them from me.

"The main point of the ward is to burn both the lavender and the sage just right as you chant the following. *Me incolumem serva, me his moenia serva.*"

A murmur settles over the room from everyone but the mages as we all try to wrap our tongues around the foreign words. It almost sounds Latin, but I have no idea. I'm just here to repeat like a damn puppet as long as it gets me the abilities I need.

"Me incolumem serva, me his moenia serva." I test the weight of the words on my tongue, then repeat them again to make sure it sounds just like he said.

"What are you stressing about, Cupcake?" Brody asks, bracing an arm along the back of my chair as he crowds my space again. "Say the word and I'll come to your room and do it for you," he promises.

I turn to him with a sigh. "I'm good."

"I'm better."

Pinching the bridge of my nose, I try to gather myself before I look back at him. "Are you always this exasperating?"

"Yes, he is," Kryll confirms. Although, when I turn to him, he's not looking my way.

Reluctantly, I glance back to Brody, who is wiggling his eyebrows at me suggestively. I'm going to need more than strength to handle this guy. Shaking him off is going to be harder than expected.

Pushing against his arm, he doesn't budge. "I'm trying to focus," I state, keeping my voice as light and airy as possible to come across as nice as I can, but it doesn't seem to register with him.

"Me too, but the direction of our attention just seems to be a little different."

Turning to face him—like, really face him—I give him a pointed look. "What is it going to take for you to leave me alone? Being here is important to me, and you're more than a handful at this point."

His smile widens as though he's pleased with the assessment and I immediately regret asking.

"Friday night. You, me, my dick. I'm a hit 'em and quit 'em kind of guy. Let me in and I'll be straight out of your system in no time. You're just not allowed to be upset when I come down firm on the fact that there'll be no round two."

He means it. He means every damn word, and I'm left wondering what my life has come to.

Leaning back, I shake my head. "Not happening," I grumble, focusing on the sage and lavender in my hands as he leans in and whispers in my ear.

"It's so happening."

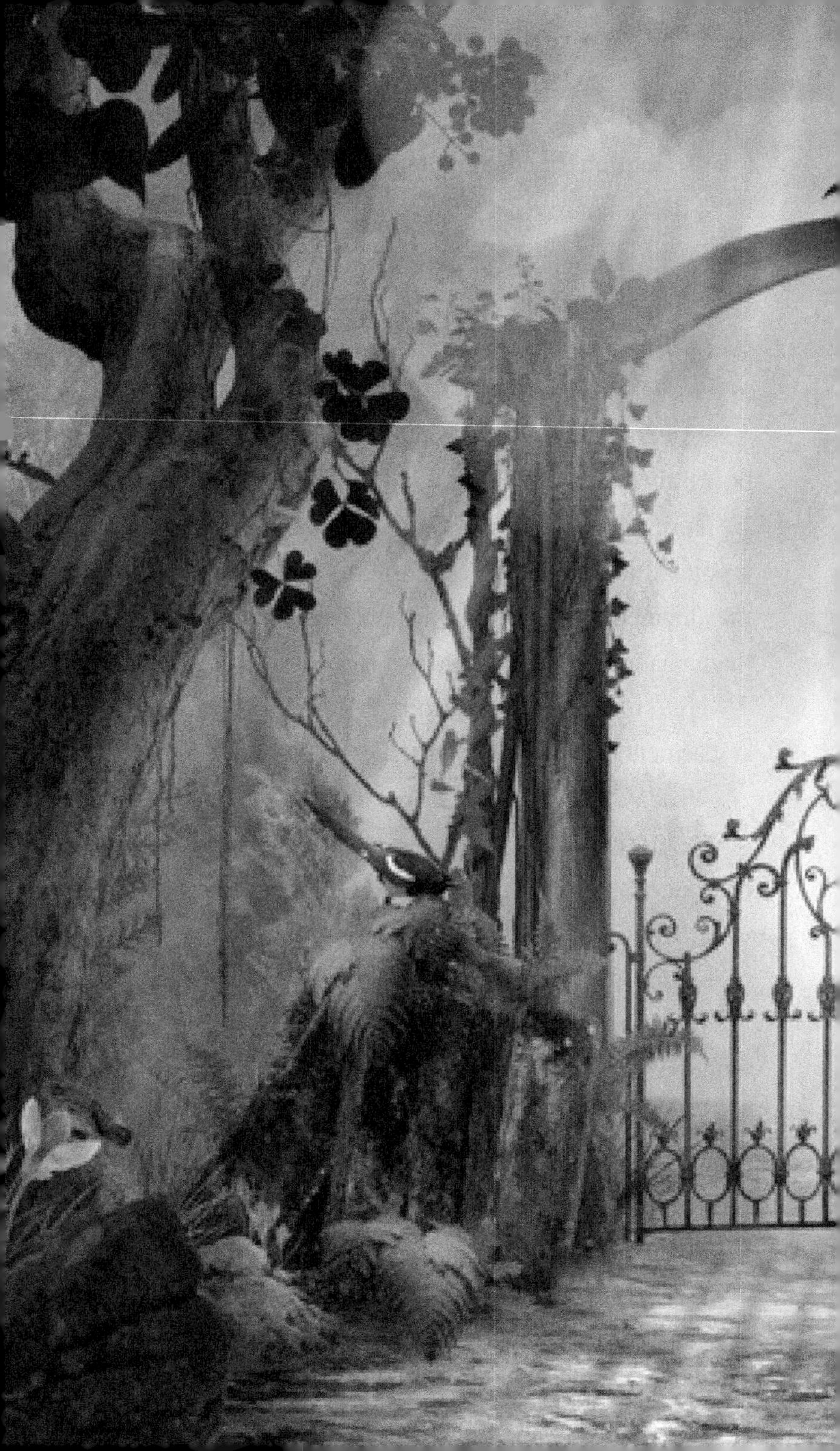

ADDI

16

I flop down on my bed with a sigh full of relief and bewilderment. I don't know how I've made it to the end of the week, but it's here, and I'm living for it. Classes have been easy enough, and the professors are focused on getting us comfortable and settled before we start taking on bigger challenges.

We haven't had combat at all this week. They're saving that for Monday, and I'm excited about it.

I make a mental note to get some exercise in this weekend in preparation. I don't want to walk into class lacking when I know I was made for it. On the ranch, my father would put me through my paces without the watchful gaze of others, but I'm more than ready to rise to the occasion now that there is a crowd.

I've managed to keep my head down and avert

Raiden's deathly stare, meaning no more power struggles or unnecessary arguments since he whisked me away and pinned me to a tree. Kryll has offered me a knowing smirk here and there but has otherwise kept to himself, while Cassian is too busy frowning at the ground as if the world rests on his shoulders, not noticing anything or anyone around him.

Even Brody has been…surprisingly quiet. My gut tells me that Raiden has reiterated his thoughts on me and the mage has fallen in line. It's a relief to have no distractions in class, but there's a part of me, a teeny, tiny part, that misses his playfulness and our interactions.

But that would be stupid, so I squash the thoughts instantly.

I didn't want any distractions. That's how I'm going to survive this place and make my claim as heir of the new kingdom.

Sitting, I cross my legs and glance at the sage and lavender still on my desk. I need to put my wards in place. I've known how to do it for a few days now, but something has been holding me back. I don't know whether it's the fear of it not working as it's supposed to or because I don't want to give myself a strong ward to allow me to let my guard down and relax here.

As much as I want to be here, it's not my first choice for getting the heir's crown. Once I can get the ward to work and allow my mind to relax a little, I'm sure I'll be more accepting of everything set out before me.

My eyes drift closed and flashes of Nora and my father appear on the back of my eyelids. If they were here now, I can picture the pointed looks from my dad and snickers from Nora as he berated me for letting my thoughts and feelings get the better of me.

The wards are necessary; not just for me to even consider letting my guard down, but also to protect me when I am most vulnerable.

Opening my eyes, I rise from the bed and swiftly grab the sage and lavender. Striking a match from the pack Professor Morgan gave us, I set it to the tips of both herbs and let the smell slowly fill the air. I dance the smoke around as instructed, walking the full length of my room from wall to wall, even clambering over my bed in a hurry to ensure there's not a spot missed.

I come to a stop by the window and repeat the words out loud as we practiced.

"Me incolumem serva, me his moenia serva."
"Me incolumem serva, me his moenia serva."
"Me incolumem serva, me his moenia serva."
"Me incolumem serva, me his moenia serva."
"Me incolumem serva, me his moenia serva."

Waiting with bated breath, I watch the smoke thicken around me until I can barely see a single piece of furniture in the room. A vortex starts in the center, coiling outward until the smoke sits around the room like a bubble. Just as I think it, it pops, the tendrils of the smoke clinging to the walls before disappearing from sight.

Holy shit.

I did it.

Giddiness tingles through me as I do a little happy dance, beyond pleased with myself that it worked exactly as Morgan explained.

I can do this. I can fucking do this.

I smile so big my jaw begins to ache. It feels so foreign on my face, but I wear it with pride. I really was doubting myself, and it was holding me back. The subconscious self-doubt really is coming out to play, but there's no space for it in my mind with everything else going on.

Stepping back toward the bed, I finally shake out of my cloak, tossing it aside without care when a vibrating buzz echoes through the room. My gaze darts to my nightstand, my feet rooted to the floor for a split second before I rush toward it.

My cell phone dances inside the otherwise-empty drawer, the screen filled with a flash of blue, and my heart races rapidly in my chest. Snatching it up, I gape at it for a moment, but before I can answer it or end the call altogether, it stops. My heart sinks along with it, regret getting the better of me, but a moment later the screen is alive again with the same image.

"I'm going to kill you," I snipe, pressing my cell phone to my ear as my free hand presses against my chest.

"Hey to you, too."

My eyes narrow like she can see how mad I am. "What are you doing?" I push, stress continuing to boil inside of me.

"Hey, Sis. How have you been? I'm missing you so hard. Do you miss me too? Oh, Addi, you shouldn't." Her teasing calms me a little, but my body is still tense as I edge toward the window and peer outside.

"I told you not to call," I grumble, despite loving the sound of her voice in my ear.

"You say a lot of things I don't listen to," she retorts, and I scoff, a smile creeping back across my face.

"You were supposed to listen to that, Nora."

"Well, Dad said I could."

I roll my eyes. "Of course he did."

Silence descends over us for a moment, and for the first time in what feels like forever, it comforts me. There is no awkwardness, no wondering what someone's intentions are, nothing but a serene sense of relief that only comes from two people in my life: Nora and my Dad.

"How are things?" she asks after a moment, and I sigh, trying to piece together a sentence that would even make sense.

"Good, quieter without you here," I murmur, not wanting to get into the drama that seemed to follow me over the first few days. She would love it. She's the biggest gossip I know, and there's no point filling her in on things that are done with now.

"I miss you."

My heart aches at her words. I'm two years older than Nora, a fact I never let her forget, even though sometimes it feels like we're twins. She's a part of me, sometimes that feels more true than anything else in this world, and hearing her voice only confirms how much I miss her now that we're apart.

"I miss you too."

"Good. Now don't give me any of that crap and tell me what's going on."

Moving away from the window and the view of a few students strolling along the pathways, I take a seat on my bed. "It's…I don't know what's going on, if I'm honest. So much is happening all at once. I'm just focusing on putting one foot in front of another. I can't really say it's not what I expected because I had no idea what to expect, but it has a way of catching me off guard." The truth falls from my lips effortlessly, even though I'm not being specific about much. She always has a way of making me loose-lipped.

"Have you gotten in trouble?"

"Define trouble."

Her laugh echoes in the air and I can picture her falling back in a fit of chuckles.

"You have. I love it!"

"Trouble? What trouble?" My father's voice washes over me, mingled with Nora's, and I feel a sense of calmness I haven't been able to manage since I got here.

"You're on speaker and Dad's here."

I mean, I gathered that now, but thanks, Nora.

"Hey, Dad."

"Hi, my love. What's this trouble I hear?"

I wave my hand dismissively, as if he can see. "Nothing crazy, just…origins being origins," I ramble, not wanting to get into the specifics with him. He has a way of overanalyzing things, which is great when he's there to help me make sense of it, but that's not the case now and it will only leave my head spinning in a million different directions.

"Do you want to talk about it?" he offers, and I smile, appreciating his calmer approach.

"I'm tired of living it, talking about it isn't going to help," I admit, and he sighs. The sound makes my chest clench. I don't want to bring him any more stress.

"Take a deep breath, Addi. You were made for this."

I feel his words deep in my soul, taking root and banishing all of the self-doubt that threatened me earlier.

"I know, but dealing with closed-minded people is

harder than I expected," I admit, wiping a hand down my face.

"It's going to take time, my love. We knew this, you especially, but you are exactly where you're supposed to be, being exactly *who* you are supposed to be. I'm proud of you, Addi. So proud."

"Thanks, Dad."

Silence dances around us for a beat before he speaks again. "They televised the opening speech from the dean."

I gulp, and I don't know why. It shouldn't be an issue, should it?

"We didn't see you," Nora adds, and I scoff.

"That's because they weren't focusing on the fae, and you know it."

"True." My father's reply is solemn, slightly defeated, but he quickly clears his throat, dismissing the doubt. "Is the support system for the fae good there?"

"As far as I know," I answer honestly, recalling my impromptu meetings with Professor Fairbourne. He's been good. Annoying, and overstepping, but he's a good support system nonetheless.

A knock at the door startles me and I frown at the offending white wood that stands between me and whoever is on the other side.

"Is that a knock at your door? Do you have friends, Addi? Friends you're not telling me about?" Nora asks, her voice rising with every word, and I roll my eyes again.

"It's probably Flora. I should go," I admit, not wanting to end the call, but also not entirely prepared for my two worlds to collide just yet.

"Fine, but I want better updates than this," she insists, and I shake my head.

"You weren't supposed to get *any*," I remind her, and she chuckles.

"Deal with it."

"I love you, Addi," my father calls out.

"I love her more," Nora quickly adds, making my heart whole.

"I love you both too much."

"Oh, and, Addi?" My father's voice pauses me from ending the call. "Happy birthday, my love."

"Yeah, happy birthday, big sis. Twenty-one is going to look so good on you."

"Thank you," I breathe, letting the call end.

I run my thumb over the screen, wishing I could see their faces, when another knock comes from the door. Holy fuck. It really must be Flora, and she's eager as hell. I have a feeling she's going to want to do something for my birthday and I'm not really feeling it. Especially not now. I finally got a brief moment to connect with my family and I'm aching from not being able to bask in the pleasure of spending time with them.

Swinging the door open, I'm ready to explain to her that I'm too busy, but I'm stopped in my tracks when I come face to face with a blond mage with a wicked grin. His gaze rakes over me until his eyes settle on mine.

"I know I'm five minutes early, but you don't look the least bit ready for our date."

THE KINGDOM OF RUIN

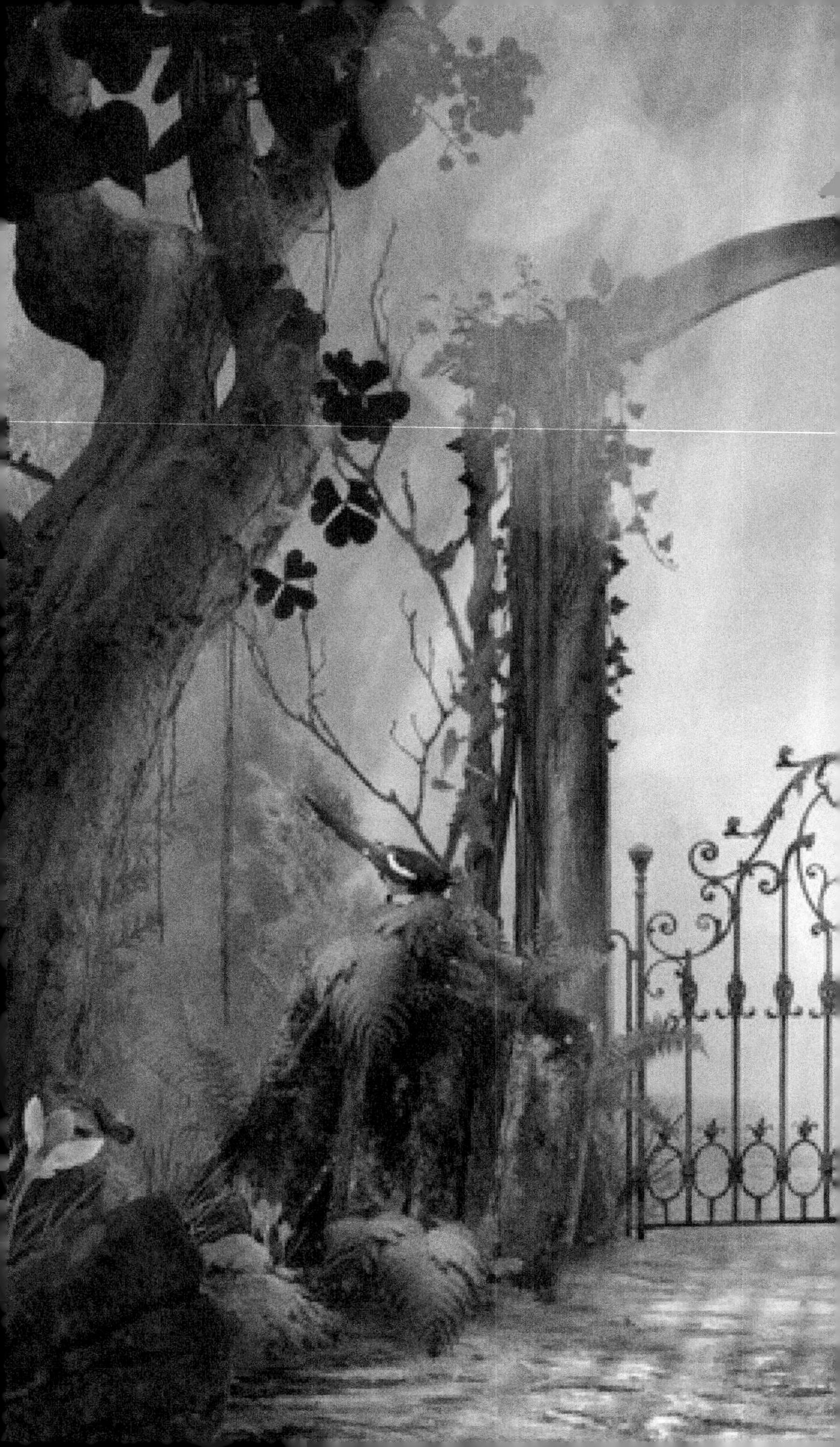

ADDI

17

His purple mage cloak is gone, revealing a skin-tight white tee that clings to muscles I didn't realize he had. Paired with fitted black jeans and worn boots, he looks sinful. When my gaze finally meets his, his blue eyes dance with amusement as he watches me take him in. His blond hair is ruffled and I can't deny the instinctive need to run my fingers through the layers.

Remembering myself, I clear my throat, aware that my skin is flushing under his knowing stare. "There is no date." The words sound lame, even to my ears, and when he rolls his eyes at me, it feels well deserved. But I genuinely thought we were past this.

"You're not dense, Cupcake. We both know this, and we both know that I specifically said Friday night at seven. And would you look at that?" he dramatically glances down at the black leather watch strapped on his wrist.

Fucker.

"I didn't agree to this," I ramble, standing my ground with less conviction than I would like, but seeing him at my door has thrown me for a loop.

"There was nothing to agree to, remember?" He cocks a brow at me and I fold my arms over my chest, trying to create another layer of defense between us.

"You're standing at my door; that seems like something we should agree to," I retort, and he shakes his head dismissively.

"Cupcake, you can drag this out however you like, but this is happening. Either you get changed and we head out, or I'm coming in there and we can get our chill on."

Smiling proudly, I shake my head at him this time. "That's where you're wrong. I have wards in place, which means *I* can stay in here, and *you* can do whatever you please, but it won't be inside these four walls." Feeling the dramatics, I grab my door, and with a flourish, I swing it toward him, ready to see the back of him, but before the satisfactory slam can ring out between us, he stops the motion with his hand.

I blink at where his hand is pressed against my door, my heart ricocheting in my chest as I process the fact that his hand is on my door...*inside* the ward.

"Can I be honest with you?" he asks, all calm and

collected, and it irritates the hell out of me.

"Sure," I rasp, not taking my eyes off his hand.

"Will it earn me brownie points?" he quizzes, and I scoff.

"Probably not."

"Then I'll keep it to myself."

My eyes rush to his, narrowing at the smugness that spreads across his face.

"Keep what to yourself?" I grumble, and he shrugs, eyebrows rising as he waits for more. I sigh, defeat getting the better of me. "Fine, brownie points."

His smug grin grows as he somehow stands taller without removing his hand from my door. "Morgan's ward is great, but it's no match for a mage. So what he should have been saying is that it will keep out anyone and everything but the mages. If you want something stronger, I can help with that."

Fuck. I would love to call him out for his bullshit, but the fact that his hand is still inside the ward I set earlier tells me it's true. Pinching the bridge of my nose, I take a deep breath, failing to accomplish anything with it.

"Of course you can," I grumble, knowing exactly where this is going before he even speaks.

"How about this: you get your sweet ass changed and come out with me, and I'll put a stronger ward in place that would keep even me out."

Now that's bullshit I can call out. "You mean a ward *you* would have control of?"

He shakes his head, lifting his free hand in the air as a show of surrender. "I'll link it to you, I swear it."

My eyes narrow. "Why?"

"Why?" he repeats, the confusion clear in his eyes.

"Why offer that?"

He stares at me for a moment before he sighs. "Because you're spoiling my Friday vibe, and by the time we're done for the weekend, I won't even want to come anywhere near your room again. One and done, remember?"

He still thinks he's getting a piece of me this weekend. He's mistaken, but if it gets me a stronger ward, the illusion that he might could work in my favor.

My lips purse as I consider his offer, but my thoughts are interrupted by the sound of laughter echoing up the stairs, followed moments later by Flora and Arlo. He's tickling her waist, making her squeal, and my heart clenches at how carefree they are. I wonder what that would feel like.

I know it's not something I will ever feel, not with the path life has set out for me. I'll either die trying to reach my goal or claim what is rightfully mine, destined to be on alert and guarded for as long as I live.

It's a decision I'm fine with until there's a small break in the clouds, just like now.

"Oh, hey, Addi. We were just coming to find you," Flora

states, stepping out of Arlo's grasp as she approaches.

"Find me?" I ask, pretending the mage before me doesn't exist, but he seems to have different ideas.

"She's busy. On a date."

Flora's eyes widen and amusement ticks the corner of her mouth up.

"Oh, for her birthday?" she asks sweetly, and I glare at her. She knows exactly what she's doing.

"Her birthday?" Brody asks, lifting his hand from my door to scrub his chin.

"Yeah." She points to the plaque on the door that reads my name and date of birth. She's dead. So, *so*, dead for this.

"Well, well, well. Would you look at that? Get yourself ready, Cupcake. You're in for a birthday treat. And you already know what my gift is."

He's either referring to his dick, which I definitely won't be accepting, or the stronger ward. The latter is the perfect gift. With my mind settled on that, I take a deep breath, exhaling slowly as I nod.

Fuck it. Here goes nothing.

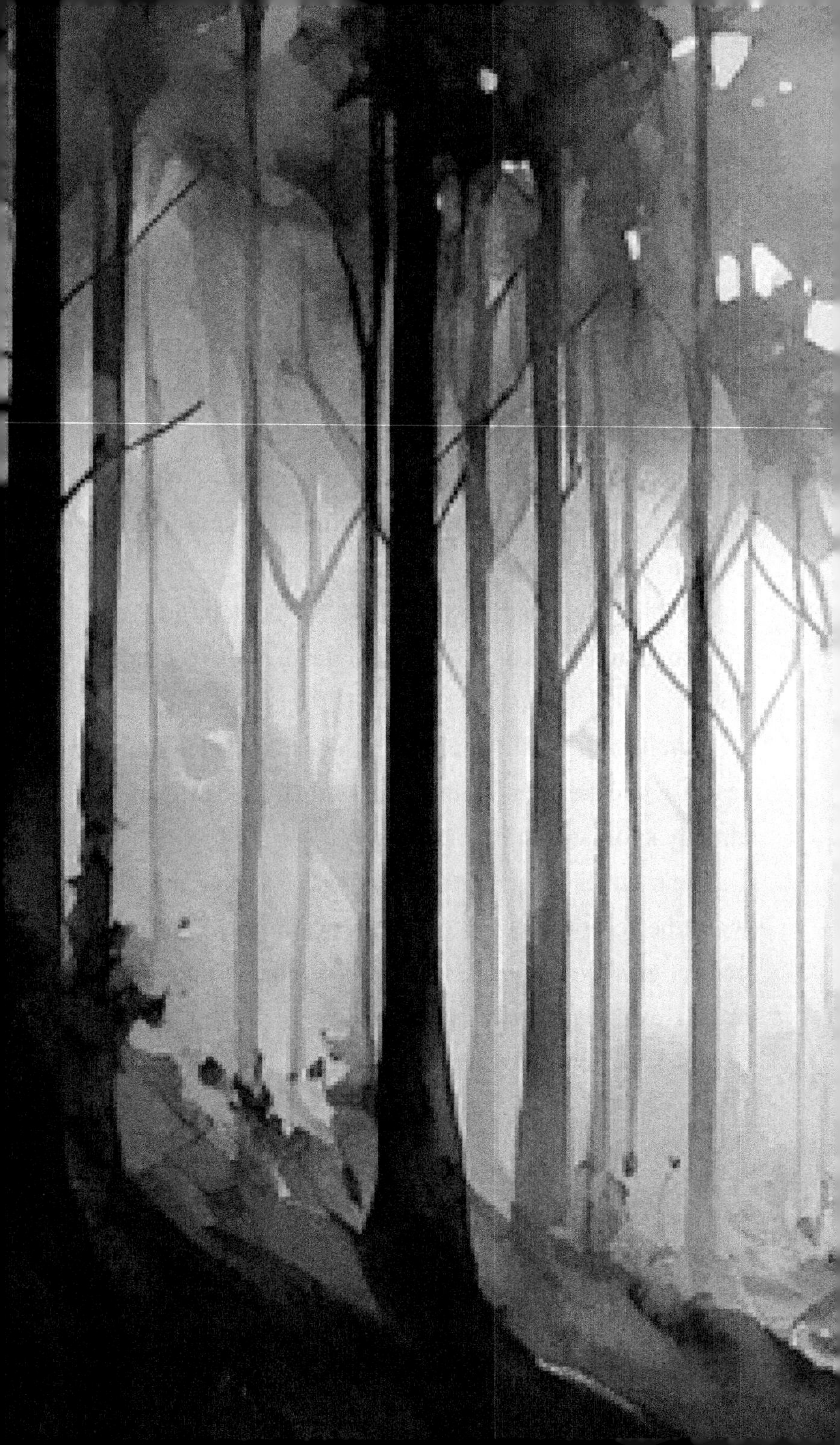

BRODY

18

I've never been patient. It's not a trait that has ever been bestowed upon me, but it seems waiting for Addi is an exception. Leaning back against the wall opposite her room, I tap my fingers on my arm as intrigue keeps me rooted to the spot.

There's something about her. I don't know what it is, but it has me tied up in knots.

I grin as I recall the look on her face when she opened the door. It'll be etched in my memory forever. I knew she would think I wasn't going to show. That was my plan; to catch her off guard, and it seems to have worked.

I really do need to get her out of my system. It's driving me insane. The sooner I convince her that fucking me is a good idea, the quicker I'll be able to think clearly again. She's consuming every part of me, on a level higher than

I've ever experienced, which will only make my release that much sweeter.

Her bedroom door opens, pulling me from my thoughts, but when only her head peers through the gap, I don't get my hopes up that we're ready to leave.

"Where are we going?"

I grin. I've been waiting for that question, and it's taken her longer than expected to ask it. "Out."

Her bright green eyes narrow at me. If she thinks it's a stern look that will make me fall in line, she's mistaken. It just makes her look hotter; a fact I opt to keep to myself. Otherwise, we're never going to get out of here.

"That's not enough to go on," she grumbles, and I sigh, relenting…a little.

"What else do you need?"

"The location."

I shake my head. "It's a surprise."

Her jaw tics, the sternness in her eyes darkening. "A surprise that could be dangerous? Do I have to be alert? Is it casual? I don't know what to wear or if I need weapons."

It's my turn to be surprised. Those aren't the kind of questions I usually get. The clothing, yeah, maybe, but danger and weapons? That's not something girls usually ask about. Although, I've never taken a fae girl on a date before, so maybe it's common with them. I don't know.

"You can wear whatever the fuck you want, but we're

leaving campus, so do with that what you wish," I offer, not really sure what situation would require her need for weapons, but as intrigued as I am, I keep my mouth shut.

She somehow manages to narrow her eyes further, muttering under her breath before she slams the door shut. She is feisty. I like it.

Glancing at the clock, I wonder whether I should have arrived earlier. As if sensing my thoughts, the door whooshes back open, stealing my next breath along with it.

Holy. Fuck.

She's...understatedly stunning.

Blonde curls float around her shoulders, with a braid still keeping her hair off her face. A black jacket sits open on her shoulders, revealing a cropped white tee underneath with a fitted bodice cinching in her waist. It's draped in silver, leaving my fingers itching to reach out and gloss over it. Fitted black combat pants make her ass look like Heaven, and they're tucked into heavy, heeled boots that lace up the front with a shimmer of silver at the sides. My head inches closer, a thought coming to mind as the silver seems to dance in the light.

Flicking my gaze back to her bodice, I notice it's the same there. The silver isn't just detailing; they're... daggers.

She's practically fucking draped in daggers.

"You are no cupcake. You're a goddamn dagger

queen," I rasp, meeting her gaze in time to see her roll her eyes at me.

"So dramatic," she grumbles, stepping into the hallway and shutting her bedroom door behind her.

"And you're hot as fuck."

The smile on her lips is hard to miss, but she still tries to tamper it down. "That's almost flattering. Now, magic my room. Please."

"No way, Dagger, we'll do it when we return."

"You can do it now," she insists, and I shake my head. She has me doing it so much that I'm going to end up dizzy.

"And have you step back in and leave me all alone? I don't think so," I retort, knowing her thoughts, and when she sighs, she only confirms it. Before she can try to continue her argument, I take a step toward the stairs. "Come on, we're going to be late."

"For what?"

"For our date."

She falls into step with me, and as we reach the stairs, I take a step back, letting her lead the way, which she does with a heavy dose of reluctance.

"The date I wasn't aware of," she points out, not looking back at me, so I wait until we're at the front door before I respond.

"When are you going to get past that? Now, or later? It'll be more fun now, but that's just my opinion."

She searches my eyes for what feels like an eternity before she gulps. "Fine."

"Good," I reply with a grin, reaching for her hand, but she whips it out of my reach before I can feel her skin against mine.

"That's not necessary."

I grin, stepping around her and through the front door. She follows a moment later, but the second I turn to her with my palm up for her to take, she pauses.

"It is."

She shakes her head, disagreeing when she doesn't know what we're doing next. I take a step toward her, and she mirrors it, edging backward from me. My dick stirs to life. I love a good cat and mouse chase. She's only making me more eager with every step she takes.

One inch forward for me, a whole inch backward for her. All the way until her back hits the wall beside her front door, giving me the opportunity to crowd her space. Her gulp is audible as I come chest to chest with her. I don't move any closer, acutely aware of the metal that clings to her waist and boots.

Lifting a hand, her eyes move to my wiggling fingers, tracking my moves as I lower it again. This time, I grasp her hand. When she doesn't protest, I kick into motion, not wanting to give her a chance to reconsider.

Her breath fans over my face as I chant the incantation

under my breath a few times before the world shifts around us. Once I'm certain we've fully transitioned to where we need to be, I let my words trail off and take a step back, despite the need to press further into her.

"You guys need to stop doing that," she rasps, breathless.

"Doing what?"

"Moving me without asking," she snaps, her eyes settling on mine as irritation swirls in her eyes.

"You'll get used to it," I say with a reassuring smile, and she scoffs, shoving at my shoulder with more force than I expect. It's not harmful, almost playful, and I like it until she speaks.

"There won't be any need for me to get used to it."

Maybe not from me, but I get the feeling Raiden hasn't even started with her yet. That's why I need to make my moves now, so I have a chance before he spoils it for all of us.

"Whatever you say, Dagger."

"Why do you keep calling me that?"

I smirk, taking another step back as I offer her my hand again, but she bats me away. "Because Cupcake doesn't really suit you when you have so much silver dancing all over your body."

"Addi is just fine," she insists, and I shrug, not really caring.

"You really are, but Dagger suits you better."

She blinks, looking around for the first time as she takes in where we are. Somewhere I know she won't be familiar with, but it will be worth it. The music starts to filter around us as we let the outside world in.

"Where are we?"

There's no use in hiding it now. We're already here. "We're at the Kenner Compound."

"Kenner Compound?" she repeats, still confused.

"Yeah, my friend's wolf pack."

"Why are we here?" Her fingers ghost over the daggers at her waist as she looks at the building a few steps away.

"Because they make the best fucking food, and I swear you're going to love it. The dining hall at the academy is fine, but one whole week without this stuff has me realizing real quick that I'm addicted to it," I admit, noting the small smile on her face, even though the sun is setting through the trees, darkening the space around us.

"I don't know if it's safe for me here," she murmurs, and my gut clenches, making me start to doubt my decision. But I never doubt myself. Why start now?

I shrug, offering my hand again as I speak. "You're never going to know if you don't live a little."

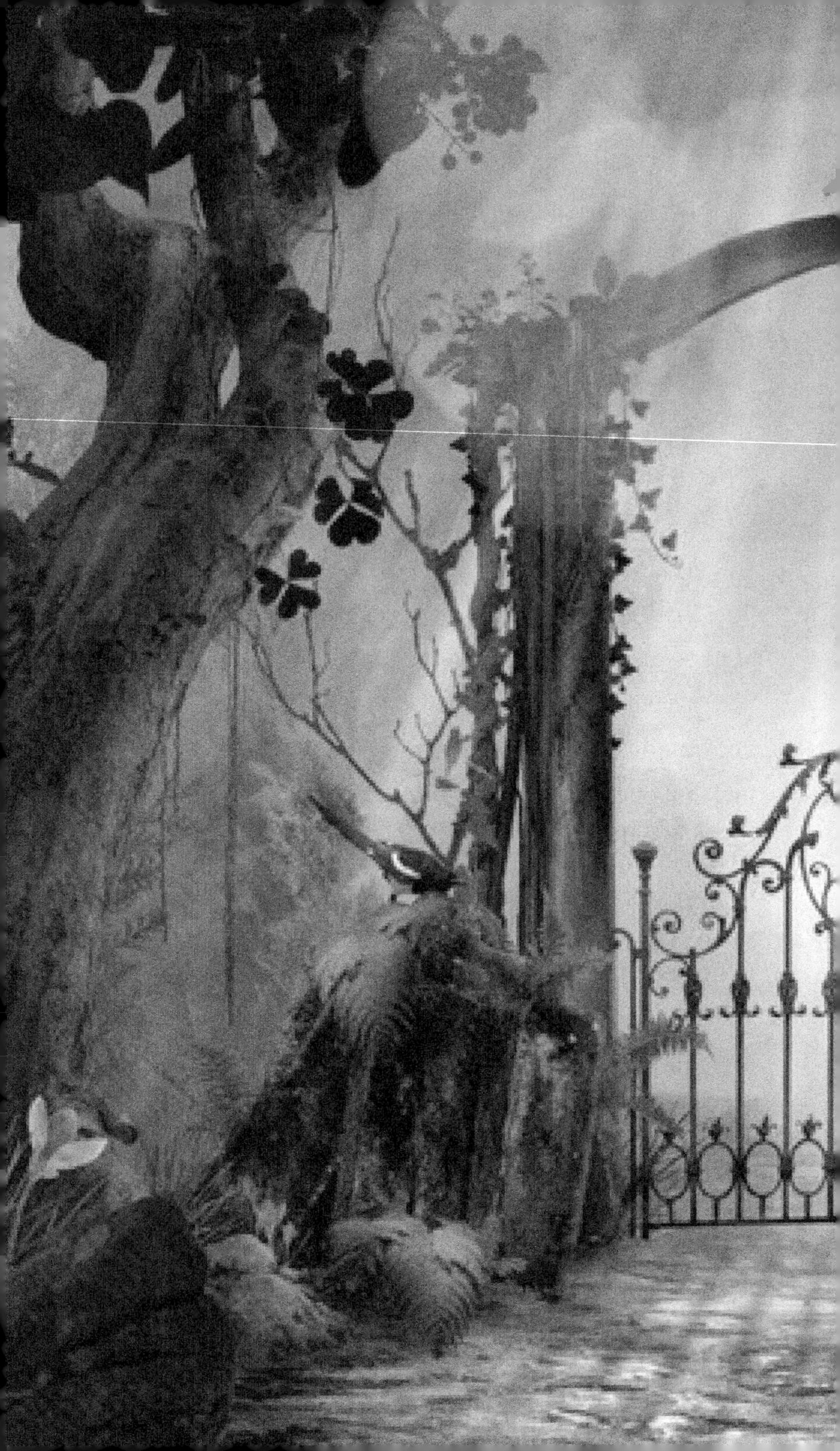

ADDI

19

Live a little? Live a little?

I've lived enough already, thank you very much. I obviously don't say that, though. The less he knows about me, the better. He offers his hand once again and I don't know why I do it. I can analyze the hell out of it later, but I place my palm flush against his.

My breath is lodged in my chest at the contact, just as it was earlier. I didn't retract by choice. Although, if anyone asks, I'll lie through my teeth. It was the initial contact, the shiver that ran across my skin from such a simple touch.

He pulls me along before I can protest and we step through the double wooden doors a moment later. The noise gets louder as the diner comes into view. The secluded setting outside made me suspicious that we were in wolf territory, but the people inside confirm it. Just because

Brody says it, doesn't mean it's true.

Tables are bunched together, a sense of warmth and family filling the space as country music plays in the background. A few people glance our way, but otherwise, they're all soaked up in their own bubbles, having a good time.

My initial walls that barricade me begin to soften but don't completely disappear. I'm not dumb. I have no idea where I am or how safe it is, but my survival instincts aren't going off.

"Oh. My. Gosh. Is that my Brody? Please tell me it is. Then explain to me how the fuck you have managed to convince someone to spend time with you. Especially someone this damn pretty."

"You don't give me enough credit, Janie," Brody protests as a woman with a slicked-back brown ponytail comes into view. She smiles at him warmly and knowingly. Not like a mother. She doesn't seem old enough for that. Maybe a big sister. I don't know, but it surprises me when he releases my hand to hug her.

Wolves are loving among themselves, not usually with outsiders. And as much as I'm an outsider, so is Brody. A mage is definitely not a wolf.

"No, the problem is you give yourself too much credit," she retorts, patting him on the back before her gaze shifts to me. The warmth remains, not as vibrant as it was for

Brody, but I don't get the sense that she wants to run me out of the building, at least not yet.

"That's mean," Brody states with a pout, and she cocks her brow at him.

"It's a fact. Something mages deal well with usually. Except for you, it seems."

"Please, if I were any other mage, I wouldn't be here," he retorts, and she huffs.

"You're damn straight, and that's because we're the Kenners. We don't let just anyone onto our land."

Noted.

Brody grabs my hand without breaking eye contact with Janie, as if offering me reassurance at her words. Glancing around the room, I notice a few more people staring our way, some with glares that are hard to deny, and my back stiffens.

This isn't a good idea. I know it.

"Is Cass joining you, or is it a table for two?" The hope in her eyes is clear, but it quickly diminishes with Brody's head shake. Cass, as in Cassian? The grump wolf on campus that is also friends with Raiden and Kryll? Dammit. I should have known.

"Table for two."

She waves him off, hiding her face as she grabs two menus and starts to lead us to a table. "I'm just wishful thinking."

"He'll come around. It's just going to take time. The pack is the pack. He doesn't know how to differentiate one person's thoughts and emotions from another. He thinks if his father believes it, you all do."

Janie stops at a slightly secluded booth and I shuffle along the red leather seat without a word as she wraps Brody in another tight embrace. "I hope he does come around. I miss him."

"You miss his grumpy ass? Please, you should be enjoying the peace and quiet."

She smirks in response, but it doesn't reach her eyes.

I'm definitely eager to know what they're talking about, but it's not my place. Besides, the information doesn't matter to me. Even if Cassian's downtrodden face and march around campus hold me captive. It's not my business. Even if he were of another origin, I wouldn't ask. Nobody gets involved in wolf business. Period.

Left with our menus, I focus on the options before me. "What do you usually go for?" I ask, bombarded with so many choices that look good.

"Do you have any allergies or dislikes?" Brody asks, and I shake my head. "The steak is insane, the ribs are mind blowing, and the crab is so good my eyes water." I snicker at his descriptions, which makes his shoulders relax and his smile match mine. "I'm going for the steak, medium rare because anything pink I can put in my mouth is like a little slice of Heaven." He winks, his words drifting over me as he leans closer, bracing his elbows on the table. "I'm referencing your pussy by the way."

Oh. My. Gosh.

"You are something else," I grumble, hiding my face behind the menu, but his chuckle still reaches my ears.

"I know. One of a kind, Dagger."

I pretend not to hear him, and I'm thankfully saved by the server, who comes over a few moments later.

"Brody. Fancy seeing you here."

"Hey, Leticia. How are things?"

The glare she gives him makes my muscles clench. If he brought me to a diner where he fucked the waitress, I'm leaving now. Not because I'm jealous, far from it, but I've had enough drama this week. This only serves to push me over the edge.

"Where's Cass?"

Brody shrugs. "I don't know. It's my friend's birthday and I wanted to treat her to some good food to celebrate. We only turn twenty-one once, right?"

She doesn't smile and her eyes narrow, darkening when she turns to me, but it's not a bad vibe toward Brody or me that I'm getting. Something tells me it links back to Cassian.

"A friend from the academy?" she asks, distaste pulling at the corner of her mouth.

"We're just here for some food, Leticia. Not to get involved in any Kenner business," Brody says with a smile, hoping to diffuse whatever threatens to rise, and to my surprise, she sighs, tapping at the device in her hand.

"Whatever. What do you want to eat?"

"Steak, medium rare, and a bottle of house beer," Brody rattles off. "And for my friend…"

"I'll take the steak, too, please. Medium, with an orange soda, please."

"You're not going to get a drink?" Brody interjects, frowning at me.

"I'm getting an orange soda."

He waves his hand dismissively. "No, I mean alcohol. It's your birthday. Celebrating age too. Don't you want your first drop of liquor at legal age?"

Shaking my head, I turn to Leticia, who is still standing beside us, her irritation palpable. "Just the orange soda, thanks," I reiterate, and she dashes out of sight a moment later. When I tilt my face back to Brody, I find a questioning look crinkling the corner of his eyes. "I don't drink. Ever."

"Like, never?"

Wetting my lips, I slink back in my seat. "Nope."

"How?" The disbelief is evident on his face, tempting me to feel a lick of embarrassment, but I don't.

"It doesn't really matter," I offer with a smile, hoping to end the conversation, but his stare only deepens.

"Tell me. I want to get to know you."

This isn't what I was expecting from him. I was expecting to be taken out drinking or dancing or something that held little to no conversation so he could get me drunk enough to fuck me later.

"I just haven't. I don't like the idea of being out of control, I don't like the thought of hiding from my problems at the bottom of a bottle, and I don't like the trust you have to put in others to not overstep when you're in that state."

He nods, and I can practically see my words turning in his mind. "Fair enough," he offers, like he understands where I'm coming from, and it leaves me a little surprised. Not that I show it. Instead, I try to redirect the conversation.

"So, tell me about you."

"There we go, she's getting into the swing of it now," he says with a smirk, and I roll my eyes.

"No, I'm just trying to steer the talk away from myself," I answer honestly. "The fact that we're in a situation where conversation can even happen is shocking in itself," I add, and he gapes at me, dramatically slapping his hand to his chest.

"I might be a player, Dagger, but I can get to know you before I fuck you."

"I think I just threw up in my mouth," I grumble, clutching my stomach, and he snickers.

"Please, do you want me to lie? Do you want me to sit

here and pretend I have pure intentions? Since you stepped out of your room, all I've thought about is wrapping your hair around my fist and running my tongue over your tits. There's nothing wholesome about me, so I'm not going to pretend there is, but I can hold a conversation. If I wanted to fuck limp limbs, I'd give good old Pamela a go," he states, waving his palm at me to reconfirm his reference.

My thighs press together despite my best efforts.

He's not affecting me. He's not affecting me. He's not affecting me.

"What else should I know about you?" I push, trying to pretend my heart isn't racing.

"Me? What you see is what you get. I grew up in Foley Hill, I'm hilarious, I don't care for drama, and I believe in trying to save people. No matter what." His eyes hit mine and I know he's referencing the human we helped earlier in the week from another one of Vallie's tirades.

"Thank you for that," I breathe, the words foreign on my tongue. I never thank anyone. Not because I'm rude, but because I do what I can, when I can, by myself.

He waves it off. "My father is also Orion Orenda."

I frown, recalling the name, but it takes me a moment to place it. When I finally remember where I've heard the name, I gape at him in surprise. "As in the member of The Council," I clarify, remembering the few times I've seen him on the television.

"Yup." He practically grimaces as he acknowledges the connection.

"You sound…ecstatic about that fact."

He scoffs. "Good assessment." He taps his fingers on the table as he looks at me. "Have you ever been forced into something because your bloodline says so? I didn't get to choose my ancestors, yet they get to choose my life choices."

My jaw falls slack as I gape at him. Despite his humor and charisma, I have to remember he's a mage; full of wisdom and prophecy most of the time, but it's strange hearing it come from his lips.

Our drinks arrive, but it's not Leticia that brings them over. I murmur my thanks, but they're gone too quickly to hear it.

"That's relatable," I admit, taking a sip of my orange soda.

"How so?"

I find him staring at me intently, intrigued by what I have to say, and I gulp.

Fuck. I should have kept my mouth shut.

Clearing my throat, I downplay it the best I can. "It's just, back home, on the ranch…ranch life isn't for me, but that didn't matter to my family. We're born into these lives with our paths already laid out for us."

"You get what I'm saying."

It's slightly impressive that he doesn't try to degrade the example I give him. He sees the connection without thinking he experiences worse than me. If he knew the truth, he would think differently, but that's not necessary. It's not for him to know. I hold my secrets closer to my chest than I do my daggers.

Food arrives a moment later and my eyes widen in delight at the size of the steak on my plate. I think I'm in Heaven from the sight and smells alone. We both cut into our food and the moment the meat melts on my tongue, I groan. "Holy fuck."

"Right?"

"I need to know how they did that," I mutter in awe, blinking at the food like it's a gift from Heaven.

"Magic, and not the real kind either. It's Janie's husband in the kitchen, Jake. He's the best chef I've ever met in my life. I've tried to replicate it with real magic, too, but it doesn't compare," he admits with a grin.

I take another bite, and another, beyond lost to the delight on my tongue, when the double doors slam open with a thunderous hit, vibrating the entire room. Everyone goes still and the music stops as we all turn to the source of the sound.

Cassian prowls through the doors, hands clenched at his sides as his gaze trails over the room before landing on Brody and me. Raiden and Kryll are a step behind him, and my chest tightens.

"Why do I think we're in trouble?" I ask, unable to tear my gaze away to question Brody, who curses under his breath.

"Because we are."

"Why?" I finally turn to glance at him, guilt etched all over his face. "Why?" I repeat, frustration creeping up my spine as I glare at him.

"Fuck." He glances over his shoulder, trying to see how far away his friends are before he quickly turns back to me. "Because Cass left the pack to attend the academy with us and he's been exiled by his father. He's not supposed to be here."

Well, fuck.

All of that, and here he is. What shit has Brody got me involved in?

Gulping, I spin back to the wolf with his eyes set on us just as he appears beside our table, palms slamming down on the wood, clattering the cutlery as he turns to Brody.

"You are so fucking dead."

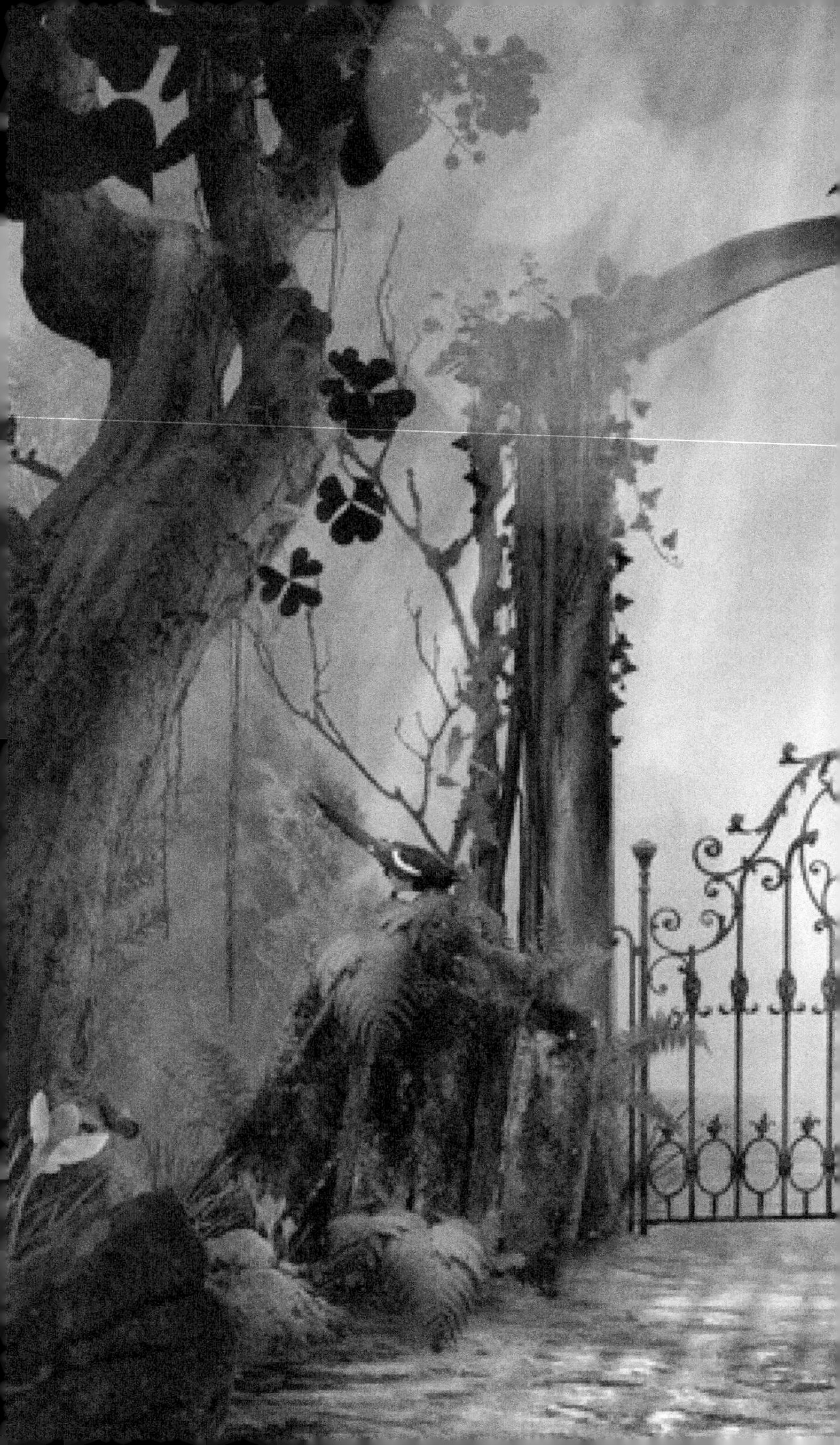

ADDI

20

One hand slips lower than my seat, resting against the leather of my boot, the raised outline of the dagger pressing against my palm. My other hand falls against my waist, finger running over the silver that awaits.

I can feel the temperature in the room drop and I'm ready to move. This is definitely not what I signed up for. This is a hefty price for a stronger ward on my room; a decision I'm currently questioning as I try to remain calm and at ease.

This shit is all Brody's fault, and the anger vibrating from Cassian confirms it. I can dwell on that fact later and give him hell for it, too—once he's warded my room, of course—but for now, all that matters is getting out of here. I can plan his demise once I'm back on safer ground. I just need to focus on an exit strategy first.

From memory, my gaze darts to the double doors Cassian and the others made their grand entrance through before slipping to the left. I also note the side emergency exit and I'm certain there will be one through the kitchen as well, but I'm hoping I can get through one of these. The kitchen just adds another obstacle to my exit attempt, and I want to keep it as easy as possible.

The double doors are my first option. There are tables crammed with customers to my left, while it's a straight line down the middle to the main entry point.

My main problem is I don't know how to get back to the academy from here, but I can figure that out once I'm outside. Once I'm outside, half the job is done.

"I just wanted some good food, man," Brody says calmly, lifting his hands in the air in surrender, but it does nothing to quell the storm brewing inside Cassian.

I don't know what's going on here. I don't understand why his attendance at the academy has led to his exile, but more than that, I don't understand why he would come back because we're eating here.

"There are other places to go. Anywhere else to fucking go," he bites out, while Raiden and Kryll glance around the room, noting the observers watching intently.

As if I thought I might get a calm evening for my birthday. I should have known that wasn't going to happen.

"You didn't have to come," Brody points out, eyes darting down to his steak like he wants to take another bite instead of dealing with his friend. I have no idea how he can think of food at a time like this, my stomach is twisted in knots and the thought of eating has long since passed.

"I didn't have to come," Cassian repeats slowly, like the words are taking a moment to register in his head.

"No." The insistence from Brody only seems to make Cassian's knuckles whiter as his hands ball into fists against the table.

"You brought a fucking fae here, Brody. A fae." He doesn't bother to glance my way, despite the fact that he's talking about me, while Raiden peers out of the corner of his eye, disgust twisting his mouth as he does. Ass. "Janie called me because the other patrons are ready to start a fucking riot," he growls, the sound so deep that I'm almost certain he's going to shift before me at any moment.

My back stiffens at the truth that falls from his mouth. I've been at risk since the moment we stepped through those doors and Brody knew it. That's why he said what he did outside. That's why he didn't confirm whether I would need weapons or not. He left it up to me. All to get a good steak? I might fucking kill him myself if Cassian doesn't beat me to it.

Glancing around the room, I look at the people instead of the exits, *really* look at them, and it's clear their narrowed eyes and muted sneers are aimed my way. A different origin on their land without authorization or connection to the pack. And not just any origin. No, a fucking fae.

Fuck.

I need to get out of here, and it has to be now. The longer I sit here letting these guys argue it out, the longer the pack has to get angrier with me. I'm not usually one to play the innocent victim card, but in this case, I really didn't do anything to piss anyone off. It happened naturally.

"I can leave," I murmur, reluctantly moving my hands from my weapons so I at least appear defenseless. I press my hands against the table, but my ass doesn't lift even an inch before Cassian's glare turns my way.

"You can sit the fuck down."

No, he fucking didn't just try to order me around like one of his pack. Fuck that.

"You can watch your damn tone," I snap back.

"I don't need to watch shit. This is *my* land you're walking on." His green eyes swirl with challenge, and it seems I'm more than happy to rise to it.

"That's not what Brody just said."

Cassian's jaw tics and Kryll rumbles a curse under his breath from behind him while Raiden gives me the absolute best deathly glare I've received from him so far.

In hindsight, this is one of those moments where I really should have kept my mouth shut, but if someone is going to push me, I'm going to push back with whatever ammunition I have.

Thankfully, Cassian whirls his glare back to my so-called date, and I don't waste my opportunity, using the break from his attention to dart from the booth. I keep my gaze locked forward, refusing to make eye contact with anyone in here since I've already pissed them off by breathing.

The cool night air wraps around me after what feels like an eternity, and the doors slam shut behind me, declaring my exit, but my heart doesn't calm.

I need to get out of here as fast as possible. The less time I give these people to attack me, the less likely it is to happen, and I really don't want to have to hurt anyone today. Not on my birthday. It almost feels like a sin.

Planting my hands on my hips, I walk toward the tree line, not really sure what I'm doing when I sense movement from behind me. It's coming at me swiftly, so I don't have time to think.

Instinct takes over and I draw daggers from my waist, twisting just in time to press them both against the throat of whoever is approaching. It's only when the silver glints against their tattooed flesh that I realize it's Kryll.

"Feisty," he grunts, a smirk teasing his lips under the moonlight. My eyes narrow. His auburn hair is swept back off his face, and his dark eyes bore into mine.

I hold my pose for a moment, considering what to do next, but I can't step back. I'm in full-on fight mode and it has me locked into position.

"Back off."

My breaths are short and sharp as I wait for him to move, but he doesn't. Instead, he shakes his head, allowing the daggers to press even tighter against his flesh, but they don't break the skin.

"I'm all for leaving you to fight your own battles, but if I move right now, there's a high chance a female wolf is going to challenge you."

My eyes widen. What the fuck? "Challenge me? For what?"

He peers down at me, the height advantage noticeable as his lips set into a firm line. "It doesn't matter."

It must matter. Why would they attack me? For being a fae? Sure. But that doesn't sound like what he's saying. There's clearly more to this that I don't know about, which isn't a surprise, nor is it a shock that he's not going to offer up the information, so I decide to act like I can't see right through him.

Irritated, my nostrils flare. "I still don't need you to protect me. Being a fae isn't new to me. It's not a surprise that I'm someone's target."

"Cute."

I roll my eyes. Of course that's all he has to say. Despite

my eagerness to nick him with my blades, I retreat, taking a step back from him, but he counters it with a step of his own.

"I'm leaving," I snap, and he cocks a brow at me.

"Do you know where you're going?"

"Nope." There's no point in lying, it's not really my style.

"Don't you care?" I can't read his expression. It's as if my admission confuses him, but I really don't have time to consider his thoughts and feelings in all this.

Shrugging, I turn away. "I've dealt with worse." I make it two whole steps before the doors behind us swing open and shouting reaches my ears.

I spin back around, refusing to give anyone a chance to jump me from behind, and see it's just the rest of the assholes storming out. Cassian strides with purpose, Brody hangs his head with a grimace, and Raiden looks like he's going to commit murder.

Likely me.

Before I can leave without any further interaction with these fuckers, Leticia comes flying out of the diner, fueled by rage as she throws a chef's knife through the air. It lodges in the grass beside Cassian, who turns and glares at her.

Yep. I really need to leave. I don't need to watch this drama unfold. Maybe it would have been entertaining under different circumstances, where I wasn't under threat simply for existing, but I don't feel like getting caught in the crossfire of all this.

"Her." The word is thunder on her tongue as she raises a finger in my direction. "You're walking out on me for her?"

Woah. Woah. Woah.

"Fuck off, Letty. I'm not walking out on you for anyone. You were never mine to walk out on," Cassian snarls, rage billowing from him.

I take a step forward, eager to get him to re-clarify that I have nothing to do with any of this, or him in general, but Kryll grabs my arm before I can get any further, shaking his head sternly.

"Our parents made a pact, Cass. Me and you—"

"Fuck our parents, Letty. That's not what I want, and it shouldn't be what you want either," he states firmly, but that does nothing to quell the disappointment drifting from her in waves.

Instead of arguing with him, she turns her angry stare my way. "Do you actually think you can just swoop in here and take my man from his pack? From his life? For what? Some academy that benefits everyone but us? I don't fucking think so."

Despite my instincts to charge her with my blades at the ready, I remember my father's words, lifting my hands in a show of surrender, all while Kryll keeps hold of my arm.

"I don't know what your issue is, but—"

"Oh, you're about to find out my issue, because I challenge you," she barks, prowling toward me with a sinister smile curling her lips. This has got to be some fucked up shit. I thought Vallie was a handful, but it seems Leticia wants to give her a run for her money.

"Challenge me?" I repeat with a frown, completely lost to whatever the fuck she's talking about as Kryll grunts from beside me.

"Ah, fuck. I warned you."

"I challenge you to a duel," Leticia declares, raising her hands at her sides. "Right here. Right now."

"Am I supposed to know what that means?" A duel doesn't sound like a good old-fashioned brawl that I could totally be down for. I've got a lot of pent-up frustration at this point, and an outlet would be great. But a duel? That sounds a little more specific, considering Kryll's concern.

"It means we fight until death or submission. The winner gets to claim Cassian."

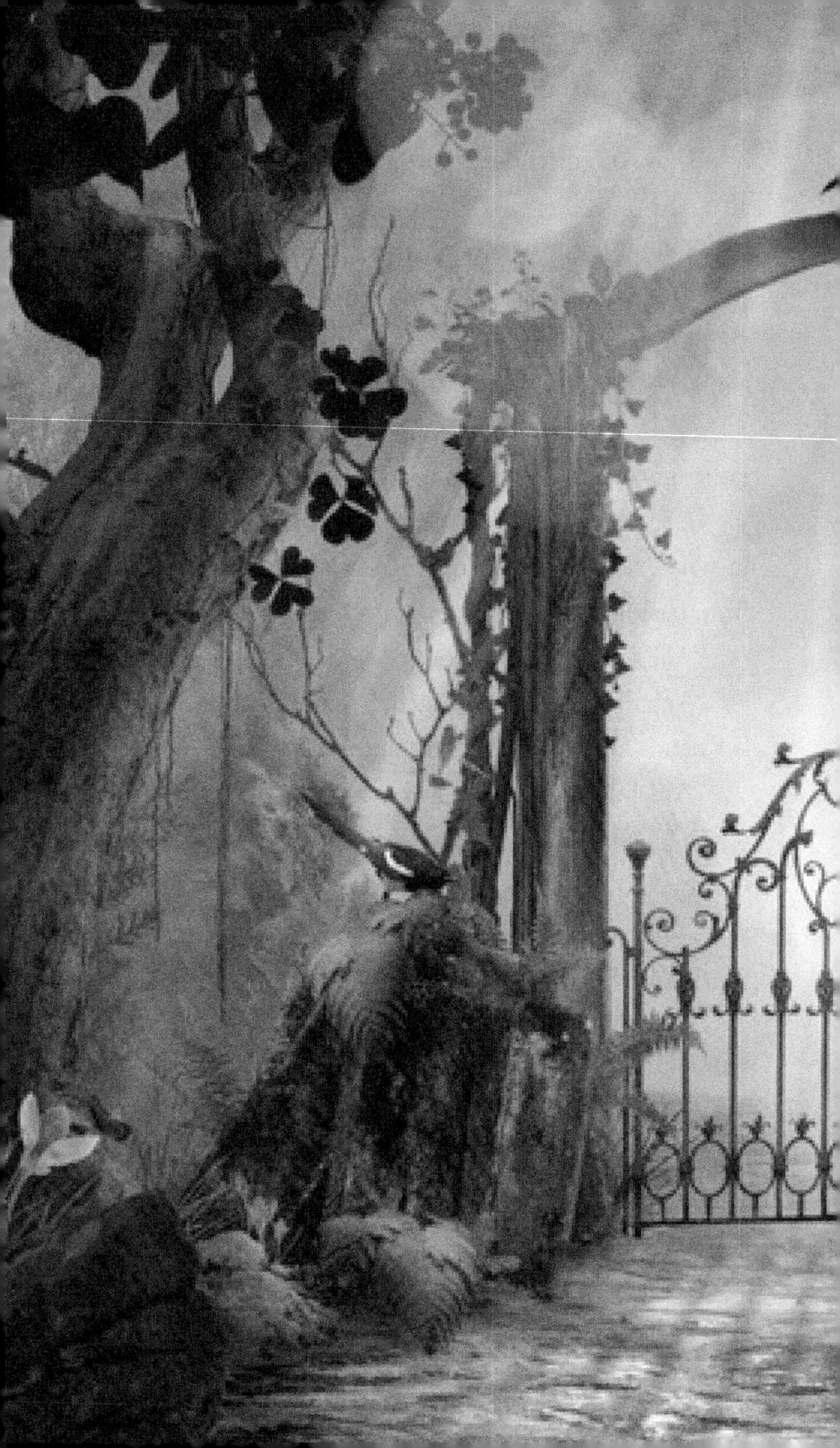

ADDI

21

Woah woah woah. Is this girl insane?

My gaze narrows on hers as she smirks, victory already licking along her skin.

"Claim Cassian for themselves? That's not what I'm here for. It's not even something I have any interest in," I blurt, but it does nothing to calm her.

"Don't worry about it. You won't be leaving with him anyway," she promises as she continues to prowl toward me.

Yeah. This girl has definitely lost it.

Flicking my gaze to Cassian, I expect him to jump in and agree with me, but he simply stands there with his arms folded over his chest, eyes shifting between the two of us. I peer at Kryll, hoping for one of them to be present enough to interject, but his eyes are fixated on the building behind Leticia. Continuing around the group of assholes, I find Brody gaping in surprise at Leticia while Raiden rocks back and forth on his heels with his hands tucked in his pockets.

A low growl ripples from my throat. "Can one of you open your damn mouth and explain to her that I am not challenging anyone for Cassian." My pleading gaze lands on Kryll as he turns his attention back to the present, but he shrugs, disregarding me immediately. "Great. You're no help," I bite out with a scoff.

Despite my gut telling me not to bother, I spin back to Raiden, who stares at me with a bored expression.

Fucking useless. All of them.

Rolling my eyes at him, I turn back to Brody again. He *has* to help me out. This is all his fucking fault. As if sensing the thoughts turning over in my mind, he lifts his hands in defense.

"She's not going to hear anything from anyone but Cass," he admits, which makes sense but does nothing to help this work in my favor.

Turning to look at him, I don't get to utter another word before Leticia speaks up.

"Don't waste your time. This is between you and me."

"Is it, though? You're not hearing anything I'm saying!" I snap. I can take on a challenge for sure, but the semantics about this being over a guy that has nothing to do with me is what's pissing me off.

"I don't need to. I challenge you—"

"You already said that," I grunt, pinching the bridge of my nose. "You can challenge me all you want, I don't mind, but don't force a prize on me that I don't want. This duel bullshit is pointless. I'm more than happy to let you have him."

"That's not how things work around here." She stops a few steps away from me, rolling her shoulders at her sides as she prepares to fight.

"Don't wolf rules apply to wolves only? I think it's quite clear at this stage that I'm fae," I point out, and she snickers.

"Wolf rules apply on wolf land, and that's exactly where we are."

Nodding, I sigh. "Okay. I can roll with that. But back to the duel shit, I would rather not, thank you. I can fight you, but there's no prize necessary."

"Oh, cute. She's playing hard to get. Maybe that's why he's so interested." Leticia's deathly glare spins to the wolf in question, who remains frozen in place, arms folded over his chest and his mouth closed. This fucker really isn't going to say anything. Such a dick.

The sound of hurried feet from the diner pull my attention as a guy rushes toward us. The moment he notices our eyes on him, he skids to a stop. "Is there a duel? I heard there's a duel," he rushes out, making my chest clench as Leticia nods eagerly.

"Yes."

It's on the tip of my tongue to clarify that it's simply a challenge, not a duel, but he's already hooting with glee as he rushes toward the diner to alert everyone else. The second he does, every damn person in the vicinity vacates the building to join us.

While their interest is occupying Leticia, I whirl my attention on the fucker who is allowing this to unravel. Marching toward him, I jab my finger in his direction. "Seriously, now would be a good time for you to open your mouth."

He shrugs. Fucking shrugs. "If she wins, there's less competition at the academy. And if *you* win, I don't have to worry about Leticia pawing all over me anymore."

I gape at him, his gruff voice rushing over me as he lays out his reasoning.

"You're an ass," I snap.

"I never claimed to be anything else," he replies, his husky voice low as someone claps their hands from behind me, pulling my attention back to the center of the makeshift circle that's now formed.

"Rules of a duel," the guy hollers, pointing at Leticia and me. "Use what you want, be what you want, we don't care. A winner is announced when someone is knocked out, taps out, or is killed. Any further questions?"

Leticia waves her hands in the air, ramping up the cheers from the wolves, which become almost deafening in my ears. How am I supposed to think of any more questions with all this noise? Fuck.

"Is this really necessary?" That's what I settle on, which only earns me a grin from the asshole explaining the rules.

"Excellent, let's go!" he shouts before tilting his head back and letting out a low howl.

I'm assuming that's the sign the duel has begun because Leticia is heading toward me in the next breath. I tug my jacket from my arms, the air around me heating from the tension building inside me.

"You know, you're pretty lacking for a fae. Your ears are embarrassing," she mutters with a cackle, and I frown as we slowly circle one another.

"Is that supposed to hurt my feelings? My ears don't determine who I am, and right now, I'm wishing when they were sliced that they had lopped the whole fucking thing off because then I wouldn't have to listen to your shit."

"Are you sure? You seem touchy, and I was only making an observation."

"Nah, observations usually contain facts, and you're just letting your opinion get the better of you. I bet you wear all your emotions on your sleeve. It's going to make beating you that much easier. I should thank you in advance," I snarl back, her eyes darkening as she bares her teeth.

"Fuck you," she bites out before charging toward me.

Earth magic. Earth magic. Earth magic.

Planting my feet shoulder-width apart, I reach into the earth beneath me, tugging on the magic inside me as vines rise around Leticia. She yelps in surprise, eyes darting to mine for a brief second, but before they can take hold of her, she launches into the air, shifting into a stunning white wolf.

She's not so stunning when she lands before me with a thud, teeth bared and claws ready to take me down. Her snarl vibrates around us as I release the magic in the vines to prepare for impact as she charges toward me.

I feel the comfort of my daggers against my palms as I pull two from my chest. Her claw slashes across my face as I manage to nick her with a blade. I hiss as she yelps. Her eyes narrow on me as the crowd cheers. The feeling of blood trickling down my face has me slightly distracted as we circle each other again.

Twirling the daggers in my hands, I take a deep breath, remembering everything my father taught me. The people around me disappear from view, the lick of pain from my cheek fades into the background, and the sounds of hollering and howls evaporate as I focus every piece of me on the enemy.

Her left paw hits the ground harder on her next step, the only hint of preparation I get before she's charging toward me with purpose. Eager to use her own weight against her, I take off too, the pair of us set to collide in the middle, but she leaps in the air at the last second, making me duck and dive, sliding across the dirt and out of her reach.

Rushing to my feet, I remain crouched as I watch her turn back to me. My heart races in my chest, adrenaline coursing through my veins, and I inhale it all, letting it fuel me.

She lowers her front legs, eyes fixed on me as her nose twitches and lip curls. I take off first this time, refusing to remain on the defensive. If she wants a challenge, I'll give her one.

My grip on the daggers tightens as I barrel toward her, but someone from the inner ring of the crowd trips me mid-step, sending me careening through the air. I land on my back with a resounding thump.

My breath leaves me with a whoosh as I blink up at the moon, but my vision is quickly filled by the frothing jaws of a pissed off white wolf. Her claws slash at my chest before I can react. Agony burns through me, forcing a scream from my lungs while channeling every ounce of my mind and body to focus on protecting me.

Leticia howls up at the sky, reaping the likely cheers

that echo around her instead of finishing me. The pain is consuming me completely. Whatever damage she's done, it's more than I've ever known or expected. I need to act fast before it worsens.

Using her victorious stance above me to my advantage, I toss aside the daggers in my hands, replacing them with those from my boots and slamming one into her left side, wedging it perfectly between her ribcage. Her howl of anguish reaches my ears as she stumbles forward a little, eyes wide as they settle on me.

I poise my other hand at her right side, ready to do what's necessary. "Does it hurt?" I rasp, glaring up at her despite my vision blurring from my own pain. Her tiny whimper is the answer I want. "That's because these daggers are a little more special than the one I caught you with at first. Want to guess why?" I twist it, her agony vibrating between us as she snaps her teeth in my face, but doesn't actually touch me. "Are you guessing it's because they're made of silver? You would be correct if you did." I can feel the maniacal smile curve my lips. "Now, it's small, so it's not flooding your bloodstream just yet, but with the other ready to slice through your body, that will change very quickly." I nod down at my other hand, ready to cut through her flesh. Looking back at her, everything around us fades away as I offer her an ultimatum "Tap out, or I add that one too."

She snarls, spit slobbering my face, but the fierceness doesn't last long as she grimaces. The dagger is doing its job, and she's struggling.

"Last chance. Tap out, or I'll kill you." My words hang heavy between us, her left side trembling, and I twist again, driving home the fact that I'm not fucking around.

I'm certain one of us isn't going to walk away from this when she lifts her right paw and taps three times on the ground beside me. A beat later, I pull the blade from her ribcage and she flops to the ground beside me, curling in on herself as she turns back into a human.

Fuck.

Everything hurts. It's like the pain from my chest is spreading throughout my body. Peering down at the wound, all I can see is the crimson blood staining my clothes. Staring at it won't heal it, and I need a second to catch my breath before I figure out my next move, so I opt to look up at the moon as the blades of grass ruffle against my knuckles.

Happy birthday, Addi. What a celebration.

No sooner do I think it am I hoisted in the air. Panic courses through my body as I start to swing my arms and legs to stop the attacker.

I grunt when my stomach hits someone's shoulder as I'm thrown over their back, and a slap on my ass follows a moment later, rendering me speechless long enough for them to respond.

"You've gotten in enough trouble as it is. Fight me, and I'll make it worse."

Kryll. Fucking Kryll? It's a little late to help now, buddy, but I don't get to say that as he moves so quickly the world blurs around us, leaving me to recoil with nausea.

Fuck these guys. They've got some explaining to do.

THE KINGDOM OF RUIN

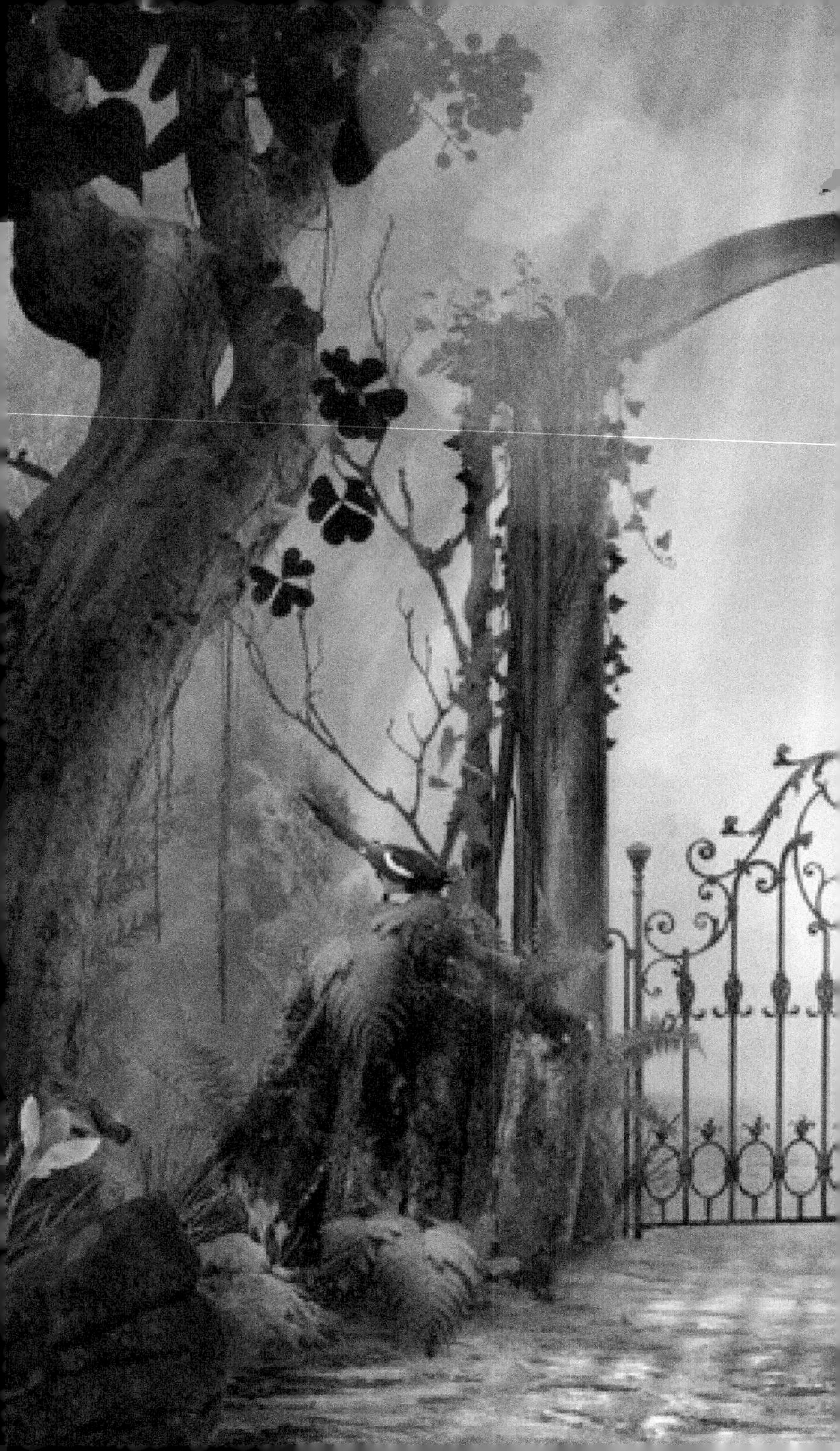

ADDI

22

Nausea burns up my throat as the world shifts. Another fucker moving me too fast without my approval. Maybe Brody was right; maybe I'll get used to it. They're doing it so often there's not much choice, but as I'm slumped into a chair, the room spinning around me, I don't think this will ever be something I get used to.

Fuckers.

Any desire to give him a piece of my mind is pushed aside as the pain in my chest heightens, making me hiss.

Fighting through it, I clutch the arms of the chair as I blink around the room. "Where am I?" I rasp, barely managing to focus on Kryll as he takes a few steps back.

"Don't get blood on anything," Raiden snaps, and I whip my head his way, which only makes the nausea stronger. I can feel myself turning green as my brain swishes in my skull, but it doesn't stop the sass bubbling from my lips.

"And where is that again? Sorry, I must have missed what you just said."

I focus on the vampire enough to catch his dramatic eye roll before he points a finger at me. "No blood."

Ass.

As much as I want to eye-roll him back, I decide to ignore him instead, peering around the room to try and piece it together for myself.

I'm seated in a leather chair, with a huge queen-sized bed a few inches away. Navy sheets are draped over it, which match the fancy curtains hanging over the arched window to my right. A huge television sits on the wall, and I can spy an en-suite and walk-in closet from here, along with another door that leads to who knows where.

"If you're just going to complain, get the fuck out of here." The snap comes from Cassian, who is standing on the other side of the bed, hands clenched at his sides as he looks at the back of Raiden's head.

"I'm struggling to understand why I'm dealing with this at all. Brody should be—" Raiden's protest is cut off by a growly Cassian, whose knuckles turn white.

"Brody can solve almost anything *but* the pain of a wound from a wolf's claws obtained during a fucking duel."

My eyebrows furrow as I sit up in my seat. "Wait, what?"

"I'll get to you in a minute," he grunts, narrowing his emerald eyes at me.

"You'll get to me now. This is all your fault," I retort, irritation curling through me.

"How do you figure that?" His slack jaw and slightly widened eyes confirm he really doesn't think he's to blame.

"Because you didn't interject and explain shit to that crazy bitch."

With his eyes still pinned on mine, he rounds the bed, perching himself on the edge as he comes to my side. He's so close that his knees brush against mine, but I refuse to falter at his proximity. I'm already vulnerable with this open wound.

He stares me down for what feels like an eternity before his back stiffens and he grunts, "Everyone out."

"Fuck that, you should have gone to your own room, asshole. This is mine," Raiden snipes, but Cassian doesn't even bother to glance back at him.

"Go into the other room then."

"Other room? Fuck. My room is smaller than half of this room," I ramble, and Raiden scoffs.

"That's because you're fae, and *I'm* elite."

That smarmy-mouthed fucker. I stumble to my feet, a little more unsteady than I would like, but I'm done with the superiority that exudes from his every pore. It's pissing me off. Before I can take a step toward him, Cassian has risen too, pushing down on my shoulder so I drop back into my seat. I can't fight against him while the pain in my chest is consuming me.

"Sit the fuck down. Raiden, give me ten fucking minutes; otherwise, there will be blood everywhere," Cassian warns.

Silence slips over the room and I finally notice that Brody is standing with Kryll by the door to the left. That must lead into the other room. Another fucking room. Oh, how the other half live.

As if sensing my eyes on him, Brody meets my gaze, a hint of guilt fluttering beneath his lashes, but before he can speak, Cassian points a finger in his direction. "You can get the fuck out too. Don't go far. There's shit to discuss," he bites, the threat evident in his tone.

Brody dips his head and slips from the room, a smirking Kryll a step behind him as Raiden sighs, joining them a second later.

It takes a moment before Cassian turns back to me, and when he does, it feels like we're closer than we were seconds ago. His knees brush mine again as his green eyes swirl with…something. I feel too delirious to put my finger on what it is, exactly.

The silence stretches, and I don't feel any control over

it, so I clear my throat and break it. "If Brody can't help me with this...who can?" I point at the blood still slowly pouring from the wound that's causing more pain than I've ever experienced, and he sighs.

"Me."

My eyebrows rise in surprise at the fact, but when he doesn't instantly get it over with, irritation creeps up my spine. "Are you going to get to it or not? Because this shit hurts like hell," I rasp, and his gaze narrows on mine.

"I can drop you back at your room," he offers, and I scoff at his threat.

"Please do. I can take care of myself."

"It seems so."

My mouth parts to give him a piece of my mind, but then I slowly process his words and it makes me pause. "What does that mean?"

He runs his tongue over his bottom lip as he takes me in. "I didn't expect you to handle yourself like that."

He's obviously referring to the fantastic duel I was forced to take part in, barely surviving. I can't tell if that's a compliment or not, but what irritates me more is the small part of me that wants it to be.

I don't rely on other people's thoughts and opinions to make myself happy, and that's not changing now. Which is why I brush it off and focus on him being a complete asshole. "I don't recall speaking more than two words to you before now. That doesn't seem like much to go on to make an assessment."

"Probably not," he replies with a shrug, pursing his lips. His eyes drop to the wound, and he sighs, running a hand down his face before his gaze flickers back to mine. "Unfortunately for you, she slashed across your chest, and I'm going to need to be able to touch the broken skin to heal it."

"It's fine." It's not fine. I'm out of my mind already, and his proximity is doing nothing to calm the storm raging inside of me.

He nods without another word, stretching out a finger, and I watch as it shifts into a wolf's claw. I gulp but refuse to reveal the slight tremor that runs through my body at the sight of one again so soon.

With a gentleness that catches me by surprise, he slices through the remainder of my white tee that's in his way, and I notice my bra is shredded beneath the material.

Damn bitch.

"Are you happy for me to remove your bodice, or do you want to do it yourself?" he offers, his voice deeper, thicker. It takes a moment to understand his question, and I know if he does it, he won't be kind; he'll use his claw. I opt to do it myself. It hurts like hell, unclipping each link, but he doesn't complain about how long it takes.

The moment it's undone, it seems to ease the pain in

my chest a little, and Cassian wastes no time getting a closer look at the damage. He runs his finger over it and I wince, despite the touch being light.

"Sorry."

"It's fine," I muster, eyes pinched shut. I take a deep breath and hold it until warmth spreads over my skin. I peer down to watch in wonder as the wound begins to heal.

"Why can't a mage heal the wound? Because it happened during a duel?" I ask to distract myself from the fact that my skin is literally knitting itself back together.

"Calling a duel adds a whole other layer of magic to the equation, which only the wolf claimed from your dueling can heal."

"So I'm guessing all of my protests that it wasn't a duel went unheard?"

"Yup."

"Well, thanks…for helping heal it, at least," I mutter awkwardly. Thanking people isn't something I'm entirely used to. I do things myself. Always. Outside of my sister and father of course.

"Yeah," he grunts in response, avoiding my gaze as he focuses on the almost-healed wound. "You showed her mercy," he states a moment later, making me frown.

"I did."

"Why?"

I shrug, instantly regretting the pain that ebbs from my

chest still. "Because I don't want my path to the throne to involve killing people unnecessarily," I answer honestly, and he snickers, but there's no humor.

"You're not going to make it to the throne."

I smile, looking around the room instead of anywhere near him. "If you say so."

"I know so."

"Okay."

I can feel his eyes on me, but I just smile despite the pain I'm in.

"Why don't you argue back?" he pushes, clearly wanting more from me.

"I'm not wasting my breath when my actions will prove my point for me," I retort, turning toward him to meet his waiting gaze.

"You're definitely feisty." His words are laced with… something; it's a little intoxicating, but I squash it back down.

"So I've been told."

He reaches out, brushing a loose curl back off my face before his thumb sweeps down my cheek, holding my chin as he stares at me.

I feel like I can't breathe all over again. It's a sensation I'm not interested in, but I can't seem to push past it with him this close.

"All healed," he rasps, making me gulp, and I scramble

to cover my chest the best I can.

"Thanks." I can feel my pulse quickening, and I can't seem to calm it down, so I decide speaking will cover it instead. "What you said back there, you were joking, right?"

"About what?" his thumb remains on my face, inching closer to my parted lips, and I can't move.

Gulping, I try to clear my throat but fail miserably. "About the fact that Leticia will know who you belong to and back off."

"That's true."

Nodding slightly, I wet my dry lips as I stare deep into his eyes, searching for the truth before I've even spoken. "Which is great for keeping her at arm's length, but it doesn't affect anyone else, right?" I'm greeted with silence. The kind of silence that makes the hairs on the back of my neck stand on end. "Right?" I repeat, eyes widening with every second that passes.

"When you're a member of the Kenner pack, exiled or not, news travels fast."

"And what news will that be?" I know the answer in my gut already, but I want to hear him say it.

He inches closer, his nose touching mine as his eyes pierce me so deeply I'm certain he's grazing my soul. "That I'm yours…until someone else beats you in a duel."

His breath fans over my face and my body reacts

completely differently than my mind as realization washes over me.

"You motherfucker," I snap, slamming my hands against his chest.

"What the fuck?" He gapes at me as I stand, needing to put as much distance between us as possible.

"Fuck you. And fuck the bigger target you just put on my back," I yell, and he's standing in front of me a second later.

I can't have him crowding me like this. It does nothing to aid my cause.

"Calm the fuck down," he snarls, reaching for my face again, but I slap his hand away this time. Much to my body's disappointment.

"I may have shown Leticia mercy, but the same won't apply to you. Mark my words," I promise, taking another step back as Brody appears in the open doorway.

"What's going on?"

I scoff at his audacity, brushing past him as I head for the exit. I need to get the hell away from these guys, but I need to make sure Brody is clear on where we stand first.

"And you can go fuck yourself too."

THE KINGDOM OF RUIN

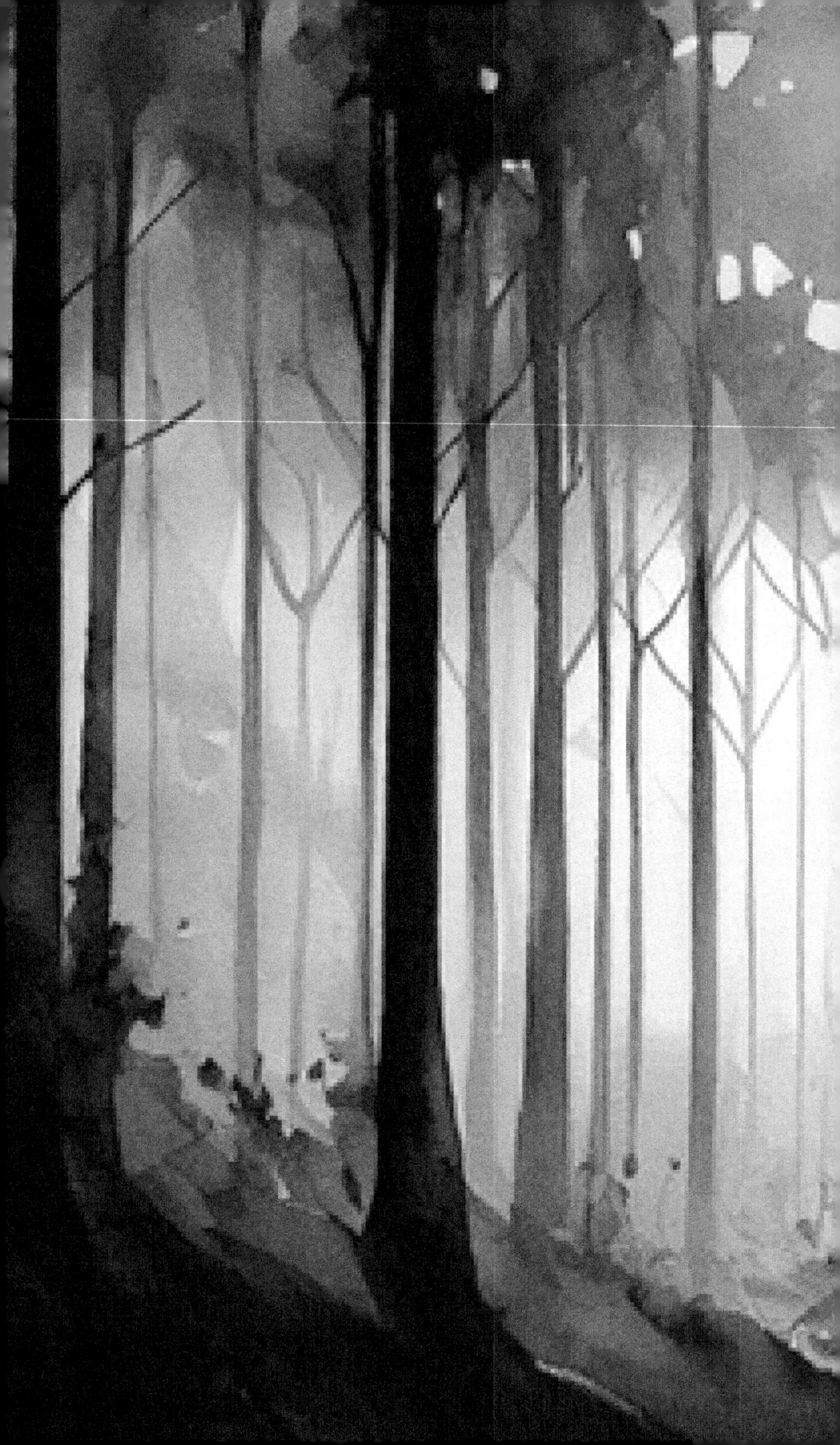

CASSIAN
23

The devilish fae saunters from the room without a backward glance, her ass swaying effortlessly. What the fuck has become of my life? I thought choosing to leave my pack, my *father's* pack, to join the academy would be the height of my downfall, but it seems I've still got much further to go.

"What was that?" Brody murmurs as I swipe a hand down my face in exasperation.

"A fucking whirlwind," I grunt, exhaustion clinging to me despite my racing heart.

"You're telling me."

I'm telling him? This guy has so many questions to answer, and he's acting just as bewildered as me. Rising from Raiden's bed, I breeze past my least favorite mage. He takes the hint to follow after me as I find Kryll and

Raiden seated on the sofa in Raiden's lounge.

A fucking lounge. Addi had every right to be surprised by the size of this place. Even the wolves aren't getting anything like this. It's a joke. I don't mind having access to it, though.

Flopping down onto the sofa with my arms braced on my knees, I level my gaze on Brody, who nervously paces beside me.

"What were you fucking thinking?" Kryll asks, beating me to it.

"What do you—"

"Don't give me that shit," I interject, all but snarling at him as he tries to give me an innocent look.

He shrugs after a moment, trying to play it off, but I'm not falling for that shit. "I wanted to wow her with some good food. Hoped I'd get in her pants too, but…" His words trail off. There's no need to continue when we all know that definitely didn't happen, and everything else that *did* happen was far from anything he could have predicted.

"Why the diner?"

"Didn't you hear the part about good food?" he retorts, like that's the only explanation necessary, and I roll my eyes at his dumb thought process.

"How did you even think she was going to be safe?"

This is what my brain is stuck on. How in the ever-loving fuck did he think this was a good idea? He shouldn't have taken anyone there, especially without me, and there was no way in hell I was showing my face yet. But a fae? A fucking *fae*? Wolves don't need to see pointy ears to know if someone is fae or not; we can smell it. I tried to tell Raiden that the first time we saw the mysterious girl in the forest by the origin houses. He was too fixated on the ears to see my point, but at the diner, everyone knew the instant Brody stepped through the door with her.

"I didn't. I was thinking food and pussy," he admits, running his fingers through his hair as Raiden slinks back in his seat with a snicker.

"You're fucking dumb, man," he bites, an air of 'I told you so' drifting around him. I don't need his ego added on top of all this.

"Aren't you going to apologize?" Kryll asks, cocking a brow at Brody, who gapes at him in surprise.

"For what? If anything, I did Cass a favor." He aims a finger at me and I rear my head back in shock. This fucker.

"How so?" I ask, eager to understand his thought process—or lack thereof.

"No more Leticia." He says it slowly, like I'm a child, and it only serves to piss me off more.

"That might sound good at first, but it's also going to travel like wildfire around the other wolves at the academy, and Addi is going to be caught on the end of it. You just linked me to the damn fae without even realizing it," I snarl, unable to bite back my anger any longer.

His shoulders slump as he tilts his face to look up at the ceiling. "I'm not going to get laid now, am I?" he mutters with a sigh, a sense of defeat drifting over him, and I shake my head in disbelief.

"I'd assume not," I snap, my hands balling into fists.

"Fuck. My dick was so hard watching her fight, too," he admits, making a show of adjusting himself through his pants.

"Tell me about it." The admission comes from Kryll, which feels more surprising than if Raiden were to say it, but I keep that thought to myself.

"I told you we should have ended her the first day," Raiden grunts, wiping his hands down his thighs as if he's not talking about killing someone so casually.

"Not doing that is the best decision ever. I definitely don't have a chance if she's not breathing," Brody grumbles, and I press my fingers into my temples, trying to calm the raging headache that's taking over from all of this bullshit.

"It's entertaining, at least," Kryll adds, and I sigh.

I don't know what it is. Drama. That's for sure.

"If you guys aren't going to agree with me, then you can get the fuck out," Raiden states, pointing to the door. His brown eyes shimmer with challenge. It's a look I'm all too familiar with when it comes to him.

He wants to purge the adrenaline coursing through his veins by arguing, and I don't have the energy to go toe to toe with him right now. So I stand, heading for the door without another word.

I have no idea what Kryll or Brody decide to do as I make my way down the six flights of stairs. Of course I have to be friends with the vampire who gets the penthouse. I'm sure it's because his mother is working here as the head of the vampires, but even Vallie is on the fourth floor, and her connections link her to The Council.

Thankfully, I don't pass a single vampire as I make my way down and step out into the night air, taking a deep breath as the cool breeze brushes over my skin. I storm down the pathway from the vampires' building, but my pace slows as I turn down the wolf path.

It looms ahead, ominous in the dark sky, with only the moon to light the way.

Everything I'm going through, every ounce of disappointment that comes from my pack, especially my father, is all because I chose to be here, and right now, I'm questioning whether that was the right decision.

Being a Kenner is highly regarded within the wolf community, even among the other packs who fall under The Council's guidance instead. When my father declined a place on The Council to focus solely on his pack, it didn't make him an outsider; it made him a fucking legend. So for his first-born son and true heir to the pack to relinquish his role to find one within the new kingdom that is forming before everyone's eyes is nothing short of a failure to him.

The disappointment in his eyes still flashes in my mind, the damage he caused to our home in his fit of rage following swiftly after. He thought his tantrum would make me fall in line, but all it did was confirm I'm doing the right thing.

Every pack should have an alpha, but when they refuse to see past their own perspective for the good of the people, it will inevitably start to crumble. Besides, when the rumors began that the academy was forming, I swore a pact with my friends that we would face this together and change the future of our kingdom. I swore it before I dedicated anything to my father, not that it matters to him. He shouldn't have to expect me to dedicate myself to him with pacts or other shit.

I'm family, that should be all that matters.

Sighing, I approach the building, and the door opens before I reach it. Two omegas step out, grins quickly spreading on their faces as they catch sight of me. I avert my gaze and try to step past them without a word, but I'm halted by a hand on my chest.

"Hey, Cass. Do you want to—"

"Don't talk to him. Didn't you hear about the duel?"

My spine stiffens as one of the girls cuts the other off, talking about me as if I'm not here.

"Duel? What for?"

"Leticia challenged someone for him and lost."

The gasp echoes in my ears as the hand slips from my body. I try to move around them, but they're both still peering up at me, waiting for confirmation that it's all a lie.

"Who?" The blonde asks, eager to reach back out for me again, but she laces her hands together instead.

"A fae," her friend whisper-shouts. The look of horror on her face is almost laughable. I consider picking her chin up off the floor but think better of it. I don't need to be getting involved in this right now. It only just happened and I need to sleep.

I shoulder past them, relieved when I reach the stairs, but the intense glares from the wolves in the communal area latch onto me, confirming that the news has already begun to spread.

Great. That's fucking great.

I don't know how I make it up to my room without another interruption, but I slam the door shut behind me, leaning against it as I take a deep breath.

Everything is fucked.

Not just for me, but also for Addi. My gut twists with the reality that it's my fault. I'm the reason this mess is unraveling. I can try to blame Brody over and over again, but really, I still let it happen.

Usually, I wouldn't care what ramifications others would face because of my actions, but for some reason, this feels different. Maybe it's because her sweet scent still lingers along my skin. Thoughts of her plague my mind despite my best efforts to squash them all down.

Fuck.

This isn't me, and I can't start acting like I give a shit now.

I need to sleep, get her out of my damn head, and tomorrow will be fine. It has to be. I refuse to accept anything else.

THE KINGDOM OF RUIN

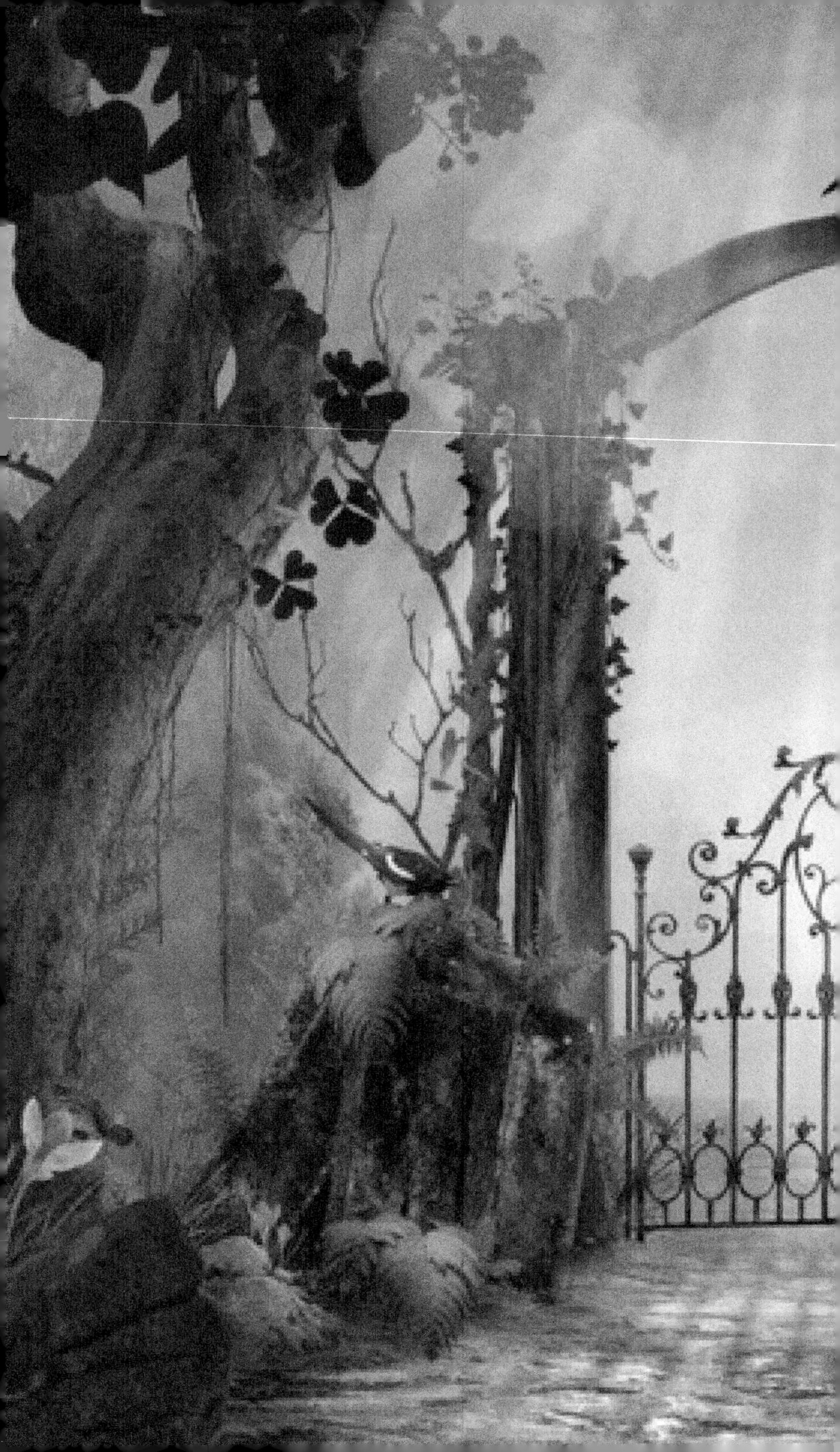

ADDI

24

I run my hands down my sides as I take a deep breath before swooping open my bedroom door and slamming it shut behind me.

There. I'm out of those goddamn four walls, and I'm not going back until I'm exhausted down to the bone.

Peering down at my bodice, I count the daggers at my waist, taking another deep breath before I descend the stairs. I've forgone the cloak, black or gray. There's no point hiding my daggers at this stage. Hopefully, if people see them it might keep them at arm's length.

I spent the entirety of yesterday hiding out in my room, going crazy so I didn't have to run into anyone, but I can't do that again today. I won't survive it.

Slipping from the house without running into anyone, I take off straight into a jog, eager to feel the breeze whip against my skin as I work my muscles.

Friday night was something else. I still can't wrap my head around how everything escalated so quickly. I signed up for a date in order to get Brody to strengthen the ward on my room. I thought I had the upper hand on him because there was no way he was getting in my pants no matter how much he hoped. Now I'm wondering if that would have been a better option, and I still don't actually know the consequences that are due to come my way.

A duel. A fucking wolf duel. Despite hiding away in my room, I didn't opt to hide away from the facts as well. I spent hours researching a wolf's duel and everything it entails.

My face scrunches with the fury that simmers in my veins at the thought of it as I run down the more secluded campus pathways.

I'm lucky Leticia didn't kill me. I'm adamant that's a testament to my strength, but my gut twists knowing there was a hint of luck in there, too. A duel among wolves over another wolf is sacred—fucking *sacred*—and Cassian just let it happen.

The moment Leticia tapped out, she practically joined me to Cassian without a word being spoken. He can fuck who he wants and do what he wants, but if he wants a relationship with anyone, they have to defeat me in a duel. It will come eventually, I assume. Mating and bonding is huge within the wolf community. So there's definitely going to be another battle on my hands.

Yay.

Despite my competitive nature and constant desire to win, I eventually came to the decision that when that happens, I'll tap the fuck out before it even begins. They can have him. They can preferably take him as far away from me as possible while they're at it. I'll be gracious in defeat, but my soul knows that it really won't be as simple as that. I'm a fae; people will likely challenge me just to have the opportunity to kill me, and I get the feeling many are going to try.

Fuck.

Shaking my head, I try to compartmentalize the thoughts that are taking over my head. I can't go back down this path again. I'm strong, resilient, and determined. No matter what is thrown my way, I will overcome it.

With a deep exhale, I focus on my breathing as I put one foot in front of the other. My heart pounds, my body warming, and I relish the effect running has on my limbs. All too soon, I approach the pathway where the fallen log rests, where I first saw Raiden and Cassian. My pulse thuds in my ears, making me tense as I try to wrap my head around my emotions.

It should be a relief that no one is out here, but I can't seem to dismiss the sense of disappointment that cascades over me. My lips purse with distaste at the reality. Despite the horrors of Friday night and the mess they've dragged me into, I'm still drawn to them. Not like a moth to a flame. No. That would be too nice. More like a lamb led to the slaughterhouse.

I'm the lamb. The fucking lamb…and they're one huge cluster fuck of a slaughterhouse, ready to dismember me one piece at a time.

Rounding back toward the origin buildings, I consider going around again but opt against it since it hasn't done much to clear my thoughts. Perspiration clings to my skin as I step inside and slip up the stairs before anyone sees me.

I'm going to have the best shower in existence, then find something to watch on television to distract myself. Or maybe I should do some yoga first? I'm not sure.

Taking the last few steps, I slow when I hear Flora yelling.

What the fuck?

My pace quickens with panic as I rush to the top step to find her standing toe to toe with Brody, and no Arlo in sight.

Her finger wags in his face as she glares at him. "Don't give me any of that crap. The sheepish look on your face screams you're guilty of something, and I won't have you waiting here for my friend. She definitely doesn't need your drama."

I'm slightly impressed. That's a lie. I'm mega impressed as I edge toward them. "What's going on?" I ask before Brody can reply, and both of their heads spin in my direction.

Flora's right. There's guilt in his eyes, and now it tinges hers. "Oh my gosh. I'm so sorry, Addi. He showed up here looking all..." She waves her hand at him in explanation, unable to find the words. "And I just knew I needed to get him out, but he's refusing to leave."

I smile—a raw, real smile that I haven't felt on my lips since I last saw Nora, which isn't all that long but feels like forever. I definitely need her as a friend, for Nora's sake, if anything. She would love her.

"It's okay, Flora. Thank you, but I've got this."

Her eyebrows furrow slightly as she assesses me before turning back to Brody. She snarls at him through bared teeth then waltzes into her room with a flourish only she could pull off. I stare at her closed bedroom door for a moment, garnering the strength to face this asshole.

I don't think I'm ever going to be ready to deal with his shit, so I suck it up and turn to him with a glare of my own. "What are you doing here?" I move toward my door, my arms folding over my chest as I get closer to him.

He rubs his lips together as he winces. "I owe you a stronger ward."

"Bullshit," I rasp with a snicker.

"What?" His body stiffens as he leans against the wall opposite my room, his defenses rising into place.

"That's not why you're here."

He rubs at the back of his neck with a sigh, his gaze dropping from mine for a moment before he finds it again. "No, probably not. I wanted a chance to explain to you, and I thought the ward was the least I could do."

I purse my lips, taking him in. I hate how vulnerable he looks, like he was the one wronged here, but more than that, I hate how much I want the stronger ward.

"You can ward away, but we're not talking," I snap, making a decision I'm not entirely certain of as I open my bedroom door and step into my space.

His gaze shifts around the bare room as he clears his throat. "I have to come in for that."

That little fact makes me pause, and my teeth sink into my bottom lip as I consider whether it's worth it or not. The main factor that has me relenting is that he hasn't stepped in automatically.

"Are you asking for permission?"

He shrugs like it's not a big deal, but a few days ago, he slapped his hand on my door without care. That guy wouldn't be teetering on the edge of my room like this. Something changed, and I don't know what.

"Fine," I grumble, hands clenching at my sides as he

steps into my room. My senses are heightened as I watch his every move, alert as hell, while he starts chanting immediately.

It's too late to back out now, and I'm putting far more trust in him than I should, but I'm holding on to the fact that he got straight to it and didn't try to push his way around my room instead.

A few minutes of tense silence drift between us before a bubble forms in the middle of the room and pops, clinging to the window, door, and walls. The second it does, Brody is thrown from the room with a tiny gasp, and I watch in shock as his back slams into the wall outside of my room that he had been leaning against a few minutes ago.

I rush to the open door, cringing as he rises to his feet and dusts off his clothes with a few strong curse words under his breath. Once he's gathered himself, he turns to me with a heavy smile.

"I'm sorry for Friday."

"Which part?" I retort before I can think better of it. He looks at me with wide eyes, fumbling over what to say, and I shake my head. "The fact is, you fucked up on so many levels that you can't even pinpoint which one might have been the worst of them, but an overall apology doesn't erase the shit you caused."

He nods, eyes darting away for a beat before finding me again. "I didn't think it would be, but I had to try." He stuffs his hands into his pants, and the way he seems to brush over it so effortlessly pisses me off even more.

"Do you realize the gravity of what you did?" I snap, my nostrils flaring with anger before I swiftly shake my head. "Don't answer that. I already know the bullshit that will fall from your lips," I grind out, earning me a nervous smile.

"Maybe we could try again?"

I blink at him, and again, and a third time as I process his dumb words. "Like fuck we can." I can't deal with him anymore. I need out of this conversation right now. "I'm going to assume that you flying from my room means the ward is in place?"

He nods, lips parting, but before he can utter a word, I slam the door shut between us, sagging against it as I try to catch my breath.

No one should be that good-looking and so overtly innocent and blasé that it makes them a fucking danger. Swiping a hand down my face, I push up off the wood as a knock sounds from the other side.

Fuck.

He's not going to make this easy, is he?

With a deep breath, I grab the handle and yank the door open, ready to give him another piece of my mind, but I'm stalled when it's Flora I find on the other side.

"Hey," she blurts, nervously looking me over from

head to toe. "I'm sorry, I just...do you want to hang out? Do something mind numbing, just...not alone?"

Her question catches me off guard, leaving me to gape at her for what feels like far too long before I nod. I need a distraction, and this might just be it.

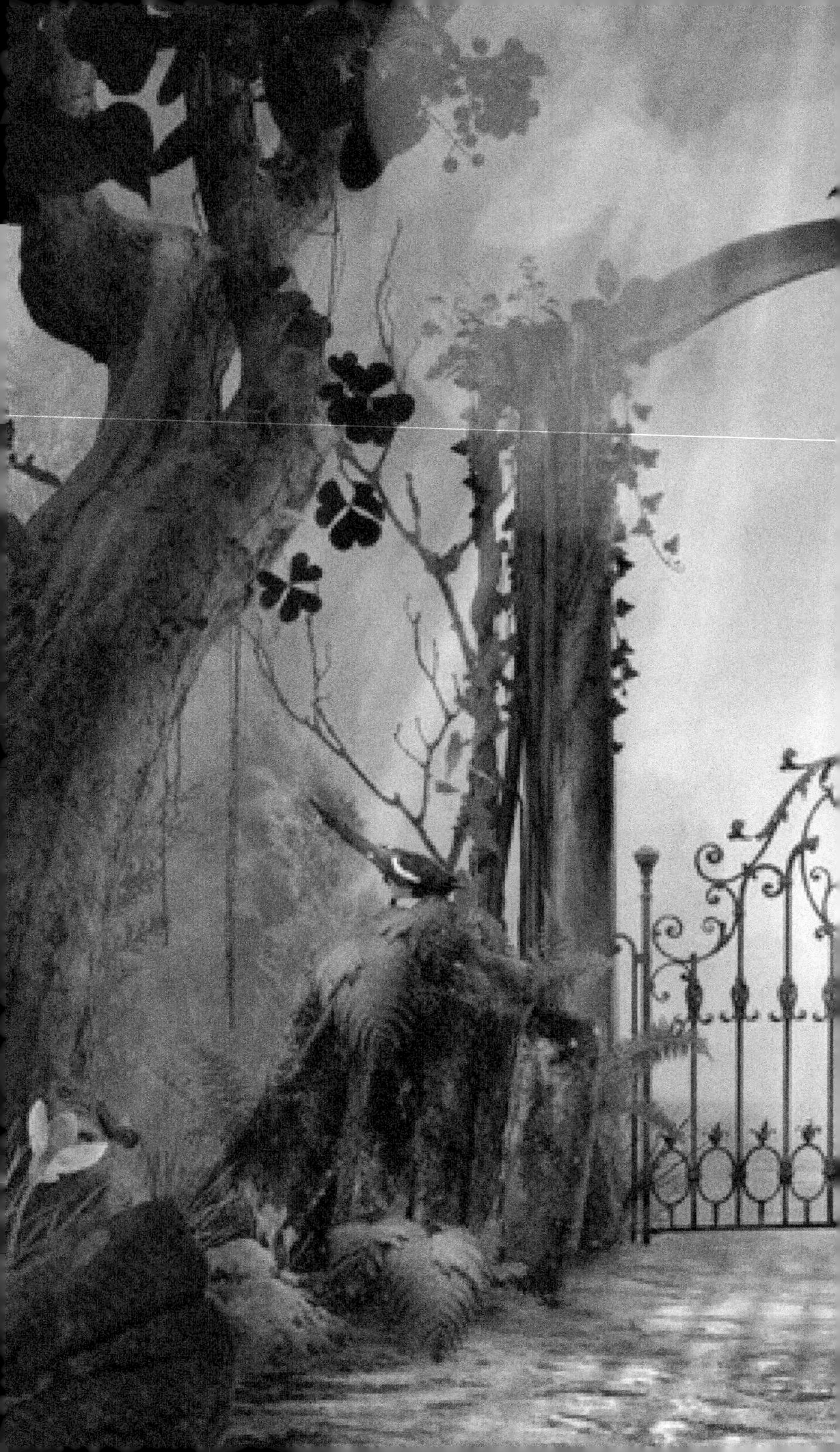

ADDI

25

Flora's bedroom door clicks shut behind me as I nervously glance around her personal space. It's the mirror image of my room, but it looks completely different, exemplifying the stark contrast between us both.

Her desk is scattered with beauty products, pink curtains drape her windows, and her bed is filled with pillows and a thick throw. Pictures of her with her family hang on her wall, making my heart clench at the reminder that I have none of mine. My room is an empty shell. Hers is all warm and inviting, like she brought a little slice of home here with her.

It doesn't take much to be girlier than me, but Flora is on another level.

I mean, right now, I'm rocking my gym clothes like a sweaty mess while she's wearing a cute red summer dress that perfectly complements her auburn hair. Her makeup is natural and fresh, and she just looks way more put together than me. It must be nice, and I almost long for it, but then I'm quickly reminded that the effort she put into all this I save for surviving. It's as simple as that.

"Get comfy, we're here for a good time," she sings, grabbing her laptop from her nightstand and getting comfortable among the array of cushions on her bed. "I have snacks, what do you want?" she asks, pulling a bag out from under the side of her bed the second my butt touches the sheets, and my stomach chooses that moment to growl. Her eyes immediately narrow as she assesses me, pulling the bag of snacks out of reach. "When was the last time you ate? I haven't seen you in the dining hall since Friday at lunchtime." I look away with a grimace, which only serves to prove whatever point she's aiming for. "Oh, you're in so much trouble," she promises, launching from the bed to grab her cell phone off her desk.

"What are you doing?" My instinct is to dive up and snatch the device from her hands, but something keeps me rooted to the spot, and thankfully so.

"Calling in a favor with Arlo," she answers, not looking up as she taps out a message. It chimes a moment later, and she smiles wide as she turns my way. "He's on the hunt to grab us some cheeseburgers and fries. What do you want to snack on until then?" she offers, approaching with the treat bag again, and I dive my hand in before she changes her mind.

When I pull out my favorite chocolate, I feel like I've hit the jackpot. "Thank you," I murmur, not really sure how to handle her attentiveness, and her smile grows.

"No worries." She takes a seat beside me, getting comfortable against the headboard, and I follow suit as she places the laptop between us. "Have you seen this?" She points at the screen, and I frown.

"*The Office*?"

"I'll take that as a no," she replies with a snicker, clicking the first episode.

"Do I even want to know what it's about?"

"It's a human classic," she promises, but my unease only heightens.

"You're not reeling me in."

She turns to me with her jaw slack and eyes wide. "Wash your mouth. It's funny as hell, completely mundane in comparison to our hectic lives, and it's all warm, like a hug. It's exactly what you need," she promises, her excitement palpable.

Her passion for it has my argument dying on my tongue. "I'm going to take your word for it."

"You're going to find out for yourself," she states, pressing play, and the opening theme song fills the air.

"Okay." The show starts up, but I can feel her eyes on

me. I try to ignore it, focusing on the screen, but after a few minutes, it's impossible to avoid. "What?"

"That feels too agreeable for you."

I cock a brow at her in confusion. "What makes you say that?"

"I don't know, but I feel like you would usually put up more of a fight."

It's on the tip of my tongue to mention Nora, but I slam my lips shut. If it were my sister and me right now, we would argue for hours over what to watch together, only for me to give in eventually to make her smile.

I can sense she wants some form of explanation as to why I'm out of sorts, but she doesn't need to know about my sister. So I give her something else entirely. Something she's already semi-aware of.

"It's just Brody," I murmur. Does he have me out of sorts? For sure, but there's so much more to it.

"That went from a hot secret to ice cold real quick," she assesses, and I scoff.

"Oh, it never got hot." I stuff a piece of chocolate in my mouth to shut myself up for a moment as her eyes narrow.

"What am I missing?" she prods, and I shake my head.

"So, *so* much."

She clears her throat and laces her fingers together in her lap. "Well, if you want to spill, I'm here. There's no pressure, but I find it's easier to get things off your chest sometimes."

"Thanks," I breathe, slightly in shock. I was certain she was going to start peppering me with questions, but instead, she's letting me set the pace. This might be the factor that separates her and Nora. Nora would never leave me alone when there's information to be had.

A knock at the door breaks the moment and Flora rushes over to reveal Arlo on the other side of the threshold with a bag of food.

His eyes narrow for a moment, as if he's concentrating, before they widen with excitement. "Is that *The Office* playing?" he asks, handing the bag off to Flora.

"It is, but you're not invited," she retorts, and he frowns.

"What? Why?"

"It's girl time," she points out, like it's really that simple. I don't mind if he's here or not, but I don't want to say that in case it's her who wants some space from him.

"I can be involved with girl time," he insists, and she shakes her head with a little cackle.

"I can see the outline of your dick through your sweats. Definitely not allowed," she declares before slamming the door shut in his face. She turns to me with those familiar pink cheeks as she heads over to the bed.

"What am I missing there?" I ask, using her own words back at her.

"What do you mean?" She doesn't look at me, opting to sort out the food instead.

Shrugging, I glance back at the door, expecting another knock, but nothing comes. "I don't know. Your connection seems completely different than...step-siblings," I admit, and she sighs.

"Yeah."

Despite there being so much unspoken in the air between us, we fall into a comfortable silence as we eat our food and fixate on *The Office*. Admittedly, it makes me grin more than I would expect, and I almost laugh at one point, but I refuse to admit it.

"I've known Arlo since I was five," she states, looking down at the few fries she has left. "I've loved him since I was eight, or I think I loved him then. It felt like it," she admits. "I knew I was crushing hard on him when I was fourteen, and when I turned twenty...my dad married his mom."

"Well fuck," I blurt, earning a smile from the defeated redhead beside me.

"Yeah, that."

"Have you guys ever talked about it?"

She shakes her head. "No, but I'm sure it's obvious to him. He's just too nice to make things awkward."

"That's bullshit," I retort, regretting it the moment she winces, but when she looks up at me with a confused gaze, I know there's a tinge of hope in there too.

"It is?"

"If that's what he was doing, then I would say that's shady as hell, but there's a level of care there for you, too. I can't decipher either of you enough to figure out anything more than that, though. But I don't get the feeling he's purposely avoiding the elephant in the room to save your feelings, because we all know that only ends in devastation anyway."

She scoffs, looking up at the ceiling helplessly. "Tell me about it. I'm a mind fae, and I can't get a damn read on him since I taught him how to shield at twelve."

"Damn, past Flora did future Flora dirty," I state, and she chuckles.

"Right?"

We laugh for what feels like forever, the weight on my shoulders easing a little. I feel lighter, and it wasn't even my problems we were discussing. It's strange to me that she just laid all that out for me, and her words from earlier replay in my mind.

"I agreed to a date with Brody so he would strengthen the ward on my room. Apparently, the one we were taught isn't strong enough to withstand mages," I admit, and she gapes at me in surprise. "I know."

"How did the date go?" she asks, a wistful romantic glint in her eyes.

"Well, I involuntarily dueled with a wolf named Leticia. I won, but the prize…is going to be more of a mess than I was already in," I admit, looking away from her.

"A duel. Damn, Addi, they're—"

"Serious, I know. It was more serious than I realized, but at the time, I was in the moment and desperate to defend myself."

"What were you dueling over?"

That's the worst part. Saying it out loud feels like setting off a ticking time bomb, but I take a deep breath and blurt it out before I can change my mind. "Cassian Kenner."

"Shut. Up. The most eligible wolf on campus?"

I frown at her as I shake my head. "No, he isn't."

"Yes, he is," she insists, sitting up to turn toward me. "His father is the elusive asshole who put the Kenner pack before all else, and his son left to be here."

"How did you know that?" I balk. I didn't know until I was right there watching everything unravel.

"You need to pay better attention to the gossip around us," she states, shaking her head, and I sigh.

"That sounds like more hard work than I'm willing to commit to," I say, and she chuckles.

"I'll focus on the gossip. You focus on keeping yourself

out of any danger." The pointed look she gives me keeps my lips sealed shut as I nod.

She's right, that much is for sure. But why does that sound easier said than done? Since I've stepped foot on campus, all I've done is wind up in some kind of trouble.

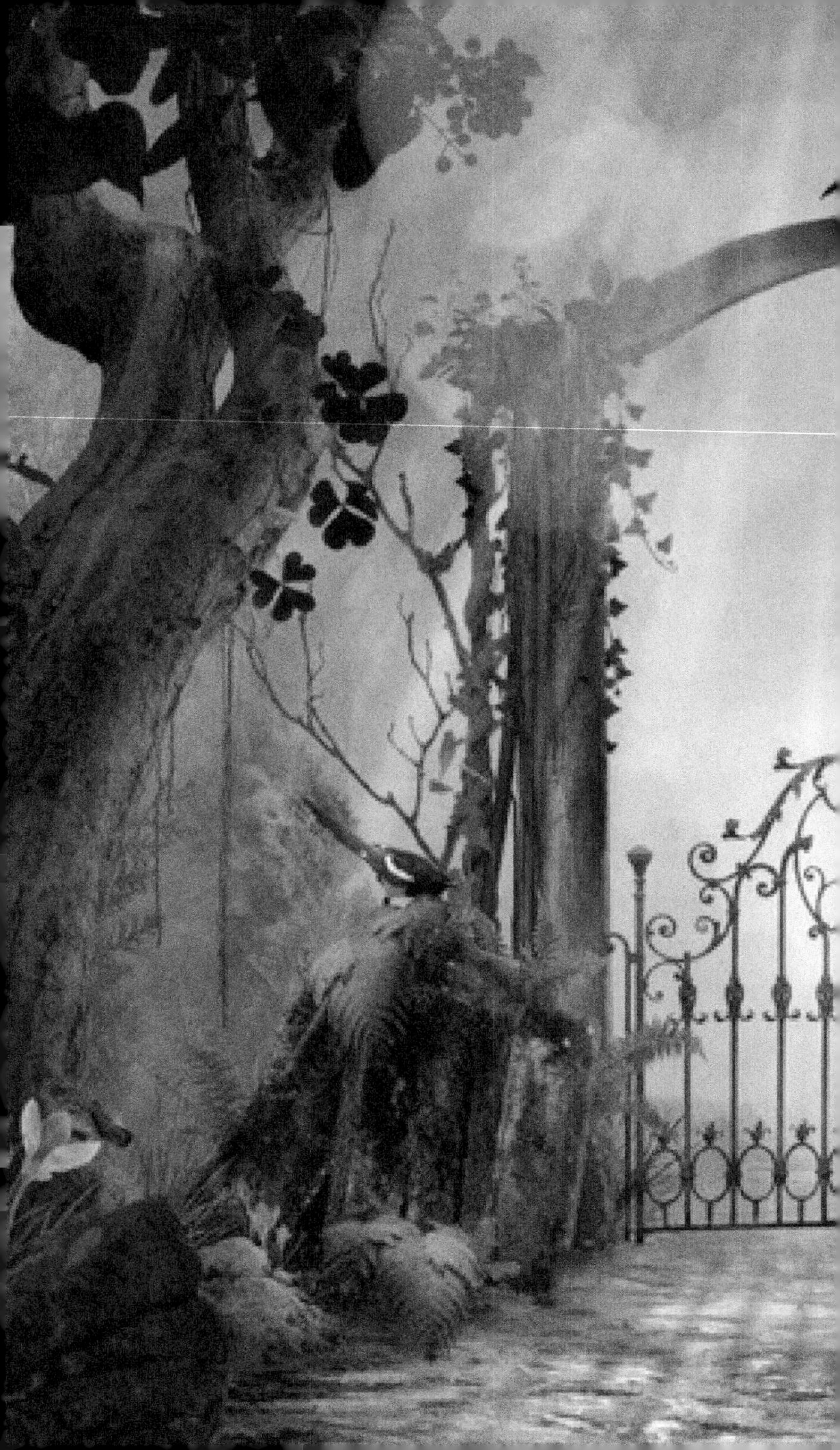

ADDI

26

Having a friend who isn't Nora is weird, but comforting. I feel protective over her, but not in the way I would be if it was Nora walking with me to the dining hall right now. The thought alone steals my breath. I would be practically feral. But Flora doesn't feel like a direct connection to me like Nora does. I have to trust that she can handle herself, while I would have Nora under my arm, throwing death glares at anyone who even considered looking in her direction. Trouble or not.

We spent the rest of yesterday watching the entire first two seasons of *The Office*—all twenty-eight episodes. We were so addicted that Arlo showed up when the sun had gone down with pasta dishes for dinner.

Again, she slammed the door in his face, and I get the feeling that something more is going on between them.

It's not my place to pry, though. If she wants to tell me, I'm sure she will. That seems to be the balance we have between us, and I like it, so as eager as I am to know, I'm not rocking the boat.

"You're definitely getting looks from at least four different groups of wolves," she murmurs as we walk past the water fountain at the end of the individual origin pathways, and I grimace.

"Great."

"I'm not getting a read that they're pissy over anything, more an air of intrigue," she adds, hoping to put me at ease, but it doesn't change anything inside me.

"Well, if that's all it is, they'll go away soon because there's really nothing to see here," I grumble, running my hands over the gray cloak that screams *I'm a fae* at everyone.

"You're funny."

My eyes narrow as I turn to her. "You're mean."

She scoffs, unfazed by my bullshit. "Please. You're a badass and you know it."

I shrug, trying to bite back the smile born of her assessment of me, but the matching tip to her lips tells me she's spotted it anyway.

Arlo walks a step ahead of us, peering over his shoulder every few moments until we enter the dining hall. Then, as we head toward the food, he moves to Flora's other side.

"Get your trays and pile your plates high. You both need to feed those egos, and those limbs need all the extra power they can get because something tells me our first combat class isn't going to be as easy as the others we've had," he states, and my gut twists, agreeing with what he's saying. I've got that same feeling in my gut, too. I don't know why, but I don't want to ignore it.

I make sure to pile my plate with eggs, bacon, and avocado with a piece of toast on the side before finding a spot at the table that's now been declared the fae pit. Flora sits beside me, and Arlo is across from her. I'm ready to get lost in my food when Arlo speaks again.

"People are definitely watching."

"Pay them no mind. They'll go away eventually," Flora insists, but her voice is softer than usual.

"Why don't you sound sure of that?" I ask, and she rolls her eyes.

"Because I'm definitely not, but one of us needs to be positive," she retorts before focusing on her food.

To my surprise, we eat without interruption, but I notice the air shift the moment the guys walk in. Raiden. Cassian. Brody. Kryll. It's clearly not just me they have an effect on. The entire room practically hangs off their every move.

Brody's eyes land on me first, then Kryll's, while Cassian and Raiden act as though I don't exist. Which is great, truly great, except it fuels the murmurs around us as people's eyes flicker from Cassian to me and back again.

Fuck.

When I'm still drowning in the intensity of it ten minutes later, with my plate now empty, I snap.

"This is suffocating. I need to get out of here," I grind out, my muscles coiling tight with anticipation.

Flora practically leaps from her seat. "Let's go."

Arlo stands without a word and the three of us head for the exit. We make it outside without issue, but I don't get a chance to breathe in the fresh air and exhale all of my problems away before a familiar vampire stands before me.

Fucking Vallie.

The sneer on her lips and her red nails aimed at me tells me I'm about to experience more of her bullshit. "You think because you have a claim on Cassian it's going to give you rights to Raiden, too?"

I frown at her, instantly irritated by her mere proximity. "Did you start half of that conversation in your head or something because I have no idea what the fuck you're talking about."

"Don't play dumb," she growls, inching closer, but I don't back away; I stand taller, using the few inches I have over her to my advantage.

"Don't stand in my way."

She cackles, head thrown back as a few of her vampire

friends step closer. "Oh, someone's getting brave because they made a little pup tap out. Newsflash, scum, I'm no pup. A duel with me would see you face first in the dirt."

"Are you forgetting what happened last week? I can remind you if you like," I offer, eager to follow through as I let my magic tap into the ground beneath us.

Watching the vines wrap around her would be the perfect start to my day, especially if I weaved them around her mouth and shut her the hell up.

Her mouth falls open, her venom ready to be unleashed, but an arm drapes around my shoulders and heaves me away from the queen vampire hell bent on causing me issues.

Confused, I blink up at the asshole getting involved to find Kryll's auburn hair and black markings along his skin. "I'm in the middle of something here."

"Not anymore, you're not."

I try to step out from under his arm, but he makes it impossible, tugging me into his side as he guides me toward our combat class. Flora is a step behind, with Arlo beside her. Neither of them say a word, happy to see what's going on, and I glare at them before turning my wrath back to Kryll.

"She was giving me shit. Again. I have to stand my ground against idiots like that. You pulling me away makes me look weak." He shrugs, not offering any kind of response, which only irritates me more, but it seems I may have to try a softer approach with this asshole to get anywhere. "What do you want, Kryll? I was hoping the four of you would forget I exist and leave me in peace," I grumble, and he snickers.

"It's nice to see you too, Addi," he muses, making my eyes narrow.

"Don't play games with me. What do you want?" I push, and his hand on my arm tightens as if he senses I'm going to make a run for it. I definitely need to, but not for the reason he thinks. It's almost nice feeling his warmth around me, and I need to put as much distance between us as possible.

"Me? Nothing. Cassian and Raiden? A moment's peace," he offers as an explanation, and I huff.

"Let me know where they find one. I could do with one of those as well."

He smirks but doesn't respond, keeping me tucked under his arm as we step into the large gym space for combat class. The entire floor is one giant mat, but otherwise, the room is bare. Everyone gathers in the different colors, confirming who is what without having to look deeper than our clothes.

"Good morning, I'm Professor Tora. I'll be your combat teacher for the foreseeable future," he announces, standing in the center of the room with his arms folded over his chest. Everyone gathers around him, and as we get closer, it's impossible not to note how stacked he is. He's not wearing colors like the rest of us, but his aura gives an easy read on him.

Nomad. Built. Strong.

He's a shifter. Thankfully, not a wolf. I've had my fill of those forever.

I try to shake out of Kryll's hold, but it only seems to tighten. "You can get off me now," I bite, glaring up at him, and he shakes his head without peering down at me.

Fucker.

"I want to know everyone's abilities from the get-go," Tora states, pacing in front of us. "Which means we're going to break off into pairs, bring it to the mat, and see what we're working with," he explains, confirming my initial thoughts. Even though part of me knew this was coming, I still feel the nerves threaten to overwhelm me.

I need to remain focused and free of distractions, so I can't let nerves take over. There's no room for that on the battlefield, and there's no room for it here, either.

He starts to rattle off names, going along the crowd before his steps slow in front of us. "Nice, Kryll and Addi, you two can go together."

Kryll grins, slapping hands with the professor, and my gaze narrows.

"What the fuck is that?" I mutter when Tora carries on.

"Tora has my back."

"And?"

"And..." He looks at me, puzzled, like he didn't just give me half a damn explanation, and I know I'm not going to get anything else from him.

Fucker.

We find a space on the mats and face off with each other. I roll my shoulders back, calculating how I can use Kryll's size against him as he assesses me, too.

"You had room for improvement back at the diner." My eyes widen at his comment, but I tamper down my defenses and shrug, acting as unaffected as possible.

"Thanks for the assessment."

"At least I have it easier than she did since you don't have any daggers hanging off you this time."

"Says who?" I retort, cocking a brow at him. He's right, I don't have any, but he doesn't need to know that. He wets his lips, looking over me once more to try and find any hints of silver. "Don't worry, I'll try and show you the same mercy too. You just have to tap out," I state sweetly, smiling wide at him, and his gaze narrows.

This may actually be fun. Despite the unfazed exterior he's always rocking, I can see the smallest crack in his walls, and trying to get to him offers a little excitement.

He charges at me first, testing my reflexes as he swings his arms at me in quick succession. I manage to deflect the first four with my arms, but the fifth catches me by surprise as he changes his angle. His balled fist connects with my stomach, but not enough to wind me. He's holding back. That's for sure.

"You hold your arms too high. You need to centralize them a little more so you can shift up *and* down when needed," he points out. He's right. I know he is. But admitting that to him feels like defeat. So I nod and carry on.

Refusing to let him continue with the upper hand, I circle him, hoping to make him feel like prey for a minute. He watches me with amusement as I hook my arms into my chest, fists balled, ready to connect with him.

I extend toward his right shoulder first, and he blocks it effortlessly. I repeat the motion with my other hand, aiming for the same spot as I stretch my leg and kick at his thigh. I catch the weak spot perfectly, and he stumbles, dropping to one knee with a look of utter surprise on his face.

"You focus too much on my hands because you underestimate what I can do. I have legs, too, and they work just as well as my fists." My pointer is definitely condescending, but I can't help it.

"You know how to handle yourself. Well, you think you do. I can prove you wrong," he says, but it's not an offer. A moment later, he's on his feet, stalking toward me with purpose in every movement.

I inch back a little before stepping sideways to circle him. He can cut the distance between us quicker than I can blink, and it's exciting how alert and on edge I am all at once.

The sound of other people hitting the mat around us echoes in my ears, but I try to block it out, focusing on him as his gaze seems to darken. I know he's going to come at me stronger this time, and I'm ready for it.

He shifts on his left foot, heavier than any other steps he's taken, and I brace for impact, wanting him to come at me. We collide a moment later, sailing through the air as his arms band around me, blocking the full impact of the floor beneath us as he lands on top of me. I wrap my legs around his waist without missing a beat, using the small pocket of energy from the impact to roll.

I'm met with little resistance, which I think has more to do with the surprise that flashes in his eyes than his inability, but I use it to my advantage, plastering his back to the mat as I lay on top of him, pinning his wrists.

I grin, victory dancing in my head as my heart races.

It doesn't last long, as he repeats a similar move on me. A second later, I'm back beneath him, the pair of us panting for breath. His eyes swirl and I get the sense his animal is right beneath the surface as he tries to catch his breath.

"This is almost fun," I rasp, acutely aware of his body

pressed against mine, and he shakes his head, trying and failing to focus.

I could take him again. I think. It's worth a try.

Hooking my legs around his, I get ready to shift my weight when a shrill voice bites through the air.

"Fuck this shit. There's no way I'm having some fae bitch infiltrate the Kenner line. I challenge her to a duel."

Fuck. My. Life.

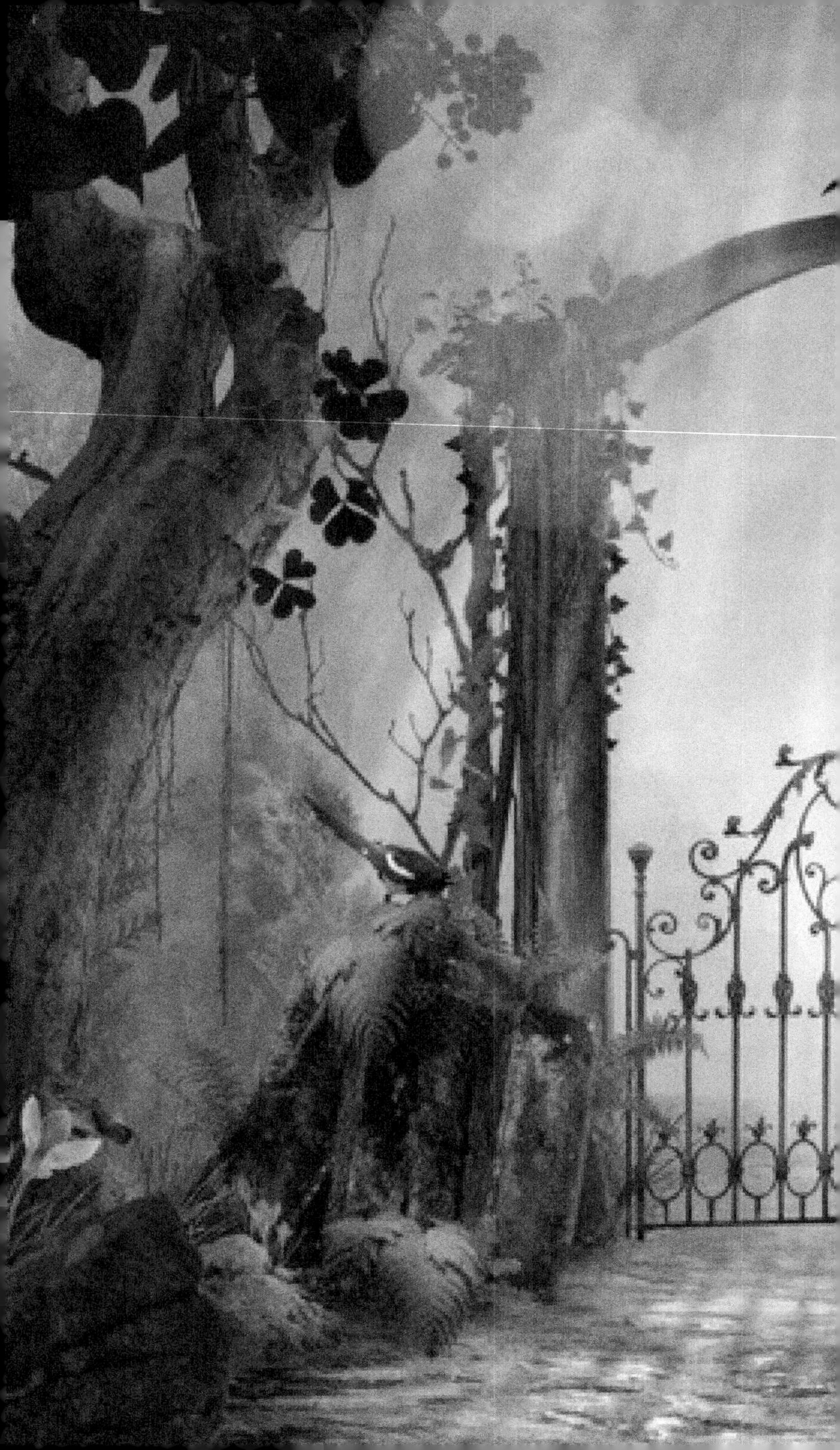

ADDI

27

With a quick breath and a failed attempt at trying to calm my pounding heart, I turn to see who has decided to cause a stir. I was finally relieving my tension in a controlled manner, and it was starting to get fun, but someone just had to go and ruin it.

Kryll remains pinned to me, so it takes a second, but I soon find a brown-haired girl with narrowed eyes standing with her hands planted on her hips.

My attention becomes slightly distracted by the smirking vampire who stands a few steps behind her. Vallie. My gut tells me she's orchestrating all of this, and there's nothing poetic about it.

Kryll curses under his breath as he climbs off me, and I instantly feel the lack of heat coming from his huge frame.

I keep my mouth shut as I stand, brushing off my clothes as I turn to face my new challenger.

"We won't be calling a duel in my class," Professor Tora grunts, storming toward us with irritation burning in his eyes.

"Fuck your class, a wolf's duel outweighs everything," she retorts, vibrating from head to toe. She doesn't bother to turn in the professor's direction, which screams disrespect, but it's not my place to say anything. I'm certain we're going to see smoke coming out of her ears like they show in those human kids' television shows, but alas, this is a lot more real than that.

Facing her head on, I decide it's quicker to rip the bandage off and get straight to the point. "If you want your precious little rights to Cassian, just say the word, and I'll tap out now. No questions asked," I offer, watching her eyes narrow in confusion. As if on command, I feel a presence at my back.

"No, you won't."

My head snaps to Cassian, who glares down at me with that feral look only he seems to be able to wear so effortlessly.

He has some fucking nerve getting involved right now, especially when it's not to help me out of this predicament. Asshole.

"You're damn straight I will," I bite, aware we have the

attention of the entire class as we stand off with each other. To everyone else it probably looks like a lover's spat, but it's so far from it, it's almost funny. He shakes his head, ready to put me in my place, but I jab my finger against his extremely muscled chest as I push on. "I do believe I've already put my life at risk because of you. I'm not interested in doing it again. I want to fight for my kingdom, not for some asshole who wants to use me to keep all the little puppies at bay."

His nostrils flare, his anger clear, but mine's right at the surface, too.

"Did you just call me a puppy?"

I peer at the thorn in my side as she balls her hands into fists at her sides, and I shrug. "I can call you a bitch if you prefer. Both feel accurate right now." I'm mentally high-fiving myself for my snark, but apparently, she doesn't appreciate it the same.

"I'm going to kill you," she snarls, taking a step toward me, and I inch closer, too.

"It's not necessary. I already told you I—" A hand claps over my mouth, cutting off the rest of my words as lips press against my ear.

"Shut your fucking mouth." Cassian's snarl sends a shiver down my spine, but it doesn't turn me pliant as I'm sure he intended. Instead, I sink my teeth into his flesh, but he doesn't flinch. Fucker. "That's not how duels work,

Becca. Addi will not face another during this moon cycle; that's the rule, and you'll do well to remember that," he snaps, aiming his words at my challenger.

Becca. I'll do well to remember that name. And what's this about the moon cycle? What does that mean for me? It feels important, even though it's just a sliver of information, but I tuck it away for safekeeping.

I see Flora gaping at me with pleading eyes, her fingers twitching as if she's about to do something, and I subtly shake my head. This isn't her battle; she doesn't need to get caught in these crosshairs.

"Are we done with the drama now? It's not what we're here for," Professor Tora spits out in annoyance. I blink up at him, mouth still covered as I try to calm the adrenaline coursing through my veins.

"We're going to cut out now," Kryll states, stepping toward Tora while Brody and Raiden appear at my left, ready to exit. It's hilarious, the control they think they have. There's no way the professor is going to—

"Fine, but keep your bullshit to a minimum or I'll report back to Mom," he grumbles under his breath, clapping hands with Kryll as he eyes me.

Mom? Is that his fucking brother? The smirk on Kryll's face says it is. Why am I not shocked? If this shows me anything, it's that you really do need connections in a place like this, and I currently have none. Which is why Tora turns away as Cassian proceeds to drag me from the gym.

There's no point objecting at this stage, not when there's still an audience. He can have a piece of my mind when we get out of here.

Cassian's front remains plastered to my back, making it difficult to walk. He must sense the same thing because in the next moment, my breath is stolen as he uses his wolf speed to hurry us along.

Nausea swirls in my stomach, burning up my throat as we come to a stop. Thankfully, he removes his hand from my mouth and takes a step back, giving me some space, but it simply allows me to collapse to my knees, palms pressing into the ground beneath me as I will the sensation away.

"We really need to talk about you assholes doing that," I bite, eyelids pressed tightly closed. He doesn't bother to respond, and if I couldn't sense his presence around me, I would assume he dropped me off and left, but I'm not that lucky.

Once I can see straight, I push up onto my feet, noticing that we're out by the forest where they first infiltrated my life. Cassian stands with his arms folded over his chest, with Raiden, Kryll, and Brody sitting on the fallen tree.

"What the fuck was that?" he bites, baring his teeth as he glares at me. The audacity of this man. I'm the one getting caught up in *his* shit left, right, and center, and he's asking me what the fuck that was? Hell no. Instead of giving him a tongue-lashing, I decide I want him to spell it out.

"What the fuck was what?"

"You don't just say you'll tap out and let them win." Ah, so that's what has him mad. Good.

"Why not?" I match his stance, folding my arms over my chest as I level him with a deathly glare.

"Because I'm a fucking Kenner."

"Was," I point out with a cock of my brow, which only makes him growl.

"Still am."

I shrug. "It still doesn't mean shit to me. I didn't ask for any of this, and I won't risk my life for some hold over you that I don't want. If anything, you should be grateful to know that there's someone out there who doesn't want to own you in that odd fucking way. No bonding here. You can go and be a free man, as far away from me as possible."

He drops his arms, tucking his hands into his pockets as a devilish smirk spreads across his face. "Well, you're stuck with it," he confirms with a shake of his head, and I scoff.

"I'm not." The words leave my mouth with such certainty, but seem to fall flat between us as he ignores me.

He closes the distance between us in a flash, forcing me to blink up at him. "I'm going to be watching your every move, every step, every breath. I won't allow it to happen."

"I'm worth more than what you're making me out to be," I rasp, irritation clogging my throat as my pulse pounds in my ears.

"You're fucking fae. If anything, I'm boosting *your* fucking value."

I rear back at his words, gaping in disgust. "You're going to be disappointed when the next challenge comes around and I do exactly as I just offered," I promise. Before I can move out of the way, he grips my chin tightly, holding me in place. He looks deep into my eyes, a breath passing between us, then another, and another until he seems to come to a decision in his mind, nodding to himself as he brings his face to mine so our noses touch.

"You can think what you want, but this isn't going away until you take your last breath."

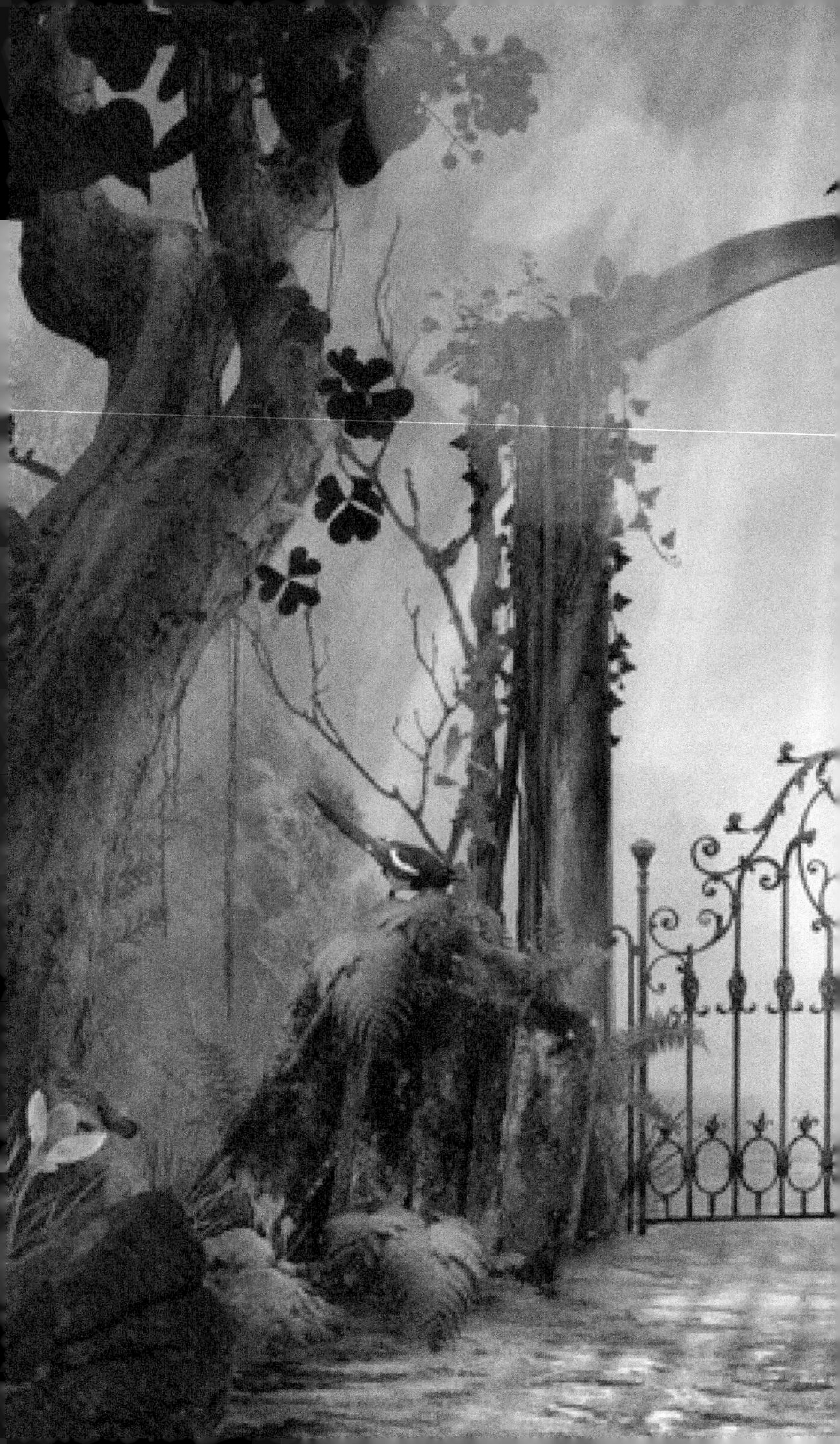

ADDI

28

One thing this whole mess is teaching me is that I am resilient. After Cassian's oath that felt more like a threat than a promise, the four of them left without another word, leaving me to walk back from the forest alone. It served as the perfect opportunity to gather myself and get my head on straight. They can play whatever games they like, but I won't be swayed from my purpose. All they're going to do is make me stronger. That's how I'm looking at it from now on.

The obstacles in my way are there for a reason—Vallie, Kryll, Brody, Raiden, Cassian, and now apparently some bitch called Becca. All of them. They're going to make my victory as the heir of this kingdom that much sweeter.

With that said, it feels like an eternity passes until lunch comes around. Being stuck in class, sandwiched between

Brody and Kryll, doesn't help the matter, but I block them out and actually listen during the lesson. Brody's knee is back to resting against mine, and I would be lying if I said the heat didn't threaten to distract me, but I somehow manage to ignore it enough to stay on task. Sure, the class is boring, some bullshit about the kingdom's palace etiquette, but I try to absorb it.

I've managed to reduce the frustration and anger that consumed me, but they still faintly simmer beneath the surface. I kind of like it, though; it's keeping me alert. If I had been able to continue with combat class and land one more hit on Kryll, the tension would have been completely gone, but there's nothing I can do about that now. They chose the course of my day, and I'm just going to roll with it.

Stepping out of class after the bell rings, Flora and Arlo appear at my side a moment later.

"Finally. I'm starving," Arlo grumbles, earning himself an eye roll from Flora. I grin at them. Their vibe is the complete opposite of everything else that surrounds me, so I let myself enjoy it for a moment.

As we near the dining hall, I note my appetite is nowhere to be seen, but I'm going to need to keep my intake up to remain alert and present. Something tells me if these wolves can't challenge me to a duel, they may just all-out attack me without warning. With Vallie's constant bullshit on top of that, I'm never going to find that moment of peace I so desperately need.

We join the line for food, grabbing our trays before Arlo turns to me with a smirk. "What are our bets on having a problem-free lunch?"

"Arlo," Flora gasps, backhanding his stomach before grimacing at me.

"What? We may as well make it fun," he insists, turning to me for backup.

I smirk. "If I bet there will be no issues, there will be more than usual, so I'm going to keep my mouth shut and play referee to your guesses."

Arlo lifts his hand for a high-five and I take it. "See, Flo. She gets it," he states, giving her a pointed look. She just rolls her eyes at him again.

"I'm sorry. He's a jerk and just can't help himself."

"I'm not offended. He'd make good money if it were real because this shit is following me around whether I like it or not," I grumble, approaching the food counter.

I should go for the chicken breast and avocado option, but my mood right now is screaming for comfort food, so I choose the mac and cheese and some crispy chicken tenders. With a bottle of water and my food, I murmur my thanks and head for our usual table.

Nervousness settles over the other fae who are already seated, more so than usual, and I understand why when I go to place my tray down.

"You can't sit here now," a girl with blonde hair mutters, tucking a loose tendril of hair behind her ear as she struggles to make eye contact with me.

"Says who?" I ask, eyebrows pinching in confusion. My words are probably sharper than necessary, especially when I can tell this isn't her decision, but I can't help it.

"Says me."

My back stiffens at the sound of Cassian's voice. I turn to face him as I sense Flora and Arlo take their seats. His arms are relaxed at his sides, not folded across his chest like usual, and I don't know whether that's to lead me into a false sense of security or not, but it's not working.

He's trouble with a capital *T*, and if he thinks he can decide where I do and don't sit, he's in for a rude awakening.

"Fuck off, Cassian," I grumble, exhaling heavily, as he tilts his head, nodding toward where Brody, Raiden, and Kryll are seated.

"You're sitting with us now."

"I'm good, but thanks," I reply with the fakest smile I can muster, but I know I'm showing too much teeth for it to look anything but feral.

"It's not an offer."

"Then there's nothing for me to decline." I pull my chair out, ready to take my seat when he places his palms on the table and leans in close.

"Don't make this harder than it has to be, Addi."

Sighing, I brace my hands on the back of my chair, knowing the second I sit down, he'll bulldoze me. "I've had enough of you all to last a lifetime, but today especially. I need five minutes with my friends to forget you exist. That's not going to be possible when I'm sitting with you, is it?"

He grins like I'm amusing him, a stark contrast to the asshole earlier who was all snarly and angry. What the fuck is going on? "Keep pushing and I'll have you seated in my lap the entire time. Come now, and I'll let you have a chair for yourself."

"Is this a fucking joke?" I blurt, aware we're garnering spectators again.

He stands tall, shrugging casually as if my blood doesn't feel like it's on fire. "I'm increasing your status, remember?"

My nostrils flare as I shove my chair back in, my anger burning to the surface as I glare at him. "I'm going to say this once, and once only. Fuck you and fuck your status."

I shoulder past him, leaving my tray of food and friends at the table as I storm for the door. Eyes trail my every move, but I make sure to keep my shoulders back and head held high.

I sag a little when I step outside and the fresh air hits me. Checking the time, I realize there's no point trying to find somewhere to isolate myself since classes will start again soon, so I find a seat on an empty picnic table, avoiding everyone's gaze as they sit in their groups.

Bracing my elbows on the top, I close my eyes, feeling the sun beat down on me. I take a deep breath, followed swiftly by another, as I try to calm the storm raging inside me. My father's mantra of being calm and collected feels like utter bullshit right now. I can't hide what I'm feeling like he can. Everything always feels too real, too raw, too close to the surface.

Shadows fall over the back of my eyelids, ruining my moment, and when I blink them open, I find Kryll, Brody, and Raiden sitting across from me while Cassian sits to my left.

Fuck my life.

A tray is placed in front of me with more force than necessary, and it takes me a moment to realize it's my food. That's the only interaction they offer as they chat about nothing like I'm not here.

"Eat," Kryll states, pointing his fork at me after a while, but I'm still far too overwhelmed with how to handle the situation to even lift my fork. When I don't immediately dig in, three more pairs of eyes turn my way wearing deathly glares.

Indecision battles inside me as I consider my options. I can make a point of refusing to deal with their shit and storm off again, or I can at least eat my comfort food first. Deciding on the latter, I ignore the four of them as I eat.

Halfway through my plate, while I'm staring off at the cute planters that frame the outdoor space, an idea comes to mind. Planting my feet only on the ground beneath me, a slight grin plays at the corner of my mouth and I have to bite it back the best I can as I finish eating.

Satisfied, I push my tray away and stand.

"Sit the fuck down, Addi," Raiden grunts the second I do, but I quickly move to the side of the table, out of Cassian's reach, ignoring him.

"Sit down, or I come and get you," Cassian warns as I take a few steps away before turning back to them with my eyebrow raised.

Cassian's eyes narrow, challenging me to take one more step, so I do.

All four of them rush to stand and charge toward me but quickly fall back into their seats with a grunt. I watch in slow motion as they peer down at their feet to find vines have creeped from the ground and laced themselves around their boots.

I snicker, and Kryll is the first to glare at me again. "Oh, she thinks she's funny," he grumbles.

"It's a little impressive," Brody states, a smirk on his lips as he looks down at the ground.

It's not enough for me to lower my defenses, though.

It won't hold them for long, but it'll give me a head start at least. "Later!" I holler, turning in a hurry, only to run straight into someone.

They catch me by the arms, straightening me, and I peer up to see Professor Fairbourne frowning down at me. There's tension in his eyes that's not usually there and my gut twists instantly, as if knowing it relates to me somehow.

"Is there a reason you're being summoned to my office, Addi?" he asks, releasing his hold on me as he glances over my shoulder at the guys filling the table I was just at.

"Wouldn't you be the one to know since it's your office?" I retort, confused about where this is going. When his eyes find mine again, a ball of dread settles in my stomach.

He sighs, dragging a hand down his face before he answers. "Not when it's the dean calling you in."

Well, fuck. That doesn't sound good. But staying out here with these guys doesn't sound much better.

Reluctant to see what comes next, I nod. "Lead the way to my impending doom," I say jokingly, and he shakes his head.

"It's not funny if that's what it actually is."

THE KINGDOM OF RUIN

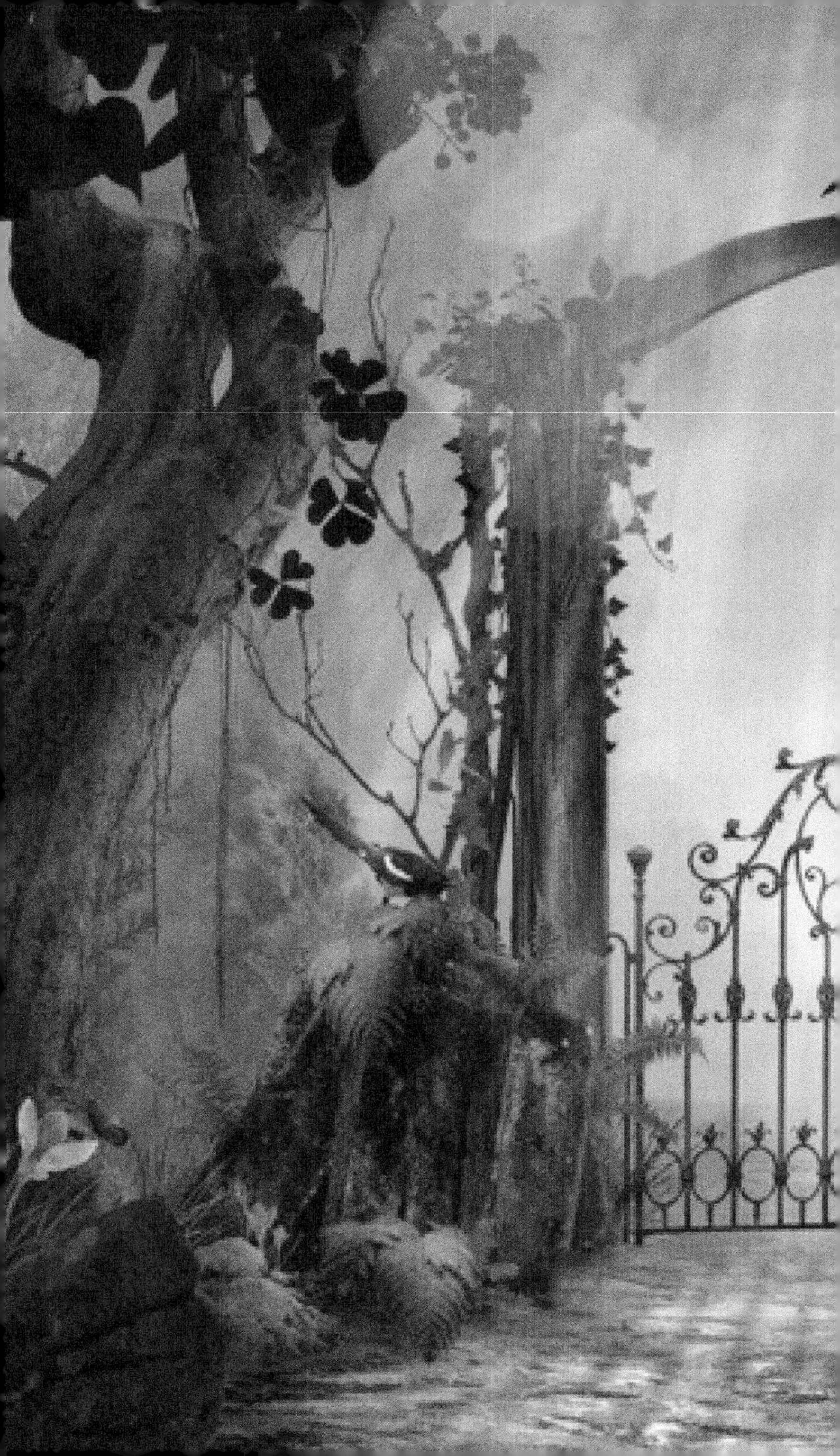

ADDI

29

The air around us shifts as we step into Fairbourne's office, and the reason for the dramatic drop is located in the high-back leather chair.

The dean.

She sits with an air of supremacy exuding from every fiber of her being as she manages to somehow look down her nose at me, even though she's seated well below my line of sight.

Her clothing is just as vibrant as it was the first day she appeared in front of the crowd of students gathering to attend the academy. Something tells me she's never had to hide away or shield herself from the spotlight. No. She's a confident vampire who destroys any obstacle standing in her way with some side eye and a pout.

Her color of choice today is yellow. A happy color, filled

with joy and hope, yet she somehow manages to make the hairs on the back of my neck stand on end. Maybe it's the sinister red lips she's paired it with, or the raised eyebrow that begs anyone to question any of her actions.

This is going to be fun. Said no one ever.

She steeples her fingers as I take my time entering the room, her eyes raking over me from head to toe before repeating the motion. She's weighing me up more than anyone else I've ever come across in my life, and I have to give it to her: it's unnerving. But once again, my father trained me well, for this kind of assessment and so much more.

"Bozzelli, you called for Addi. I'll step out and give you a few moments," Fairbourne states, and I can't stop myself from turning to gape at him. That fucker is just going to hang me out to dry, and I don't even know what for. I could have sworn it felt like he would have my back a few days ago, but now, at the first hurdle, he's ready to sidestep so he doesn't get caught in the crossfire. No wonder the walk over here was so damn quiet.

"You should stay, Professor Fairbourne," Dean Bozzelli insists, a hint of disdain in her eyes when I turn back to see her giving him the same once-over I was privileged to experience moments earlier.

The door clicks shut behind him, deepening the dwindling energy that fills the room.

"Take a seat, Miss Reed," Dean Bozzelli orders, waving her hand at the seat on the other side of the desk.

I'd sat in that same seat last week, being showered with words of confidence from Fairbourne, but I know when I drop into it this time, it will be to receive the complete opposite.

"You're causing quite a stir," she states, and I frown.

"I'm not sure I know what you're referring to."

I mean, I do, but I'd rather she be more specific. There are a lot of things she could be pulling me in here for; which one of them is the real question, and I deserve to know what I'm defending myself against.

She laces her fingers together with a glare, silently calling me on my bullshit before she finally offers anything in the way of explanation. "I have the vampire head of council demanding you be escorted off campus immediately."

"Why would they even know I exist?" I blurt before I can think better of it. But realization washes over me as she explains.

"I believe you've caused issues for their daughter. Vallie."

Fucking Vallie. Nothing irritates me more than her damn existence right now, and that's saying something since there's a running challenge for the top spot on my shit list.

Rolling my eyes, I take a deep breath, but processing the fact that this is actually happening leaves me speechless. She stares me down for what feels like an eternity, making it clear that she wants my thoughts on the situation before she proceeds.

I clear my throat, finally finding the ability to speak again. "Why does another student's opinion of me in this competition warrant expulsion? I thought we were here to learn how to work together and show who's the best candidate for the heir." I ask, and Dean Bozzelli's gaze narrows.

"Did I say it did?"

I shrug, clearly having hit a nerve. "You're insinuating it."

Adjusting herself in her seat so her spine is straighter, she peers at me with distaste. "*I* make the rules at this academy. The new heir will be announced by myself, not The Council," she bites, but it's a complete contradiction to why we're even here to begin with. Clever. We all know the decision doesn't rest solely on her shoulders, but the way she says it would make you think so. She's full of the power moves it seems, even if they are an illusion.

Her ego just grew before my very eyes with the power she believes she wields. Combined with the defensive undertone of her words, though, it's clear she's easy to falter. I could sit here and point out all of her flaws, but instead, I decide getting out of here is the best option.

"Great, are we done then?"

She shakes her head with a smile that looks more like a grimace. "I've also had the Kenner pack calling to pull you from the academy too."

I stiffen at the mention of Cassian's pack, or old pack, whatever the semantics are. Of course they had to wade in with their opinions, too. Assholes.

"How have I upset them?" I ask, intrigued to understand what they said.

"By claiming his son."

Ah, so it was Kenner himself. Great. Not Leticia causing more issues because I won, but their alpha. That's not what I need right now, but there's nothing I can do about it.

Dean Bozzelli gives me that same look, waiting for information, and since she seems intent on keeping me here longer than necessary with this shit, I give it to her.

"I did no such thing. I defended myself, albeit on their land, but I didn't technically agree to the duel. If someone comes to attack me, I have a right to defend myself. If that weren't the case, I wouldn't even be at the academy as a student."

My jaw tightens with annoyance as she eyes me. She doesn't even bother to look behind me, where I can still feel Fairbourne's presence, even though he keeps his lips tightly shut.

"The Kenners may not be on The Council, but they are still highly regarded within the community," she states, the corner of her mouth ticking up, and I know what she's saying without letting the words actually leave her lips.

Even though they don't fall under The Council's ruling, they are still regarded more highly than the fae. Everyone is always ranked higher than the fucking fae. Because people like Mildred fucking Bozzelli allow it.

Irritated, I clear my throat, knowing I may regret what I'm about to say, but I'm done pretending this shit is going to fly. "I'm here at this academy because I believe in my people, and I believe in myself. Just like the enrollment to the academy states. No origins are stronger than others. Everyone is seen as equal. That's what it said, but I think that's bullshit in your eyes. That's just to show that an opportunity was offered to us. But what is more noticeable to me, which is astounding because I have to live every day as a fae who is downgraded and disregarded without plausible cause, is the fact that things aren't changing as promised. If we're going to let people's thoughts and feelings cause disarray in the academy, how are we ever going to create a solid foundation for our future?"

She laces her fingers together as she braces her elbows on the table, and I sense Fairbourne shifting nervously from foot to foot behind me.

"Carry on."

"Sorry?" I have no idea what she means this time. I'm not even trying to play dumb.

"You clearly have a vision. Explain it to me."

Shifting in my seat slightly, I shake my head. "It's not that I have a vision; it's a clear assessment of everything I've seen and experienced here since we began. Changes need to be made to the structure of our leadership, which is the entire reason the academy was built, was it not?"

Calm and composed. I mentally high-five my father for the strength right now.

"It was," she bites out, glaring at me, but now the gates are open and there's no stopping it.

"So if we're here to find the heir, but are going to let The Council and other members of high society dictate our every move still, then we may as well continue as we are. There's no need for the academy if The Council will continue to wade in whenever they feel it's necessary. That leaves them as the true leaders still."

Her nostrils flare. It's obvious she hates my evaluation of the situation, but she can't deny it, either. Not when she just sat there and listed off two different people wanting me off campus, thinking they'll get their way because they rank higher in society than I do. She runs her tongue over her teeth as she continues to narrow her eyes at me. I think what pisses her off more is how spot-on I am; adding to the fact that I'm a lowly fae will only make the poison all the more bitter.

"Do you think I don't know what I'm doing?" she asks after a beat, and I shrug.

"I didn't say anything of the sort."

"You insinuated," she retorts, using my own words against me, and I shake my head.

"No, I explained my point of view, as you asked. If you're taking it as the points raised being aimed at you, then that's your problem." She's not putting any words in my mouth. I'd say it's a good thing I've got Fairbourne in here as a witness, but he's been useless.

Dean Bozzelli stands, wiping her hands down her blazer. "Everything you say may be true, but another point that remains true is how low the fae have fallen. They're disregarded because they deserve to be. Our kingdom was left in ruins at their hands, and I don't believe the throne should have to suffer the weight of them once again. The crown belongs to stronger origins like the vampires, or maybe even the wolves." My blood runs cold with anger at her words, but I still scoff at the fact that she spits out the word *wolves,* like it's an annoyance that they're even a consideration for her. All she wants is for the vampires to be in control. Period.

I may be a lowly fae, but she regards anyone who isn't a vampire in the same light.

Standing, I match her stance. "Well, it's a good thing it's not a decision that rests solely on your shoulders then, isn't it?"

"You aren't going to reach the top as you hope, Miss Reed," she snipes, sneering at me as I roll my shoulders back.

"Are we done here?" I ask, my tone bored, which pisses her off, but I'm done showing this woman respect when she's so openly willing to tear me down based on my origin.

A fake smile spreads across her face. "If my words offend you, that's your problem, not mine." Her attempt to throw more of my words back at me is embarrassing. How unoriginal.

"Your words would have to mean something to offend me," I bite, my teeth bared in a lackluster smile. "Is there anything else for us to discuss, or can I get back to class?"

Her lips purse as she drags her eyes over me from head to toe, just as she did when I first walked in, but it doesn't hold the same level of power as before. Now it just feels spiteful and arrogant, and I don't care for it.

She sighs, glancing over my shoulder at Fairbourne for the first time since he shut the door before finding my eyes once again. "You can leave, but don't think this is the last you will be seeing of me," she promises, and I turn the second the words are out of her mouth.

I'm not sticking around to deal with any more of her shit if I don't have to. Especially not when it's clear she's going to make my life hell just for breathing.

Join the club. There are plenty of them painting targets on my back. What they don't realize is that I can adapt, adjust, and aim for the fucking sky.

When I'm declared the heir of the kingdom, I'll be ticking off everyone on the damn list that stands in my way.

THE KINGDOM OF RUIN

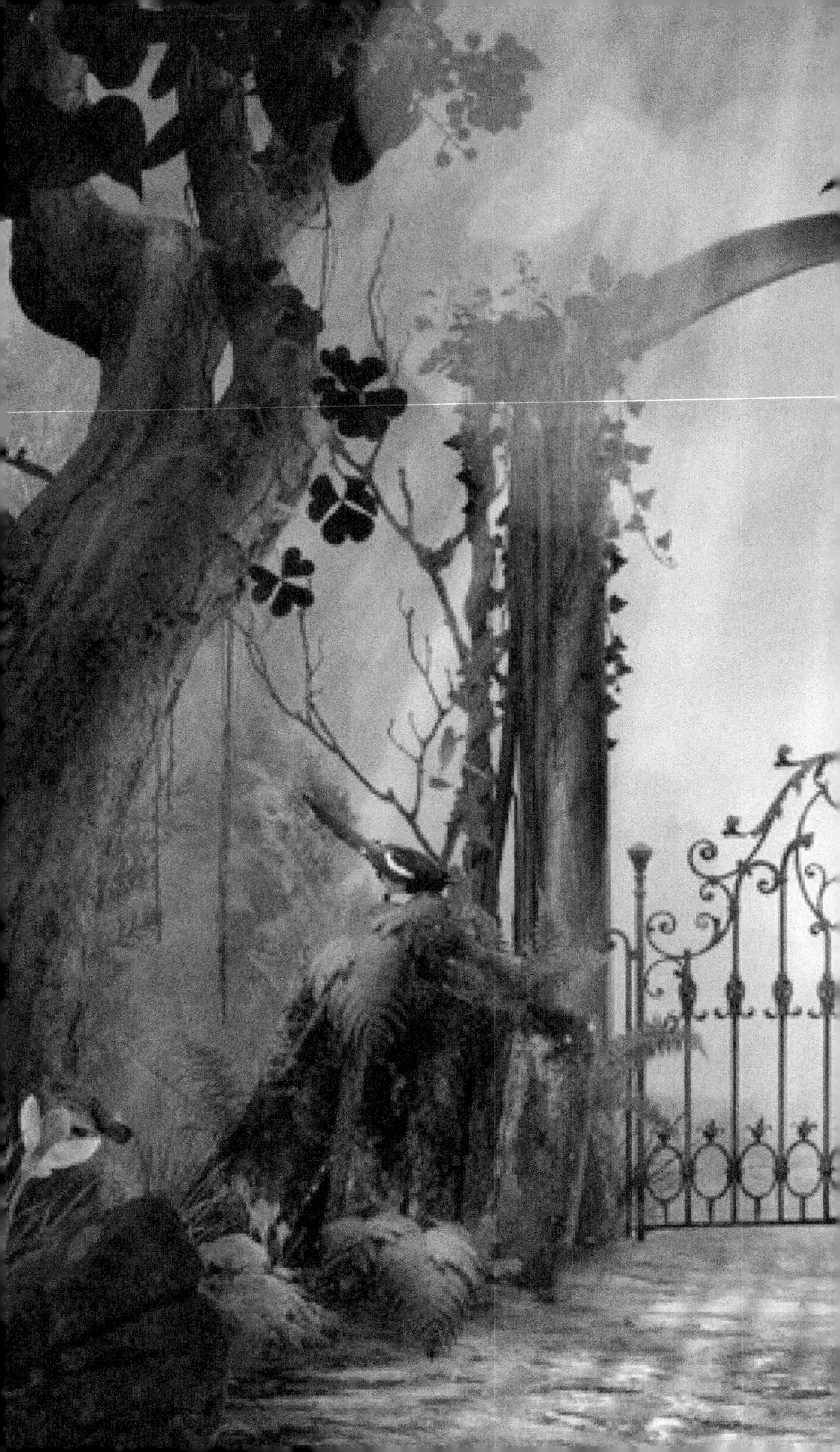

ADDI

30

My irritation hasn't flagged nearly enough as I step into my next class, and I find myself wrapping my gray cloak around my body as an extra shield to protect me from the assholes I can't seem to escape.

I find Flora first, concern shimmering in her eyes, and try to offer her a reassuring smile before I take my seat. The professor pays me no mind, despite the fact that I'm later than everyone else, but I take that as a good sign. I have to find positives somewhere in all of this. It's most probably because I'm fae or something, but I don't care. Another lecture isn't needed at this time.

Settling between Brody and Kryll, I keep my gaze set forward, only to earn a scathing glare from Raiden as he peers over his shoulder at me. It's just like the face he made outside when he realized I had used my magic to wrap the vines around his boots, holding him in place. I smirk at the memory, which only makes him frown further.

"You know I could have helped you if you hadn't used your magic on me," Brody says under his breath, and I turn to look at him, eyebrow raised in confusion.

"How so?" I ask, intrigued enough to forget that I'm supposed to hate and ignore him at all costs.

"I could have come up with an excuse to get you out of the meeting."

"Why would I need to get out of the meeting?" He's bullshitting me. I know it.

"Nobody wants a meeting with the dean. Ever."

He's right there, but he doesn't need to know that.

"It wasn't that dramatic, but thanks," I offer, turning back to the professor as he addresses the class, but his words aren't registering in my head.

"I forgive you," Brody whispers, and I rear back, blinking at him in wonder.

"What do I need to be forgiven for?"

"The vines. You're an earth fae, remember?"

Earth fae? Apparently so. "Oh, I don't need forgiveness. You deserved that," I reply with a smile, turning away again, hoping this time I'll be able to ignore him. As if hearing my thoughts, his knee presses against mine.

Fucker.

"How so?" he presses, leaning in closer just as the professor claps his hands.

"Today, we're going to be delving into the realm of kingdom etiquette," he announces, earning an echo of groans from around the room.

"Why do we need to know this?" Everyone turns to look at the source of the question, and I'm surprised to find it's a fae. I vaguely recognize his face, but I haven't had any interaction with him at all. He smirks at everyone's attention, and when his eyes find mine, he winks.

No thanks. I've got enough to handle. I don't need another.

The professor clears his throat. "Because one day, someone in this academy will be our new heir, surrounded by a network of support from within these very halls."

"Don't you think it's pointless to step backward and reaffirm traditions that didn't work so well for us to begin with?" The guy pushes, and I can't decide if I agree with him. The question is valid, but his tone sets it all off wrong, and I don't know why.

"This class is going to happen whether you take part or not. What will it be?" The professor retorts, leaving me slightly impressed as I turn to the guy in question, who silently lifts his hands in surrender.

A beat passes as everyone returns their attention to the professor, who shakes off his blazer and smiles. "One of the many traditions the kingdom still observes today is the hosting of celebratory balls." I'm pretty sure every guy in the room—bar the professor—groans in distaste, making him smirk. "Calm your excitement. There's a lot to get through, and you're going to reach your peak way too soon."

"This guy actually has jokes," Brody states, leaning against my arm, but I ignore him.

"The summer solstice and the winter solstice were the two most important events of the year, but there are several other lesser events sprinkled throughout the calendar that make these balls a regular occurrence. Almost monthly," the professor explains as a projection appears before him. It's a ballroom filled with elaborate decor and well-dressed people. "The heir would take their seat at the center of the long table, their loved one to their right, and their close confidants filling the remainder of the space. A feast is served, origins mingling among the crowd as live music plays."

"He seems to be enjoying the thought," Brody states, a little louder than I think he intended based on the look on his face when the professor turns to him a moment later.

"I am, they were a thing of wonder."

"You went to them?" I blurt in surprise, and his smile grows.

"I organized them. That's why this is my favorite

subject to teach," he explains, a wistfulness dancing over his eyes.

"But you're a human," Vallie calls out with a level of snark only she can accomplish.

"And?" The professor turns to her with a determined challenge in his eyes, and I love it.

"The fae were in charge," she grumbles, flicking her hair over her shoulder as the professor shrugs in response.

"King Reagan didn't discriminate."

My heart pounds at the mention of our history, of how things once were. Everyone complains that the fae ruined it all, but even though I don't really remember anything from that time, my gut tells me that's not the case.

The professor claps his hands again, his smile gleaming from ear to ear. "We're going to hold a ball at the academy at the end of the first semester." Groans ring out once again, making him roll his eyes, but he continues on. "The dean has decided it's necessary for everyone to learn how to do the waltz."

"The what?" I'm not sure who the comment comes from first because so many people holler it at the same time.

"The waltz. A two-person dance that is believed to represent freedom, passion, and expressiveness. Quite fitting if you ask me," the professor explains, leaving grumbles in his wake again. "The fact that none of you really have a clue is exactly why work must begin as soon as possible. Luckily for your class, there's an even number of males and females, so partnering works well."

"I'll take Raiden," Vallie blurts, standing with a flourish.

"You'll take who you're given, Miss Drummer."

She scoffs, flicking her hair over her shoulder again as her gaze narrows. "My daddy is—"

"None of my concern within these four walls," he retorts, making me snicker.

"Raidy, tell him," Vallie whines, but the grumpy vampire ignores her, which only makes it harder to bite back my smile.

Of course her eyes happen to find mine in that moment, and she glares at me like always.

"Vallie, you will be paired with Grant," the professor states, reading from his electronic device.

"But he's a shifter!" she retorts with anger. I'm certain she's going to stamp her foot at any moment, but it sadly doesn't come.

"Did you miss the part where I said the origins mingled effortlessly?"

"Whatever," she grumbles, dropping back down into her seat. I'm sure she'll be calling home about the professor to try and get him kicked off campus, too.

Bitch.

"Arlo and Delia." A petite fae girl waves nervously at Arlo, who grins in response. "Flora and Kryll." I glare at the guy to my right, but he ignores me. He better be nice to her, or he'll have me to deal with. "Kimi and Cassian." A wolf turns to me with a sparkle in her eyes and a smirk on her lips, but I turn away to ignore her. "Polly and Raiden." A blonde vampire I've seen with Vallie a few times claps her hands excitedly as Raiden shakes his head, not even bothering to look her way. Vallie, however, tries to cause a stir with the fact that they're both vampires after the professor's prior comment, but he continues to ignore her outburst. "Which leaves Addi and Brody," he finally calls out, making my body stiffen.

I chance a look to my left to find a shit-eating grin on Brody's face. Fuck my life. It didn't even cross my mind that his name hadn't been called out yet.

"I recommend watching some videos online to get a good gist of the dance. We'll begin in-depth practice during our next lesson. For now, we're going to focus on the other areas of etiquette that come with being present at a ball. From your attire to dining, we're covering it all."

He definitely loves what he's talking about, that's for sure. My father taught me everything about the dining experience, but unfortunately for me, I don't know the dance at all. The professor's words start to go over my head as I get lost in my thoughts, trying like hell to recall the dance from memory, but it's nowhere to be found. I'm hoping the grumbles that filled the room mean I'm not the only one at a disadvantage. I hate not knowing something. Even something as trivial as this gets under my skin.

My brain wanders for the rest of the lesson until the bell rings and everyone starts to move around me. I rush from my seat, but it's useless because the second I step outside of the classroom, Brody is right beside me.

"Have you done the dance before?" he asks, draping his arm around my shoulders, and I shake out of his hold, giving him my best glare as we step out into the afternoon sun. When it's clear he's not going to give me any space, I shake my head.

"No. Have you?"

"A little," he replies with a shrug, making me pause mid-step before quickly remembering myself. That's helpful. I guess.

"We can practice, get ahead of the game," he offers, coming to a stop beside me. I move out of the way of the other students trying to move around us, giving myself a second to consider his offer, and a hand lands on my shoulder.

"Hey, Addi, I'm Neo." I turn to find the fae who questioned the professor earlier. When I don't immediately move to shake his hand from my shoulder, Brody does it for me. My stomach clenches, and I don't even want to begin to think of why. He eyes Brody for a moment before turning his bright green eyes back my way. "I'm familiar with the waltz. I know we're not partners, but I thought I could escort you home and we could—"

"Let me stop you there, asshole," Brody bites, his aura darkening around him. "We both know she would be protecting you and not the other way around because you're weak and needy as fuck. Nice try, but fuck off."

"I wasn't asking you."

Is this about to turn into a pissing contest? If so, count me the fuck out.

"You don't need to be asking Addi either. She's my partner for the dance, fucker. But please, test me. I love it when I get to knock someone down a peg or two," he snarls back, his usual casual demeanor completely evaporating before my very eyes.

What the fuck is going on right now?

Searching around me, I hope to find Flora, Arlo, or hell, even Raiden at this stage, but I come up empty. Typical.

Eager to get the fuck out of here, I sidestep Neo, only to have Brody's arm drape around my shoulder again, but this time it seems impossible to shake him off.

"Fuck off, Neo, before I do it for you." Neo's gaze flickers between Brody's and mine. I can't figure out his sudden interest; it seems off, but I'm not going to call him out on it right now. That will only make the situation worse, and Brody really doesn't need any further encouragement. "Fine, we'll leave instead."

Before I can turn my head to look at Brody, we're moving. The world spins around me as nausea rises to the surface.

This motherfucker.

THE KINGDOM OF RUIN

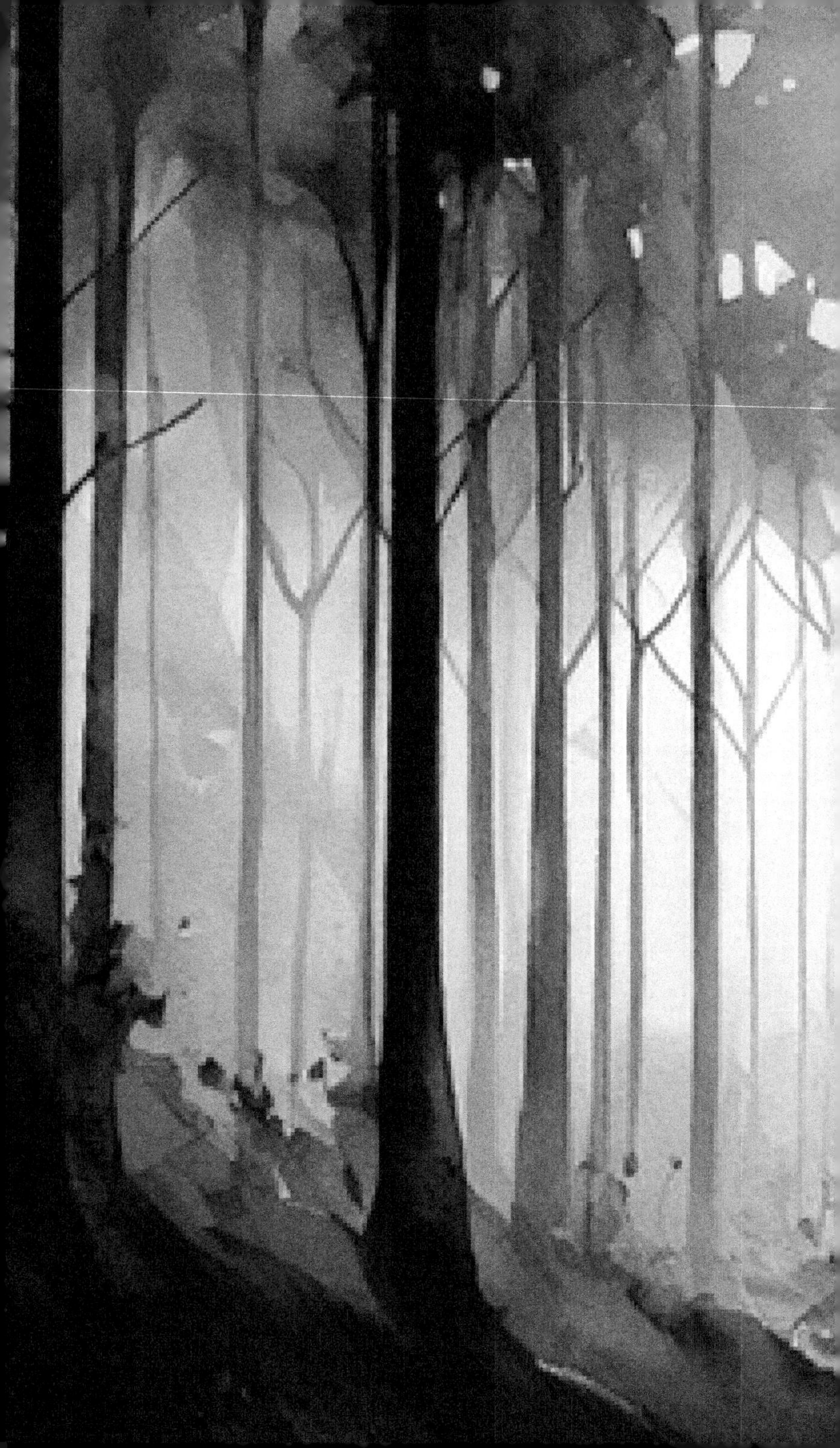

BRODY

31

I mutter the enchantment under my breath, transporting us like I did on Friday night, only this time, I opt for somewhere a lot less…dangerous. My dick wants me to take her back to my room at the mages' building, but I don't need to piss her off any more than I already have.

Despite my desires, I'm acutely aware that she'll be raging mad at me when we stop moving since I didn't get her consent, but I can apologize for that when she needs to hear it.

I take a deep breath as we come to a stop, my magic falling around us as the familiar forest comes into view. I press her back against the nearest tree, which offers the most privacy from the walkway nearby, watching as her eyes practically roll in their sockets as she tries to focus.

Her face has paled from the movement, but she still

remains the same crazy girl underneath. I don't think I've ever been this obsessed with someone who has so much fire in everything they do. If I'm honest with myself, that's more than half of her appeal.

She's a fae—without the typical ears, sure—but one would assume she'd be timid and meek, yet she's nothing like that at all. Circling back to her ears, I can only imagine the pain she must have endured, yet here she stands, unwavering in spite of whatever is thrown at her.

I get a whole five seconds before her eyes settle on mine, narrowing as anger swirls in her orbs.

"What the fuck was that?" she snarls, pushing against my chest, but I don't budge as my dick stiffens. She really is something else.

Keeping my gaze locked on hers, I smile softly. "I'm sorry."

"You're...what?" Her eyebrows pinch in confusion as she continues to glare at me. The press of her palms remains against my chest, intoxicating me with her damn presence.

It's not often I apologize, so she better appreciate this.

"I'm sorry. I know you don't like it, and I was totally selfish."

She blinks up at me, even more confused than she had been a moment ago, and it feels like an achievement. Grinning wider, I only make her glare deepen.

"What the fuck is this, Brody? Why am I here?" She peers around me, confirming we're alone like I know we are. No one comes out here so soon after classes. In an hour or so, maybe, but for now, it's just the two of us.

I probably should have considered where we are since my every thought has been consumed by a damn earth fae, but hopefully, the misstep can be overlooked.

Wetting my lips, I place both of my hands on the tree by her head. I can't help but notice the way her eyes track the movement of my tongue before she gulps.

Fuck. Please.

"I can't get you out of my head," I rasp, admitting the truth, and she scoffs.

"Try harder." Her snark just serves to make my cock harder for her.

"How is it this easy for you to deny?" I ask, genuinely curious as my heart races in my chest and my pulse rings in my ears.

"What are you talking about?"

She's full of shit.

Full. Of. Shit.

I might not have heightened senses like the others, but it's written all over her, just as it's written into every piece of me.

Inching closer, I expect her to put more force into her palms, keeping me at bay, but she does nothing. "I didn't get a good night kiss, never mind a chance to get you out of my system on Friday, Dagger."

Her jaw falls slack as she gapes at me before she shakes her head subtly. "Move on, fuck someone else," she grumbles, and I only wish it was that easy.

"I tried."

"What?" She rears her head back like the fact is a kick in the teeth. If I were a guessing man, I would believe that's jealousy in her eyes, but I know more than anything she would deny it until she's blue in the face.

"I tried. Getting over someone is easier when you get under someone else. I tried it. Tried doesn't feel like a strong enough word, but here I am, still obsessed with you."

She searches my eyes. For what? I don't fucking know, so I let the silence consume us until she scoffs. "Do you want me to give you a pity handjob or something?" she asks, cocking a brow at me as she tries to laugh this away.

"Fuck no," I grunt, my muscles tensing with a need like I've never felt before. How can someone have such an effect on somebody else while trying to remain unfazed like this?

"What do you want then, Brody?" she repeats, only this time her voice is laced with anger. "I don't like you." Not true, I can see it in her eyes. "I'm certain I might hate you for the shit you pulled." Fuck that. "Accident or not, and—"

Fuck all of that.

I cut off her next words with my lips against hers, fusing us together as heat swirls between us. Her lips are soft, full, and hot as sin.

I need more.

Stroking one hand down her cheek, I cup her chin, deepening the kiss when she still doesn't push me away. Tipping her head back a little, I get to delve between her lips and claim even more of her for a split second before she starts fighting back.

Not for me to get off.

No.

For control.

Fuck.

Her hands ball into fists, tugging at my t-shirt beneath my cloak, bringing me closer to her as I shift my hand to her throat, pinning her in position. The groan that vibrates against my palm brings my dick to full mast as I press against her. She's flush against my body, not an inch of room between us from head to toe.

I bring my other hand to her waist beneath her cloak, a little disappointed to not find any daggers along her ribcage like on Friday, but at least she can't use one against me this time.

My blood is a raging inferno from her touch, ready to

tear through my body and envelop us both in a heat like no other.

Fighting for control, our lips and tongues dance together as our hands roam. Her hands tug at my t-shirt, and a satisfied moan parts her lips a moment later when her palms touch my bare skin.

Fuck. Fuck. Fuck.

As much as I don't want to ruin the moment, I don't want her to regret this later, feeling like I forced this. "Hate fucking is far superior to any sympathy shit you were talking about. Tell me you're in," I breathe against her lips, not giving her much room to escape me, but I'm asking at least.

She ignores me at first, continuing to kiss my lips, which I gladly reciprocate, but when her fingers dance along the waistband of my pants, I know I need to hear those words from her.

"Tell me, Dagger. Give me the words."

"No," she rasps, shaking her head as her eyes pry open and settle on mine.

"Why?"

"Because…"

Nothing follows but silence. She can't even finish the damn sentence. Her gaze travels back to my lips, her fingertips dancing over my skin as she tries to find a reason not to.

"Say yes, Dagger."

"Then I'll be out of your system?" Her eyes meet mine, sending me into a spiral because right now, I don't think I ever want this feeling to end. I can't lie and agree to that.

"Say yes, Dagger," I repeat, refusing to confirm or deny.

"Just this once, Brody," she states, breathless, and I raise an eyebrow at her, refusing to agree to anything at all. Taking my hand, she guides me to her core, her combat pants separating me from her pussy, but the heat against my touch is undeniable. "Yes."

We collide together at her admission, control flicking between us as we take and take. Our cloaks fall first, our lips still fused together as I chant against her mouth. I sense the shift around us. If she does, she doesn't utter a word about it, but the magic ensures we're protected from any stray observers.

It's just the two of us, the grass beneath our feet, and the bark at her back.

Grabbing her waist, she understands what I want, letting me lift her into the air as she wraps her legs around my hips. Fuck. I'm closer, but not close enough.

I fall to my knees with a thud, laying the sinful beauty before me. Hands roaming, I slip under her fitted black top, hissing at the feel of goosebumps along her skin as I search out her tits. Taut nipples pebble beneath my touch and I bite back a groan, kissing her harder as I try to get my fill of her.

"Hate fucking doesn't involve getting me ready, Brody. Just take," she snaps against my mouth as she shuffles to her elbows, peering at me with challenge in her eyes.

If I don't take, then she will, and as tempting as the latter sounds, I'm going to get exactly what I want from her.

I reach for the button of her combat pants, yanking without care as the button pops. She gasps but doesn't utter a word. If she wants this rough and fast, then that's what she gets, but on my terms.

Grabbing the waistband of her pants, I pull them to midthigh before I hook my arms under her legs, hoisting her in the air again as I stand. Her hands wrap around my neck as she squeals, and a moment later, she's back pressed against the tree with her legs splayed, dangling over my arms.

At this height, her eyes are level with mine and my dick is mere inches from her core. Using the tree to hold her in place, I blindly dig a condom from my pocket and unbuckle my pants just enough to free my length before sheathing my cock.

Her movements are restricted by her pants, which are still mostly on, and I like having her at my mercy like that. Pulling the material of her panties to the side, I line my cock up with her entrance, but before I push inside and find Heaven, I meet her gaze once again.

Pupils blown, jaw slack, and pulse vibrating at her neck, she looks so fucking hot I could come without ever getting inside her.

As if sensing her final opportunity to back out, she rolls her eyes before dropping in my hold, pressing my dick at her entrance, and I hiss at the immediate heat that consumes me.

Hot fuck.

I slam all the way inside her, my lips crashing against hers again as my body thrums with ecstasy. She's so fucking tight, so fucking hot. It's too much.

Too fucking much.

I can't think.

"Please move, you have to move," she pleads against my mouth, and I lean back enough to look down at where we're truly connected. Slowly, so damn slowly, I retreat until only the tip remains before slamming back inside her hard and fast.

Her head falls back on a groan, her nails piercing the flesh at my neck as I repeat the motion again and again.

All I can hear are her breaths, all I can see is the euphoria in her eyes, all I can feel is her hot pussy claiming me, and all I can taste are the sweet remnants of her lips against mine.

Adjusting my hold on her, pressing her into the tree even more until I'm certain there will be marks along her back once we're done, I shift angles slightly.

"Holy fuck. There. Right there," she chants, her voice light and almost whimsical, moments before she cries out with pleasure. Her core clenches around my dick, taking everything from me as she climaxes.

The sight of her, the sound of her, the feel of her as she comes apart is too much. Never in my wildest fucking dreams has anything ever been so…this.

I can't hold back. I don't want to.

My forehead falls to her shoulder and my fingers dig into her thighs as I find my release. My movements turn jagged, desperate, and intoxicated as we ride out wave after wave of pleasure.

Slowly, once I can even consider moving, I drop to my knees again, lowering her to the grass before I pull out. My eyelids fall closed as I try to catch my breath.

"Holy fuck." My words are a rasp, my throat burning from fuck knows what as I force my eyes back open so I can look at her. I instantly frown when I find her standing before me, tugging her pants back into place before she starts fixing her shirt and bra. "What are you doing?"

"Leaving."

"Not yet, you're not," I grunt, my mind a damn vortex of thoughts that I can't piece together.

"I am," she states, reaching for her cloak. She drapes it over her shoulders like I'm not still a trembling mess on the ground right now.

"We need to talk about this, Addi."

"We don't need to talk about anything, Brody." She gives me a pointed look, like that's the end of it, but it's so far from it that she has no idea.

"Addi." It's a plea, a fucking plea from my lips, and she offers me what I can only describe as a sympathetic smile in response.

Crouching before me, she leans forward, pressing a featherlight kiss to the corner of my mouth.

"Thanks, but you were a means to an end."

"What the fuck does that mean?" I bite, my cock still semi-hard and exposed with the condom in place. I'm a mess. A fucking mess. It's all her fault, and there's nothing I can do about it.

"It means you fucked me out of your system, and I ensured Cassian fucks all the way off," she explains with a smile, standing again.

"How do you figure?" I ask, intrigued with where her head is at since mine is a fucking mess.

She shrugs. "I fucked his friend. He'll leave me alone now."

I laugh. The sound gives me the strength to stand and remove the condom from my dick before I tuck myself away. She stands, frowning at me as my laugh softens into a chuckle.

"What's funny?" She can't help but ask, and the uncertainty in her eyes only confirms that she's not ready for the answer.

"You'll see," I reply with a wink before eliminating the distance between us. I lift my hand to her cheek, and when she doesn't immediately bat me away, I grin triumphantly before running my tongue along her bottom lip. The shiver that consumes her is bliss, and I'm not the one feeling it. "And by the way…definitely not out of my system."

THE KINGDOM OF RUIN

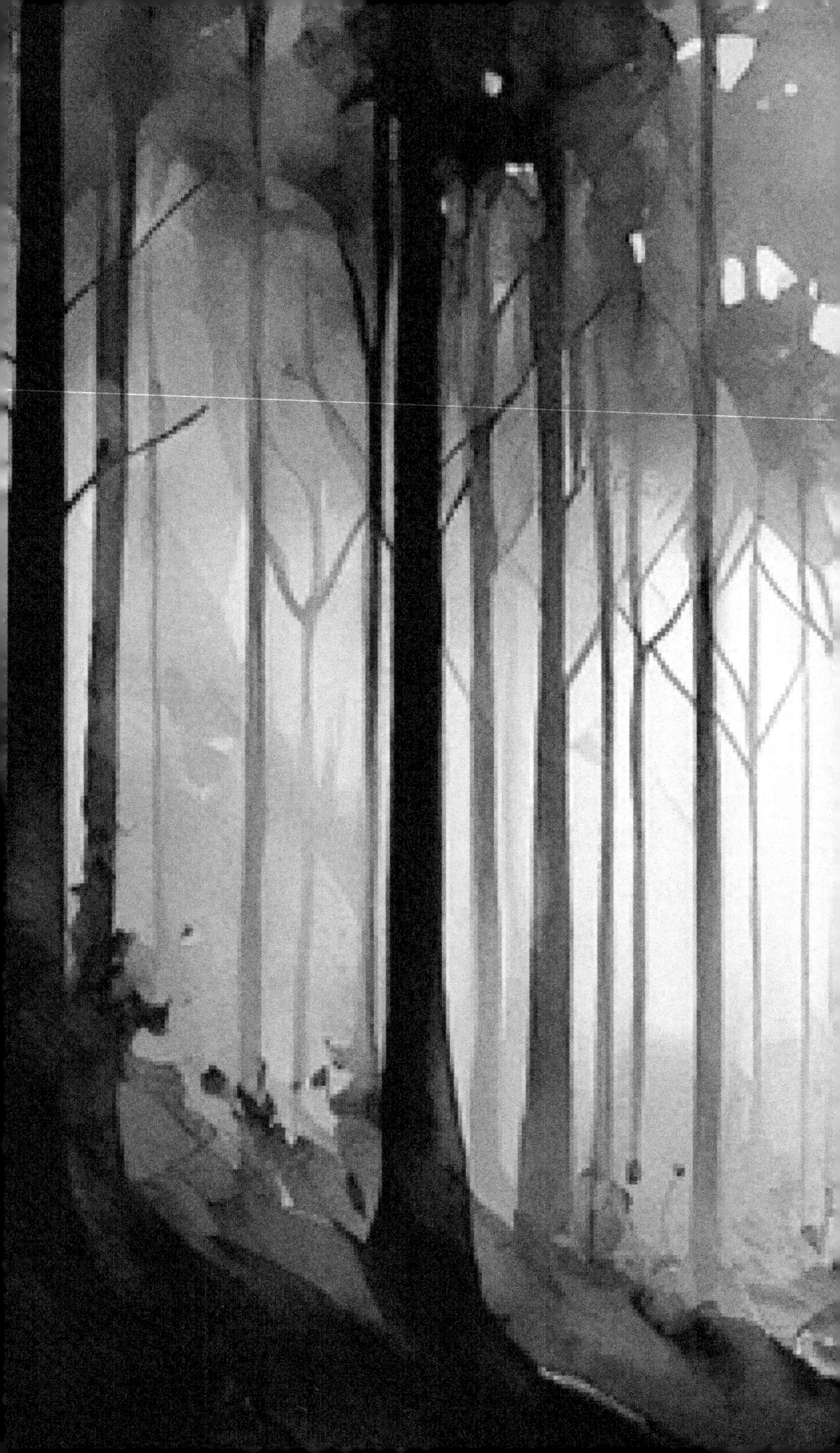

RAIDEN

32

"Where's Brody? He was supposed to be helping us," I grind out, pacing the lounge area of my room as I wait for the most infuriating mage that I've ever met.

Kryll shrugs like it's not really a concern, earning a glare from me, but it goes right over his head like usual. How I've survived so long with these fools is beyond me. They leave me second-guessing every decision I've ever made, but somehow, I can't walk away from them.

I think that's what annoys me the most. They're the sort of family that gets under your skin, forcing unconditional love from you without your permission, and somehow, I'm not even mad about it.

It really does need three of us, but Cassian is off sulking somewhere, and Brody is fuck knows where. I can't keep up with my friends on their damn emotions at the moment. Cassian seems to be consumed by all of the shit that went down at the diner Friday night. I don't understand why he was pissed with Addi in combat class. She offered him a free pass to be rid of her and he refused. That's some bullshit right there. And to top it off, *he* decides she has to sit with us.

We don't need this drama. I've already got my hands full with Vallie without the added layer of some annoying fae that enjoys getting under my skin more than Brody does.

Sighing, I pinch the bridge of my nose, trying to calm the stress rising inside of me, but it's pointless at this stage.

The memory of the vines wrapped around my boots as she sauntered away flashes in my mind, irritating me even more. I can feel my chest tightening, which is not what I need right now. I need to stay focused.

Fuck.

"Let's just get it over with," Kryll states, as if he can sense the inner turmoil consuming me, and I shake my head.

"We need another man."

"I know that, but we don't have anyone else we can trust, so it's the two of us, or we don't show." He's so matter-of-fact it pisses me off.

"We can't not show," I grind out, and his eyes widen

like he already knows that and I'm just being dumb.

"Then let's get on with it." I march to my front door, swinging it open with fury, to find Brody standing on the other side with his hand raised, ready to knock.

"Hey, you guys," he says, all calm and chill, sauntering past me to high-five Kryll, who looks at him in confusion.

"Where the fuck have you been?" I snap, my anger rising when he shrugs.

"Around."

"What's that smug fucking grin on your face?" Kryll asks, folding his arms over his chest as he assesses our friend with me.

"I don't know what you're talking about," Brody answers too quickly, a grin tipping the corner of his mouth as he looks anywhere but at us.

"Yeah, you do," I grumble, now eager to know what the fuck had him so busy he was late, but all he does is shrug again.

"He got laid. It's obvious," Kryll states, making me freeze as I whirl to find the fucker.

"Does that mean you're finally over the wretched fae bitch?" I ask, aware of the troubles he had over the weekend trying to get over her to no avail.

"Don't call her that," he snaps, turning to me with rage in his eyes. It seems I've hit a sore spot. What's that about?

"You need to get over it, man. You're fighting a losing

battle with that one. She's never going to go near you," I grumble, annoyed that we're still having this discussion, but I don't miss the shit-eating grin that spreads across his face before he turns away, offering both Kryll and me his back.

I chance a glance at Kryll, who nods in silent agreement before I gape at the fucker ignoring us.

It's her.

He fucked her.

He definitely fucked her.

If the grin on his face didn't tell me that, my ears do with the wild racing of his heart.

My gut clenches, my nostrils flare, and my pulse quickens. I refuse to look any closer at the reasoning behind it, even though my subconscious knows exactly why.

"How the fuck did you make that happen?" Kryll asks, calm, cool, and collected as always, making Brody turn with another shrug.

"I don't kiss and tell." He also doesn't want to meet our gazes right now either. Asshole.

"Yes, you fucking do. Every time. It's annoying as shit," I bark, recalling every time I've had to endure one of his stories.

"Well, not this time."

"And why's that?" Kryll asks, and Brody shrugs. Again. I'm going to snap his damn shoulders if he does it one more time.

"You usually fuck them out of your system, brag about it, and move on to the next. What are we missing?" I ask, tapping my chin as I look at him. Brody runs his tongue over his lip, no answer readily available, so Kryll spells it out for me instead.

"She's not out of his system."

A burst of laughter tumbles from my mouth before I can stop it, earning me a glare from the mage in question. "Oh, fuck. Wait until Cassian hears about this," I say with a snicker, and he scoffs.

"He can thank me when he's ready."

"For what?" I ask, confused as to what he thinks the situation is, because he's clearly way off from where I'm at.

His eyes flicker to Kryll's before settling on mine. "Making her ours."

It's my turn to scoff this time. "She's not fucking ours," I grind out, my gut twisting, and I can't figure out if it's at the thought of it or the words coming from my lips. But I'm not looking further into it. Not when these assholes are here.

Brody ignores me, heading back toward the door with Kryll behind him, leaving me to blink after them.

Fuck.

Addi Reed has wormed her way under everyone's skin.

It's annoying and intoxicating all at once. But one thing is certain; if she's going to fall from the pedestal she put herself on, it will be at my doing. Not theirs.

THE KINGDOM OF RUIN

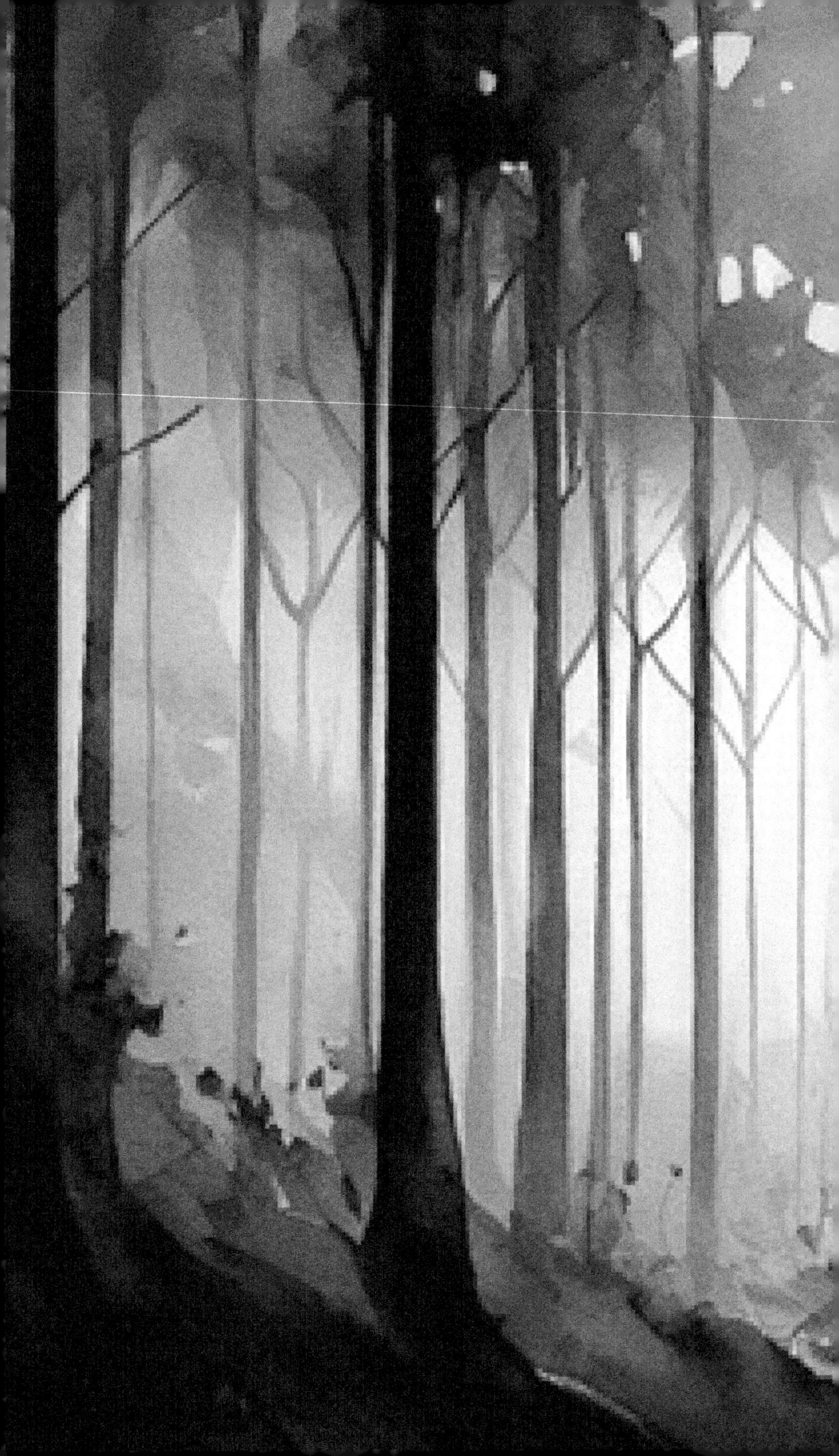

CASSIAN

33

I slice my knife effortlessly through the steak on my plate while keeping my head down, avoiding any onlookers hoping to start a conversation. This is all Brody's fault. The mention of one of Jake's steaks has me crawling back. Thankfully, Janie hasn't uttered a word, she just ushered me to the most discreet booth possible with a knowing smirk on her lips that tells me I haven't seen the end of her tonight.

A few betas have spotted me from their table by the window. I can feel their eyes on me as they whisper among themselves like I can't fucking hear them, but I choose to let it go over my head. I'm avoiding any kind of drama tonight. Which is exactly why I called ahead to check if Leticia was working or not. She isn't, but I can't stay longer than necessary because fuck knows someone will tell her, and I really can't handle her right now.

I love being a wolf. My origin makes up a huge part of who I am, but fuck me, some of the shit it comes with drives me insane. Duels, for one. Needy women for another. The idea of finding a true mate that fills my thoughts instead of someone who takes, demands, and offers nothing to the partnership, feels impossible. I'm not holding out hope anyway.

Slipping another piece of steak in my mouth, I swallow it down as someone slides over the leather seat across from me. She gave me longer than expected, at least.

"It's good to see you, Cass, but not when you're like this."

I look up at Janie, her concerned smile in place as she tucks a loose tendril of hair behind her ear. She's the closest thing to a sister that I've got. Her enjoyment at bossing me around stems back as far as I can remember, and I can't deny that it feels weird…this new barrier between us. Since I walked out on the Kenner pack, I didn't just turn my back on my father; I turned my back on everyone. Friends and loved ones included.

"I don't know what you're talking about," I grunt, making her scoff.

"Of course you don't. You don't show your face forever, no matter how many times I plead with you, then, when you do show that ruggedly handsome face of yours, it's to protect some fae girl. A fae girl who wins a fucking duel against Leticia, to be precise, and now you're back again looking all…you."

Her assessment seems accurate and my shoulders sag with relief when I realize that she's not snapping the words in anger like I half expected. She's just as concerned as she always is, but she's not mad at me. Never mad at me.

"Life is full of surprises at the moment," I admit, earning a snicker this time as she places her hand over mine. I look down at her touch as she squeezes in comfort before retreating so I can carry on eating. Not that I do. My focus is on her.

"When isn't life just a spoonful of madness? You're a Kenner, pack or not. It has a habit of following you around." She leans back in her seat, folding her arms over her chest as her eyes settle on mine. "Besides, you're attending an academy to find the new heir to reign over the future of our kingdom. You're asking for drama right there."

"Maybe," I grumble with a shrug.

"There's no *maybe* about it. But you're not alone, Cass. I know you have Kryll, Brody, and Raiden, but I'm here for you as well. Jake, too. You know that."

She's right. I do. But she shouldn't have to deal with the burdens I bring because I wanted out; I wanted a chance for a better future. My vision of a new kingdom doesn't have to be hers as well.

Smiling at her, I place my cutlery on my plate. "I know that, Janie. We promised, didn't we?" I cock a brow at her, making her smile soften as she takes a trip down memory lane with me.

"We always do."

She curls her little finger, inching it toward me, making me glare at her for a split second before I copy the motion and lock in the pinky swear with her. I'm certain she had me doing this when I was just a newborn baby and she was the bossy six year old that always told me what to do.

My cell phone vibrates on the table beside my arm, breaking our stare-off as I glance down at the offending interruption. Brody's name flashes across the lock screen with an incoming text. I consider ignoring it, but something in my gut has me reaching for it anyway.

Brody:
We need you.

Fuck.

Cassian:
Where?

"I have to go." My finger slips from hers as I rise from my seat, tucking my cell phone into my pocket.

"Don't be a stranger," she warns with a familiar challenge in her eyes as she opens her arms, wrapping me in her warm embrace a moment later.

"I won't." Another promise. I'm always too damn soft with her.

"Good, and bring that girl of yours back around," she adds as I step out of her hold, frowning down at her as she moves in time with me toward the door.

Girl of mine? That girl belongs to no one, no matter how hard I seem to be trying. Even if it is an illusion. My reasoning seems to be fucking with my head more than anyone else's, and I'm in no position to deep dive into it all. I can't think about that right now, though. It seems my friends need me.

As we step out into the evening air, Janie grabs hold of my arm, the pointed look on her face rooting me to the spot as I shake my head. "I'm not promising that shit. It's more complicated than that."

"Like that wasn't obvious when you were here, and don't think anything that happens at the academy doesn't reach my ears. I like her. I like the challenge she brings you. I think we could be besties."

I snicker in disbelief. "Right, sure." My cell phone vibrates in my pocket, another message from Brody with his location pinpointed. "I really do have to—"

"Go, I know. Be safe, Cass." She rubs my arm, rising

on her tiptoes to press a warm kiss to my cheek before she heads back inside.

It's strange, the difference I feel from the other students on campus, even the other wolves. Janie's warmth, Jake's too, they've always been an extension of me. Glancing back over my shoulder at the closed door, I sigh.

Maybe I messed everything up. Maybe I am as selfish as my father says I am.

I'm not going to get answers tonight, though, so I can assess this more at another time.

Taking a deep breath, I rush from the dark and quiet corner of Kenner land and across the City of Harrows to the opposite end of the cobbled streets where the vampires run every inch of the ground they feed on.

I slow half a block from the street Brody sent. My speed returns to normal as my hearing takes over, and barely a beat later, I hear the grunts and thuds of a brawl unraveling.

Great.

I should have been expecting this shit.

Rounding the corner, I find Kryll repeatedly slamming his fists into the guy's face beneath him, blood splattering in every direction as he moves to the next target. Raiden's eyes flash red as he approaches another vampire from behind, wrapping his arms around his throat in a swift move as he effortlessly snaps his neck. The target clatters to the floor in a pile of limbs while Brody stands under a shadowed arch, hands in front of him as he chants, bringing the magic at his fingertips to life.

There are three of them, half a dozen men scattered across the street, and another five charging at them.

"Anytime, Cass. There are more on their way," Raiden grunts, pulling a small dagger from the waistband of his pants and aiming it at the nearest of the approaching vampires.

I'd love to send him an eye roll and give him a piece of my mind, but the two vampires inching toward Brody catch my attention and I take off.

Quickly considering my options, I shift midair, letting my wolf take over. It always startles the other origins, but vampires tend to react the most, especially new walkers like these. The pair of fuckers pause midstep, gaping in surprise as I land a few feet away from them. Their eyes burn red, raging brighter a few seconds later as they set their sights on me.

Perfect.

Charging toward the one on the left, my wolf consumes me, snarling as my teeth snap excitedly. I aim for his throat, the sweet satisfaction of his flesh piercing beneath my bite rippling through me as we fall to the ground. He doesn't stand a chance, his cries of pain wilting into the wind as I take his life before moving on to the next target, only to find Kryll beating me to it.

Literally.

His anger issues run *way* deeper than mine. The appreciation for blood splattering his knuckles is a level of sadism that holds no appeal for me.

Running my claws along the cobbled road beneath my paws, I hunt down the next closest vampire, ready to eliminate that threat. Once my wolf has had the taste of blood, it leaves him insatiable. I'm pretty sure I'm not blood-haze crazy like these guys, but the need is high.

Brody's magic holds one in place, their arms stiff at their sides, and it's almost too easy. Leaping through the air, my jaws open, a sense of calm washing over me as I connect with the target and knock him to the ground. But before I can sink my teeth into him, I'm knocked aside. Snarling, I stare down at the new vampire who thinks he has the upper hand.

I can hear the need for blood zapping through his veins as his eyes search me erratically. Raiden is behind him in the next instant. The telltale sound of his neck snapping fills my ears a moment later as Kryll attacks the guy on the ground.

Silence descends over us as dead vampires lay scattered across the road. The stores that line each side of the street are closed, leaving no one to watch on. Certain the danger is gone, I transition back to my human form.

"What the fuck happened?" I ask, wiping a hand down my face. My fur may be gone, but the blood that coated it moments ago still clings to my skin.

"Something that could have been avoided if you were here to begin with," Raiden snaps, finally earning the eye roll that takes over my face.

Of course, this is my fault.

Kryll scrubs at the back of his neck, his fiery auburn hair darkened with splashes of crimson blood. "They were feeding on the humans again."

Fuck.

"Is that why some of them were so…"

"Fresh? Yeah," Raiden grunts, taking a handkerchief from his pocket to clean off his hands.

"Why is The Council allowing this?" I ask, looking at each of them, but my gaze settles on Raiden, knowing he's the most likely to have the answer.

"Vampire numbers are a priority to them."

Of course they are.

"It's going to create an internal war throughout the fucking kingdom if this carries on," I grind out, irritated by the hierarchy of origins that seems to plague the kingdom. Especially the City of Harrows, but my concern is it's already bleeding into the academy too.

Raiden scoffs in that manic way that makes him look like a nut job. "If you're going to get pissy over this shit, then we won't call you for help next time."

"I'm just calling it how I see it," I retort, and he shakes his head in disbelief before settling his gaze on mine.

"How about you worry about the issues we have going on instead of a potential war? I really think it's the least of your problems."

He glances at Brody and I follow the movement.

"How so?"

"Not now, Raiden. Fuck me. He still has blood all over him," Brody grumbles, not looking at me.

"What the fuck am I missing?"

Raiden grins, and even Kryll peers at me from my peripheral vision as my eyes narrow on Brody.

"Brody fucked Addi," Raiden declares, clapping his hands as I freeze on the spot.

He did what now?

THE KINGDOM OF RUIN

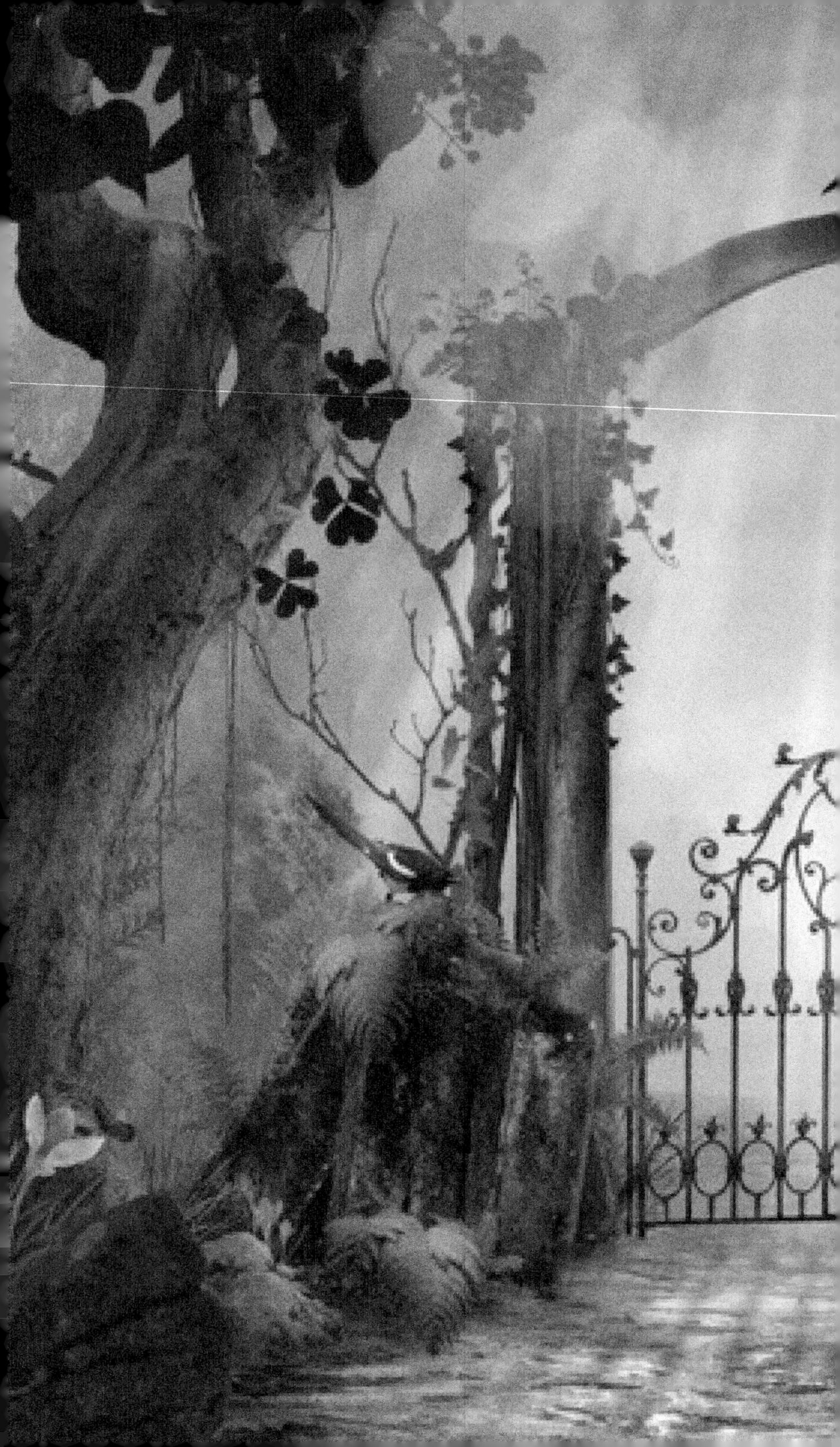

ADDI

34

As I turn off the water, soap suds gather at the bottom of the shower. I don't feel any lighter like I was hoping. My mind is still wrapped up, consumed with thoughts of the exact person I was trying to work out of my system.

Brody.

Fuck.

That escalated quickly. I don't know what I was doing. My body took over, and the second his lips pressed against mine, I lost every piece of logic that I'm usually so careful to keep at the forefront. Apparently, I'm strong, but not stronger than the needs of my lady parts. She's the real boss around here it seems.

Was it worth it? Hell yeah.

Am I wondering if there's regret mixed in there now?

Definitely.

Is there hope it will all be over with now? That they will all leave me alone? I think so.

Fuck, I don't know.

I should want that. I should want to go back to living my quiet life without those four assholes, but it seems I'm a glutton for punishment.

No, Addi. It was just sex. Once. One and done. That's what Brody had promised. Until he didn't.

Swiping a hand down my face, I grab the navy towel I hung earlier, wrapping it around my body as I step from the shower stall. I look at myself in the vanity mirror that stretches the entire length of the opposite wall.

I can see the ghost of a small mark on my throat from Brody's touch and it makes my thighs tingle. I know if I look at my back and my legs, I'll find more.

I shouldn't like it as much as I do.

Abandoning my reflection, I turn for the door. I just need to hide away in my room for the night and give myself some time, focus on some self-care before I turn all of my attention back to my classes.

With a nod, I step into the hallway, but the newfound spring in my step is paused when I see someone braced against my bedroom door.

Not just someone.

Cassian.

His brown hair is messy from running his fingers through it, and his head is hanging low as he braces his arms against my door. A white fitted tee is sculpted to his abs and the jeans he's wearing mold around his ass like sin. With open-laced boots, he looks far better than he should.

His head whips to me instantly, his eyes darkening as his nostrils flare. His green eyes are narrowed and consuming, while his jaw tics with irritation. My grip on the towel tightens as I open my mouth, but I don't get to release a breath, never mind a single word, before he's barreling into me.

My body stiffens at the impact, but we don't hit the ground like I expect. We're moving, not far, and a moment later, we're still again. My back is pressed against the mirror in the bathroom, the vanity right beside me, and the empty shower stalls across the room.

Fucking hell.

Stuck between fight, flight, or freeze, I gape at him, eager to slam my fist into his face and get the fuck out of here, but the hold he has on me isn't going to be easy to escape.

Chest to chest, he tilts his head down, running the tip of his nose up my throat, and I shiver at the contact, failing to come up with anything to say. His hands shift, gripping my hips over the towel, and it sparks my brain back to life.

"What the fuck are you doing?"

He runs his nose along my jawline, his fingers digging into my sides as I gasp.

"It's true," he rasps, more and more intoxicating with every breath I take as I frown in confusion.

"What is?" I sound far too breathless, and it pisses me off.

"Don't play dumb."

"You're the one showing up at my room out of the blue claiming things are true. I have no idea what you're referring to," I state with a pointed look, and he cocks a brow at me.

"Technically, we're in the bathroom."

I roll my eyes. "Technically, you're pissing me off. What the fuck do you want, Cassian?" I bite, my heart rate accelerating as he leans back, emerald green eyes meeting mine.

"I want to hear you say you fucked Brody."

My chest clenches. I was hoping he would just be pissed at me and ignore me for the rest of time. Apparently, I was wrong.

Gulping, I fail to hide the smallest hint of nerves that creep up my spine. "I fucked Brody."

The words hang in the air between us for a beat before his hand snakes around my throat, mirroring Brody's mark from earlier.

"What did you think that would achieve?" My eyes

narrow further, unsure of what he wants me to say, and he shakes his head in annoyance. "Brody told me what you said. What you thought would come from getting under him."

"Technically, it was against a tree," I snap, using his own sass back at him, but it doesn't hit the mark like I'd hoped.

"Technically, it doesn't make a difference. His dick went right here, is that correct?"

I gasp as he flicks the towel open, cupping my pussy in the next breath.

My body tenses, but not with the desire to fight, no matter how much I try to summon it.

Fuck.

"Get off me."

He fucking smirks as he shakes his head.

"Say it like you mean it, Addi." The challenge is clear, fueling the anger I'm desperate to launch at him, but he moves the tip of his finger just an inch and we both feel it. He looks down at where we're connected, swirling the pad of his finger softly before looking at me with a gleam in his eyes I've never seen before. "Say it while you're not getting wet against my hand, Addi."

"I don't know what you mean," I rasp, hands clenching at my sides as I try to push him away, slam my fists into his face…anything, but I'm frozen and at his mercy.

"Don't play dumb, Addi. It doesn't suit you."

I shrug, trying to act as unaffected as possible, but we both know it's a sham. "I fucked your friend. Now you have to let someone else challenge me." That's the logic I'm sticking with, but any hope of it sticking evaporates when his smirk turns into a full-blown grin.

"And that's what you told Brody?" he asks, his finger still dancing the gentlest sequence over my entrance. I nod, unable to find the words as I focus on keeping my breathing even. "And what did he say?"

The memory flickers in my mind, but I shake it off. "It doesn't matter."

"I think it does," he pushes, earning another eye roll.

"Of course you would."

"How sheltered has your life been, Addi?"

My nostrils flare, and I'm not sure if it's because of his bullshit question or the fact that his fingers have paused. "Not very."

"Are you sure?" he presses, leaning closer so his lips drag over my cheek as he speaks.

"What does that mean?" I hate that I keep asking this question. Every situation, every moment, I'm out of my depth, eager to know more. My curiosity is becoming a burden, and at this stage, I'm certain it's going to be the death of me.

"It means that there are more men than women in this

world."

"I know that." What does that have to do with right now, though?

He shifts, tilting my head back to look down into my eyes as he speaks his next words. "You should also know that it means men share." I gulp, and he feels the movement against his palm, his grin turning more sinister with every second that passes. "Do I need to spell it out to you?"

His asshole attitude pisses me off, bringing me back to the present and making me acutely aware that I need to put as much distance between us as possible, right the fuck now, before I do something stupid.

"No. You've made yourself clear. You can leave now."

"I'm not going anywhere," he breathes against the shell of my ear as he drags his finger to my clit, spreading my folds so fucking slowly as he draws circles around the already tight nub.

Fuck.

I slam my palms against his chest, silently proud of myself for doing so, but as I shove at him, he increases the pressure at my core.

"Harder, Addi. I like it harder," he rasps, pressing his length against my thigh, and I force back a groan. "And honestly, knowing that my friend, my brother, fucked you hours ago only makes me want to be inside you even more now."

Scoffing, I shake my head as he tightens his hold on my throat. "Forget it."

"Are you telling me you don't feel it, too? Deep down, you know you love the fact that you claimed me in the duel. You like how strong it makes you feel, but most of all, you like how you get the big bad wolf in your pocket. Admit it or I'll happily prove it to you." He hammers the words home by thrusting two fingers into my core.

My back arches as my fingers curl into his t-shirt.

Fuck. Fuck. Fuck.

"Now the question is, do you like the advantages that come with you winning the duel more or less than the title you now wear?" His fingers swirl, making my legs weaken.

He senses the desire in my veins, and a moment later he's placing me on the vanity. The towel falls open, leaving me on display as he takes his fill. His fingers don't stop. Not that I want them to; my body is in control now.

I grip the edge of vanity, at a loss for words as he blows his breath over my nipples, smirking when they pebble, eager for his attention.

"Tell me you don't want it," he murmurs, grabbing my waist so my pussy is at the edge of the vanity. He maneuvers my legs until he has easy access to what he wants before dropping to his knees. "Tell me you don't want me to get a taste of you."

My heart races out of my control as I gape down at

him. "I don't," I croak, the lie evident even to my own ears.

"Say it louder." He swipes his tongue from my entrance to my clit. The groan that parts my lips is raw, desperate, and needy.

Dammit.

He repeats the motion, and my body jerks with need. My head falls back, my eyes falling closed, but I wince as my head cracks against the mirror behind me. Fuck, it hurts, but the adrenaline coursing through my veins makes it impossible for me to focus on anything but Cassian between my legs.

His fingers find the most satiable rhythm as he nips at my clit, and I'm helpless to the ecstasy that takes over. I have nothing to blame it on but myself. I want this, whether I want to admit it out loud or not is another story. A story I'm not even willing to entertain at this moment, but the only thing stopping me from reaching the peak of euphoria is definitely myself.

Blinking at him, I find his eyes already locked on me, and as he swirls his fingers and grazes his teeth over my clit, I fall apart.

I can't control my cries as I ride out wave after wave on his tongue. My limbs fall limp as I come down from the pleasure coursing through me, but I don't get a second to bask in the afterglow before I'm placed on my feet. I lose my balance as he spins me, and I have to blink a few times before I can force my gaze to settle on our reflection in the mirror, just in time to feel the tip of his cock at my entrance.

Our eyes meet in the glass, my pulse thundering in my ears, but as the silence descends over us, it's quickly broken by the creak of the door opening.

"Get the fuck out," Cassian growls, his voice dark and twisted as it quickly falls shut again.

It's enough to bring me to my senses, and I stand tall, ready to push away from him, but he uses the movement to his advantage, driving his cock deep into my pussy as I cry out with pleasure again.

"Tell me you don't want it, and mean it. Really fucking mean it, Addi."

I blink at his reflection, noting the blood smeared across the glass, and my gut knows that's from where my head collided earlier.

It's intense. *He's* intense. Maybe if I give in just one more time, it will be enough. It *has* to be enough.

Acceptance drapes over me in a warm embrace, and instead of using words to agree, I shift, grinding against him. It's his turn to moan, the sound feral, setting off a bomb inside of him as he grips my hips and slams into me with raw, desperate need.

Holding onto the vanity, I watch him watch where we're joined, sweat beading at his temple as he snarls with every thrust. There's nothing sweet about this, just feral ferocity that is driving me to the top of the mountain at a breakneck pace.

"That's it, Alpha, clench around my cock. I fucking love it."

Alpha? What does that mean?

I don't get to ask as my body screams at his words. My climax starts in my toes, claiming every inch of my body one piece at a time until there's nothing left but my release. His hand wraps around my throat, tightening as he finds his release along with me.

It goes on forever, every drop wrung between us until we're a panting mess.

The reality of what I've just done washes over me more quickly this time, and I curse, wiping a hand down my face as I look anywhere but at him. He must sense the shift in me because he wordlessly slips from my body, giving me enough space to grab my towel and wrap it around me.

"You're bleeding. Let me heal you," he murmurs, and I shake my head. The reminder instantly makes my head hurt.

"I'm fine." I head for the door, but he grabs hold of my arm, halting me in my tracks.

"Let me heal you, Addi," he repeats, grabbing my chin with his free hand to force me to look at him.

"Get the fuck off me," I bark, yanking my arm out of

his grasp, and he lets me go. I take a step back, irritated that I hate the distance between us, but when he doesn't barrel toward me again, I slip the door open and make a run for it.

A moment later, the sound of my bedroom door clicking shut behind me rings in my ears, offering me the slightest teasing of a sense of peace I'm not sure I want. I hear the floorboards creak from the other side of the door, and I know it's him.

Holding my breath, I wait for what comes next, but nothing does. After a few minutes, he retreats, leaving me alone with my thoughts, and I'm not sure I like them right now.

THE KINGDOM OF RUIN

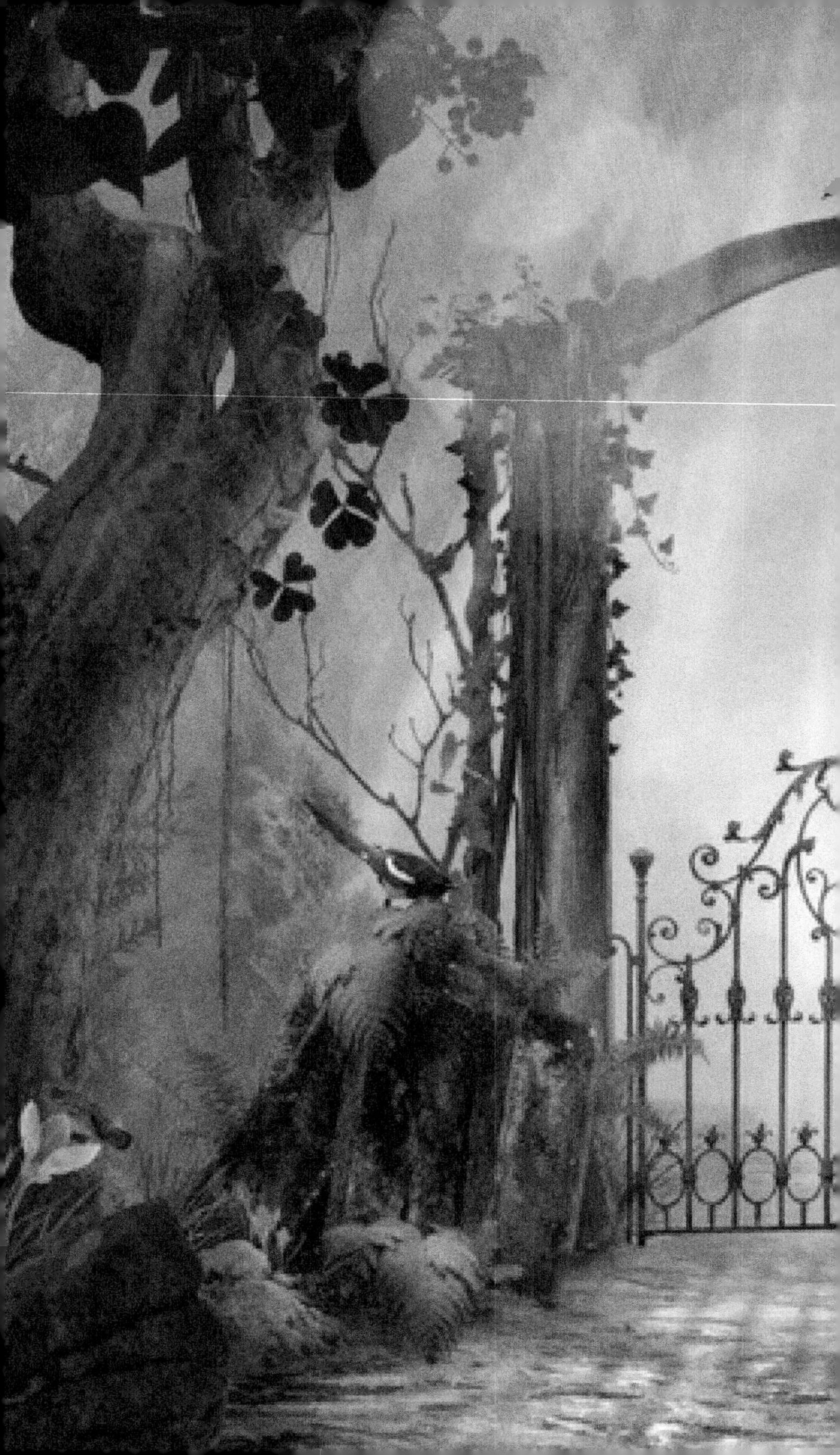

ADDI

35

Morning comes too quickly, and before I know it, I'm dressed and standing in front of the mirror wondering who the fuck is looking back at me. I'm exhausted, I can see it in my eyes, but the color in my cheeks is new. Probably from the sex, just like the bruises that are now scattered all over my skin.

The evidence of yesterday's events leaves me torn. I like them, along with the ache between my thighs, but the reminder of who put them there pisses me off. I'm drawn to them. It's undeniable at this point, but that doesn't mean I have to be happy about it.

Yesterday…was a lot of dick. Good dick, I can admit that, at least, but I can't continue to be distracted like this. If my father and Nora could see me now, they would definitely have different opinions. My father despises distractions of any kind, and even though he wouldn't be aware of what, or who, is distracting me, he would sense it. While Nora would be high-fiving me, desperate for all the details over cake and a rerun of her favorite movies.

Instead, I'm left trying to figure out how I'm going to handle all of this by myself. After a restless night, I'm opting to bury my head in the sand and hope nobody sees. Although, I'm aware someone stepped into the bathroom last night. I don't know how much they saw, but I'm sure it was enough.

I cringe, pinching the bridge of my nose in irritation as a knock sounds from the door.

Dammit.

I can't avoid whoever it is. I've spent so much time procrastinating that I'm barely going to make breakfast, and all of the extra physical activity has me starving.

Moving toward the door, I press my hand against the wood, but they speak before I can try to piece together who it is.

"Come on, Addi. I know you're in there."

Flora.

Taking a deep breath, I swing the door open with the best smile I can muster plastered to my face. "Hey."

"We're not going to be able to eat if we don't go now," Arlo states from behind her, glancing at his watch, and I join them out in the hallway.

"I'm ready."

We head downstairs in comfortable silence. The building is quiet since it's later than usual. Everyone will either be in the dining hall or heading for their first class.

I sigh with relief as we make it outside without someone calling me out for the bathroom last night, then Arlo clears his throat.

"So, are we going to talk about the elephant in the room? Or should I say air?" He points around, indicating we're outside.

My pulse quickens with panic as I try to keep my response as calm and collected as possible. "What elephant?"

Flora whacks Arlo in the chest, but he just chuckles as he wiggles his brows at me. "About what the bathroom is supposed to be used for."

My eyes widen in horror. "Oh my gosh, did you walk in?"

His nose crinkles. "What? No!"

I frown. "Then how…"

"Honey, you are not quiet," he states with a wink, and I can feel the color already draining from my face as I stop, shying away from them both with my head in my hands.

"Oh, fuck," I grumble under my breath, but it seems Arlo is eager for more gossip.

"Who was the lucky guy?"

"We're not having this conversation," I state, lifting my face as I point a finger at him.

"Okay, lips are sealed," Flora promises. "But if you do need to talk about anything, I'm here," she adds. Arlo opens his mouth again, but she claps her hand over it, effectively shutting him up, and I grin.

"Thanks, Flora."

"No worries. Ignore Arlo's teasing. He's just jealous the girls aren't tripping all over him here like they do back home."

"If you say so," he retorts, winking at her, and I watch in amusement as her cheeks turn pink.

Thankfully, Arlo doesn't try to push for more as we head over to the dining hall. Stepping inside, I'm praying to anyone that will listen that the assholes plaguing my thoughts and life are nowhere to be seen, but the moment I step through the doors, my gaze locks on theirs.

Brody and Cassian are sitting side by side, with Raiden and Kryll across from them.

I can avoid them. I know I can. Turning, I move toward the food trays, but an arm drapes around my shoulder, pulling me into their side and redirecting me. I'm not surprised to find it's Brody who's making the first move, like the whole fucking room isn't watching.

"I already got your food, Dagger."

I frown but don't stop walking with him. "Why?"

"Because."

"Because…"

"Get your ass over here and eat, Dagger," he says with a sigh, maneuvering us through the crowd with ease.

"I said yesterday that I wasn't doing this," I point out, and he shrugs.

"And then you fucked me."

He says it way louder than necessary, making me glare at him. "To get it out of our system," I bite out through clenched teeth, and he smirks.

"Not out of my system, remember?"

"That's not what you promised," I retort, floundering under his close proximity yet again, but if he notices, he doesn't seem to mind.

"I didn't promise shit. Besides, then you got handsy with the big bad wolf. I feel like this only serves to work in my favor."

"That doesn't mean I have to sit here," I scramble as we come to a stop beside the table.

"You can sit where you want. It just has to be at this table," Cassian grunts from his seat, not bothering to glance my way. I sigh, looking around the room to see all eyes pointed our way.

Dammit.

I can cause a scene or eat the bacon, sausage, and egg on the plate that Brody's pointing to.

"My friends are coming too."

"They can do what they want," Kryll answers, and I quickly search them out, waving them over before I take my plate and move around the table. I leave a spot beside me open but drop down closest to Raiden. If anyone is going to leave me alone here, it's him.

Flora and Arlo appear a moment later. Flora takes the spot directly across from me while Arlo sits between her and Cassian. The table falls into silence as everyone eats. I can sense the uncertainty from Flora and the need to check that I'm okay, so I offer her a small smile. It will have to do for now.

I'm halfway through my food when a shadow falls over me from the edge of the table, and I don't need to look up to know it's my least favorite vampire.

"Move," Vallie bites, and I look into her eyes to see venom dancing in her orbs.

Sighing, I ignore her as I turn to the table to find all four guys staring my way. "Do you see my predicament? That's all I want to do, but now that she's demanding it, it makes me want to dig my heels in more," I grumble, irritation zapping through my body.

"Good. Keep going, Vallie, this is working in our favor," Brody says with a victorious grin.

Ass.

"I said, move," she snarls, only this time she grabs my

hair and drags me from my seat.

What the fuck? I knew I should have put it up in my usual crown braid this morning, but I was too distracted.

She manages to drag me to my knees before I can get a handle on the situation. I slam my fist into her stomach before swiping at her legs to knock her down with me. Her grip on my hair tightens, yanking on where I hurt it in the bathroom yesterday, but I use the pain to fuel me.

"Stay down, bitch!" she yells, making me snicker at her bullshit as I repeat the movements again, jabbing her in the stomach before hitting her thighs. Her chest hits the floor, but her hold on my hair only tightens more, so I push up to my feet, fighting against the pain as I get a better angle to slam my fist into her face. I do it twice before she relents, releasing me to cup her face.

Hovering over her, I want to keep going, pummel her into the ground and get some rest from her bullshit once and for all. But once again, my father's voice in my head stops me.

Mercy.

Fucking mercy.

She doesn't deserve it anymore.

"You're making it harder and harder for me to not just kill you," I growl, sweeping my hair back off my face. She cups her nose, blood pouring down her chin.

"Wait until my father hears about this," she seethes,

and I scoff.

"I believe he already tried to have me expelled. How's that working for you?"

"It will stick this time."

I roll my eyes. "Good luck with that." Taking a step back, she rushes to her feet and two of her friends hurry over before they head for the exit. She's never going to learn. She's persistent, that's for sure. That's twice she's caused a scene with me that's ended physically, and both times she's ended up worse for the wear. Maybe the third time is when I snap altogether.

"Her father tried to get you expelled?" Cassian grunts with furrowed brows, and I nod.

"And yours. Does anybody else's parent want to add their name to the list?" I ask, looking at Brody, Raiden, and Kryll.

"It is *hot* when she's angry," Kryll states, making my jaw fall slack as I stare at him.

Flora chuckles until I glare at her and she covers her mouth, but a frown quickly transforms her face as she points at me.

"You're bleeding."

I lift my hand to my hair, the thick liquid familiar against my fingers, and sigh.

A breeze flutters around me, and a second later, Cassian is standing in front of me. His gaze is set on my head at the wound that has been reopened from last night. His jaw is set in a firm line as he reaches out to run his hand over it. A warmth blossoms at his touch. Instinctively, I panic that my body is overreacting to him again, but I quickly realize it's magic that's dancing along my skin.

Before I can react, he leans forward, pressing his lips against the crown of my head. "All healed."

I gape at him, unable to find any snarky words to make him back off, when a siren blares, jolting me.

"What does that mean?" Flora asks as everyone starts to rise, and it's Raiden who has the answer.

"It means the dean is ready to give a speech."

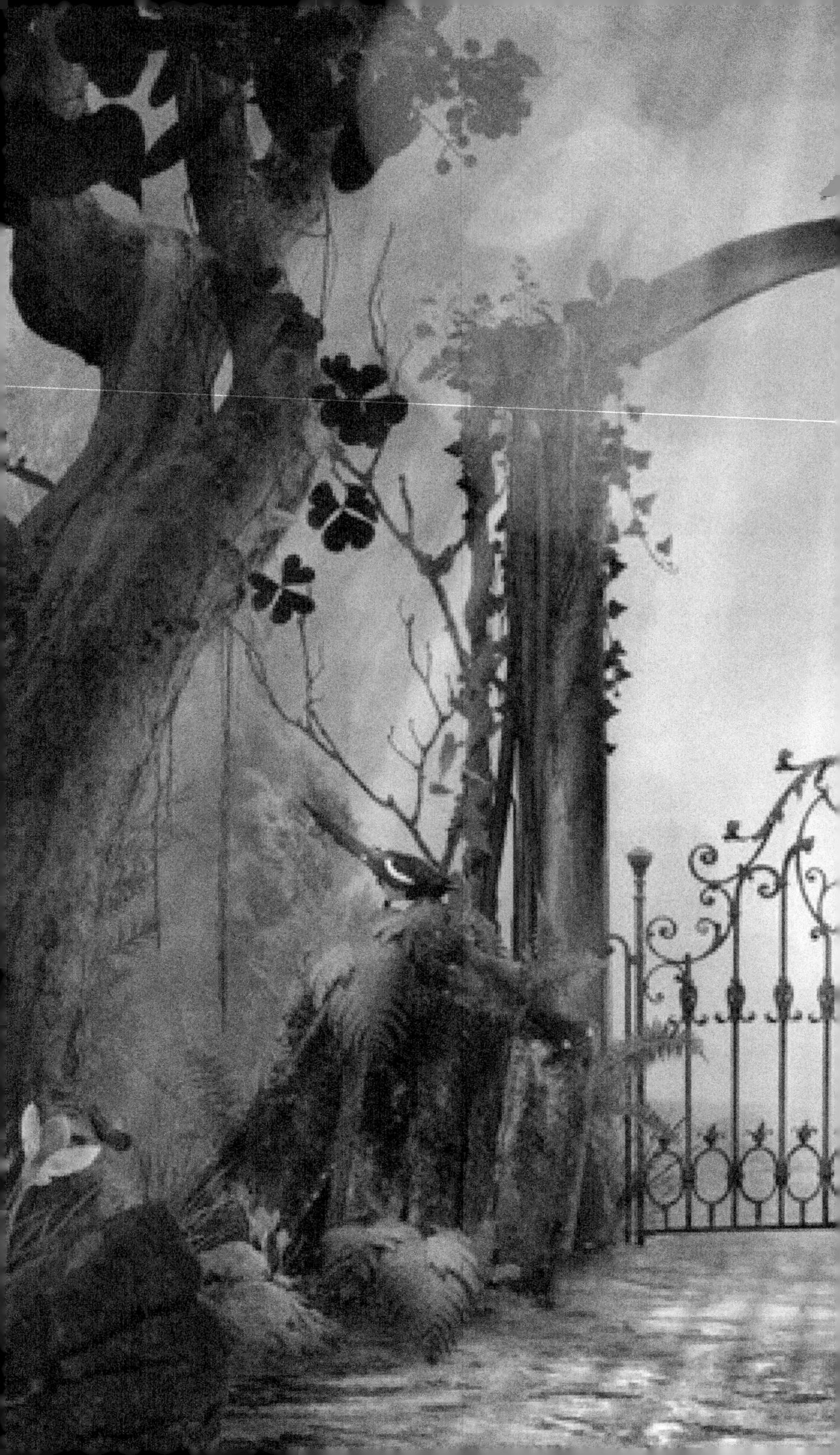

ADDI

36

Adrenaline still courses through me as I follow the crowd outside. I'm acutely aware of the wide berth everyone seems to be offering me, and I appreciate it. Maybe Vallie's repeated attempts to bring me down are working in my favor a little. I don't want everyone to fear me too much, but at least they know I'm not a pushover.

"Where are we supposed to go?" I ask, keeping my head tilted toward Flora on my left. Arlo flanks her other side, and although I can sense the assholes hovering nearby, too, they don't cause any further irritation than usual.

"To homeroom," Arlo explains, and I nod in acknowledgement as we head in that direction. When we near the entryway, I spot Vallie off to the side, dramatically sobbing as she points to her bloody nose before her red-tipped finger aims in my direction.

Professor Holloway, the vampires' guide, follows the direction of her extended arm, frowning at me as she continues to listen to whatever bullshit Vallie is feeding her.

Amazing.

"It looks like you can add my mother to that list of yours," Raiden states from a step behind me. I glance back at him with a frown as I slowly understand what he's saying.

"Your mother," I breathe, slowly turning back to Vallie and Professor Holloway, who is now glaring at me.

I sigh. Honestly, fuck my life.

I knew coming here, I would have the odds stacked against me, but this is on another level. No one could have predicted this.

Upping my pace, I dart into our homeroom, taking my seat before Brody and Kryll in hopes of building invisible walls around myself. The mage to my left makes it impossible when he drops into his chair and instantly places his hand on my thigh.

Fuck.

Warmth blossoms from his touch, but before I can enjoy it too much, I shove his hand away. A soft chuckle parts his lips and I can feel his eyes on me as he places it on my leg once again.

"Have you ever been told no before?" I grumble, hands fisting on the table as I glare at him. My annoyance with him only seems to make his smile spread wider.

"When you mean it, let me know." He squeezes my thigh, punctuating his statement, before turning forward, leaving me to narrow my eyes at the side of his head.

"What did you expect would happen after you let him between your thighs?" Kryll asks, and I whip my irritated stare his way, but he doesn't react.

"We were getting it out of our system. Nothing more. I *expected* him to fuck off," I bite, not entirely sure why I'm even answering him.

"Not out—"

"I know. You've made that very clear since the fact. Thanks," I snap, interrupting his repetition of the same line he's been giving me since the moment we finished.

Kryll chuckles behind his hand, trying and failing to hide the smugness that naturally exudes from him.

They're all assholes. That hasn't changed. Good dick or not.

A projection screen descends against the wall at the front of the classroom, drawing everyone's attention, and a moment later, Dean Bozzelli appears on the screen. She's sitting behind a desk, fingers laced together on the table as she sits tall. A lime-green blazer sits perfectly on her shoulders, with a silk white shirt beneath. It seems her love for neon colors knows no bounds.

"Good morning, students. I hope you are all doing well and settling into your new surroundings." The corners of her mouth lift just enough to be considered a smile. A fake one, but most people won't care to notice. "Now that the introductory period is over, it's time to buckle down and start looking at the trials and challenges the academy has to offer. We do have to find our new heir after all," she declares with a real grin this time, excitement dancing in her eyes.

It's contagious. I'm desperate to focus on the challenges laid out for us instead of the drama that has sought me out. Anticipation zings through me, but I can feel the nervous energy in the room from some of the others.

"Have you ever seen someone look so excited for people to die?" Brody whispers, fingers flexing on my thigh. His question leaves me speechless. The truth in his words is startling.

"In three months' time, we will begin the first Heir Academy battle."

Battle?

"You will spend the lead-up to this learning the intricate details of what will be required of a leader within the kingdom, which will include a field trip to the dormant castle. It will be a great opportunity to breathe in the power it holds, leaning into the history of our kingdom, along with the etiquette you all need to embrace in order to lead the realm. While all of that is somewhat whimsical, combat classes will be the opposite. I think it's safe to say this will intensify, and it must, if we are to find our strongest citizens. Combat classes will begin to prepare you for the battle with smaller, less vital training sessions. Information on those will be given as they are confirmed, but please bear in mind that they may be sporadic and declared with short notice because, of course, a kingdom can come under attack at any time without warning."

I can barely breathe as I cling to every word when she parts her lips with a twist of venom. The castle? Whimsical? Battles? They're definitely turning the heat up. We all registered to be here, but the details of what that would entail were never specified—until now.

"I'm sure some of you are nervous. It's understandable, but the purpose of this academy is to weed out the weak and find our inner strength. Our new heir."

"I bet she thinks she's going to weed out all of the fae. But not you, Dagger," Brody breathes against my ear, making me tense. The words leave a chaotic feeling in their wake. I shouldn't like them, but I do.

Suppressing the smile tempting my lips, I keep my gaze focused on the projector.

"The main battle you will be preparing for will take place outside of the academy. A specific location will be declared closer to the time. It's important to express now that origins will be mixed together to create teams that will be designated by the origin guidance team." She presses her palms flat against the desk in front of her, nodding to someone off-camera before continuing. "All further communications regarding the matter will be shared at the earliest opportunity. To the future heir, whoever you are, we're watching."

The screen cuts out and murmurs pick up around us as students talk among themselves.

"I'm choosing you for my team," Brody declares, bopping me on the nose. I swipe at him, but he already moved.

"They just said it's assigned," I retort, pointing to the blank screen, and he shrugs.

"Yeah, but I'll get Raiden to put in a good word."

"I'd rather you didn't," I insist, and he pouts.

"You would rather go up against us instead?"

I falter.

Fuck.

He has me there.

I know in my gut they're strong; their presence seems highly regarded, too. I'm in no position to confirm or deny right now, though, so I turn to the front where the professor now stands, the projection gone.

The usual saying is to keep your friends close and your

enemies closer, but I don't really know what they are or where I want them. Yet the words hold weight in my gut.

Swiping a hand down my face, I relax in my seat.

I guess I'm facing more than one battle here at the academy.

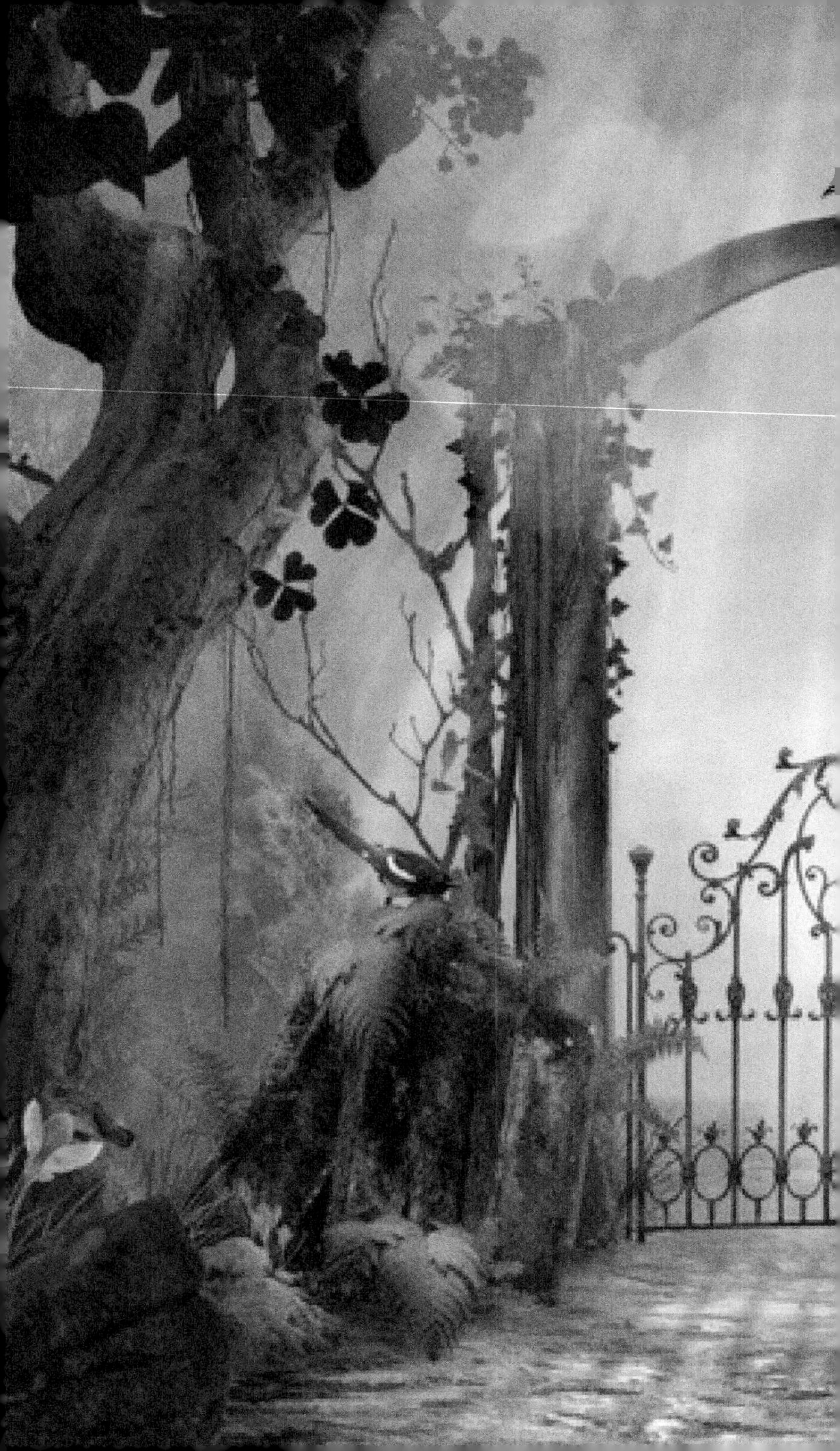

ADDI

37

A hectic morning dwindles into a somewhat mundane day as each lesson that succeeds Dean Bozzelli's declaration begins to blur together. The hype she was trying to build doesn't seem to be matched with any action taken. Maybe when we have our next combat class the training will ramp up, reflecting what she promised.

I smile my goodbye to Flora as I step into my bedroom and kick the door shut behind me. Dramatically unclipping my cloak and letting it form a puddle on the floor, I flop down on my bed with a sigh.

The lessons may have been average, but they were still mentally taxing. Or was that the constant presence of the guys now haunting my every move?

Wiping a hand down my face, I close my eyes as

Brody's words from this morning play in my mind. *"You would rather go up against us instead?"*

I don't know the right answer to that question. I think that's what's irritating me the most.

Are they my friends or enemies? I have to take fucking them out of the equation to really consider it, but no matter how much I try to fight it, when I look in their direction, all I can feel is the memory of their touch along my skin.

Shaking my head, I refocus my thoughts and consider each of them on an individual basis.

Raiden is an asshole and he's never pretended to be otherwise, but in this instance, it doesn't work in his favor. His ridiculing comments about my being a fae ring in my ears. The fact that he's a vampire should also be a negative, but that would only lower me to his standards for disregarding me for being fae-born, so I keep that off my mental list. It's his fault I have Vallie to deal with, and he doesn't seem to care about the drama he brings my way, so he has to be an enemy, right?

Cassian's bullshit runs just as deep as his. I was forced into a damn duel because of him, and his lack of desire to get me out of it puts him in the same category. Now his new demands that require me to sit with him in the dining room get under my skin, too. It's another ploy to keep other women at bay. He's using me as a shield against the women who want him, so they're not an actual distraction for him. Ass. Definitely on my enemy list.

Brody is…Brody. He hasn't really been an ass, but he's associated with them, and that has to count for something. I guess he would be considered more of a friend than an enemy, but the use of the word friend should be taken with a grain of salt. There always seems to be an undertone with him that I can't quite put my finger on.

Kryll, the last of the pains in my side, is an enigma. I wonder if anyone has ever had a glimpse of what's under the mask he puts on for everyone. He's always calm and collected. My father would be impressed, but to hold that level of patience and attention is surely exhausting. I guess he's more friend than foe, too, but he's too impassive to make a clear judgment.

I've got my hands full in more ways than one.

A vibration echoes from my nightstand, making me roll toward it with a sigh. Pulling my cell phone from the top drawer, it's no longer a surprise to see Nora's name flashing across the screen. Really, who else is going to be calling me? Nobody else apart from my father has my number.

I accept the call, smiling as soon as I bring it to my ear and hear her voice.

"How's my favorite sister doing?"

"I'm your only sister," I retort, making her scoff.

"I can still find a way to knock you from the top spot if

necessary," she challenges, and I roll my eyes.

"You wouldn't." I roll to my back on the bed, looking at the ceiling.

"So, how are you doing?"

"I'm okay." I pull at a loose thread on my t-shirt, acutely aware of the lie that falls from my lips.

"Are you sure? It was announced today that Heir Academy's battles will be held in three months, and it's going to be televised."

My body stills at the new revelation as I sigh.

Of course it is.

"That's what I'm here for, Nora. Participating in the battles isn't a concern. It's what I've been preparing for," I reply. It's the truth, and I'm truly not worried, but I know she will still be concerned for me.

"I know that. I've watched you train all my life, but that doesn't mean the anticipation doesn't get to you. It's okay to be a little bit like the rest of us mere mortals and have feelings, Addi."

"Hmm, maybe," I mutter, not wanting to get deeper into the subject with her. Embracing my feelings goes against literally everything my father spent all that time teaching me, but she doesn't know that because I ensured she was taught the complete opposite.

"Something sounds different with you."

My eyes widen as if she can see me and I shake my

head like it makes a difference.

"There's nothing different with me," I defend, but the slight lilt to my voice gives me away and I know it.

"Bullshit."

"Nora—"

"I'm switching to a video call," she interjects, and I pinch the bridge of my nose to try and calm the growing fluster that tries to take over me.

"Nora, there's no need for—"

A notification makes my cell phone vibrate, and I don't need to look to see that it's for a video call.

"Either switch to the video, or I'll head toward the academy," she warns, making my blood run cold.

"You will not. It's not safe," I bark, rushing to a sitting position at the edge of my bed. My brain is already calculating the easiest and fastest route home from here.

"Then take the call."

I sigh but relent, as she knew I would, clicking the button to switch over. A moment later, her face appears on my screen.

She smiles at me with the sweetest expression in her arsenal. Her heart-shaped face, big blue eyes, and rosy pink cheeks gleam at me, and it warms my heart, making me forget anything and everything that weighs me down.

"Ah, it's a boy," she assesses with a wink, making me scoff.

"I don't know what you're talking about," I grumble, unable to look at the cell phone as I lie.

"It's amusing to me that you don't think I know these things. The glint in your eyes reminds me of when you used to go and see that guy in the village. Josh?"

My nose scrunches in distaste. "He was an ass."

"Yet you still continued to let him put his peen in your—"

"Ew, that's enough, Nora."

She chuckles, loving the way she gets under my skin so effortlessly. "What? Don't worry, Dad's not here."

"Where is he?" I question, rising to my feet as I start to pace back and forth at the side of my bed. "You shouldn't be alone."

"Fuck off, Addi," she mumbles, narrowing her eyes at me through the phone.

"Did you just cuss me out again? That's twice in a short span of time."

She rolls her eyes at me as she purses her lips. "I'm nineteen, not nine. Do we need to recall what you were doing at nineteen, or have we covered it enough with the mention of Josh?" She cocks her brow at me, all sure of herself, leaving me with no choice but to concede again.

"Fine, but you really do need to prioritize your safety. Dad knows that," I point out, and she smiles.

"I know, and so does he, but he needed to restock

groceries. He won't be long. And now you're deflecting instead of talking about the boy causing that shimmer in your eyes."

Of course she would find a way to turn the conversation back to me. "There's no one to talk about." Technically, there's more than one, so I'm more omitting than lying, but she still sees right through me.

"Are we keeping secrets now? I'm lonely without you, Addi. You have to entertain me in some way." She flutters her eyelashes and sticks out her bottom lip, knowing full well that I can't say no to her. I don't think I've ever found someone who can.

"Why do you always make me soft on you?" I grumble, and she beams, knowing she has me in the palm of her hand.

"Because you love me."

"Hmm, I'm reconsidering."

"Of course you are," she says with a roll of her eyes as I try to find the words to explain.

"The fae guys here are pretty quiet, or maybe that's just in comparison to the other origins," I explain, getting comfortable against my headboard.

"So it's not a fae." How do I even articulate that I have my hands full with two guys, neither of which are fae? "Is he dreamy, at least?" she asks when I don't respond right away, and I scoff.

"No, dreamy would hint that they're nice."

"They?"

"Hmm?" I frown at her in confusion as she gapes through the cell phone at me before her mouth spreads into a huge smile.

"You're so cool, Addi. It's clear that the new world changes are starting to take shape."

My frown deepens. "What does that mean?"

She shrugs. "I just mean the whole creating partnerships between one woman and multiple men."

"You knew that?" Did everyone but me know this?

"While you're outside practicing until all hours, I like to know what's going on in the world outside of the ranch," she retorts, a smug grin tipping her lips further.

"Of course you do." She always likes to remind me that she's far smarter than I give her credit for.

"When you become the heir, I'll be your top confidant. I'll keep you in the loop on all things, don't worry," she promises, and my heart lurches as I quirk a brow at her.

"Do you really think I'm going to let you show your face to the world and make you a target simply because you're at my side?"

"You're just begging for me to rebel. You know that, right?"

"You wouldn't."

"I feel like I could rise to this challenge," she insists,

making my chest ache. I know I'm overprotective, but with good reason. Our history is painful. She's suffered enough and I want to shield her from the rest of it. I know I shouldn't, and deep down, I know I can't forever, but I'm just not ready to admit that to myself yet.

She's so strong-spirited, despite everything we've been through. It only illuminates how much love I have for her.

"I love you, Nora," I breathe, letting my heartfelt emotions rise to the surface, if only for a minute.

"I love you too." A knock at my door startles me, and the knowing look in her eyes that I have to go tightens my chest. "Is that one of them?"

"I hope not," I retort, and she chuckles.

"Have fun and make sure you use protection," she sings before ending the call, leaving me to gape at a blank screen.

Protection.

Last night, with Cassian, did he...?

Fuck. I don't recall any mess, but that guy's dick is huge so it could still be lodged all the way up there. I don't fucking know.

Another knock echoes from my door, pulling me from my thoughts. Placing my cell phone in the drawer, I place my palm against the door for a brief moment before I swing it open to find Kryll standing before me.

His auburn hair looks darker without the natural light

glowing down on him, and it only deepens the black markings that cover his skin. In black jeans and a quarter button-up, he looks as sinful as ever. It's a shame he's half-hidden by his origin-assigned cloak too.

"What can I do for you, Kryll?" I ask when he doesn't immediately speak.

He takes his time, letting his gaze travel up my body before he meets my gaze and shrugs. "You can come to dinner."

There's no please, no question, no option. Nothing but a demand.

Fuck that, and fuck him.

"I'm good, but thanks," I blurt with a sickly sweet smile before slamming the door shut in his face. Friend or foe, I'm not dealing with that mess tonight.

THE KINGDOM OF RUIN

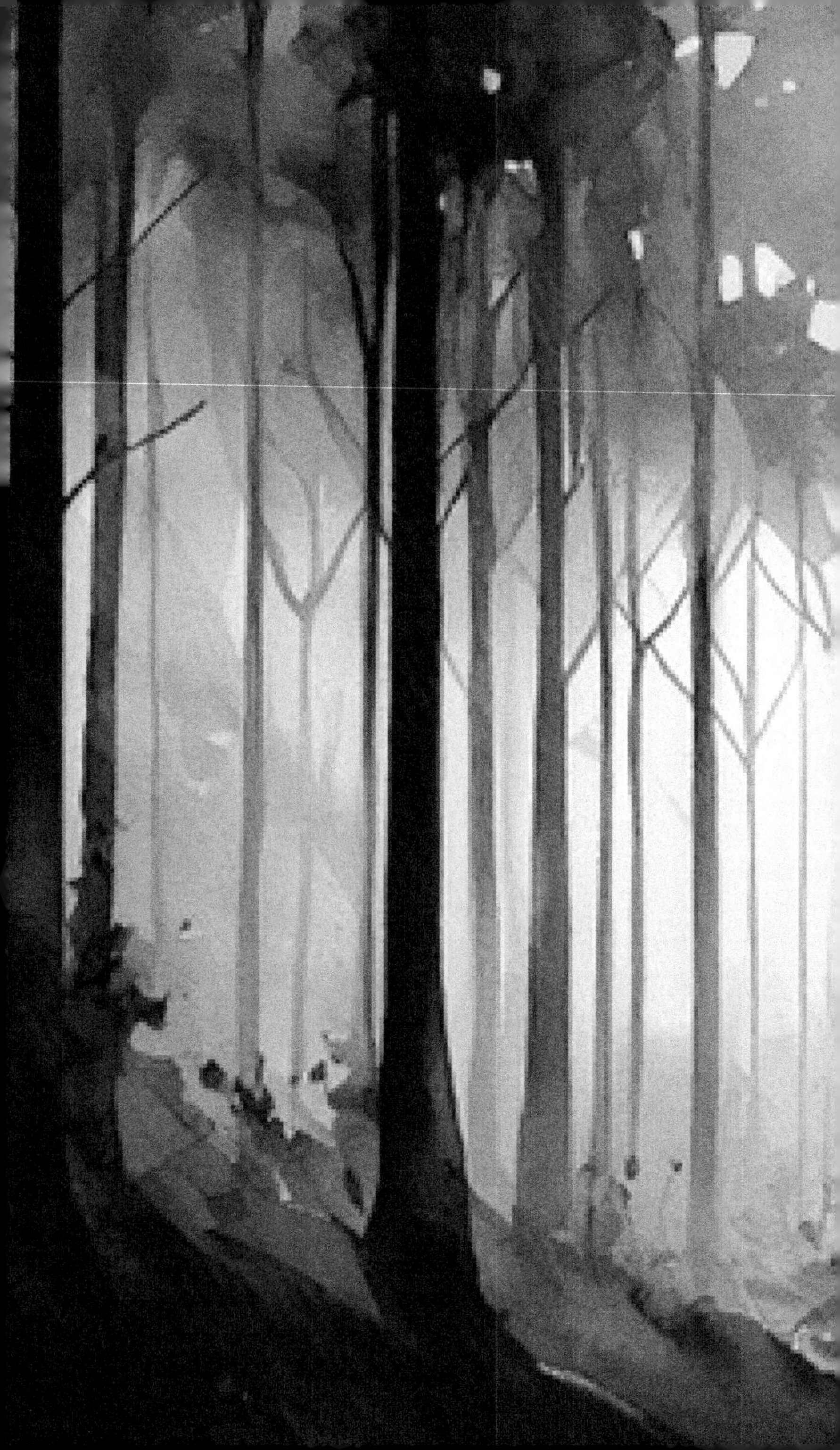

KRYLL

38

I wasn't expecting the most joyous of greetings, but slamming the door shut in my face is not necessary, is it? I've been cordial. I think.

Maybe I've been too nice? Maybe I haven't been nice enough? Maybe I don't care.

Wiping a hand down my face, I head back down the stairs. Reaching the communal area on the ground floor, I'm greeted with nervous stares as they watch me with a level of uncertainty you only ever get from a fae.

I step outside without acknowledging anyone, simply because doing so would only stress them out more than they already are. My presence rolling through like mist will offer them more peace than a friendly wave or smile.

Pursing my lips, I take a few steps back as I look up at the building. It takes me a moment to locate the window

I know belongs to her room. If my excellent orientation skills weren't working their magic, then the lack of life coming from that glass square reflects it, too.

I barely got a glimpse inside her room—or lack thereof—and I can't decide if I'm surprised by it or not. Irritated that I'm thinking so deeply about this stuff, I shake my head and focus on the task at hand.

Get Addi to the dining hall.

Luckily for me, her window is slightly ajar. Just enough for me to get up there and get in. She won't be able to slam it in my face then.

Rolling my shoulders, I let my magic dance through my veins. The telltale flapping of wings thrums in my ears, bringing me to life as I shift. Hitting the ground, I launch into the air and take to the sky. My lungs feel full for the first time in forever as I let my inner beast take flight, both in the sky and inside of me.

I give myself a few minutes to enjoy the moment, letting every worry and stress float away as my mind clears. There's something about my shifted form that completes me in a way I can't even begin to explain. With a mental promise to do this again soon, I set my sights on Addi's window.

My claw hooks around the window pane, swinging it open as I transition back to my human form. My feet hit the floor with a thud. At the same time, an almighty scream rings in my ears, but before I can find the source of the sound, my body is sailing through the air. The tugging sensation ripples through my body as I'm launched with raw force. My back slams against the wall, leaving me dazed as I slump to the floor. I've never been more relieved that shifting didn't leave me stark naked when I turned back.

I quickly push on my palms to sit up, using the wall behind me to keep me propped up as I try to process what just happened.

"What the fuck?" I groan as I take stock of where I am. "How am I back here?" I grumble, noting that I'm in the hallway outside Addi's room. Her bedroom door is open and she stands at the threshold, gaping at me while I rub at my head.

"Apparently, Brody's ward actually works," she muses, unable to hold back the smile curling her lips.

"Wait, you have one of Brody's wards up?" I clarify, and she nods. "Fuck, no wonder it hurts," I grunt, feeling the ache from the impact throughout my body.

"What does that mean?"

I shrug, and it fucking kills. "It means I'm going to give him a beating for this when I see him."

Pushing through the pain, I stand, brushing off invisible lint from my jeans as an excuse to brace myself for a moment. When I look back up, it's to see Addi giving me a pointed look with her arms folded over her chest.

"What is it you want so badly that it has you climbing through my bedroom window, Kryll?"

"Technically, I flew in," I retort, and her eyebrows rise a little.

"Your shifter has wings?" She seems slightly impressed, but I brush it off. I'm not getting distracted.

"That doesn't matter."

That earns me an eye roll as she takes a step back, reaching for the door. "Okay, then, as I already said, thanks, but no thanks."

She goes to slam the door again and I panic.

"Wait!"

I'm not expecting anything at all, but to my surprise, she pauses.

Shit.

What am I supposed to fucking say?

Clearing my throat, I give her a pointed look. "Do you really want Cassian or Raiden to come find you instead?"

She shrugs. "It seems to me that they're not going to be able to get in here. So I'm good with taking my chances."

She's so smart, but sometimes she's too naïve.

"And when you finally leave your little shoebox, you don't think they'll be waiting?"

The way she gulps confirms that she understands the truth. She knows they're relentless.

She sighs, folding her arms over her chest again. "Why is this necessary?"

I'm wondering that myself right now as pain continues to cling to my limbs from the force with which I was launched from the room. "It's all about status. Especially since you're technically Cassian's—"

"I'm not Cassian's anything," she interjects, wagging her finger at me.

"Okay," I reply with an eye roll. It's clear she doesn't want to get into that right now, which is cool and all, but there's also the other fact. "Besides, we heard a rumor that they're assessing groups and considering who to place together for the battles. If you're not in the dining hall at all, you may be an afterthought when decisions are made."

Her lips twist and I bite back the surprised smile threatening to take over. It was Raiden who said to bring up the battles and teams, and it seems he was onto something.

"Fuck, fine," she grumbles, turning away from me. I watch as she grabs her cloak from the floor, draping it over her shoulders before patting her hands over her hair. The braids are intricate and make her look way too pretty for how fierce she actually is, but I suppose that's part of her charm.

A beat later, she steps out into the hallway and clicks the door shut behind her.

"My friends—"

"Are not on my list to collect," I interrupt, heading for the stairs without glancing back.

"But—"

I spin on the balls of my feet, cocking my brow at her, and she growls under her breath.

"You're an ass, you know that?"

"Yup," I reply with a wide grin before heading outside.

I sense a few double takes from the fae in the communal room, certain they've already seen me leave once, but none of them utter a word in my direction.

A somewhat-comfortable silence washes over us as we take the pathway that leads toward the academy building. We make it to the fountain that joins all of the pathways when I spot my brother walking toward us.

"Kryll."

"Asshole," I retort, smirking at him, and he grins, leading me into a false sense of security before he has me caught in a headlock. Fucker always moves too quick.

A bubble of laughter escapes Addi's lips as she gapes at us, and my brother proceeds to rub his knuckles over my skull.

"Do you want me to embarrass you in front of your girl?"

"Not his girl!" Addi hollers quickly with a shake of her head.

"Yet," I say with a wink, and I watch in amusement as

her cheeks heat.

It was a joke, but maybe there's some truth to those words that I'm not ready to address yet.

Thankfully, my brother releases me, pulling me from my thoughts as I rub at my hair.

"Mom said you haven't called," he states, raising his eyebrows at me, and I frown.

"To tell her what?"

"Anything."

"There's nothing to tell." I rub at the back of my neck nervously. I know I should probably just call to say hi, but it feels like a harder task than I'm willing to admit.

"She heard about the battles through the news. She seemed upset by that."

"That sounds like a you issue since you knew before me. It seems you're not the one giving anyone a heads-up," I retort, feeling my defenses rise, but the way his brows furrow tells me there's more to it than that. He doesn't leave me guessing, though.

"I didn't get one, asshat."

Concern overwhelms me as I sense it pour from him. "Is everything okay?" I ask, acutely aware that Addi is still present so he's probably not going to say much, but I need to ask anyway.

"It's fine." He pats me on the shoulder, a smile that doesn't quite meet his eyes stretching across his face. "Go and make an appearance in the dining hall. They have eyes everywhere and they're watching interactions," he adds under his breath, and I nod. Fun. The rumors are true. Waving me away, he turns to Addi. "Nice to meet you again, Miss Reed. I should probably warn you away from him," he states, pointing my way, and she rolls her eyes.

"He's not taking the hint."

My brother chuckles. "He never does." With one final wave, he stalks off without a backward glance.

Addi falls into step beside me as we continue toward the dining hall. An awkwardness shifts between us, forcing me to glance her way. The second my eyes lock on hers, she speaks.

"Is it weird? Your brother working here?"

Shrugging, I consider her question. "Not really. We love each other, of course, and I have his back just as much as he has mine, but really, we're quite independent. He leaves me to my devices and I don't overstep with him, so everything should work out fine."

"I can't imagine a sibling that doesn't want to know anything and everything," she states before clapping her hand over her mouth as if she instantly regrets the words slipping past her lips.

I could delve deeper, but that's not my place. If she wants to talk, I'll listen. I can't say that I'll care, but I'm not one to pry unless it's necessary, and this doesn't feel like one of those moments.

The silence between us shifts to a different kind of awkwardness that I can't quite put my finger on as my mind drifts. We're about to step in there, and the need to put on a show of some kind feels expected, but completely unnecessary in my opinion.

It's hard to decide whether to give them nothing to see or everything to watch. The fact that my brother didn't know about the battle details prior to the announcement doesn't sit well with me. He's the combat professor, which only confuses me more. Unless he's been prepped to go full force anyway. No matter which way I look at it, it doesn't sit well with me.

Nothing here sits well with me.

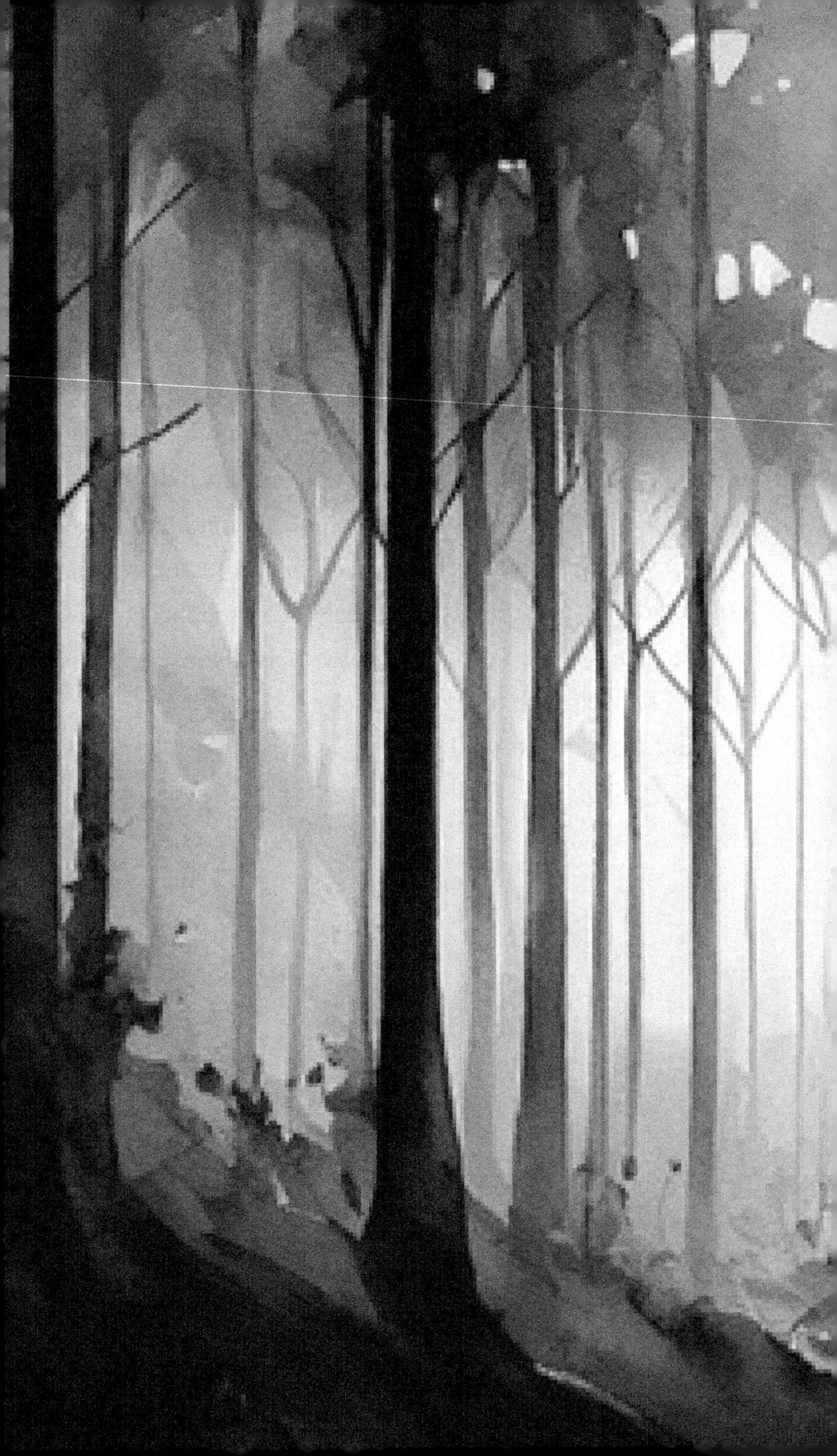

CASSIAN
39

My attention snaps to the double doors the second I recognize Kryll's flash of red hair, along with the sweet blonde at his side. Her green eyes shimmer as she glances around the room.

He got her here. He *actually* did it.

I track her every move. Her posture is straight yet agile, like she's walking with a storming purpose while being prepared for an attack at any given moment. She's an enigma—a vision. I can't guess anything about her. I especially couldn't have predicted that she would taste like Heaven, or that her moans would be as smooth as honey. She has me in a chokehold and there's nothing I can do but succumb to her.

Her hair is braided back off her face, drawing my attention to her clipped ears for a split second before I focus on her pouty lips. All too quickly, they turn toward the food counter, leaving me to look at the back of her head and the gray cloak draped over her shoulders.

I internally curse at the material for denying me the view of her ass as she walks. I've seen her natural sway. It's intoxicating, just like every other part of her.

My cock stirs, eager to find the opportunity to have a repeat of last night, minus the slight head injury she incurred. I'll avoid that this time. Maybe. My fingers flex, recalling her soft skin beneath my hands. She's a distraction, that's for sure. One I'm happy to get lost in, despite my responsibilities.

I had been aware of her existence since Vallie started shit with her from day one, but I ignored her, like I did everyone else, as I grappled with my own issues. But all that stopped when I walked into Janie's and saw her there. Add to that her ability to fight like she did, taking Leticia down effortlessly, and I'm a goner.

She didn't put up too much of a fight this morning when I pushed her to sit with us. Although, I could see the irritation thrumming through her and hear the racing of her heart, despite her efforts to remain impassive. News of the battles didn't seem to stir her like the other fae students. It's as if she's ready for it, expectant. She's definitely not like any other fae girl I've met before.

Now, I want her in my squad. I want to have her back,

and somehow, I already know I can trust her with mine. My gut twists, knowing exactly why, but I tamper the thought back down. She's under my skin, there's no denying it.

I take a bite of my burger as they approach. Jealousy swirls through me when Addi throws her head back with laughter. Kryll snickers along with her, but the second she stops at the table, a sullen look transforms her face.

"What's funny?" Brody asks, reminding me that he's here too. Raiden grunts from across the table, also letting his presence be known. Addi takes the seat at the end of the table again, leaving a spot free between her and Raiden, while Kryll takes the chair on the other side of him.

"Nothing," Kryll mumbles as Addi smirks down at her tray of food. When it's clear they're not going to let us in on their little joke, I find myself scrambling to think of something to make her look at me.

"I'm impressed you're not kicking up a fuss like usual," Raiden states, waving his fork in Addi's direction. She simply glares at him, refusing to respond.

"Oh," Kryll mutters suddenly, rising from his seat, and I frown.

What's going on?

Before I can ask, he saunters around the table to Brody at my side and punches him in the arm.

"What was that for?" Brody complains, rubbing at the spot as Kryll strolls back to his seat and continues to eat.

"The ward on her room," he replies after a few moments. Brody's brows furrow for a second before realization washes over him, and he grins, pleased with himself.

"Sucks to be you," he states, winking at Addi as Kryll sighs.

"I think I cracked a rib," he retorts, lifting his t-shirt to reveal a small smattering of bruises. Addi peers around Raiden to get a look, and as much as I agreed to share with my friends, that doesn't count when things feel weird like this. When she's looking at my abs eagerly like that, too, then it won't matter.

"Cover yourself up," Raiden grunts, shaking his head as he focuses on his food.

"Any word on who is selecting the groups?" Kryll asks as I stretch out my leg, nudging Addi's leg with my own.

I get comfortable, appreciating the feel of her against me, and when she doesn't move away, I take it as a win. It's more likely that she's refusing to falter at my touch, wanting to demand the upper hand between us, but I'm going to pretend it's because she likes it as much as I do. Which I truly think she does. She just doesn't want to admit it.

"No," Raiden replies, bringing me back to the present.

"My brother just mentioned that the professors weren't aware of the battles in advance."

My jaw tics at the revelation, but I can't say I'm truly surprised. Growing up in my father's pack feels just like this, like there's always a step or move that you haven't seen until it's too late.

Nobody else offers a hint of shock at the news as I chance a glance around the room, trying to discern who is paying closer attention to their surroundings than the rest.

"Do you think it's a member of the staff?" Brody asks, clearly doing the same as me, and I shrug.

"There's never really any staff in here. Not unless I'm causing a scene, of course." She rolls her eyes and I grin. "That would make me think it's more likely a student trying to blend in, but who would be given that kind of control?" She rounds her eyes to Raiden. "Maybe someone whose parent is at the academy, or whose family member is on the teaching staff," she adds, glancing past him to look at Kryll.

Fuck, her mind has me just as excited as her body.

"Excellent thoughts, Dagger, but if Kryll's brother didn't know about the battles, I can't imagine he's been made aware of the selection process and Raiden…well…"

"My mother possibly likes you more than me, and that's saying something," Raiden finishes.

"That pretty much sums it up," Brody adds as Addi leans back in her seat, deep in thought.

"Maybe it's a mage, you know, with their magical

abilities," Kryll states, and Addi frowns.

"Fae have magical abilities." The bite to her tone is clear, but it seems to go straight over Kryll's head.

"Yeah, but—"

"But what?" she snaps, hands balling on the table as she stares him down.

My cell phone pings in my pocket, breaking the moment, and despite the amusement of watching someone else be on the receiving end of her wrath for a change, I check to see what it is.

"Fuck."

"What's wrong?" Brody asks, and I sigh.

"My father is here."

"*Here?*" Raiden repeats, his eyebrows knitting together as I nod. "Why?"

"I don't know," I murmur, placing my cell phone on the table. "It's probably to throw his weight around like usual."

"But you're not part of the pack anymore," Kryll points out, and I nod again.

"I know, but that doesn't really matter to him. He thinks he's above the law, remember?"

"Why now?" Raiden asks, confusion dancing in his eyes, but I see what this is.

"My little alpha over here has probably piqued his interest." I point across the table at Addi, watching in amusement as her eyes widen and her hand flies to her chest.

"Me?"

"You," I confirm.

Her lips purse and annoyance scrunches her face as her eyes narrow on me. "Then maybe you shouldn't have let the duel happen," she says.

"I didn't say I was mad about it," I retort, taking a drink of my water as her glare darkens.

"Well, you should be."

I wink at her as Raiden sighs. "Are you going?"

"No." Grabbing my cell phone, I quickly type out a message, hit send, and place it back on the table.

Finishing my burger and fries, I turn my focus to the pretty blonde at the table, but before I can enjoy staring at her, a shadow falls over me. A quick glance to my right reveals Professor Whitlock, the head of the wolves, beside me.

Fuck.

"Mr. Kenner, you're being summoned."

"I'm aware, but I declined." I turn away, hoping he'll take the hint, but unfortunately for me, he leans closer, bracing his palms against the table.

"Mr. Kenner, it's not an option. To keep the peace, the faculty have let him on campus, and he's awaiting your arrival."

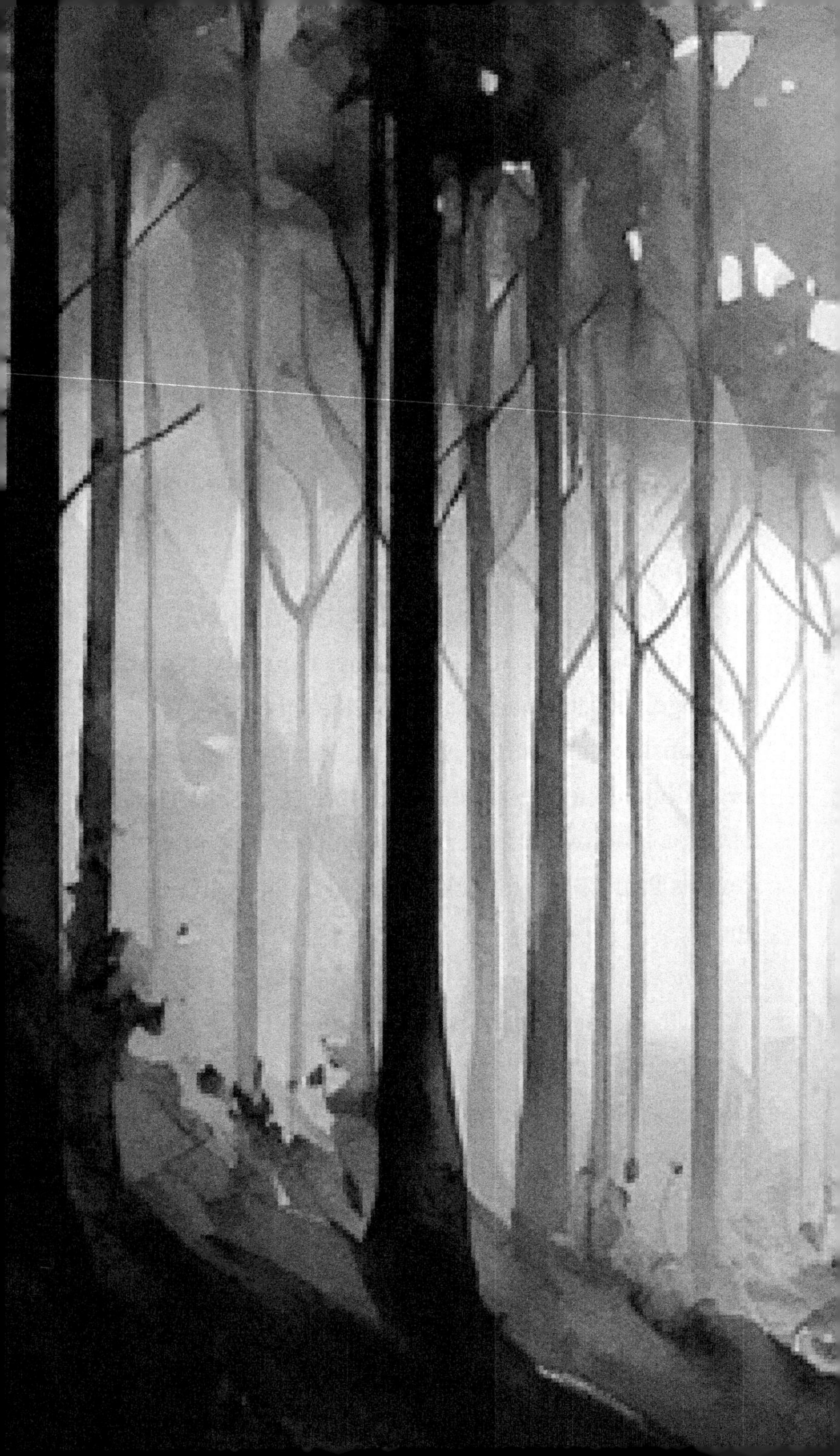

CASSIAN
40

I trudge behind Professor Whitlock toward his office. He doesn't offer me a single word of guidance, like his job title implies, knowing full well that I'll be on my own when I step through those doors.

My father is feared by everyone, and it seems that panic filters all the way through the academy, too. When I was small, he scared me, but as I got older, wiser, I learned a lot of his crap is all smoke and mirrors. He also taught me to fear no one. He probably didn't mean to include himself in that equation, but here we are.

The professor's office door creaks open as he pushes it with his hand, but he steps to the side so my father only sees me standing at the threshold. Loser. Stepping into the room, I note the small lamp offering the only source of light so my father can look even more dangerous now that the sun has set.

He leans back in Whitlock's high-backed leather chair, ankle propped on his knee and his fingers laced together, offering me more of a sneer than a smile. His brown hair is long and uncontrolled, covering half of his face, but his piercing blue eyes are prominent, even in the low light.

The door clicks shut behind me as I edge farther into the room. My father waves at the seat on the other side of the desk and I take it with a sigh.

"You've been avoiding me," he grunts, shifting in his seat so both of his feet are on the floor, and rests his elbows on the desk.

"Yet you still didn't get the message," I retort, and his failing attempt at a smile disappears altogether.

"Watch your tone," he warns, the rasp of his wolf slipping through into his gravelly words.

"What do you want, Father?"

"Alpha," he snaps, slamming his fists on the table in a fit of rage, and I shake my head.

"You're not my alpha." I keep my voice even and any hint of emotion locked away.

"I am until I say so." This has been his reaction since I cut ties. He didn't like my announcement, and he didn't like me leaving his pack—or his control—which, in his words, *forced* him to exile me. Exile is a lonely place for a wolf, but I still have a lot of people around me, so I don't mind it as much as I could.

He doesn't like me basking in his punishment, so he's reverting to imaginary control that he still believes he has. Because of other people's fear of him, he truly thinks he has it.

Taking a deep breath, I inch back in my seat, but I'm far from relaxed. I'm more alert now than I was at the diner on Friday. I may not fear him, but that doesn't mean I shouldn't anticipate his moves.

"If you're here for a power trip, I'm going to have to cut it short," I state, and he shakes his head, disappointment oozing from him.

"To leave the pack is one thing, Cassian, but to allow another origin to win in a duel for you is something else entirely."

Ah, so the news got back to him. Good. I knew it would piss him off. Not that I take pleasure in doing it purposely, but it's just another reminder for him that he doesn't control me anymore. He may be annoyed it's someone from a different origin, but I bet he's more pissed that she beat the girl he had betrothed me to. The strongest beta for me, or so he said, was beaten by a fae. I think it's fantastic; he, however, would not.

He wants me to call him out on it. He wants to get under my skin. He wants to get any kind of emotion from me, and I refuse.

"It's none of your business," I breathe, reminding him that he's not my alpha without saying the actual words again because I know it will have him charging at me with his fists raised.

"It *is* my business when it reflects badly on me," he snarls, and my eyes narrow.

"Does it, though? I'm not a member of your pack and you publicly exiled me. If anything, it's a reflection of how terrible *I* am, and proves that you made the right choice exiling me. It works in your favor if anything," I ramble, watching as his hands ball into tight fists on the table.

He purses his lips, eyes drilling into mine. "I want to meet her."

"No." My answer is instant, but it doesn't really register in his mind.

"It's not a question."

"The answer is still no," I push, refusing to give in to the man who has always been too selfish to be a true alpha.

"I will meet her, Cassian. I'm throwing a moon party on Saturday. You will come, and you will bring her," he orders, still not getting the message. Sitting tall in my seat, I lean a little closer to the desk.

"I said—"

"If you don't," he interjects, projecting his voice so loud that the desk rattles between us. "I'll meet her on far less amiable terms, with you nowhere in sight."

Fuck.

The promise in his eyes is certain. I can see right through him. He already has a contingency plan in mind if I don't take her to the moon party and my gut tells me it wouldn't be good. Before the duel—fuck, right after the duel—if he had tossed this threat my way, I would have backed away without a word. Unfazed, uncaring, and glad to be rid of a fae girl who has done nothing but leave chaos in her wake.

Now, however, I can't say I'm as impassive as I was.

I can't let him get his hands on her. My wolf won't allow it.

"Is that a threat, Father?" I ask, refusing to acknowledge that I care enough about her to do as he demands.

A sneer spreads across his face as he sweeps his hair back. He stands, leaning over the table in an attempt to dominate. "Defy me and find out."

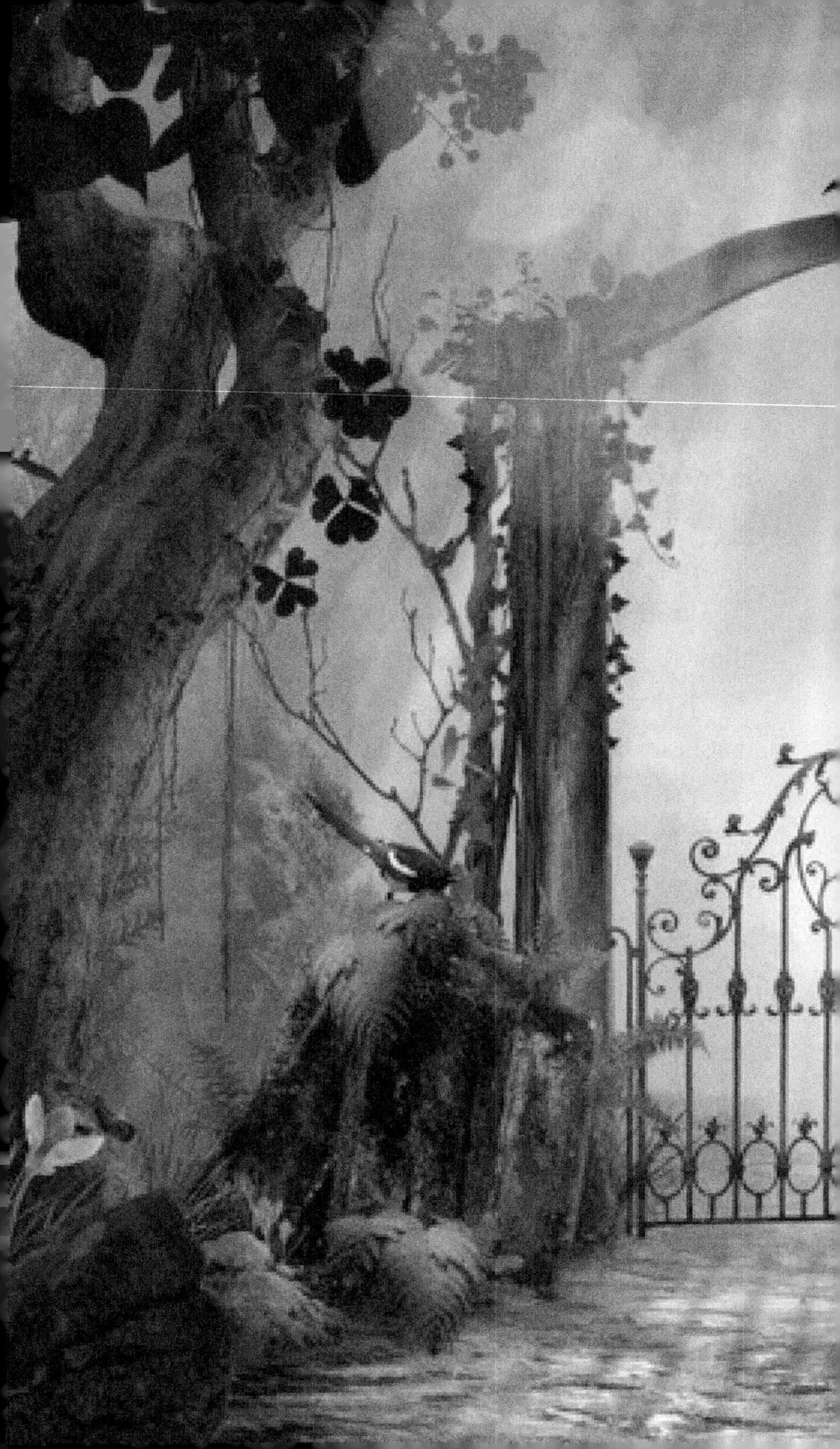

ADDI

41

Dressed head to toe in black with my gray cloak over my shoulders, I'm ready for another day in paradise. I consider tucking daggers into the pockets of my combat pants, but opt against it at the last minute.

Nightmares plagued me for some reason last night, and they seem to have filtered through into my morning, leaving me on edge despite the fact that I remember nothing of the terrors that crept into my dreams. I have to remember they're just dreams and not my reality, no matter how jittery they're making me.

I run my fingers over the braids pinning my hair to my head, making sure there's nothing for Vallie to get her grabby mitts on today.

After Cassian was pulled away last night, I mumbled

some bullshit excuse, grabbed my burger, and hightailed it out of there. Battle groups be damned. Thankfully, I made it back to my room without any further issues. Even better, Flora caught me on the way back in and dangled my new favorite series in front of me. *The Office* is a gift from someone high above who wants to shed a sprinkling of light on my life and I'm here for it.

What I'm not here for is the fact that I fell asleep in the process. In Flora's room. My gut twists with the thought again, just like it did when I woke in the middle of the night, startled and disoriented from my first nightmare.

She's tearing my walls down, one brick at a time, and it seems I'm helpless to the fact. I snuck out without disturbing her, and as much as I feel off kilter from the nightmares and falling asleep in a space that wasn't my own, I'm more worried about trying to figure out where we were up to in the series before I passed out.

A knock at the door startles me from my thoughts. Glancing at the time, I notice it's a little earlier than usual, but Flora probably wants to make sure I haven't disappeared altogether.

I swing my bedroom door open without further thought, freezing in place when it's Cassian I find on the other side of the threshold. My heart rattles in my chest before I can calm it and I clear my throat, giving myself a chance to act unfazed before I speak.

"What are you doing here?"

His green eyes clash with mine, emphasized by his emerald cloak. "Can I come in?"

I frown at his soft tone but still shake my head. "No."

"Please," he grumbles, leaving me even more confused. I don't think please is a popular word in his vocabulary. So what has him saying it now?

"Brody's ward is in place," I ramble, pointing behind me like it's visible, and he shrugs.

"I'm aware, but if you take my hand, it will let me in." He extends his arm, palm up, as he looks at me. I don't know what the hell is going on, but a part of me wants to do just that, yet the other, the protective side, has me shaking my head again.

"No."

His eyes close as he sighs, and I note the slight tic to his jaw. Whatever is bothering him is really doing a number because the Cassian I'm familiar with, although it's a rather limited familiarity, really, wouldn't continue to try and compose himself like this. He blinks his eyelids open again and exhales slowly. "I need to talk to you, and a little privacy would be appreciated."

"Why?" I push. He has to give me something. Instead, he cocks his brow.

"The privacy part is pretty important. Otherwise, I would have discussed it with you over breakfast." My lips twist with uncertainty as I stare at him, earning me another sigh as he curses. "Fuck. If Brody put the ward in place, he doesn't fuck around. The second you don't want me in here anymore, the ward will know and throw me out."

Do I trust that? I don't know, but I do know the way it tossed Kryll from the room yesterday. Whatever he wants to say, he seems determined that I need to hear it. Before I change my mind, I place my palm in his. His fingers wrap around mine, and a moment later, he tugs himself inside.

I gulp, uncertain about having someone else in my space. Especially him. The walls feel closer and the roof feels lower. His mere presence makes everything shrink around me and I feel like I can't breathe.

He kicks the door shut without a backward glance, only intensifying the feelings swarming inside of me. *Is it hot in here? It feels really fucking hot all of a sudden. Maybe I should open a window?*

The thought quickly fizzles out in my mind after remembering Kryll's intrusion yesterday. That damn thing is staying shut for the foreseeable future. His hand keeps mine captured in his grasp as his gaze flits around my room.

I don't like him looking at my personal space—or lack thereof, if I'm being honest. "What did you want to talk about, Cassian? We're going to be late for class and I need to eat first." I try to retract my hand and take a step back, but his grip only tightens.

"I met with my father last night."

"I'm aware." I was literally there when he was summoned. This isn't new news or news that requires entry into my room.

"He's an asshole," he states, and I smirk.

"I assumed that's where you got it from."

His eyes narrow on me as I offer him an innocent smile in response. He sees right through it, just like usual.

"He's throwing a moon party on Saturday," he explains, the tic flickering in his jaw again.

"Good for him."

"He wants me to be there."

"Good for you."

"With you."

"Hell no," I blurt, my head rearing back as I frown at him, failing to tug my hand free of him, despite my best efforts.

He sighs, eyes dropping to the ground for a split second before he finds my gaze again.

"I know what you're saying, but—"

"There are no buts," I interject, trying to tug my hand away again, but his knuckles turn white as he clings to me.

"There are," he retorts, his voice edging toward a growl.

"Cassian," I start, taking a deep breath, but he's not hearing me.

"Addi," he replies, his eyes widening with a plea I don't truly understand.

There's more going on here that I obviously don't know. What am I missing? "Why?"

"Because he's an asshole, remember?"

I shake my head. He might be an asshole, but that's not enough of an explanation for me. "No, but for real, Cassian. I have no desire to meet your father. Why would that not work both ways? Maybe tell his ass I'm a fae. That will scare him away."

"I think it's *because* you are fae that he wants to meet you," he admits, his voice barely more than a whisper, and my chest clenches. "I told him no myself and challenged him repeatedly until the conversation became...less than friendly. And honestly, I don't want to find out whether he was bluffing or not because I've never known him to do so before, so I can't imagine him starting now. It may have been veiled, Addi, but even veiled his threats aren't something to be taken lightly."

My pulse quickens with every word he says. He's taking this seriously. I can feel it in my bones.

"Is the threat for you or for me?" I breathe, my subconscious already knowing the answer, but I want to hear it for myself.

"Both," he admits, his thumb stroking across the back of my hand like he isn't holding it in a deathly grip.

"What would he possibly want with me?" I ask with a frown. I can't wrap my head around it.

"I don't know," he replies, but I can tell he's been thinking it over on repeat since they parted ways. "But I would rather find out in a more controlled environment than see him act erratically because he didn't get his own way to begin with." His eyes darken as if recalling a memory where something similar happened, and it sends a shiver of uncertainty down my spine.

"He would hurt me." The words fall from my mouth before I can stop them, my mind needing clarification of another danger I'm suddenly facing.

"Definitely." He doesn't miss a beat or sugarcoat it. I have to be thankful for that, I guess.

Wetting my parched lips, I take a deep breath and repeat everything he said so far. One fact weighs heavy in my stomach as I lift my gaze to his again: "A moon party; does that mean…"

"A new moon, yes."

Fuck.

Is this the opportunity I want or the challenge I'm suddenly fearing the most?

Fuck.

I can't even think about that. Emotions and feelings are only going to cause me more harm. I know that.

"He's setting me up to face another duel," I murmur,

and the corner of his mouth flicks up.

"You're smarter than you look."

"Fuck you," I grumble, whacking his chest with my free hand, but he doesn't flinch. Instead, he presses my palm against his chest with his own. His eyes soften as he steps in closer and looks down at me.

"That's what I think it is, too, but I won't let that happen." It feels like a promise—one I'm not sure he will keep.

"Why not? It would make both of our lives easier," I breathe, reminding myself just as much as him that he's not supposed to be claimed by me, a fae.

"Says who?" he rasps, and I feel a slight jolt to his heartbeat beneath my palm.

"Says me."

"And you seriously believe that?" he pushes, eliminating the minuscule distance that remains between us. His hand releases mine at his chest to cup my cheek, crowding my space as my mouth opens and shuts, but nothing comes out. "Because I think you like it just as much as I do."

"I don't," I stumble, shaking my head, but the words fall flat between us.

"If that were true, I wouldn't be standing in here right now. The ward would be separating us." Fucker. He knows he's right, and I hate it. Even as I mentally yell for him to get out, the magic doesn't react because they're not true thoughts. "Coming with me is more for yourself than it is for me," he adds, his thumb trailing over my bottom lip, making my throat dry up.

"I highly doubt that." My pulse is thumping so hard, I feel like it's vibrating my whole damn skull as I peer up at him.

For the first time since he stepped in here, he releases my hand and I flex my fingers to ease the growing ache, but it's quickly forgotten when his hand moves to cup my pussy over my combat pants.

I bite back a moan, hating how fucking good it feels when he does that.

"Come to the party with me, Addi. I'll protect you and make it worth your while." Now *that* is definitely a promise. I don't believe he'll protect me. I never believe that from anyone. Somewhere along the way, someone always lets me down. It's not always intentional, but it happens all the same. Which is why it is definitely safer to keep everyone at arm's length. It's been a long time since I let anyone in, other than my sister and father, and I prefer the isolation.

I know my presence is going to be necessary because he's right, I don't want to call his father's bluff. Not when I can see the uncertainty swirling in his eyes. Besides, I don't back away from shit like this. At least this time, I'll have a few days to prepare for a duel.

With my mind made up, I press my pussy against his

grip, watching his eyes flare with desire.

"Do I get to request payment in advance?"

He grins. It's so delicious I almost forget how much of an asshole he is. He leans in close enough for his lips to brush against mine as he speaks. "So fucking needy. It's hot. But no, we have breakfast and classes to get to, remember?"

"Ass," I bite, hating him throwing my words back at me.

"Say yes." The trail of his lips against mine makes my whole body tremble. "It's for your safety, that much I can promise you."

"Fine," I rasp, and he grins wider.

"Good girl."

It's on the tip of my tongue tell him to go fuck himself with his good girl appraisals, but he cuts me off by crushing his lips against mine.

I give in, fighting for power between us as our lips collide and our tongues dance together. He presses his palm against my pussy, making me gasp as my back arches while bringing his other hand from my cheek to my throat.

He devours me, leaving me pent up and wanting before taking a brisk step back.

The distance between us is suddenly too much, but it does the trick of bringing me to the present.

"Let's go, Alpha," he mutters, dark eyes set on me as

he backs away toward the door. It seems I'm not the only one struggling to part ways right now. But it's for the best.

Clearing my throat, I straighten my cloak and head for the door. "Why do you keep calling me that?" I ask, unable to stop myself. He's said it twice now. Alpha. In a pack, that's your leader, and that's not what I am.

"Because I see what you are," he admits, reaching for the handle and waving for me to step through the doorway first.

"Which is what?" I ask, my heart racing in my chest.

"Capable of being anyone and anything you believe. You have the alpha spirit in your bones. A strength and power that is undeniable. Either that, or you just have me so captivated that I would follow you to the pits of Hell without a care for anyone or anything but you."

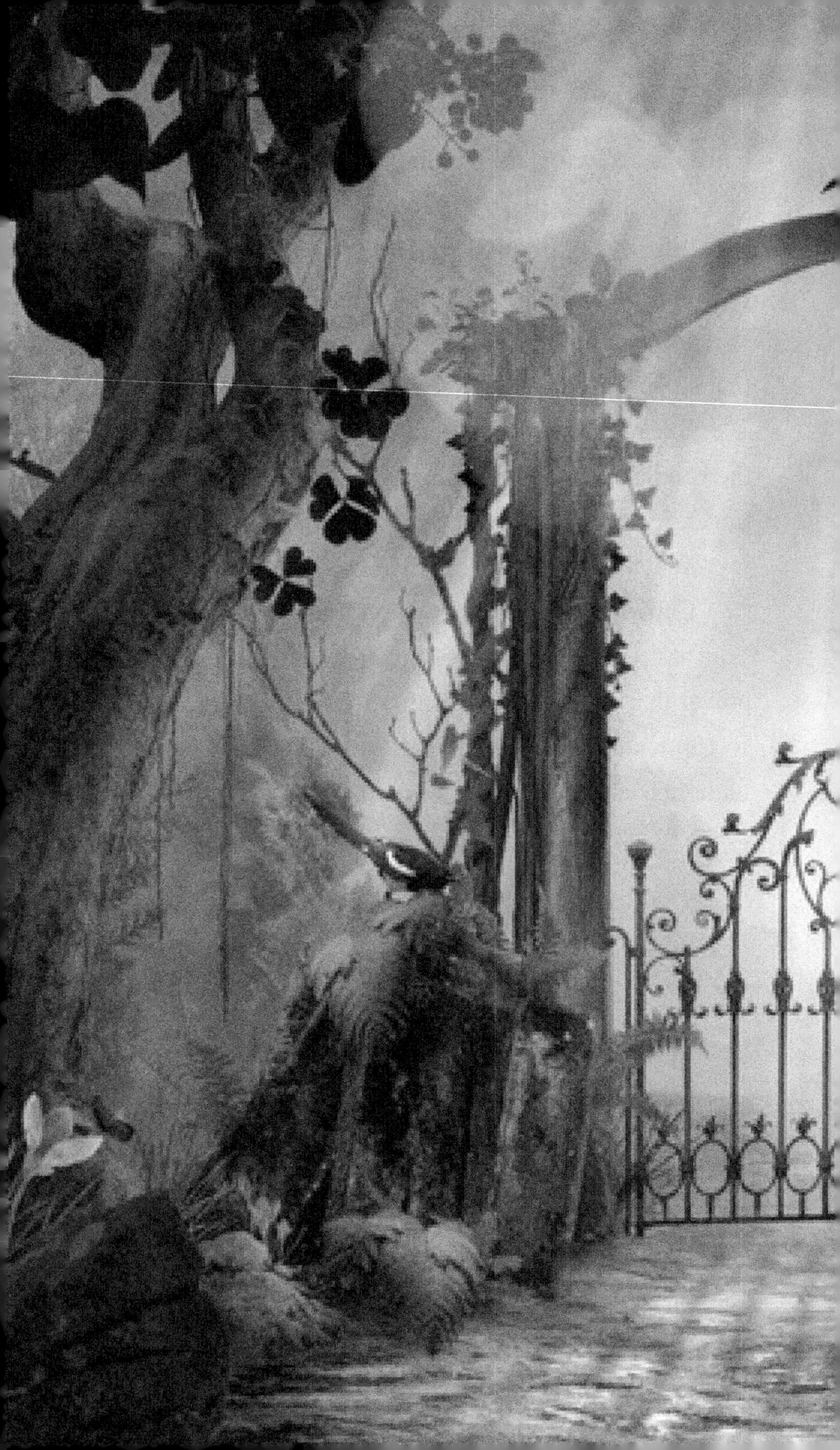

ADDI

42

I don't know how, and I'm trying not to jinx it, but this week has been calm. Definitely too calm, and the feeling that things are going to get worse only intensifies as the moon party looms over me.

It's tonight.

T.O.N.I.G.H.T.

And I don't know what I'm supposed to do. I'm extremely outside my comfort zone. There's no denying it. My memory of the panic in Cassian's eyes fades, leaving me to wonder if it's really necessary for me to go, but then I somehow get a passing breeze of his scent in my room and I'm warped back to that moment.

I'm going. That much is for sure, whether I like it or not, and no matter what, my daggers are coming with me.

"You're focused on all of the wrong things, Addi. What

are you going to wear?"

I glare at Flora, who shrugs, unfazed by my deathly stare. When it's clear she's not going to relent, I sigh.

"I don't even know," I admit, willing an outfit to magically appear before me.

Flora is adamant that tonight is a date, no matter how many times I explain to her that my life is in danger. That part seems to go right over her head.

"He's here."

I frown at her, and a second later a knock comes from the door. "How?"

She taps her brain. That's stronger than—I cut off my thoughts, worried someone could hear them as I circle to face the door with my hands planted on my hips.

"No one should be here yet, I have another hour," I mutter, but I'm not going to get any answers standing here. Stomping toward the door, I whirl it open to see the wolf in question.

He's wearing a fitted black tee with black jeans and black leather combat boots.

Fuck.

He can't be my savior tonight, not when he's such a distraction.

"Addi," he breathes, making me shiver.

"Cassian."

Silence descends over us as we stare off with one

another until Flora clears her throat from behind me.

"I'll leave you to it, but holler if you need me," she mutters, squeezing my arm as she passes. I murmur my thanks as she disappears, but not before winking at me behind Cassian so he can't see.

I roll my eyes at her, wishing she could stay as a buffer between me and the wolf, but that would only put her at risk. Not that I necessarily think he would hurt her right now, but having been on his radar for the past week or so hasn't done me any favors, and I refuse to be the reason she comes to any harm.

Turning my attention to Cassian, I make no attempt to let him in. Yet. "You're early."

"I thought you might need help choosing what to wear." The bullshit is dancing in his eyes, blazing for me to notice.

"You mean you thought I might run," I retort, and he shrugs.

"There's that too. Are you going to let me in?" he asks, rubbing the back of his neck nervously.

"I'm considering my options," I mumble, my lip twisting as I let him stew for a minute before offering out my hand.

His fingers wrap around mine as he steps over the threshold, filling my room and invading my space once again.

"Okay, Mr. Stylist, what should I wear?" I pull my hand from his, and he lets me go. I can't decide whether I like it or not.

"Casual. Like what you wore to the diner with Brody. I would probably recommend flat boots this time, though, and definitely bring the daggers."

Someone paid a lot of attention to what I was wearing if he even noticed my boots. Hiding my smile, I nod.

"Noted." I move into my closet, already piecing the outfit together in my head. While I get changed, Cassian can hit me with all the information I need before we arrive. I need a run down of who is who at this damn thing. "Tell me everything I need to know. What should I watch out for, who should I be most wary of, and who should I avoid at all costs? All of that crap," I holler, whipping my oversized tee off. I'm acutely aware of him in the other room, but I'm out of view at this end of the small walk-in closet.

"Me."

I startle at the close proximity of his voice, whirling around to watch his eyes land on my exposed breasts.

"I'm getting dressed," I blurt, making no move to hide an inch of my exposed skin. All that stands between us is my panties.

"I don't think you should bother," he rasps, eyes darkening with every breath he takes.

I frown, but I don't move as he slowly prowls toward me.

He approaches with a finesse that leaves me breathless, and he hasn't even touched me. The second he's within arms reach, he moves lightning fast, snatching at my panties, which crumple on the floor beside me a moment later.

"Cassian," I mutter, unsure what it is I'm asking for.

"Don't finish whatever bullshit is about to come out of your mouth. If I'm still in the room, we both know it's a waste of breath for you to tell me you don't want me."

He cups my pussy with his next breath, his go-to move, and the heat that rises between us becomes an inferno.

"Fuck, you're hot."

I know he's talking about the connection too. My chest rises and falls uncontrollably as I stare up at him, revealing my desire despite my will to shield anything and everything from him. "If you do this now, I'm going to walk into that party freshly fucked," I croak, and he smirks.

"I like the sound of that."

His lips crash against mine as he completely crowds me in every way. His body presses against me, his breath mingles with mine, and his mouth consumes me.

I cling to his neck, my nails digging into his skin as

I battle for control, but it's too much. *He's* too much. I'm helpless to do anything other than concede.

He lifts me in the air, sweeping my feet straight off the ground, only to lie me down on the floor in the next moment. I want him as naked as I am this time. Last time, in the bathroom, I was exposed while he remained dressed. Not this time.

Blindly searching for the hem of his t-shirt, I scramble to untuck it from his jeans to be met with soft-yet-hard skin a second later when my fingers splay across his abs.

"Fuck," he grumbles, tearing his mouth from mine as he reaches behind his head to tug the material off. I blink at his muscles, the tension running through him as he hovers above me. I need more.

Sweeping my hands down to the waistband of his jeans, I undo the button and he takes the hint. I'm left cold and needy for a few seconds as he kicks off his boots and jeans, and it doesn't go unnoticed that there's nothing else beneath the denim, just his thick length jutting in my direction, eager for attention.

He drops to his knees with a thud, and my throat goes dry with anticipation. My head pulses where I slammed it against the mirror last time, a silent reminder of how hard and rough we were. Maybe we can take it easier this time. Maybe. But the feral look in his eyes tells me it's unlikely.

Without a word, he crawls between my thighs,

grabbing my right leg and pinning it against my chest as his vision locks on my core. Tingles dance over my skin with anticipation, but I'm not left wondering long before he leans down and swipes his tongue between my folds.

"Fuck." It's my turn to curse this time as one soft sweep leads to another before his movements become more urgent. He reaches for my left leg, pressing it against my body along with my other so he can devour even more of me.

I try to grasp the carpet beneath me, desperate to cling onto something as my body swirls at his touch, but it's pointless, so I grab onto the only thing in reach: his hair. My fingers tangle in his cropped brown locks at the exact same time he thrusts two fingers deep into my core, matching the rhythm of his tongue without giving me a second to adjust.

We're desperate, needy, and rough.

I don't think I like it any other way.

My hips lift from the floor, my back arching as I match his pace with my own, and a few moments later, I feel the telltale sign of my climax tingling in my toes. My hold on his hair tightens as I moan in ecstasy, bathing in the glow of my release as he laps eagerly at my folds.

He doesn't stop until I'm completely wrung out, slowly lifting his gaze to meet mine.

With one swift swoop, he lifts me into his lap, hands

engulfing my ass cheeks as he grinds me down against his cock. My nipples grow taut pressed against his skin as we stare at one another. Panting, sweat clings to my skin, my hair loose and pressed against my neck as we remain frozen in place.

"Ride me," he rasps. "Show me you want it just as badly as I do."

My throat dries out as my body moves of its own accord. He delves into his jeans pocket from beside us, retrieving a condom a moment later, and my eyes grow wide. I was about to do as he commanded without even considering protection.

"You used this last time, right?" I ask, nerves tingling through me as I wait with bated breath for his response.

"Of course. You would know if I didn't," he grunts, and I lift off him just enough for him to sheath his dick.

"What does that mean?" I frown, the question lost on him as he grabs my waist, lining me up with his length before thrusting inside me. He pulls me down hard, making me groan as my head falls back with ecstasy.

All I can feel is him. I'm full, so fucking full, and he doesn't wait a single beat for me to adjust as he tightens his hold on my waist, lifting me and dropping me on his dick over and over again. My body heats, goosebumps ghosting over my skin as I press my palms into his shoulders and dig my knees into the carpet.

He wanted me to show him I wanted it too, yet he's taking all of the control. His hold at my waist doesn't slack, but his movements slow as he offers me a chance to gain the power between us. We both know he's offering it. For how long, I don't know, so I grind down on him, grinning at the curse that falls from his mouth as I try to match the pace he had just set.

I slam down on his length again and again, crying out every time as he fills me completely. I'm intoxicated by him, but the confusion over what he meant a moment ago still lingers in my brain.

"How would I know?" I ask, my pace unwavering as he frowns at me. "If you didn't use one last time. How would I know?" I reiterate, his eyes darkening, and I know at that moment that his answer is going to knock me off my feet.

His fingers press deeper into my waist as he regains control, forcing me to rise and fall on his cock like a ragdoll made solely for his pleasure. I almost like the idea of that as pleasure licks over my skin until his answer echoes in my ears.

"It means if I didn't wear one, I'm pretty sure I would have marked you as mine."

My eyes widen in surprise, my jaw falling slack as I gape at him. Our eyes clash a split second before his mouth crushes against mine and I succumb to another orgasm. It tears through me, hard and fast, prolonging as I feel his movements stutter and his cock pulse inside me a moment later.

I cling to him as we topple over the edge together, my limbs weak and exhausted as I rest my head on his shoulder. I have no idea how long we sit like this, basking in the energy between us, before he shifts to press his lips against my neck.

I lift my head and his mouth follows after me, trailing up my throat and over my pulse in slow, purposeful moves. It's tantalizing until he nips at my delicate skin, making me shriek.

Glaring at him, I shiver at the sight of his dark eyes swirling with emotions I have no desire to tangle with right now. Clearing my throat, I shift in his lap, biting back a moan at the loss of his cock when he retreats, and to my surprise, he lets me go.

He stares up at me with a grin that shouldn't look so sinful as I fold my arms over my chest and glare at him.

"I still don't like you," I grumble, making his grin widen.

"The feeling is mutual, Alpha."

THE KINGDOM OF RUIN

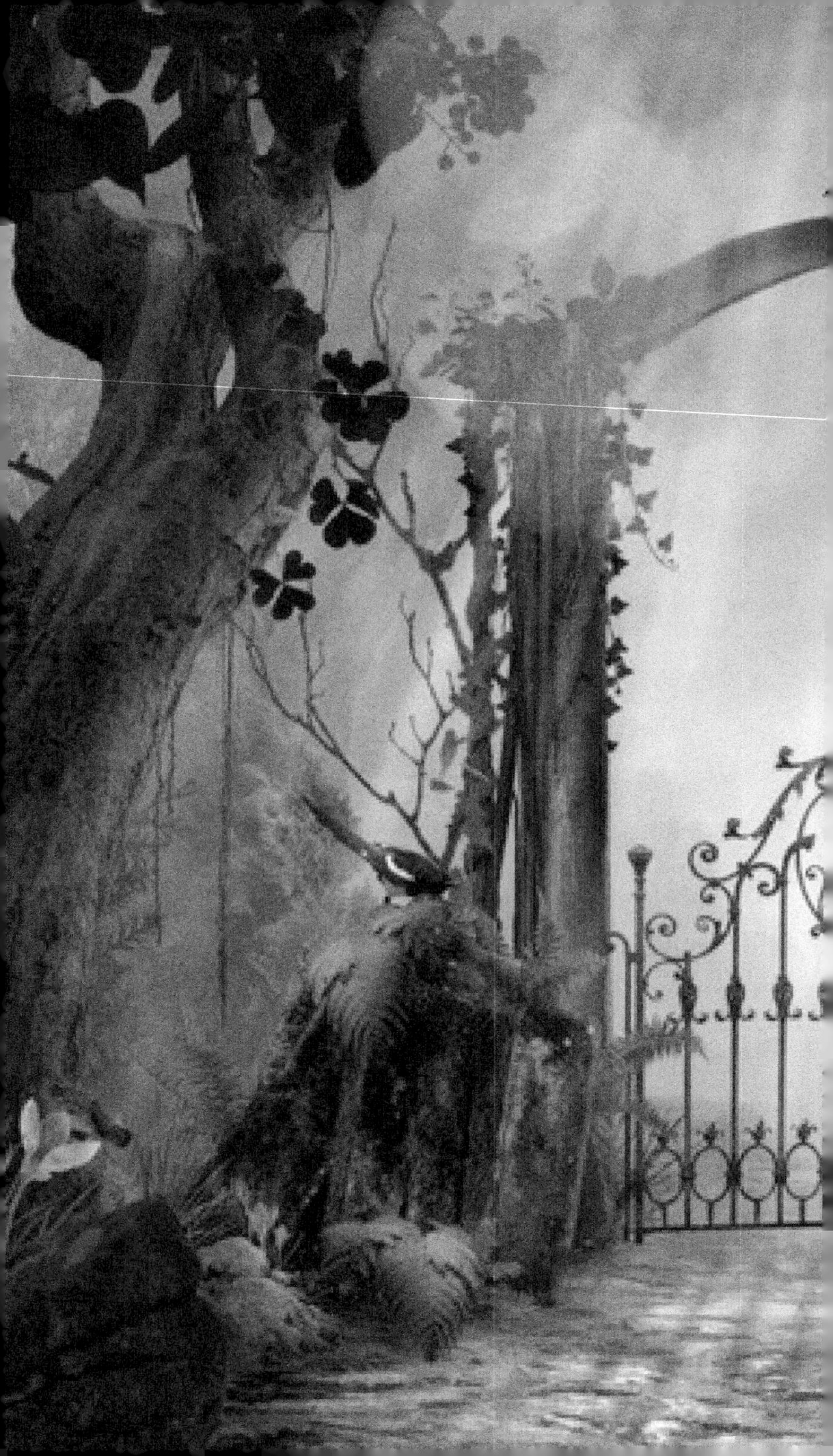

ADDI

43

I haven't dared asked him for confirmation, but I feel thoroughly fucked, so I'm certain I look it no matter how much I've tried to shield the fact. I rebraided my hair and opted to wear fitted combat pants tucked into flat, black combat boots, with a long-sleeved white tee and my adapted corset beneath my leather jacket.

If anyone remembers me from the night Leticia challenged me to a duel, I'm sure they'll recognize the shimmer of daggers around my waist too. The only difference this time is every single one of them is made of silver. Since I know where I'm going, I can plan accordingly.

"I'm sure we can get there some other way," I grumble, pouting at the wolf standing toe to toe with me, back to his usual grizzly self.

"You're making this harder than it needs to be." I'm sure he's right, but he's not the one left with the nausea churning inside of them.

"Do you not have access to a vehicle?" I press, hoping for something else, and he cocks a brow at me.

"Why would that be necessary?" The challenge flashes in his eyes. Since he can use his wolf speed, it makes sense it wouldn't be needed, but that's beside the point.

"The vampires drive around in flashy cars, and they have vampire speed," I retort, and he rolls his eyes.

"The vampires are assholes. I'm not. Now, come on," he grumbles, offering me his hand again. I can sense the tension growing around him, probably regretting the extension of courtesy instead of just grabbing me and running like he's done previously.

Fuck.

"Fine. Get it over with," I mumble, my stomach clenching in preparation, and he wastes no time wrapping his fingers around mine and pulling me in close.

The world shifts a second later and I press my face into his chest, trying to shield myself from the sickness I know is coming. He stops quicker than expected, and I'm relieved to note that the waves of nausea aren't as bad this time.

My eyes fix on his as the world settles around us, and before I can take a confident step back, he leans in and presses his lips against mine in a ghost of a kiss. He's gone too quickly, putting a large step between us as I find Raiden, Brody, and Kryll waiting by the tree to our left.

I can hear the sound of music in the distance, but it seems as though there's a little distance between us and the party. Thank goodness.

Raiden is dressed head to toe in a navy suit tailored to perfection with a pristine white shirt underneath. He's forgone the tie and his top button is open. The way the moon beams down on him, he looks even more sinister than usual.

Brody stands beside him, his usual grin in place as he winks at me. He's wearing stone-colored chino pants and a white polo top. He looks so casual and put together—nothing like a mage walking onto wolves' land.

Kryll, however, almost looks like he could fit in. Maybe it's the shifter in him. Not that I know what he is, except for the fact that he mentioned wings. He's dressed in a fitted white tee and black jeans with unlaced leather boots. The tattoos that cover his body look darker in contrast to the white top, and his auburn hair looks almost brown beneath the dark sky.

I don't know what brought the four of these guys together, but here they are, and I seem to have found myself tangled in the middle of it.

"Are you ready to dance, Dagger?" Brody asks,

sauntering toward me with a grin on his face. Before I can answer, his arm is around my shoulder, pulling me toward the noise in the distance.

"Dancing, not really, but I'm ready for someone to give me a hint as to what we're walking into. Who I should be on the lookout for, who I should avoid at all costs, who is safe to breathe around," I ramble, looking up at him with pleading eyes, and I don't even care if it makes me look weak. I need the facts however I can get them.

He frowns down at me. "That's what Cassian was supposed to be telling you. That's why he came to get you and we met you here." He looks at me expectantly before glancing at the wolf in question. He puts two and two together and quickly gets four. "Fuck. Now I'm jealous."

My cheeks heat and I'm thankful for the night air hiding it from him.

"You two were fucking? Again?" Raiden grunts, and I refuse to glance back at him to see the disapproval that undoubtedly matches his tone.

"Fuck off, asshole," Cassian grunts, while Kryll appears at my right side.

"The low down is, Cassian's father is…there's nothing more accurate than calling him a cunt." I cringe at the word, but no one disregards his assessment. "Stay away from him at all costs. I know that's why we're here, but even Raiden won't leave you alone in his presence." A few beats pass and Raiden doesn't correct him, which fills me with a little bit of hope.

"Who else is off limits?" I ask, my body relaxing under Brody's guiding arm.

"Dalton. Kenner's right hand man. He's worse than the rest. Ruthless, brutal, and will kill you first and reap the consequences after." Great. Sounds like a nice guy. "You're safest with Janie or Jake. I'm assuming you met Janie at the diner?" I nod. "Good, her and her husband love Cassian, which will extend to you unconditionally."

I open my mouth to correct him on the situation, but Brody squeezes my arm. "Winning the duel matters more than your origin or any other factor that could make them hate you. That's why she called Cassian the moment we sat down. That was all completely my fault, and she ensured you were safe before you won the duel. Now, her respect for you will have only grown."

I nod, not really sure what to say while my thoughts swirl with the entire situation, leaving me feeling a bit helpless. I want to say I'd rather not be here, I want to confirm that I don't ever want to cross paths with Cassian's father, but more than that, I don't want some victory of a duel to gain me things I have no business receiving.

The music gets louder as mellow lights illuminate the trees, revealing a huge gathering of people dancing and laughing along with the music as they clink their beer bottles and move to the beat. The energy quickly shifts around me and trepidation clings to my limbs.

Everyone seems familiar with one another, all touchy-feely, as wolves are known for being, until their eyes find me and their joy falters.

Cassian silently steps forward, semi-blocking me from view as Janie approaches. She wraps her arms around Cassian's neck, murmuring into his ear. He nods and she walks around him to stop in front of me.

"It's good to see you again. I didn't really introduce myself properly last time. I'm Janie." She offers out her hand and I take it, but instead of shaking it, she pulls me from Brody's grasp and into a hug.

"Be careful of my daggers," I yelp, and she chuckles in my ears.

"I'm good, but the heads up from you earns a little more respect from me," she states. "Now, are you going to introduce yourself or leave me guessing?" she muses, leaning back and releasing me from her hold.

"Addi. I'm Addi."

"Nice to meet you. Do me a favor, yeah?" I nod, and she smiles. "Stay at Cassian's side, okay?"

Great. The concern for me is extending past the small group I'm here with. It's appreciated, but it doesn't leave me feeling any safer here.

"When was the last time you ate?" she asks, looping

her arm through mine as she pulls me toward the barbeque set up in the far corner.

"Oh, I'm not really hungry," I insist, and she shakes her head.

"That will just show them that you're nervous, Addi. You've got to walk in here exuding that confidence you were bathing in when you took down Leticia," she murmurs against my ear. My gaze darts around the space, and I find a large percentage of the crowd watching my every move.

Fuck, she's right.

"Lead the way," I reply, making her smile spread as I absorb her words and channel my confidence into every step I take.

I may be out of my comfort zone, but that doesn't mean I don't know my own abilities. I can handle myself. Being here doesn't change that.

Janie releases me as she approaches the guy at the grill. He sweeps her off her feet and plants a kiss on her lips with a big goofy grin on his face before he swiftly gets back to manning the meat. She reappears at my side a moment later, the guy waving at me as she places a plate in my hands.

"How am I supposed to eat all of this?" I ask, glancing down at the meat, potatoes, and corn piled high before me.

"Do fae not eat this much?" I shake my head as she leads me toward a table. "Maybe it's just a wolf thing," she adds, and I grin.

"Maybe."

The second I sit down across from Janie, I'm shuffled along the bench so Cassian can sit beside me, and Brody takes the spot to my left. Kryll and Raiden sit on the other side with Janie, and they all have their own plates stacked high.

Thankfully, the table settles into a comfortable silence as we eat. The music is good, and the longer I sit here, the calmer the general atmosphere tends to be. Not that I'm going to bask in that fact too much. The second I let my guard down, I know the rug will be pulled from under me.

As if sensing my inner thoughts, a guy appears at the end of the table. "Cassian, your father is looking for you." He's speaking to Cassian, but his dark gaze is settled on me. A jagged scar runs down his cheek, slipping down his throat and disappearing beneath the collar of his t-shirt. His tongue sweeps over his bottom lip as his stare intensifies, and without being told, my gut confirms this is who I was warned about. Dalton.

"You can let him know where you've spotted me," Cassian grunts, not lifting his gaze, but his hand quickly lands on my thigh, squeezing with confidence.

"I think we both know that's not how it works," he retorts, his voice deepening as he leans forward, bracing his hands on the table. Cassian sighs, seeking my hand with his, and the moment our fingers are laced together, he pulls me to my feet.

The second we're standing, Kryll, Raiden, and Brody rise too.

"Alone," Dalton bites, glaring at the entire table. Janie included.

Fucker.

I definitely don't like him.

"I don't think so," Cassian grunts, and the guy shrugs like he's more than happy to report back to his father how uncooperative he's being.

"That's cool. He mentioned something about causing a scene, and we all know how much I love those."

The stare-off between them dances in their eyes, both of their muscles flexing, begging for the other to make the first move, until Kryll speaks.

"Go, we've got her."

I gulp, uncertainty twisting in my gut. I don't need anyone to have my back, but I'm not dumb enough to forget that I'm in unfamiliar territory, and they know more than I do.

Cassian squeezes my fingers, silently sending a message. What he's trying to say, I'm not entirely sure, but I muster the best smile I can before he saunters away with his father's right-hand man.

Settling back into my seat, Janie offers me a tight

smile. "He won't be long."

I open my mouth to answer when another shadow casts over the table, and I turn to see a familiar snarl glaring down at me.

"Fuck off, Leticia," Raiden grunts, but she doesn't even acknowledge his words as her stare hardens and she inches closer to me.

"You only beat me in the duel because you used weapons," she states, jaw tight, rage pouring from her in waves. Half of me wants to pat her on the back, call it an unlucky event, and move on, while the other half wants to remind her exactly who she came for. Instead, I settle on using my snark.

"And you shifted into your wolf within the first five seconds. Using your inner weapon instead of facing me in your natural form."

"My wolf *is* my natural form," she retorts, nostrils flaring with fury. "You think you know everything, and I'm more than eager to prove that you don't."

"When did I say that I know everything?" I challenge, quickly growing tired of the bullshit she's throwing at me, and she scoffs. "What do you want, Leticia? You're boring me."

I know it before I ask, the answer shimmering in her eyes with a deathly promise.

"I want a rematch."

THE KINGDOM OF RUIN

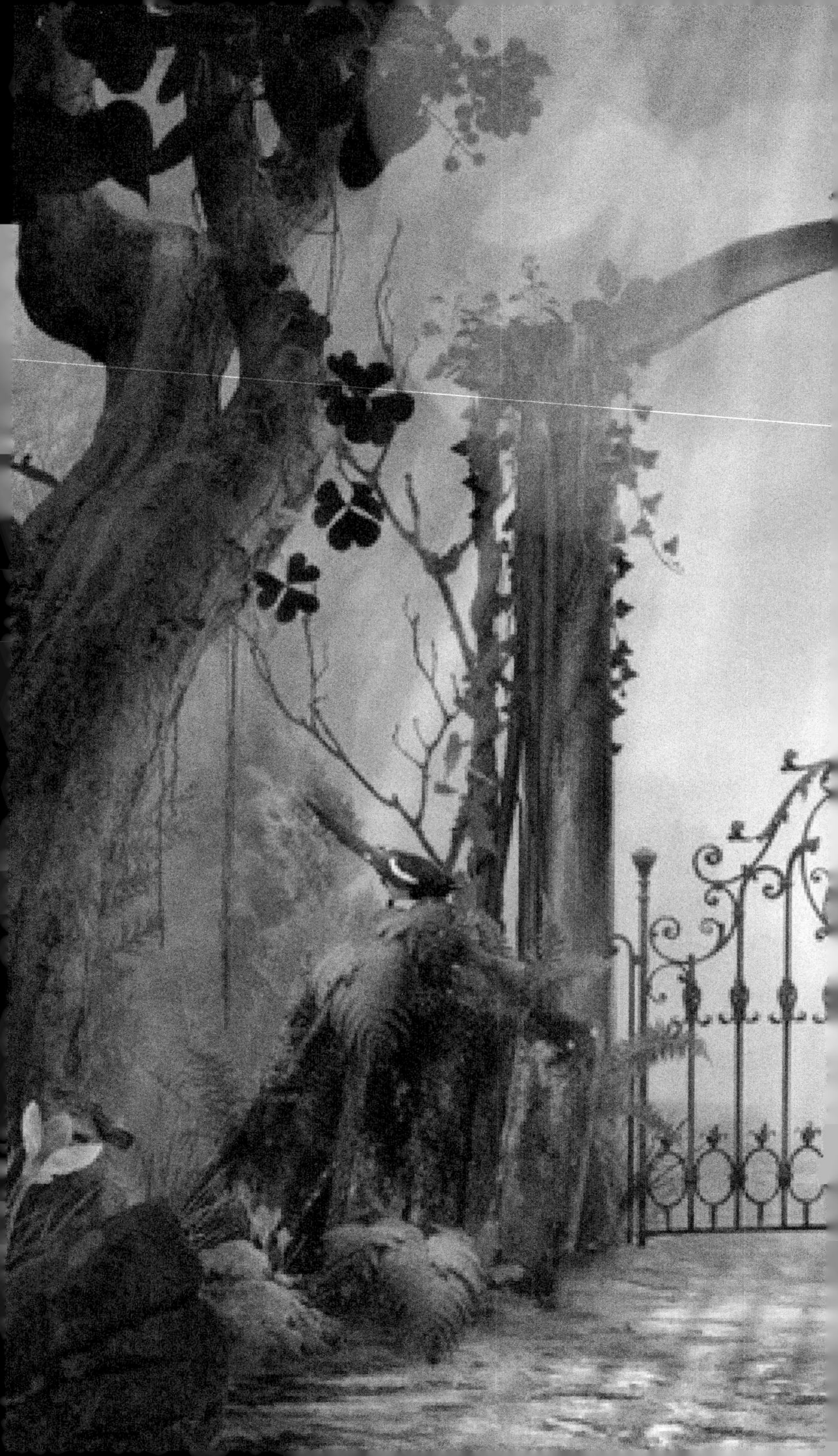

ADDI

44

"Is this really necessary?" Janie asks from across the table, glaring at Leticia like she's the outsider, not me. Leticia doesn't pay her any mind as she leans in closer to me.

"When the clock strikes midnight, I can challenge you again. Be ready." It's a promise, not a warning, and my gut clenches.

She doesn't get to have him.

I'm not saying I want him; I just….fuck.

Emotions I refuse to let out rattle inside of me as someone looms behind Leticia.

"Now, now, girls, we don't truly want to celebrate the new moon with a duel, do we?"

Leticia stills, eyes wide when she hears the voice, and I look behind her to see who it is. The air that exudes from him screams leader, and the way both Janie and Leticia respond to him only confirms my suspicions. It has to be Cassian's father.

A deadly grin spreads across his face as he meets my stare. "You must be Addi Reed, the girl causing quite a stir."

Clearing my throat, I nod, standing as I remember my father's lectures on greeting other origins. "Alpha Kenner."

Leticia shifts from between us, and I groan, hating that there's no longer anything standing in his way.

"What the fuck was that about?" Cassian growls, storming toward us with his hands fisted at his sides.

"Son."

"Don't play coy; it doesn't suit you," he bites, facing off with his father.

"I don't know what you want me to say. When Dalton didn't come back with you straight away, I came looking. I just happened to find the lovely Addi Reed in the process."

Cassian turns to me, scanning his eyes over me to make sure I'm okay. His jaw tics, making it clear his father is full of crap, and Dalton pulling him away was all part of a plan to separate us.

Alpha Kenner follows Cassian's line of sight, turning to me with an assessing stare. "For a fae, your ears are... lacking."

Asshole.

"I'm aware."

He inches closer, assessing exactly what I'm self-conscious about. "The scars are neatly done. A professional, for sure. Was it done on purpose?"

What the fuck?

I shake my head. "Not by me," I grumble, ready for him to leave already. Deep in my soul, I know I'm being lured into his trap, and he's in no way done with me yet.

"So you're happy being a fae?"

What the fuck kind of question is that?

"Always."

He reaches out, and it takes everything in me not to shrink away. The tip of his finger ghosts over the scar on my left ear as I sense Brody inching closer behind me and Cassian snarling behind his father.

"Who did this to you? It must feel like your identity is incomplete."

His words are like poison. Just as he intends.

"I feel perfectly fine." It's the truth. I may be self-conscious about them, but it doesn't make me feel any less of a fae without my signature pointed tips.

"How?"

I know what he's asking, and as much as I scramble for an answer, I know there's no use in lying. I'm not the best at it, my heart always giving a little murmur, and he'll be able to see right through me. My pulse is already erratic enough, a sensation I don't hide because that would only cause more confusion as he tries to get a read on me.

"I was attacked as a child."

His eyes widen as the corner of his mouth turns up just an inch. "You poor thing." I've sensed more sympathy from a wilted flower. If he thinks I'm falling for that, he's truly mistaken. "By who?"

I frown at him. Nobody asks that. Not that many people know the details behind my ears, but still. There's intrusive, and then there's that question. There's no use lying, though. Despite how awkward the truth may be.

"By a wolf."

A gasp echoes from my left, and I know it's Janie. It cuts through the rising tension thickening around me, but the same shock isn't evident on Alpha Kenner.

No.

Instead, there's a sparkle in his eyes.

"How?" he pushes, and I shrug. "How?" he repeats, more demanding this time.

"Father, that's enough," Cassian bites as Alpha Kenner leans back, tapping his finger against his chin.

"I'd recognize your eyes anywhere," he murmurs, so quiet I'm unsure if I heard him correctly. Whirling around, he finds Dalton a step behind him. "Fetch her." There's glee in his voice as he turns back to me, and with every passing moment, my gut sinks.

"What's going on?" Kryll asks, and I wince, panicked that Kenner will lash out at him, but he seems to go unheard. Not by Cassian, though, who turns to me, storming by his father to get to my side.

"We're leaving."

"You're going nowhere," his father snarls, pointing his finger at his son in warning before turning back to me.

I'm acutely aware that the entire gathering is staring this way, and the music doesn't seem as loud as it did earlier. Here's the scene Dalton was talking about. I was just hoping it would center around Cassian and not me.

I should have known I wouldn't be that lucky.

A menacing smile takes over Kenner's face as his presence seems to loom around me even more. "I've sliced the ears of a fae before." I freeze, blinking at him as his words take root in my veins. "A small girl," he adds, an air of triumph oozing from him. "Not just any small girl… you."

My pulse rings in my ears. "Me."

The word parts my lips as I try to wrap my head around what he's saying. I don't think, I don't consider, I don't do anything but launch myself at him. I reach for two daggers at my waist, ready to pierce this fucker with them, but Cassian manages to intercept me, pinning me to his chest.

"Somebody spell it out for me," Cassian growls, and I wiggle against his hold to no avail. I need to use my magic, even if I reveal…no, earth magic will do. It has to.

"Let go of me, Cassian. He needs to pay," I snarl, my blood burning through my veins with the need to get my revenge. Kenner laughs, arms out wide at his sides as he basks in my rage. Let him. "What you did to my sister." My heart aches, and it fuels his sadistic glee.

"Ah, little Nora, right? Was that her name? I can't remember."

Fuck him.

Fuck him. Fuck him. Fuck him.

"She was just a baby," I spit, the world fading away until all I see is him. I need Cassian to put me down so I can connect with the ground.

"How is she?" he asks, but I understand what he really means.

"Alive, no thanks to you." Agony twists into fury through every ounce of my body.

"How are her legs?"

Fuck this.

Fighting against Cassian's hold, I try to reach him again as his voice booms in my ear. "What the fuck is going on?"

A cry echoes from behind Kenner, drawing his attention away from me for a second, and I let the world seep back into my vision. I need to think, and I need to think fast if I'm going to bring him down.

Dalton parts the gathered crowd, pulling along a

woman. He comes to a stop a few steps away from us, letting the woman's gaze dart around. Her frantic eyes settle on mine. Eyes so similar that my heart practically rips from my chest.

"Adrianna."

I gulp, biting back a whole different kind of nausea threatening to consume me.

"Is that Queen Reagan?" Raiden asks, cutting through the darkness seeping into my limbs.

"That's right, everyone," Kenner announces, gaze flicking between the woman and me. "Please gather round and meet Queen Reagan." His gaze settles on mine as I brace for the words I know are going to come from his mouth. "And Adrianna Reagan, daughter of King and Queen Reagan, the fallen king and ruiner of the fae origin. Which makes her the rightful-yet-despised heir to the kingdom."

AFTERWORDS

What bitch of an author leaves it there like that?

I hate her.

Jokes.

I think.

This book took form all on its own and it's taking me on the best ride. I can't get enough of it. If I reach burnout it will simply because this story will not let me relent, but in the best way possible.

I don't know whether it's because I wrote without having breaks in a chapter and kept it flowing differently, but I genuinely just wanted to keep writing every day.

I hope you love it as much as I do, and I can't wait for the next book to drop next month!

Yup, that's right.

Roll on June 28th, you deserve it!

THANK YOU

I feel like I should create a song at this stage. Haha. Clears throat…
Jokes. Maybe a rap one day.

Michael. What a fella. I love you. Have I mentioned that? We're on this journey together, and there's no one else in the world I would have rowing this boat while I pretend to sit and look pretty upfront. Love ya boo.

To my babies, every day you tell me you want to write a book too and it fills my heart. All I want in this world is for you to have a good life. To dream, to thrive, to see it all. Don't ever be afraid. I love you.

Nicole and Jeni. You guys are my queens. Imagine me trying to do this without you? No thanks haha Thank you for being so fabulous!

Kirsty, mate. Absolute superstar. We're growing fam, we're thriving, we're making memories, and you're a boss bitch. Thanks for being her friend.

To my beta readers, your comments give me life. I love taking this journey with you guys.

Thank you to Sarah and Lily for making everything perfect. You gals are superior.

About KC Kean

KC Kean began her writing journey in 2020 amidst the pandemic and homeschooling… yay! After reading all of the steam, from fade to black, to steamy reads, MM, and reverse harem, she decided to immerse herself in her own worlds too.

When KC isn't hiding away in the writing cave, she is playing Dreamlight Valley, enjoying the limited UK sunshine with her husband, children, and furbabies, or collecting vinyls like it's a competition.

Come and join me over at my [Aceholes Reader Group](), follow my author's Facebook page, and enjoy Instagram with me on the links below.

Also by KC Kean

Featherstone Academy
(Reverse Harem Contemporary Romance)
My Bloodline
Your Bloodline
Our Bloodline
Red
Freedom
Redemption

All-Star Series
(Reverse Harem Contemporary Romance)
Toxic Creek
Tainted Creek
Twisted Creek

(Standalone MF)
Burn to Ash

Emerson U Series
(Reverse Harem Contemporary Romance)
Watch Me Fall
Watch Me Rise
Watch Me Reign

Saints Academy
(Reverse Harem Paranormal Romance)
Reckless Souls
Damaged Souls
Vicious Souls
Fearless Souls
Heartless Souls

Ruthless Brothers MC
(Reverse Harem MC Romance)
Ruthless Rage
Ruthless Rebel
Ruthless Riot

Silvercrest Academy
(Reverse Harem Paranormal Romance)
Falling Shadows
Destined Shadows
Cursed Shadows
Unchained Shadows

Heirborn Academy
Kingdom of Ruin
Reign of Blood

Printed in Great Britain
by Amazon